The book is based on the life experiences and recollections of the author.

The book consists of nineteen chapters and one hundred and twelve-thousand words.

The book contains explicit descriptions of sexual behaviour and is therefore intended for adult reading only.

Table of Contents.

Painful Visit (circa-1984)

Playground of Delights (circa-1986)

A Moment of Madness (circa-1988)

The Last Time (circa-1990)

Nothing Else Matters (Nov-2005)

Foreword

In our pursuit of sexual discovery our actions are sometimes achieved without sincerity or conviction. Whether the sexual act involves infidelity or just impulsive and irrational misbehaviour, it can often be conceived that the risks are gratuitous and frequently undertaken without remorse, incrimination or consequence.

The chapters unfold in a sequence of true events. Each short story follows the journey of a young man growing through his adolescent years into middle-age. In his quest for Human Sexual Response he discovers that the entrance to the sexual arena can be fraught with an element of uncertainty, intrigue, risk, danger, and sometimes a touch of light-hearted humour.

The book is based on the life experiences and recollections of the author. Although some of the stories have been slightly embellished and a small amount of fiction added, all the events, incidents and characters in the book are rooted in fact.

The book contains explicit descriptions of sexual behaviour and is therefore intended for adult reading only. To protect the privacy and reputation of individuals, all the names, dates and places in the book have been changed.

'Persuasive Approval' published January 2017 is the first book in the 'Persuasive' listing of erotic books by Ethan Dorian. 'Beverley Grainger, Persuasive Intent' is the second book published July 2018 and is available on Amazon Books.

Other work by the author comprising of romantic poetry and song lyrics have been published in the Musical Category under the pen name of James Marlowe.
Song Lyrics (Volume 1)
Song Lyrics (Volume 2)
Song Lyrics (Volume 3)
Song Lyrics (Volume 4)

A Helping Hand (circa-1966)

The full-length mirror on the bedroom wall threw back an image of a fit and healthy young man, boasting an impressive sculptured and toned physique.

"My first record," he proudly smiled, lifting the lid of the record player and carefully lowering the needle onto a black piece of vinyl, cursing to himself when the needle missed the start and scratched the surface.

'In the chilly hours and minutes of uncertainty,' Donovan sang. *'To feel you all around me,'* he chirped in, letting the wet towel drop to the floor and smiling with admiration at the perfect specimen of manhood, hanging in a gentle curve over his left thigh.

Even at a very young age some of his friends often teased him about the size of his penis. And when he was in his early-teens and taking showers after school sports, he noticed that compared to other boys of his age, he had been gifted with an exceptional attachment.

Eric Clapton and Bob Dylan looked down from posters on the bedroom wall, as he slipped into a pair of tight beige shorts and a white t-shirt.

He looked in the mirror, checking his winning smile, his immaculate appearance and the impressive bulge, straining inside his shorts.

With temperatures reaching into the high-seventies, it was only late morning and even with all the windows open, his bedroom was incredibly hot and uncomfortable.

After a splash of after shave, he glanced in the mirror one more time, making sure everything was perfect before he left the house and headed off to meet his best friend, Andy Dobson.

Ruth Dobson lived with her teenage son in a detached house on a private residential estate on the outskirts of Gateshead. In all the time, he had known Andy and Ruth they had never once discussed or even mentioned the subject of her divorce, almost six years ago.

According to gossiping neighbours when Ruth discovered her husband was having an affair with his secretary – apparently, a woman half his age, with loose legs and firm young tits – he came home one night, packed a bag and walked out of her life.

The divorce was messy, but the settlement left Ruth financially comfortable. She kept the house and bought a new Austin Mini for her sons seventeenth-birthday.

In the girls and sex department, Andy claimed to have lost his virginity to a girl he met when he was on holiday with his mother and father, in southern France.

He was still a virgin. Probably because he had been going out with a girl for almost two-years, who constantly reminded him that the Catholic Church advocated that sex before marriage was an unholy act. Her parents didn't make things any easier. They were over-bearing and over protective with their daughter's social life, both lecturing her from a very young age about the merciless wrath that would befall her if she ever gave in to temptation and that boys were the evil seed of Satan and if she ever explored such wicked and unholy temptations, God would come down and pierce her eyes with fire.

But the day she let him touch her breasts for the very first time would be embedded in his memory for life. He wasn't sure whether it was her final pledge of endearment or just a parting gift, but there was an uncanny coincidence on that particular day.

Not long after he had fondled her breasts, she told him that her parents were going to live in Australia and she would be going with them.

Up till now, sex had been nothing more than imagination and endless hours of masturbation.

"Come in Mark," Ruth invited, fanning her face with her hand and sipping a cool drink. "Isn't it hot. Let me get you a cold drink," she offered, smiling into his eyes and turning on her heels.

"Come with me into the kitchen," she added, her shapely bottom bouncing delightfully inside a pair of white shorts, the curves of perfection waving invitingly beneath the tight fabric, revealing shrouded hints of the alluring nakedness that lay beneath.

"Andy said you were coming here to discuss your camping holiday to Barcelona. He's outside on the patio. He's very excited," she smiled, pouring liquid into a glass, her shapely breasts making a brief appearance through a small gap in her blouse.

"Be careful. Hitchhiking can be dangerous," she sighed, handing him a glass of orange juice and giving his hand a gentle squeeze, the warmth of her touch sending a shiver up his spine and leaving him with an iceberg of an erection straining inside his shorts.

Even with all the windows rolled down, the heat inside the Austin Mini was unbearable. Andy was at the steering wheel and he was sitting in the passenger seat, accepting the role of navigator. Ruth was sitting comfortably in the back, casually thumbing through a magazine and playing with a silver pendant hanging on a chain around her neck.
"Thanks for driving me to Ipswich to see my mother," Ruth said, catching sight of her son in the rear-view mirror. "Your grandmother hasn't been well lately," she sighed. "It'll give me time to look after her while you're on holiday," she added.
"And don't worry about your precious car. It'll be locked in my mother's garage until you get back from Spain," she smiled, twisting the buttons on her blouse and fanning her face with the magazine, her white summer dress creeping slowly above her knees, the slightest movement in the seat offering hints of the enchanting treasures that lay beneath.
"Would you two boys like a mint?" Ruth asked, searching inside a straw bag, the question giving him another excuse to crane his head and look back over his shoulder.

"Take one for Andrew," she smiled, her dress riding high on her thighs and her white knickers in full view, his decadent subconscious flashing images of the buttons on her blouse springing apart and a surge of pure woman spilling out.

In the claustrophobic closeness, heart beats raced, and hormonal chaos stirred genitalia, filling the car with the aroma of sex.

Was it the humidity of the afternoon sun, or was it the heat of sexually charged bodies, he thought.

Whatever it was it had left him with a throbbing nuisance inside his shorts and he wondered how many times he could discretely lower his hand and make an adjustment without making it too obvious.

It was late in the afternoon when they finally reached Ipswich.

Although Edith Webster had recently suffered a stroke which left one side of her face and body semi-paralysed, she showed amazing courage to ensure that her disability wouldn't prevent her from the life she had cherished with her late husband, Arthur.

The six-bedroom Victorian house set in an acre of land with two sun terraces, a large gazebo and an orchard at the bottom of the garden, held many memories of her late husband and Edith made it very clear that she would only leave when heaven calls her name.

During dinner that evening, Ruth had been sampling the red wine a little too much and a little too often, and it was evident from her slurred speech that she was heading for a severe hangover the next day.

After putting Edith safely to bed and making a short detour to her wardrobe, Ruth walked back into the living-room wearing a figure hugging red skirt and a blouse with too many buttons undone.

"let's have some music," she smiled, pouring wine into a glass and lifting the lid of the record player, the crooning voice of Frank Sinatra filling the room with romantic suggestion.

'*Strangers in the Night,*' she sang, kicking her shoes across the floor and floating on air around the room to an imaginary waltz.

'*What were the chances, we'd be sharing love, before the night was through,*' she harmonised with Frank, swaying her curvy bottom and blowing the occasional kiss from the palm of her hand, when she thought her son wasn't looking.

"It's getting late. I think we should all get some sleep," Andy sighed, lifting off the sofa and pointing a finger at the clock above the fireplace.

"After you've danced with me. You know how I love to dance, Andrew," she smiled, taking his hand in a gesture of melodic movement.

"I'm not in the mood, mother. I'm too tired. And you're embarrassing me," he sighed, pulling his hand away.

"Will you dance with me Mark?" she asked, flashing her eyes and pursing her bottom lip. "You don't look tired and I promise not to embarrass you," she smiled.

"I'm not…I'm not…I mean I don't," he stammered, searching for the right words, eager to say yes, but not wanting to offend his friend, Andy.
"I'll take that as a yes," she smiled, lifting him off the sofa and pointing a finger at the door. "You can go to bed Andrew. We'll follow you up as soon as we've finished our dance."
"Don't be too long," Andy, sighed, grunting his frustration through hissing teeth and lifting his shoulders in defeat, as he headed for the door.
"Dance with me, Mark," she whispered, wrapping her arms around his neck and pulling him close, swaying her hips and moving back and forth to persuasive urges.
"You're a good dancer," she smiled, feeling his growing flesh pressing against her burning heat, smiling into his eyes and pushing back, letting him feel the heat of arousal, the urgent sexual desire of a wanting woman.
"Fuck me. What if Andy decides to come back," he thought, the swollen limb inside his shorts threatening to make an appearance and his balls about to erupt at any second.
He wanted to tell her to stop but that was never going to happen.
He couldn't remember the last time he'd slept on dry sheets. The sleepless nights creating images of her lying naked in his bed and a running commentary of filth to stimulate the countless hours of masturbation and the powerful orgasms that followed.

And now the woman who had helped to launch a trillion sperm was pushing her body against his swollen flesh with lustful intent, teasing his senses and corrupting his mind with potential and suggestive implications.

"Christ. Is this really happening," he thought, hormonal chaos spinning inside his head and his body responding in ways he could never have imagined.

It felt like he was caught in a dream. If it was a dream he never wanted to wake up.

The pulse of her lips and the warmth of her breasts flattening against his chest, promised him the moment was real.

"You've got sugar lips," she whispered, smiling into his eyes, a thousand butterflies fluttering inside her stomach and the ache between her thighs pleading for attention.

"Kiss me," she breathed, eager tongues joining together in a ballet of heightening endearment, impatient hands responding to the persuasion of touch, sweeping over fabric, over curves, over bulges, over flesh, searching and probing, fondling and squeezing, two hearts beating in an intimate union of surreptitious flutters and anxious confusion, two heads swimming in a sea of mixed emotions, two people losing control of rational.

"You've got beautiful breasts, Mrs Dobson," he uttered, arousal and expectation sweeping away caution, pushing and thrusting his hips, letting her feel his hardness pressing against her softness.

"Thank you," she smiled. "Would you like to feel them," she offered, reaching back and unclipping her bra, two weighty breasts spilling from their bondage and into his hands.

"Wow," he gasped, lowering his hand and making a quick adjustment to the swollen limb inside his shorts. "They're magnificent," he croaked, feeling the warmth and the softness between his fingers, the acquaintance of touch stealing his heart and the breath from his lungs.

"I've always admired them, Mrs Dobson," he confessed, pulling and squeezing her nipples a little more than he intended.

"Be gentle," she whispered, breaking away from the embrace and smiling at his innocence as he searched for apologetic words.

"Don't say anything. It's not necessary," she sighed, placing a finger over his lips.

"Sex is a perfectly natural biological function and I'm rather flattered that at my age, I still have that effect on a young man," she added, removing the finger from his lips.

"I also have needs, Mark. It's been a long time since my divorce and far too long since I had…," her voice trailed off as she considered her next statement, the brief interlude giving her a moment to admire his physique. *His fit young body. His firmness. His endless stamina. The gruesome muscle hidden beneath his shorts.... Christ. I'm old enough to be his mother,* she thought, shaking her head and banishing the corrupt thoughts from her mind.

"Well let's just say far too long since I enjoyed the comforts of a man," she sighed, the sound of elephant-like feet thudding on the stairs interrupting their moment of passion.

"That's Andrew," she panicked, slipping her bra under a cushion and buttoning up her blouse, making sure there were no signs of mischief when he burst through the door.

They looked at the door. They looked at each other. They waited anxiously for the lecture that never came.

"Just getting a drink of water," Andy grunted from the kitchen, the unnecessary clashing of cupboard doors and the frustration in his voice as he headed back up the stairs, a clear sign that he didn't agree with leaving his mother alone with his friend.

In a room, full of emotions, they forced smiles and spoke in surreptitious whispers, watching the fire crackle, the mood unavoidably broken, the intimacy and the passion, the excitement and libido consumed in the flames.

Ruth emptied what was left of the wine into two glasses and made the best attempt to apologise for her son's protective behaviour.

"Ever since the divorce, Andy's been very protective. He means well," she sighed, lifting the glass to her mouth. "He's still young and sensitive but it's just a matter of time before he grows out of it," she smiled, draining the wine from her glass.

His bedroom was spacious, with a double bed, a hand basin in the corner of the room and fitted wardrobes running the entire length of one wall.

He removed his t-shirt, dropped his shorts to the floor and took himself in hand.

It was time for the tissues.

"This shouldn't take long," he smiled, images for masturbation already forming inside his head. *The kiss.... The heat of her breath.... Her stunning body.... Her shapely bottom.... Her weighty tits falling into his hands.*

"I want to touch you, Ruth," he fantasised, his mind creating images of her nakedness and the bulging veined beast growing rapidly in his hand.

"I'm want to fuck you, Ruth," he grunted, wrapping his fingers around the girth, tugging and pulling, working the length back and forth, fast and slow, up and down, the sound of the bedroom door closing against the latch and the shapely silhouette of an unexpected visitor, dressed in a white robe, interrupting his moment of pleasure.

"Who's there?" he whispered, choking back lump in his throat and pulling a bed sheet over the swollen limb, blinking his eyes and trying to focus in the darkness, the shapely curves visible through the diaphanous material and the familiar smell of perfume, informing him that Ruth Dobson had just entered his bedroom.

"It's only me," she announced, floating across the room in a whisper of silent footsteps, her shapely breasts bouncing beneath the robe and a thin smile lifting the corners of her mouth.

"I couldn't sleep. I had to see you," she whispered, the bed creaking slightly as she settled her weight on the mattress.

"Are you pleased to see me?" she asked, smiling into his eyes and kissing him softly on the forehead.

"Yes. Yes, I am, Mrs Dobson," he replied, choking back a lump in his throat, hormonal chaos rattling around inside his head and his heart banging like a drum inside his chest.

"You are pleased to see me," she smiled, the phallic object poking beneath the white cotton sheet, teasing her curiosity and bringing a smile to her face.

"I think I got here just in time," she frowned, lifting off the bed and loosening her robe, smiling into his eyes before brushing it from her shoulders and letting it drop to the floor.

"I think you were going to start without me," she giggled, the smile of a temptress dancing behind closed eyes, twirling on her toes and flaunting her body with flirtatious suggestion, her shapely breasts bouncing with every movement and the mysterious shadowy triangle of pubic hair clearly visible beneath a pair of white panties.

His penis twitched, and his heart missed a beat. His eyes were bulging, and his mouth was wide open. He was afraid that if he blinked his eyes the erotic images would vanish forever.

"I can help you with that." she offered, stepping over the garment and sitting back on the bed. "If you'll let me," she added, leaning over and pulling the bed sheet from his naked body.

"What a gorgeous body," she whispered, blinking her eyes and scraping a finger nail over the hard indents and valleys and the proportional bumps of his abdomen, pausing when she felt his penis brushing against her hand.

"Wow. It's huge. I wasn't expecting that," she gasped, brushing hair from her face and staring wide eyed at the swollen limb bobbing and swaying in front of her face, thoughts and images of the gruesome muscle stretching and filling her body teasing her senses and wetting her thighs.

"And thick," she breathed, studying the shape of the bulbous head and making a mental note of the awesome length, marvelling at the substantial girth and watching the sticky white fluid oozing from the open eye.

"So, you've always admired my breasts," she said, a flirtatious smile lifting the corners of her mouth and a familiar wetness manifesting between her thighs.

"Give me your hands," she smiled, squeezing them gently before placing them firmly on her breasts, letting him feel the warmth, the weight, the softness and the hard nipples rubbing against his sweating palms.

"I think you're ready," she breathed, feeling a familiar fluid brushing against her leg.

"Let me take care of you," she said, smiling into his eyes and wrapping her fingers around the fleshy column, feeling the firmness of youth filling her hand.

"You're so hard," she whispered, moving her hand up and down the length in slow measured strokes, tugging and pulling, stroking and squeezing, back and forth, faster and faster, gripping the girth and dragging the loose foreskin over the smooth head, feeling his sticky solution coating her hand.

"I'm coming. I'm coming, Mrs Dobson" he moaned, closing his eyes and sucking in gasps of air through clenched teeth.

"Come for me. Let it all come out," she said, in a persuasive whisper, just as the dam broke and his balls exploded, his life source shooting into orbit in never-ending streams of seminal fluid before falling back to earth, coating her hand, decorating her breasts and spilling over the bed sheet.

"I'm sorry about the mess, Mrs Dobson," he croaked, breathing in urgent gasps of air through his nose, his limp flesh hanging like a quivering serpent over his thigh and his balls drained of liquid passion.

"You don't have to apologise," she said, smiling at his innocence and kissing him on the forehead before rolling off the bed. "I just wanted to make you feel good," she smiled, the messy offering cooling quickly on her hands as she skipped across the room to the hand-basin.

"I'll just wash my hands," she said, ignoring the old taps groaning in protest and smiling into a mirror as she cleaned the sticky mess from her hands.

"I can't let you sleep on a wet bed," she smiled, taking a handful of paper tissues from a box and humming a love song inside her head.

'Love was just a glance away, a warm embracing.... Dooby-dooby-do,' she whispered, cleaning his attachments,

the sensuous movement of a paper tissue brushing over his fallen champion and her pendulous breasts swinging with the motion of her hand, bringing a smile to his face and his flaccid penis back to life.
"Have I done that," she giggled, dropping the sticky tissues on the floor and curling her fingers around the long-veined column, feeling the firmness of youth growing rapidly in her hand. "You're an insatiable young man," she said, smiling into his eyes and working the length back and forth, pulling the foreskin over the bulbous head and watching it smooth away over the thickening girth.
"What a beautiful specimen," she thought, pausing momentarily to admire his physique and his growing attachment. *The length...The girth...The firmness.*
"Haven't you had enough?" she smiled, the question sweeping away the corrupt images from her mind, remembering that he was only eighteen and his body was still growing, mindful that she was in his bed and the ache between her legs needed urgent attention.
"Not yet," he casually answered, his head and his heart floating somewhere in heaven.
"That's good," she whispered. slipping out of her knickers and dropping them on the floor next to the paper tissue.
"I need to be touched," she breathed, kneeling on the bed on all fours with her bottom perched precariously above his face, the folds and petals of her sex peeking through a forest of dark pubic hair.

"Touched," he croaked, blinking his eyes into focus and pausing briefly to admire her sex. "Touched," he nervously repeated, sweeping his hands over feminine curves, exploring and probing, discovering unfamiliar territory, before sliding a finger through the dark bush of pubic hair and parting the delicate flaps and folds of her moist entrance.

"Wow, Mrs Dobson. You've got a beautiful body," he whispered, feeling the heat, the textures and the wetness, watching the cheeks of her bottom opening and closing as she shifted her weight on the bed and gazing at the hairy valley and the dark pigmented skin around her anal opening, breathing in the musty smell of sex and waiting for his balls to erupt.

He couldn't believe what was happening to his body. It felt like he was in a dream, floating somewhere above the ground. Somewhere in paradise.

Up to this point in his life, Ruth had been nothing more than a fantasy in his thoughts. A visitor in his imagination. A vision of wonder, who had guided his hand through tireless hours of masturbation.

"But now it's real and she wants me to touch her. Christ, she might want more than that," he thought, his imagination running wild with conflicting thoughts that he might have to perform sexual intercourse.

The warm melting pleasure of her mouth and a wet tongue marking a sensuous trail of oral fluids along the swollen shaft, broke his mental dilemma.

"Does this make you feel good," she smiled, easing him in and easing him out, sucking him in and spitting him out, sweeping her tongue over the sensitive head and wiggling the tip inside the small eye, sucking and blowing, feasting on his essence of youth.

"Yes. Yes, Mrs Dobson," he grunted, moaning and groaning and sucking in air through his nose, closing his eyes and gritting his teeth, before blurting her name in a final warning.

"I'm coming...I'm...I'm coming...I'm commiinngggg," he moaned, his balls exploding with a frenzied force, emotional ballast spewing in copious streams from the open eye, the untimely communion splashing inside her mouth and decorating her face, stinging her eyes and making her gag.

"I can't breathe," she gasped, easing the meaty object from her mouth and staring inquisitively at the endless surge of sticky white substance, as if fascinated by the exceptional quantity.

"You're going to have to control your emotions when you make love to me," she smiled, leaning over the washbasin and cleaning the sticky residue from her hands for the second time that night.

"Make love...Mr's Dobson," he gulped. "I…I Should tell..."

"You don't have to explain," she smiled, interrupting his confession. "I understand your inexperience. But that's another thing I can help you with when I come to your bedroom tomorrow night," she whispered, a furtive smile curling the corners of her mouth.

"And after what we've just done tonight, I think you can call me Ruth," she said, slipping into her knickers and picking up her robe from the floor.

He wasn't sure if it was the enthusiastic knock on the bedroom door or the delicious smell of bacon and eggs drifting up from the kitchen that woke him from his sleep, but his eyes were just coming into focus when Andy barged into his bedroom.

"Breakfasts ready," Andy barked, sweeping back the curtains with infuriating enthusiasm and filling the room with sunlight.

"It smells delicious," he croaked, trying to disguise the guilt in his voice and trying to hide his embarrassment behind a forced smile.

"Good morning," Ruth greeted the boys, as they walked into the kitchen, a surreptitious smile lifting the corners of her mouth.

"I like this song," she announced, turning up the volume on the radio and humming along to the music, trying to break the nervous tension hanging between them.

'In My Life,' she sang with the Beatles, twirling in graceful steps, her breasts bouncing hypnotically inside a white blouse and her trousers clinging to her figure like a second skin.

"Sit down at the table," she smiled, placing breakfast plates on the table and finishing the song line. *'I've loved them all.'*

"After you've had your breakfast, I've got a little job that needs done in the gazebo. It's not a difficult task. Just a light bulb," she confirmed, leaning over the table and pouring coffee into cups.

Changing a light bulb would normally be a simple task. But hovering at the top of an unsteady pair of step ladders, with a bothersome wasp buzzing around his head and a permanent lump inside his shorts screaming orders in a coital language that he couldn't comprehend, didn't make the job any easier.

"Fucking light bulb," he sighed, thoughts and images of the previous night flashing inside his head. *The warmth of her mouth...Her shapely breasts...Her curvy bottom and bushy vulva...The blow-job...The aroma of sex still teasing his nostrils.*

"Fuck off," he cursed, swatting away the pest with a sweeping hand and almost losing his balance, catching a glimpse of the vision of beauty walking down the garden path, towards the gazebo.

Framed in a halo of sunlight with one hand raised to protect her eyes from the sun, her hips swaying like a cat-walk model and her breasts bouncing freely beneath a white cotton blouse, Ruth Dobson looked like an angel.

"Can I help?" she breathed, raising both hands and playfully squeezing his buttocks, the smell of her perfume teasing his nostrils and the touch of her hand, enough to wake the sleeping monster inside his shorts.

"I would like to see what mouth-watering delights are hidden inside those shorts, but I'm afraid I must go and prepare dinner. And don't forget our rendezvous tonight?" she prompted, as she left the gazebo, just as quickly as she had entered.

With a light bulb sweating in the palm of his hand and the visitor inside his shorts twitching as if it had a mind of its own, he sighed and went back to work. After drowning in a sea of hormonal promise for almost an hour there came a point when he thought if he didn't masturbate soon his balls would explode. After checking his watch for the millionth time the sound of his bedroom door closing against the latch and a whisper of movement gliding across the floor in the hide and seek of shadows, signalled the beginning of a momentous night of passion.

"Sorry I'm late," she sighed, brushing her robe casually from her shoulders and letting it fall to the floor, a pair of white knickers hugging curves and dipping into valleys, twisting and twirling in stockings and suspenders, swaying her hips and flaunting her body with provocative suggestion.

"I had to make sure Andrew was sleeping," she whispered, shuffling her feet and wiggling her hips, sliding her panties over her thighs and letting them drop on the floor. "I'll make it worth your while," she smiled, flashing her eyes with flirtatious intent before rolling her stockings down her legs and slipping them off her feet.

"I've thought about you all day," she whispered, climbing on the bed, kissing his lips and blowing a whisper of hot breath into his mouth, feeling the throbbing limb pushing urgently against her body and a familiar moisture gathering between her thighs.

"You and Andrew are heading off to Barcelona tomorrow, so this is probably our last moment together. I want to make it special," she smiled, moving her hips and pushing back, letting him feel the warmth of her tits flattening against his chest, letting him feel the intense heat of arousal and the emerging heat of passion between her legs.

"Very special," she whispered, lowering her head and sweeping her warm wet tongue over his chest and then moving south over his muscular stomach, dipping into his naval and brushing her hand through his pubic hair.

"Keep still. Don't move," she smiled, dragging her finger nails over the hairy scrotum and gripping his meaty cock, wrapping her fingers around the thick girth and stroking the length, feeling it growing rapidly in her hand.

"Enjoy the moment," she grinned, snaking her wet tongue up the length and easing him into her mouth, easing him out in trailing strings of saliva, pulling the foreskin back and sweeping her tongue over the bulbous head, probing the small eye and feasting on his seed of life.

"Ah. Ah. Oh. Oh," Mrs Dobson, he announced, closing his eyes and shuffling anxiously on the bed, moaning and groaning and breathing in urgent gasps, euphoric mutterings signalling his premature release.

"Don't you dare come," she sighed, letting him slip from her mouth, a frustrated voice joining an unforgiving stare.

"I desperately need you inside me tonight," she said, an uncompromising smile lingering long enough to make sure he controlled his emotions.

'They were going to fuck,' he sighed, choking back a nervous lump in his throat, the cold realisation of performing sexual intercourse suddenly feeding his panic.

'She doesn't know I'm a virgin…? Should I tell her…? What if I can't get it up...? What if I get it up and she's disappointed?' he thought, the sound of squeaking bedsprings and a demanding voice interrupting his sexual torment.

"Let me get on top," she volunteered, shifting her weight on the bed and squatting over him with both knees on the mattress and his swollen limb throbbing against her bottom.

"Okay," he croaked, closing his eyes and clenching his teeth, trying to control his emotions.

"Let me do the honours," she insisted, shuffling on her knees and lifting her bottom slightly, opening her legs and lowering her hand, wrapping her fingers around his cock and easing the swollen limb inside her body.

"Oh. Ah," she gasped, gritting her teeth and sucking in air through her nose, whimpering through a painful cry when she felt the length and girth stretching the flaps and folds and filling her moist entrance with hard flesh.

"Give me a moment," she sighed, easing him out slowly and brushing wet hair from her face, waiting patiently for her body to adjust to the brutal invasion.

"I'm okay now," she smiled, moving her hips to the persuasion of touch, a mature woman submitting to the compelling needs of nature, a clear sign that Ruth Dobson had gone too long without having the pleasure of a man inside her.

"That feels good," she moaned, lifting and lowering, easing him in and easing him out, rising and falling, drawing him in and slipping him out, up and down and in and out, fast and slow, slow and fast, softness against hardness, skin smacking against skin, moans following groans, wheezes chasing grunts and pants forcing sighs.

"It's been too long," she whispered, working him tirelessly, thrusting and grinding and wriggling and twisting, easing him in and easing him out, wriggling her hips and taking him deep, lifting up and easing down, two people joined together in a moment of intimate connection, two voices exchanging compliments and words of endearment, loving and giving, giving and taking, moving back and forth to impulsive urges, rejoicing in a mutual courtship of sexual discovery.

"Let me help," he offered, holding her hips with both hands, lifting her up and pulling her back, up and down and back and forth, bucking and thrusting, pushing in and pulling out, penetrating deep inside the vaginal vault, reaching the limits of her inner core and fucking the last breath of air from her lungs. Sensation followed sensation, two hearts racing in timeless beats, sweat and perspiration fusing in the momentum of give and take, hands searching and fingers gripping flesh, euphoric whispers growing into blissful cries, genitalia embracing genitalia and body fluids blending with the heat of passion.

His release was powerful and sustained, streams of liquid lava firing up his shaft and shooting through the open eye, a million trillion sperm splashing with reckless abandon inside her innermost depths, flooding the inner walls of the vaginal vault in a sea of seminal fluids.

"I'm exhausted. That was amazing," she gasped, lying on her back and staring at the ceiling, breathing in precious air through her nose and trying to calm the heart banging like a drum inside her chest.

"You were very good. You certainly lasted longer than I expected," she smiled, breathing in and blowing out, waiting for the welcoming calm.

"How do you feel. Was it good. Was it all you expected it to be?" she asked, smiling into his innocent eyes and brushing strands of wet hair from her face.

He tried to speak. His mouth was moving but nothing was coming out. He was floating somewhere in heaven, marvelling at his achievement and wanting to shout at the top of his voice that he was no longer a virgin.

He resisted the temptation.

"I'll take that as a yes," she smiled, leaning over and kissing him softly on the lips, the warmth of her breasts brushing against his arm, stirring the sleeping muscle and bringing him back to reality.

"Are you getting an erection again. You're a machine. You don't know when to stop," she giggled, kissing him on the forehead and running her soft hand over his hairless face.

"It's not every day you lose your virginity, Mrs Dobson" he said, a triumphant smile lifting the corners of his mouth and a massive wave of relief sweeping away the burden of adolescence turmoil.

"Especially to a beautiful woman like you, Mrs Dobson," he uttered, words of endearment and the promises of eternal affection waiting anxiously behind tight lips.

He wanted to celebrate. He wanted to tell her how much he loved her. He wanted to ask questions. He needed reassurance.

He would have to wait. She had other things on her mind.

"I think I need to do something about that," she said, pointing a finger and smiling at the fleshy column bobbing and swaying in front of her eyes.

"Get on the floor. I want you to make love to me from the back," she said, shifting her weight on the bed and kneeling on all fours, with her hands flat on the mattress and her bottom raised submissively in the air, her smile widening and her legs following suit.

"Put it in" she said, glancing over her shoulder and brushing hair from her face, watching him shuffling his feet on the floor and moving his hips back and forth in a simulation of coital enquiry, trying to penetrate the burning inferno between her legs.

"Let me help you with that," she smiled, reaching back with her hand and guiding him in, two lovers joined in a sea of blissful sensation, moving to persuasive urges in a progression of give and take, flesh to flesh, skin to skin, joining and separating, a mature and wanting woman giving way to the force and the energy of youth.

"Oh. Yes. Oh Yes," she gasped, gripping the bed sheet with both hands, feeling him pushing in and pulling out, in and out, forward and back, hard and fast, easing from her body and then sliding back in, entering and retreating, soft and slow, breathless gasps stumbling over pleasurable cries, moans and groans and frustrated sighs turning into a vocal demand that caught him by surprise.

"Push that big cock inside me. Fuck me faster. Fuck me harder. Hurt me. Make me come," she pleaded, impulsive urges spilling from an abandoned mouth and stealing her dignity.

"I'll try, Mrs Dobson," he sighed, pausing momentarily and choking back a lump in his throat, the crude obscenity something that he didn't expect to hear from a Christian kind of woman as refined and innocent as Ruth.

"Let me know if I'm doing it right," he croaked, swallowing the lump in his throat and moving back and forth to the persuasion of touch, knowing that her choice of words was nothing more than a spontaneous reaction caught up in the heat passion, storing the filthy obscenity in his memory files for future use during solo stimulation.

"You're doing it right. In fact, you're getting very good at this," she smiled, pulling him close, two lovers fused together in pools of sweat and perspiration, moving back and forth to persuasive urges, in and out, pushing in and pulling out, hard and fast, all the way in and all the way out.

"Oh…Yes," she moaned, feeling the tight labia lips gripping the girth on the way in and the moist flaps and folds clutching the length on the way out, in and out and back and forth, sliding in and slipping out, all the way in and all the way out, filling her body with hard flesh and sucking the last breath of air from her body.

"I'm, coming. I'm, coming," he grunted, moving his hips back and forth, the bed rocking, the floorboards creaking and the bedsprings squeaking in a fanfare of perpetual give and take. "I'm coming…I'm coming," he gasped, a sea of liquid passion rushing through his shaft with a burning intensity, streams of seminal fluids splashing the walls of the vaginal vault and reaching the cervix, the heat of passion exploding inside her vulva, teasing her senses and bringing her to the edge of euphoric bliss.

"Don't stop. Keep it in. Oh…Ahhh. Fuck. Fuck. I'm, comiinngggg," she hissed, sucking in air through her nose and blowing out through her mouth, arching her feet and curling her toes, vaginal fluids flooding her thighs and euphoric mutterings smothered behind tight lips, a breath-taking orgasm celebrated in blowing whispers of silence.

"Are you okay, Mrs Dobson," he innocently asked, easing the softening limb from her body, the intimacy and passion and the physical endurance of orgasmic release consumed in racing heartbeats, breathless pants and restless flutters.

"I'm fine," she gasped, brushing hair from her face and sucking in air through her nose, waiting for her heart beat to calm and the euphoric tremors to melt away.

"That was amazing," she smiled, breathing in through her nose and blowing out through her mouth. "You certainly hit the spot. And twice in one night. You're the perfect lover," she added, the ego-boost bringing a smile to his face and making him feel an inch taller.

"This must be our secret," she whispered, staring into his eyes and speaking in conspiratorial whispers. "No one must know. Andy would be devastated if he ever found out we had slept together," she added, shifting her weight on the bed and looking in his eyes for reassurance.

"I'm tired. I'll have to get back to my room," she purred, yawning into her hand and snuggling her face into the pillow.

A questioning voice and the sound of fingers tapping impatiently across the bedroom door, broke them from their slumber.

"Are you awake, Mark?" a familiar voice enquired.

"It's Andy," they whispered in unison, rolling off the bed in a panic and gathering their clothes from the floor.

"Christ. How did we let that happen?" he cursed, pulling on his briefs and staring at the bedroom door in utter shock and disbelief.

"He mustn't find me in here," Ruth sighed, choking back guilt and slipping into her nickers.

"You'll have to get rid of him," she insisted, grabbing her robe and disappearing into one of the double wardrobes.

He took a deep intake of breath, braced himself and opened the door.

"Hi, Andy," he croaked, a lump in his throat threatening to stop him breathing and a knitted weave of agonising knots turning like a nauseating vice inside his stomach.

"You're up early. Couldn't you sleep with all the excitement of the holiday?" he muttered, forcing a smile and covering the door with an outstretched arm, hoping it would prevent him from coming into the room.

"I can't find my mother," Andy announced, brushing past him as if he wasn't there, scanning the room suspiciously, before turning to face his friend.

"I've knocked on her bedroom door, but there's no answer. I've also looked downstairs but she's not there either. My mother's always out of bed before six," he added, pointing at his wrist watch and muttering the time under his breath.

Six-thirty for fucks sake. She's only a half-an-hour late. Ruth was right about his controlling influence on her life, he thought, the chaos inside his head filling with

impulsive thoughts of how to salvage the situation and furthermore protect Ruth's dignity.
"Your mothers probably exhausted and don't forget she had a lot to drink last night, so she's probably nursing a hangover," he said, exaggerating a yawn and feigning a smile.
"Go down stairs and put the kettle on. Once your mother hears you clattering around in her kitchen, she'll appear," he said, forcing another smile. "I'll get dressed and follow you down in a couple of minutes," he added, pointing a finger at the door.
"You're probably right," Andy sighed, lifting his shoulders and glancing around the room one more time before heading out the door.
"That was too close for comfort. I can't stop shaking. I certainly don't want to go through anything like that again," Ruth sighed, blinking her eyes and stepping from the claustrophobic darkness of the wardrobe.
"I'd better go," she said, in a nervous whisper, slipping discretely out the door and tiptoeing across the landing with uncanny silence, avoiding the floorboards that always creaked outside her bedroom door.
Andy was pouring tea into a cup when he walked into the kitchen.
"Any sign of your mother," he asked, hiding his guilt behind a well-practiced poker face, a familiar voice at the kitchen door, interrupting his nervous dilemma.
"Good morning," Ruth announced, draped in a white bathrobe with her hair wrapped in a towel above her head. "Forgive me for not having breakfast prepared

but I've just stepped out of the shower," she said, apologetically, forcing an innocent smile.
"Was that you, banging on my bedroom door, Andy?" she enquired. "It seems I can't use my bathroom these days without first informing my son."
"Sorry," he sighed, shrugging his shoulders and taking two more cups from the cabinet.

The weather forecaster was right when he said the recent hot weather was about to change and we should expect a few days of heavy rain.
"Fucking British weather," Andy cursed, as the Dover to Calais ferry headed out of port. "You don't expect this kind of weather in August," he added, watching the rain spilling in waterfalls over the deck and swaying with the boat, as it climbed the waves of the cruel sea.
"I'm not a very good sailor," he nervously announced, wiping his brow with his hand and holding his stomach, a feeling of nausea turning his face green and his breakfast threatening to make an early appearance. "I'll try and sleep through the journey. Wake me up when we get to Calais," he sighed, lying on a bench seat and resting his head on his backpack.
After suffering from a severe bout of seasickness for most of the journey, it was no surprise that Andy was one of the first to disembark from the ferry.
In the vaporous humidity of a French café, they sipped coffee and talked for almost an hour, mostly about Andy's first and last time on a boat. Once the

colour had returned to Andy's face and Mark had listened to his compelling storey of the ferry crossing for the millionth time, he brushed his hand over the misty window.

"The rains stopped, Andy," he said, interrupting another story. "If we want to get to Paris before midnight, we'd better go," he added, forcing a smile and draining the last of his coffee.

Even without the traditional beret perched on his head and a string of onions around his neck when you looked at Marcel Dubois you knew he was French.

"I can take you into the next village," he offered, pulling to a halt at the side of the road and sticking his head out the window of a rusty old Renault van.

"It's near to a main road, so you'll have a better chance of getting to Paris," he smiled, peering through a pair of beer-bottle glasses perched on the end of a bulbous nose, a cigar sitting permanently in the corner of his mouth with an inch of grey ash hanging precariously from the end.

"One of you will have to get in the back," he said, stepping from the vehicle, his jacket and trousers soiled with several indescribable stains, the origin of which you would hazard a guess at but would never dare ask.

In a challenging protest of groans, creaks and splutters, Marcel fought frantically with a vehicle desperately in need of urgent maintenance and four tyres lacking air and tread.

"Thank you for the lift. Your English is very good," Mark smiled, climbing into the passenger seat and catching a whiff of a disgusting smell coming from the back of the van.

"I picked some of it up during the war, but I also have relatives who live in London," he replied, puffing on his cigar, oblivious to the grey ash falling onto his jacket and trousers.

"Sorry about the smell," Marcel said, in an apologetic voice. "I'm a chicken farmer. I hope your friends okay in the back," he added, rolling down the window to get fresh air into the vehicle.

"This is the village. And that's the main road," Marcel announced, pointing a finger at a road sign and pulling the car to a halt at the side of the road, just as Andy threw up in the back of the vehicle.

After swearing on oath never to eat chicken again they sat on a grassy verge by the side of the road waiting for their next lift, breathing in precious air and watching the Renault van chugging up the road with clouds of black smoke spewing from the exhaust and the engine protesting against the reckless misuse of the clutch and gears.

In a moment of collective silence, they looked at each other in disbelief.

"He can't be serious. Tell him thanks, but no."

"Don't be too hasty. Let's see where he's going to first" Andy replied, picking up his bag from the ground.

“je vais a Paris,” the Frenchman confirmed, as he dismounted from his motorbike, his leather jacket and heavy boots creaking as he lifted the side-car and helped Andy to climb inside.

After the second down stroke on the pedal, the BMW 500cc engine started with a deep throaty roar. With his arms wrapped around the Frenchman and his face pressed hard against a symbol of a blood-soaked dagger imprinted on the back of his leather jacket, they headed for Paris.

The haunting images of his lifeless body lying in an open coffin suddenly fed his panic.

He tightened his grip. He cursed Andy. He prayed.

They had only travelled about ten miles when it started to rain.

After standing on the roadside on the outskirts of Paris for more than an hour, cold and wet from the bike ride and the smell of chicken shit still lingering on their clothes, they wondered if they would ever reach the Spanish border.

With green and purple images and psychedelic symbols designed to demonstrate and support the revolution for love and peace, the Volkswagen Camper Van was a work of art.

“Welcome aboard,” a friendly voice invited, as they climbed into the vehicle, the sweet smell of cannabis and incense mixed with the unmistakable body odours of the unwashed, greeting them with a bottle of beer and a cigarette.

‘Christ! A Volkswagen Camper was never designed for so many people. There must be ten bodies. They made a

mental count. Ten.... No twelve, including the spaced-out driver and the young girl giving him a blow-job.

In the comfort of the warm vehicle they smoked weed and drank beer, watching a group of hairy people sitting cross-legged on the floor, all lost in their own little world, smoking weed or tripping on a more lethal cocktail and all dressed in a way to express rebellion against social citizens of the contemporary world.

A young girl with Che Guevara's face printed on the front of her t-shirt rocked on an old cigarette burnt leather seat, singing and strumming a guitar with a string missing. It appeared to be an off-key rendition of a Joan Baez song, but sadly without the aid of the high-e string her performance gathered little interest.

Once the guitarist realised she had no future in the music industry, the croaky voice of Bob Dylan crackled from a battered old radio. *'Like a Rolling Stone,'* sang alcohol and dope inspired voices, struggling with meaningless words and singing lyrics that didn't exist.

They travelled the rest of the journey south to Montpellier, in a friendly and claustrophobic atmosphere, drinking beer and smoking weed, listening to their compelling narrative of why the hippies had given up their boring lives back in the U.K. and were now heading off to spend the rest of their days living in love and peace on the island of Ibiza.

After arriving at Perpignan and passing through the French border into Spain, they thanked the hippies for their hospitality and boarded a train that would take them along the Spanish coast on their way to Barcelona.

The campsite near Barcelona was modest and inexpensive, but more importantly it was close enough to the nightlife and the inviting buzz of the city centre.

After a night of drinking and flirting with a couple of girls against the splendour of the fountains and the magic of Gaudi's architecture, they quickly settled into holiday mood and soon forgot about their precarious journey through France.

After taking a gap-year before attending Boston University to study architecture, Sally and Kelly were in their last few days of a four-week vacation.

In a café opposite the monumental majesty of Antoni Gaudi's *'La Sagrada Familia,'* the two girls asked them to take a photograph against the backdrop of the magnificent cathedral.

The flash of a Nikon camera was enough to make the introductions.

Over a drink in a nearby bar, the two girls said they were in Barcelona to visit the museums and look at the architecture, so most of the conversation was steeped in historical significance.

Gaudi's architecture. The work of Picasso. Renaissance Art. Canaletto. Michelangelo and Leonardo da Vinci were all subjects joining the conversation with spirited enthusiasm.

Mark and Andy forced smiles and nodded their heads at every appropriate junction, trying to look interested and hoping there would be no questions to answer.

After an hour of listening to the two girls talking about architecture and their ambitions in life, an invitation to join them for a drink at their campsite near Tarragona the following day and a promise not to discuss 'The Arts,' helped to ease their embarrassment.

It was late the following morning when the taxi approached the entrance to the El Cordoba campsite near Tarragona.

"No. Carretera cerrada," the resolute voice of a Spanish Policeman informed the taxi driver, motioning with his hand to pull to a halt against the temporary barrier.

The Police had taped off the main access road and all pedestrian routes into the campsite. Nobody was allowed within fifty yards of the entrance other than the emergency services.

It was utter chaos. They couldn't believe their eyes. It all seemed like a bad dream. They were both speechless.

A young female reporter pointed over the campsite and talked into a TV camera and curious onlookers stood in a line against the barrier, staring into viewfinders and pressing buttons, camera shutters snapping at the speed of light and film capturing timeless images of sadness and tragedy.

Trees around the site were incinerated by the heat and pieces of green and white fabric - presumably the remains of what used to be tents - hung limply from metal posts and the remains of personal possessions, burned clothing and shoes littered the site.

The campsite was swarming with emergency vehicles.

The Fire Service worked tirelessly, trying to extinguish the last of the fire and ambulances sped in and out of the site in a fanfare of sirens and flashing blue lights, taking the dead and injured to hospital.

The pungent smell of human flesh hung in the air and rows of green plastic shrouds embracing lifeless human beings lined the entrance road to the campsite.

Everywhere you looked you saw death.

A news reporter said a tanker delivering liquid gas to the campsite exploded under pressure and within minutes a cloud of propylene gas had spread across the site. When someone unknowingly lit a stove, it ignited the gas and a devastating ball of fire consumed everyone in its path.

The fire at EL Cordoba campsite claimed more than a hundred lives.

The taxi drive back to Barcelona seemed like an eternity. Hardly a word was spoken. The devastation, the haunting images and the uncertainty of Sally and Kelly had left them both speechless.

They prayed in silence.

After purchasing two train tickets that would take them from Barcelona to Paris the following day, they decided to spend their last night in the city.
The clock on the church tower had just registered midnight when they met two girls having a drink by one of the coloured fountains.
The two girls weren't really interested, but nonetheless they listened to their compelling narrative of the fire at the El Cordoba campsite.
They were only interested in sex and money and they intended to make their last night in Barcelona, a night they wouldn't forget.
The sixties were the decade of free love and a liberated society free of any boundaries and furthermore, the advent of 'The Pill' had provided a promiscuous path for those who were willing to take it.
"Have you seen what they're wearing. It's almost verging on indecency," Andy whispered in his friend's ear, clinking glasses with the two girls and trying to look cool.
"The only thing missing is a 'fuck-me-quick' hat on their heads," he discretely added, staring approvingly at endless legs disappearing into micro mini-skirts and pieces of fabric the size of a handkerchief, barely covering their breasts.
"It looks like our lucks about to change for the better. If we don't get a fuck tonight, I'll give you five pounds," Andy said, with the confidence of a lawyer.

"Wake up Mark!" Andy shouted, pacing the floor in a nervous panic.

"She's gone, and the bitch has taken all my fucking money," he cursed, twisting his face in rage and searching inside his pockets. "Have you checked your pockets?" Andy barked at his friend, choking back a nervous lump in his throat and making urgent gestures with his hands.

"Although I can't imagine why they would take my money and not take yours," he sighed, answering his own question.

"FUCK," he spluttered in reply, searching through pockets he didn't know he had, shaking his head from side to side and cursing under his breath at the inevitable outcome.

"You're right, Andy. They've taken all the cash I had in my jeans and shirt pockets," he confirmed, lifting his shoulders in defeat and snarling his anger through gritted teeth.

"Fortunately, I still have a few pesetas and some francs, which I had hidden inside my money-belt," he declared, snorting a sigh of relief and counting the money. "We were lucky. If we hadn't purchased the train tickets to Paris yesterday, we'd be right in the shit," he added.

After swapping notes about their sexual experiences, they accepted what money had been taken was a small price to pay for what the girls had offered in return. And furthermore their holiday was almost over, and it wouldn't be long before they were back in the UK.

As they left Ipswich and headed back to Gateshead, Ruth appeared to be a little subdued. She seemed to lack her usual enthusiasm and her smile held a trace of sadness.

"Andy, I'm concerned about your grandmother's health," she said, in a sympathetic voice.

"She requires daily care and attention that I can't give her living in the North East," she added, pausing to blow her nose in a paper tissue and collect her thoughts.

"I've asked her to come and live with us in Gateshead, but she refused. She said she wants to spend her final days living in the house she shared with.... your grandfather."

"I'm just letting you know that if things don't improve, we might have to move to Ipswich."

The seasons slipped slowly away from warm summer days into cold winter nights, eventually melting into the welcoming spring of a new year.

Mark and Andy both found employment that year and although they had separate careers and worked in different parts of the city, they still remained close friends.

At times, they were inseparable, which unfortunately made it difficult for Mark and Ruth to continue their relationship, but it kept him informed of Andy's whereabouts at all times.

They waited patiently for opportunities. They didn't come. Ruth couldn't wait.

After a lot of subtle persuasion from his mother, Andy agreed to carry out some urgent maintenance work at his grandmother's house in Ipswich.
No risk. No uncertainty. No conspiratorial apprehension. Just a week-end of amazing sex.
Ruth showed him different ways to make their bodies connect and how to arouse a woman during foreplay, making sure she reaches ultimate pleasure.
She spoke with authority, much like a school teacher giving advice to a pupil.
"Ask her what she likes. Find out what turns her on and what turns her off. Remember there are some women who enjoy oral sex and anal sex but there are others who are offended or embarrassed by it. So, if you don't ask, you'll never know."
The sex was physical, heated and extremely vocal.
They fucked in the missionary position. They fucked standing up against a wall. They fucked in the bedroom, doggie-style in front of the mirrored wardrobes. They fucked on the couch. They fucked over a table. They fucked on the floor. They fucked over the kitchen sink. They dropped onto the floor in the sixty-nine-position. Her on top of him. Him on top of her. Two people joined together in a union of suffocating passion, two lovers copulating in an endless display of oral and anal sex.
She mothered him. She fucked him. She sucked him and fucked him again. She swallowed his swollen limb. She swallowed his life source. She stole his heart.

It was early in June when he received the news that would change his life forever.
Ruth informed him that she was moving to Ipswich in September to live with her mother.
Although the news was somewhat expected, and he knew he would miss Andy's friendship, the pain he felt in his heart for his mother would always have a deep and everlasting effect.
Saturday the 30th September 1967 was a day he would never forget.
It was 6.45.am and he hadn't closed his eyes all night.
He had spent most of the night casually thumbing through a book and admiring the parting gift from Ruth, the new wrist-watch and book a precious reminder of their time together.
Ruth told him the book was an informative study carried out by 'Masters and Johnson on the reaction of Human Sexual Response' during different stages of sexual arousal.
Wiping a tear from his eye and choking back a lump in his throat, he read the inscription.
"To my dearest Mark...You will always be in my thoughts. All my love...Ruth."
The clock on the bedside table told him it was almost 7.00.am.
He leaned over and pressed a black button on the radio.
Tony Blackburn greeted the early morning listeners.
"Good morning everyone....Welcome to the exciting new sound of Radio 1."
The Move started singing, *'Flowers in the Rain.'*

Sleep of the Guilty (circa-1967)

Jimmy Boyd was a hard man. Towering over most people at six feet tall his casual persona hid the physical, threatening and violent tendencies that earned him his reputation.

The long white scar running across the left side of his neck was given to him by a nightclub doorman, just before Jimmy got the better of him. After Jimmy, had finished with him his injuries were so bad an ambulance had to rush him to the nearest hospital.

Jimmy had an opinion that was without compromise. You either agreed with him or you were wrong. He drank his whiskey by the bottle rather than by the glass and if you were to ask him how he ever managed to get through life, he would be the first to tell you that he had a lot of help from his best friend, Jack Daniels.

Some people called him 'the butcher.' Others called him 'scar face.' But nobody would ever dare say it to his face.

Frank Brand said Jimmy was a fearless maniac and probably the reason why he had his blood-type tattooed on his right arm, the day he joined the British Armed Forces.

Sandra Boyd never used any of these names. She just called him, 'that fucking arsehole.'

Before joining the army, Jimmy lived with his parents in a modest council house in a working-class area of Gateshead. He was only fourteen when his

father fell to his death whilst erecting scaffolding on a multi-storey building.
After the funeral, he refused to go back to school. He told everyone that he would get a job and look after his mother.
But Jimmy never lived up to his mother's expectations. From the age of fourteen he spent most of his teenage years in and out of young offender's institutions. Although most of his offences were for minor thefts and ant-social behaviour, when he was eighteen he spent nine-months in prison for GBH.
Like most young offenders, he avoided rehabilitation and acquired a hatred for authority. When he was inside he spent most of his time either boxing or pumping iron in the gym.
The only three things that prison gave Jimmy Boyd was independence, a reputation and an amazing physique.
The night Frank Brand called into his local pub and offered a lending hand to Jimmy Boyd, it forged a bond of friendship between the two men.
Jimmy was already punching and kicking at two men on the floor while a third man swung punches at the back of his head. But even though he was outnumbered, he fought like a man possessed.
That's when Frank decided to make the fight a little more even.
After placing a firm arm around his throat, he pulled the third man away, dragging him like a rag doll until he was clear of the action.

After feeling the brutal force of Jimmy's violent temper, it wasn't long before the three defeated men escaped through an exit door at the side of the building.

After an exchange of hands and a beer at the bar, Jimmy told Frank that the three men had bullied and beaten him through his early school days. Lifting his glass to his mouth he confessed that being a skinny kid with a stammer and his hands and face covered in warts, he was a prime target for bullies.

Fortunately, by the time he reached his late teens his stammer had gone and so had the warts.

Jimmy Boyd had suspected for some time that his wife was having an affair with someone she worked with at the local council office.

Desperate to find out the truth about his wife's infidelity he constantly racked his brain, hoping he could resolve the situation before the army sent him on his next tour.

There were lots of rumours and speculation about Sandra's infidelity. Jimmy was a little naïve at first, but after a little snooping, he soon discovered that his suspicions were correct.

Sandra was having an affair with her boss, a married man in his mid-forties. In his remit as Housing Manager he was responsible for the maintenance, allocation and subsequent letting of all council houses, so there was no surprise when Sandra and Jimmy were unexpectedly offered a fully modernised council house, only a few hundred yards from his mother.

In the early years of married life, they struggled emotionally and financially and there were times when the strain became unbearable and after too many arguments and physical abuse their future together, looked increasingly doubtful.

Jimmy had blackened Sandra's eyes so many times you rarely saw her without dark glasses. But for the sake of their son they made the best of a volatile relationship. They gave up sharing a bed together and although they slept under the same roof, they both led separate lives.

Jimmy first became suspicious when Sandra started to wear sexy underwear and about twice a week she would go out in the car and wouldn't return until the early hours of the next morning. Whenever Jimmy questioned her, she always had a reasonable explanation and a girlfriend that was always willing to provide her with a watertight alibi.

Although their marriage had reached the end of its life and a divorce offered the best solution, Jimmy's male chauvinistic attitude wouldn't be compromised until he knew the truth about Sandra's affair. He also knew that the only way he was going to know for sure was to catch her red-handed with her lover.

And that's when Frank came up with a brilliant plan. Like most young men in their late teens the availability of money was always at a premium, so when Frank Brand offered his brother a substantial amount of cash for a few hours of his time, it didn't take him long to make up his mind.

On a blistering hot August evening, Jimmy Boyd opened the boot of his wife's car and helped Mark Brand to crawl inside. The plan was that he would remain inside the boot and hopefully catch Sandra having sex with her lover.

Lying on his side in the foetal position he tried to adjust himself to his new environment. Jimmy smiled and threw a packet of chewing gum, hitting him on the side of his head.

"It's going to be a long night, so put it in your pocket in case you get hungry later," he sniggered sarcastically, before closing the car boot.

The sound of the engine followed by a squeal of rubber confirmed that Sandra had pulled out of the drive and was heading off to meet her lover.

Aware that he probably had a long night ahead of him he tried to manoeuvre his body to get as comfortable as possible, although he quickly realised that the boot of a Ford Cortina Mk1 was never designed for human cargo.

It was dark, hot and uncomfortable and there was that distinctive smell of engine oil and exhaust fumes that you always associate with garages.

As he shifted his weight inside the tight enclosure, a sense of claustrophobia suddenly fed his panic.

He knew he had made a wrong decision.

But it was too late. It had gone too far. There was no going back.

He nervously chewed the inside of his mouth.

After travelling for about twenty minutes the car pulled to a halt. The sound of the passenger door slamming shut, and the muffled sound of a male voice signalled that their night of misbehaviour was about to begin.

As he willed his eardrums to capture a slight hint of their conversation the doors suddenly opened and they both stepped out of the car.

In the uncanny silence, he held his breath, listening for sounds, trying to figure out why they had left the vehicle. His only thought was that they had decided to go for a drink until it was dark enough to prevent any unwanted spectators.

As the minutes crawled by with tedious trepidation he cursed himself for his stupidity.

After almost an hour of muttering profanities, the ensuing silence was suddenly interrupted by the sound of the driver's door opening. Only this time Sandra was alone.

Clouds of cigarette smoke began to drift inside the boot and although the unhealthy environment urged him to cough, he made sure he resisted the temptation.

With her heart beating at the speed of sound and her foot pressed hard against the accelerator pedal, Sandra followed her lover to their destination.

When the car eventually pulled to a halt, the door opened, and a man climbed into the passenger seat. They talked for a few minutes but again their conversation was vague.

With hormones reaching boiling point their night of passion soon got underway.

Through a fanfare of squeaking springs and a vocal commentary of muffled promises, two impatient lovers groaned out their pleasure in a chorus of euphoric grunts, moans and groans and breathless gasps.

A furtive voyeur alone in the darkness, a packet of chewing-gum his only companion, listening for sounds and making mental notes, easing into the role of a private investigator.

After a moment of unnerving silence, the rear doors opened and they both climbed into the back seat of the car. This time the action got physical and heated.

In no time, the car was rocking back and forth to the motion of two people fucking through a running commentary of filthy curses and crude obscenities.

"YES! YES! Fuck Me Harder. Fuck Me Faster. Harder. Faster," Sandra pleaded, her lustful demands echoing inside the boot and bringing a smile to his face.

"Yes. Yes," he whispered under his breath, shifting his weight and reaching inside his pocket for the packet of chewing-gum, the pretence of conspiratorial smugness lifting the corners of his mouth, knowing that when he gives Jimmy his PI report it would surely get him a well-deserved bonus.

"She can't get enough," he thought, as their lustful passion and vocal persuasion quickly gathered speed. *"They're like a couple of dogs on heat,"* he grinned, the increasing momentum of give and take tossing the vehicle from side-to-side, the sudden

movement throwing him against the side of the boot and forcing a nervous gasp.

He swallowed the gum. It was caught in his throat and blocking his windpipe. He couldn't breathe. He was hyperventilating. He was going to choke to death. He panicked.

"LET ME OUT OF HERE...! GET ME OUT!" he shouted, launching into a fit of choking coughs and breathless gasps and banging his clenched fist hard against the inside of the car boot.

"What the hell's going on?" Sandra barked, holding the boot open, as he scrambled out and fell to the ground in a gasping heap.

Kneeling on all fours with his arms outstretched in front of him and his face turning a deep shade of purple and a choking sensation in his throat that threatened to stop him breathing, he frantically sucked in air through his nose, trying to get oxygen into his lungs before he passed out.

"Let me help you," said a faceless man appearing from the shadows, the urgency to straddle over his limp body with his arms wrapped firmly around his stomach, signalling his intention to undertake the 'Heimlich' manoeuvre.

"Don't move," he insisted puffing and panting and pulling hard on his chest, the sustained pressure on his lungs forcing a reaching gasp.

"Again," the man announced, shuffling his feet on the ground and repeating the manoeuvre, another gasp forcing the blockage from his mouth and dropping to the ground in a stream of choking saliva.

The car door slammed shut and tyres screeched over tarmac, leaving clouds of exhaust fumes spilling in his wake, a clear sign that the faceless man was in a desperate hurry to leave.
"I'm sorry, Sandra," he sighed, removing strings of saliva from his chin and coughing and wheezing through a lingering trail of choking exhaust fumes.
"He was in a bit of a hurry," he added, knowing that a good private investigator would have taken his registration number, lifting his shoulders in defeat, aware that his future as a PI was sadly coming to end.
"You would be in a fucking hurry if you found someone hiding in the boot of your car," Sandra bellowed, raising both eyebrows and pointing a finger.
"Get in the fucking car. You've got some explaining to do." she barked, her voice growing in volume and her eyes narrowing with questioning uncertainty.
Over the next twenty minutes the story unfolded, and he had no option but to give Sandra a detailed account of the cunning plan devised between Jimmy and Frank.
But when he told her that Jimmy would probably beat the shit out of them when he finds out about her sexual liaison with the faceless man, her mood unexpectedly changed.
After muttering something under her breath that sounded like, *'that fucking arsehole,'* she rolled the car window down and took a packet of cigarettes from her handbag.

After removing two from the pack she lit them both and handed him one of the cigarettes.

He raised his hand at the offending weed. "No thanks, Sandra. I don't......"

"I know you don't smoke. But this is probably a good time to start," she said, interrupting his declaration, a thin smile lifting the corners of her mouth.

"Take it. It'll calm your nerves," she insisted, handing him the cigarette.

They talked for a while, mainly about her volatile relationship living with Jimmy.

Sandra said that his arrogance and uncaring attitude was the main reason which ultimately led to her affair with the faceless coward in the fast car.

She confessed that when she found out Jimmy was playing around with other women, she felt used and humiliated. She said there was one occasion when she overheard Jimmy telling Frank that he wouldn't let a wedding ring get in the way of a good fuck.

In a nervous voice, she told him that Jimmy had knocked her down so often there were times when she thought she would never get up again.

After searching his face, hoping to see a trace of understanding she sighed and pulled on her cigarette, the sorrow in her eyes and the regret in her voice, choking back anger and pain.

"The act of infidelity and the danger it brings seems to be so exhilarating at the time," she declared, through a fog of smoke. "We try to convince ourselves that it's nothing more than two people having a bit of fun and trying to bring a little excitement into their dull lives. Love sometimes demands that we take risks, but we all know life's never that simple," she added, wiping a tear from her eye and forcing a smile.

"It's never simple. Tonight's a good example of that," he sighed, rolling the window down just enough to drop his cigarette through a small gap.

"And risk," he blurted, thinking about his eventual encounter with Jimmy and the inevitable outcome for Sandra when he tells Jimmy about his wife's infidelity.

A long silence of suffocating uneasiness consumed the air inside the car before Sandra's questioning voice broke the apprehension.

"That's the first time I've fucked with an audience," she whispered, raising both eyebrows, the boldness of her statement sweeping away the tension and changing the mood.

After a brief moment of light-hearted humour, he casually cleared a layer of condensation from the inside of the glass and glanced at his watch.

He was surprised to see it was only eleven thirty.

"I won't say anything, if you don't Mark," a voice said, breaking the silence.

"We don't have to tell him anything. Fuck Jimmy," she barked, fumbling nervously with a packet of cigarettes. "We both know he's nothing but a fucking arsehole," she added, handing him another cigarette and nibbling on a finger nail, waiting patiently for a response.

"I....I don't understand. What....What will I say?" he stammered, choking back a lump in his throat and searching her eyes for reassurance.
"What will I say when he eventually opens the car boot to let me out?"
Sandra chose her words carefully.
"It's simple," she said, reassuringly. "You just tell Jimmy that the voice you heard inside the car was female. I'll tell him that I met a friend and we went clubbing together. Don't worry. I'm a very good liar," she smiled, handing him a cigarette.
"That sounds like a reasonable explanation," he croaked, nodding his head and pulling on his cigarette, the anguish and uncertainty joining the miasma of nicotine inside his lungs.
"But will it convince Jimmy?" he sighed, coughing into his hand.
"What can he do. There's only me and you that know the truth," she whispered, flicking her cigarette ash out the window, her voice and demeanour growing in confidence.
"If you convince Jimmy that all you heard were two female voices, he'll have no other option but to accept what you say," she smiled, gazing into his confused eyes and giving his hand a gentle squeeze.
"Trust me. If we both stick to the same story, Jimmy will never find out," she said, with the conviction of a barrister.
"Fucking arsehole," she uttered, removing a compact mirror from a bag and tracing a finger over an

eyebrow, the reflection throwing back an image of a defiant and bitter woman.

After repairing her eye-shadow and cursing into a mirror for almost ten minutes, Sandra's questioning voice broke the uncertainty hanging between them.

"It's only midnight....The nightclubs don't close until two in the morning....We can't go home too soon," Sandra said, placing her handbag on the floor and shifting her weight in the seat.

"We're going to be here for a while, so why don't we...," she smiled, lowering her hand and squeezing the sleeping monster inside his pants.

"CHRIST! Sandra," he barked, blinking his eyes into focus.

"What the fucks happening. And where's your blouse and bra?" he gasped, shuffling nervously on the seat and lowering his voice slightly. "I thought any issues we had with Jimmy were resolved and now you're half naked and you've got your hand on my...."

"Cock," she answered for him, smiling and flicking up the hem of her skirt in a flirtatious gesture, a dark bush of pubic hair easily visible against the smooth white flesh of her thighs.

"I'm not wearing any panties either," she said, with mocking tease. "There in my handbag. And they can stay there until I've finished with you," she smiled, leaning over and peppering warm kisses over his neck, the persuasive words in his ear, fuelling his libido and sweeping away the need for caution.

"Remember what I said. Life sometimes demands that we take risks," she whispered, the pulse of her lips marking a warm wet trail from his ears and across his forehead, kissing his eyes and his lips, slipping her tongue into his mouth and pressing her breasts against his chest, letting him feel the softness and the weight, letting him feel the emerging heat of passion, the sexual demands of a wanting woman.

"But Sandra," he croaked, his head swimming in a sea of emotional confusion, the closeness and familiarity, the flirtatious intent and intimate suggestion increasing his heart rate and sending a visceral surge of blood flooding into his genitals.

"Just relax," she whispered, an inquisitive hand finding the growing lump inside his pants.

"It'll be our secret," she smiled, mouths connecting, lips flirting and tongues dueling in a flirtatious dance, sweeping over teeth, wiggling and dancing, swirling and sucking, feasting on the intoxicating heat of each other's breath.

"Lift up a little?" she whispered, fumbling with the zip on his pants, the fullness of her breasts and the acquaintance of her hand brushing away caution and any lingering anxieties.

"Okay," he said, hesitancy turning into submission, leaning back in the seat and sliding his jeans and briefs over his thighs, the white veined column springing free from the fabric and bringing a smile to her face.

"What a massive cock," she gasped, blinking her eyes into focus and wrapping her fingers around the thick girth, working the length with eager enthusiasm, quick strokes, slow strokes, back and forth, fisting and pulling, gripping the fleshy limb on the way down and easing her grip on the way back.

He was in uncharted waters, swimming in a sea of emotional tides and turbulent currents and riding the waves of an unpredictable storm.

"Do you really want to continue with this," a voice inside his head asked, the haunting images of Jimmy's violent temper when he finds out he's been shagging his wife, finding their way inside his head.

The Hospital... The Surgeons... All working tirelessly trying to repair his battered face... 'But Jimmy would never find out. Sandra would never tell him.... would she'?

'There's still time to stop this.' The voice inside his head chirped in.

Part of him wanted to end it now but another part of him was drawn to the danger, excitement and the emotional challenge of a sexual wanting woman.

"Fuck it," he sighed, aware that hormonal chaos had now taken control of his senses, purging his brain and making it impossible to think logically.

He knew he was sinking fast, but he had convinced himself that Jimmy would never find out.

The warmth of her mouth and a whisper of hair brushing over his thighs, eroded any indecision from his mind and brought him back to reality.

"Long and thick. Hard and tasty. Just the way I like them," she breathed, gripping the gruesome limb with both hands, pulling and releasing and dragging the foreskin over the sensitive head, easing him in and easing him out, dragging her teeth on the way back and wiggling her tongue inside the small eye, feasting on his sticky arousal and bathing the smooth head in a wash of saliva, sucking him in and swallowing him deep until her jaw ached and she had to let him slip from her mouth to take in air.

"It's too big. I can hardly get it in my mouth," she gasped, the promise of deep penetration and a familiar moistness manifesting between her legs, lifting the corners of her mouth.

"But I do know where it will fit," she grinned, letting him slip from her mouth, hormonal chaos teasing her senses and her heart beating in an urgent rhythm of lust and expectation.

"I want that inside me," she said, the authority in her voice getting his undivided attention.

"Okay," he replied, casually lifting his shoulders. "Do you want it in the front. Or in the back…Or shall we…?" he muttered, a serious face staring back at him and an urgent voice demanding action.

"I don't care where it happens. I just want fucked," she snapped, removing her blouse and skirt, smiling at his innocence and shifting her weight in the seat.

"Help me into the back," she smiled, taking his hand and squeezing between the two front seats, the moonlight casting alluring shadows over a delightful shapely body, a peach shaped bottom and an amazing pair of tits that couldn't be ignored.

By the time they hit the back seat they were naked, overheated and primed for action.

"That's so fucking good," she breathed, feeling his fingers parting the moist lips of her labia and sliding between the slippery flaps and folds.

"How many fingers have you got in there?" she asked, through a whisper of breathless moans and pleasurable groans.

"More fingers," she pleaded, grabbing his hand in a gesture of urgency. "Oh Yes," she purred, when he inserted a second finger inside her burning heat.

"Deeper. Harder. Faster," she insisted, gasping and wheezing and moving her hips back and forth, euphoric mutterings blowing between tight lips when he slid a third finger inside her body, followed quickly by a forth.

Sandra was hot. She was wet. She was ready for cock.

"Let me get on top of you," she said, discomfort giving way to necessity, shuffling on the seat and straddling over his thighs, the vinyl seat, cool against his back and the feint slithers of moonlight casting phallic shadows inside the car.

"I'm not sure if I'll get this all in," she said, with mocking tease, hovering precariously on both knees, opening her legs and adjusting her body for entry.

"But I'm going to try," she smiled, wrapping her fingers around the meaty girth and easing him into her body, an inch at a time.

"It's so big," she breathed, through a chorus of moans and groans and breathless whispers, pausing momentarily until the inner walls of the vaginal vault had stretched enough to make way for the gruesome muscle to slide inside.

There wasn't a lot of flexibility in the back seat of the car and the confined space forced them into unfamiliar territory and made the sexual act frustrating and sometimes a little clumsy.

"That's nice," she moaned, lifting and lowering over the formidable length, easing him in and easing him out, twisting and wriggling, up and down, joining and separating, feeling the vaginal muscles embracing the length and gripping the girth, feeling her body moulding to accept the penetrating force.

"Keep going," she urged, bouncing up and down with increasing urgency, sucking in short gasps of air through her nose and blowing out through her mouth, guiding him along the coital path of deceit and infidelity in a persuasive whisper of encouragement, cursing and sighing in frustration, when his cock slipped out of her body.

"Don't stop. I'll get that," she insisted, shifting her weight on the seat and slipping his cock back inside her body, moving her hips to the persuasion of movement, lifting and lowering, easing him in and easing him out, all the way in and all the way out, thrusting her hips and wriggling her bottom, embracing the awesome length and rejoicing in the exceptional girth, probing and penetrating the limits of her inner heat.

"What a great fuck," she gasped, shifting her weight on the seat and moving her hips in a seductive rhythm of pleasure, lifting and lowering over the fleshy limb, easing him in and easing him out, making sure she was receiving everything he had to offer.

"Feel my tits," she grunted, blinking her eyes into focus and pushing her tits into his face, watching his hands reaching out and cupping her breasts, squeezing one and kissing the other, biting one and nipping the other, pulling and tugging her nipples between his finger and thumb, her whimpering cries of pleasure lost in the discomfort of a painful sigh.

"I'm getting cramp in my leg. I need to change position," she announced, lifting from the seat and letting his cock slip from her body, a voice of authority and a persuasive gesture of movement, motioning him to change position.

"Fuck me from the back," she said, looking back over her shoulder and shifting her weight on the seat, opening her legs and pouting her bottom, blinking stinging sweat from her eyes and gripping the car seat with both hands.

"Put it in," she said, gazing in admiration at the perilous limb bobbing and swaying in the shadows.

"You don't have to be gentle. I want it rough and I want it hard and fast" she added, opening her legs and gritting her teeth, shuffling on the seat and bracing herself for action.

"Rough, hard and fast," he repeated, shuffling his feet on the floor and a hovering precariously with one knee on the car seat, one hand gripping his cock and the other hand holding her waist to give him leverage.

"You're very wet," he uttered, breathing in the musky smell of sex before easing the throbbing flesh between the warm wet folds of her vulva.

"Oh, Fuck," she gasped, as he eased the gruesome limb inside her body, his libido in overload and his teenage stamina unrelenting, moving his hips back and forth, pushing in and pulling out, joining and separating, entering and retreating, in and out, hard and fast, battering and bruising her body in a merciless demonstration of brutal force.

"Is this rough enough for you," he grunted, moving his hips back and forth and increasing the pace, faster and faster, pushing in and pulling out, beads of sweat dripping from his brow and disappearing between the cheeks of her bottom, two lovers grunting out their pleasure in an exchange of filthy curses and promises that would never be kept.

"Fuck. Yes," she cursed, blinking sweat from her eyes and brushing hair from her face, every movement, every gesture and every word, adding to her moment of pleasure.

"FUCK ME! FASTER! HARDER! FUCKING HURT ME!" she screamed, pushing back to meet the force, driving him deeper and deeper inside her body, two lovers fused in perspiration, moving back and forth to impulsive urges, buttocks clenching and relaxing, skin against skin, genitalia embracing genitalia, thrusting faster and pushing harder, penetrating deep, sliding in fast and pulling out slow, in and out, hard and fast, battering and bruising her body with brutal and uncompromising determination.

"Oh, Yes," she hissed, moans and groans and euphoric mutterings spilling from a helpless mouth, a wanting woman hanging on a precipice of orgasmic heights.
"I'm Coming....I'm....I'm Coming....I'm Fucking Coming," she gasped, the mantra repeating in a chorus of piercing cries, moans and groans joining the momentum of give and take, muscle contractions exploding inside her vulva in an ocean of pulsating waves, the ultimate release consuming her body and stealing the last breath of air from her mouth.
"I'm coming," he croaked, groaning out his pleasure through euphoric grunts and breathless wheezes and reaching the summit of no return.
"Fuck. Yes," he gasped, his balls exploding with an uncompromising force, firing a copious amount of molten hot lava up the shaft and erupting from the eye with the force of a volcano, a tidal wave of white sticky ballast shooting indiscriminately against the inner walls of the vaginal vault and flooding the cervix in streams of emotional fluid.
"I'm empty," he uttered, letting his softening cock slip from her body and collapsing in a heap on the back seat of the car.
"I'm full," she mockingly replied, wiping stinging sweat from her eyes and brushing wet hair from her face. "That was amazing," she added, breathing in short gasps of air and trying to get precious oxygen into her lungs.
"You can tell when you've had a good fuck when the seats are wet, and the windows are covered in

condensation," she giggled, shuffling on the seat and gathering her clothes from the floor.

It was almost two in the morning when she drove the car out of the sea front car park.

Neither of them said very much, as they headed home. No eye contact, just a few grunts and the occasional forced smile, the guilt and deceit hanging like a lead weight in the pit of his stomach and Sandra's infidelity hanging by a thread.

"Are you okay?" she asked, breaking the silence. "Take one of these. It'll calm your nerves," she smiled, handing him a cigarette.

"What do you think," he replied, pulling on his cigarette. "I'm about to confront a maniac who knocks teeth out for fun," he sighed, staring at his face in the car window and wondering what it'll look like after Jimmy gets through with him.

The deep intake of smoke into his lungs made him cough but that didn't matter. He had other things on his mind. *'Fuck it.* He thought, dropping his cigarette out the window and nervously chewing the inside of his mouth. *Every condemned man is granted a last request. After all what more had he got to lose. The nervous tension and anxiety had probably set him on the path to becoming a confirmed smoker. And now he was heading home to confront a man who he had just betrayed. And that man was Jimmy Boyd, a self-confessed homicidal maniac, a man who enjoyed inflicting pain on people before beating them unconscious.*

About a mile away from the house, Sandra pulled the car to a halt and cut the engine.

"Fuck me. This is it." he thought, choking back a lump in his throat, the haunting reality of a confrontation with Jimmy only minutes away.

"I'm not sure If I can pull this off, Sandra," he croaked, beads of sweat forming on his forehead and on the palms of his hands and a lump in his throat threatening to stop his breathing.

"Don't worry. You can do this," she said, with confidence, kissing the side of his face and giving his thigh a gentle squeeze. "Remember what we talked about. Follow the plan and everything will be fine.... Trust me," she smiled.

"As soon as I've parked the car on the drive, I'll go straight to my bedroom. Once Jimmy knows I'm home, he'll let you out of the boot," she said, with casual ease, removing a compact mirror from her handbag and refreshing her lipstick.

"And remember, you're supposed to have been in the boot for hours, so when Jimmy lets you out, you'll have to give an Oscar winning performance," she added, a smile lifting the corners of her mouth.

"It's time to get back in the boot."

The ominous sound of a key turning in the lock and the haunting click of the boot opening, suddenly fed his panic, bringing hundreds of small goose-pimples surfacing on his arms and legs. He was no trained actor, but he knew as soon as Jimmy opened the car boot he would have to give the performance of his life.

Even in the darkness surrounded by a million stars he could still make out the shadowy outline of Jimmy's threatening physique and his penetrating eyes staring down at him, ready with questions and demanding answers.

"Help me out, Jimmy," he barked, taking his outstretched hand and climbing from the boot.

"Never again Jimmy. Never again," he sighed, slipping quickly into character, feigning a limp and shuffling his feet in a comical Charlie-Chaplin-like-walk.

"My legs are fucking numb. I can't walk properly," he cursed, stumbling around with theatrical exaggeration and holding his chest with both hands.

"What a waste of time that was," he croaked, glancing at his watch.

"Seven fucking hours, cooked up inside the boot of a car, just to find out that Sandra was meeting another woman," he lied, lowering his head and clutching his thighs, making sure he avoided any eye contact with Jimmy.

"Is that right," Jimmy replied, his half smile and cold eyes indicating disappointment.

"It's getting late. You'd better get yourself away home," Jimmy said, squeezing his hands together and cracking his knuckles.

"I might need to talk to you again, after I've spoken to Sandra," he said, suspiciously. "So, don't leave the fucking country" he barked, clipping him playfully across the head.

Mary Boyd had never been a beautiful woman.
She was only in her mid-fifties, but she carried another ten years on her shoulders.
Her eyes were deeply hollowed, and her face was heavily lined with fatigue, no doubt brought about from years of smoking and living a life of pain and suffering.
Mary had every right to live on her nerves. Suffering from anxiety disorders, she had no trouble getting through a bottle of vodka and three packets of cigarettes a day. And if it wasn't for the repeat prescription of Valium and the many other pills and medication keeping her alive, she would have probably ended up in a mental health institution.
It had been a long time since anyone had seen Mary Boyd smile.
Everyone was looking forward to the New Year's Eve party. Mary had spent most of the week baking food and preparing the house for her sons coming home party. After finishing a short tour in Northern Ireland, Jimmy was back in the North East on two weeks' home leave. Although Jimmy and Sandra's marriage continued to be estranged, they continued to live under the same roof, but still slept in separate bedrooms.
Most people who lived on the council estate rarely set foot inside the local pub, but for some reason they always felt an obligation to show their faces on New Year's Eve.
They met people they hadn't seen for years. They shook hands with strangers and talked to people

they didn't even like. They bought drinks at the bar and cursed at the prices. And after an hour of being pushed and squeezed in the mayhem of cheerful celebration, most of them couldn't wait to get back home in front of a warm fire and the TV.

After pushing their way through a human tide of spirited people, Mark and Frank were immediately confronted with Sandra and Jimmy in a heated exchange of abusive language.

As the argument gathered pace it quickly became apparent that Jimmy had discovered the name of the faceless man who had been shagging his wife. And furthermore, after Jimmy had finished with him his injuries were so bad he had to be rushed to hospital.

It was fast approaching midnight when they eventually arrived at Mary Boyd's house.

Mary made everyone welcome with a drink, including a couple of strangers who were staggering around clearly unsure of where they were, or how they had got there.

As the coloured baubles and silver glitter on the Christmas tree twinkled in the glowing coals of the open fire, someone announced the countdown to the New Year.

As Big-Ben chimed the departure of 1967 and the arrival of 1968, raised glasses and spirited voices greeted the New Year with a chorus of *'Auld-Lang-Syne'*.

After the usual protocols of shaking hands and too many overenthusiastic kisses, everything was back to normal.

"Are you okay?" Sandra, he asked. "I overheard the commotion in the pub," he added, looking nervously over his shoulder and keeping his eye on Jimmy.

"I'm fine, Mark. But I can't say the same for Simon," she sighed, adding a name to the faceless man lying in hospital, trying to eat his food through a wired jaw.

"Jimmy's been drinking all day, so I'm trying to keep out of his way," she said, lighting a cigarette and placing a Procol Harum record on the turntable.

"I'd better get my dark sunglasses ready," she sighed, forcing a smile that quickly faded.

"Fucking arsehole," she cursed, blowing smoke in the air above her head and humming quietly to *'A Whiter Shade of Pale.'*

Jimmy had fallen over so many times the situation had reached the point where he was becoming a nuisance to others trying to enjoy the New Year celebrations, and after insulting some of the guests with his aggressive behaviour and foul language, he was beginning to embarrass everyone, including his mother.

It was time for Jimmy to go.

"Can you help Sandra with Jimmy," Frank asked. "He can hardly walk. She'll never get him home on her own," he added, giving his brother a friendly pat on the shoulder.

The journey to Sandra's house wasn't considered a long walk, but when you're carrying a dead weight he knew it would be some time before they could return to the party.

"He's a lot heavier than I thought. Let me take most of the weight, Sandra" he volunteered, wrapping his arms around Jimmy's back and dragging him along the slippery footpath.

"He doesn't look like a big man now," Sandra sniggered. "But he still looks like a fucking arsehole," she cursed, smiling at his incapacity and lighting a cigarette.

Getting Jimmy to the house and opening the front door was the easy part. Dragging him up the stairs and getting him into bed was more of a challenge.

He wasn't surprised to see an overflowing ashtray, a few empty beer cans and a whisky bottle littering the bedroom floor, but he was surprised to see Jimmy's Royal Northumberland Fusiliers uniform hanging proudly on a coat hanger and his boots gleaming like a mirror on the floor by the bed.

"Sleep it off Jimmy," he grunted, throwing him on the bed and removing his shoes.

"He's been sick on his shirt," he informed Sandra, pointing a finger at the mess and looking back over his shoulder.

"I'm not surprised, he finished off a bottle of Jack Daniels before he left the house tonight," she sighed, staring at the pool of vomit on his shirt.

"I'm not cleaning it off. He'll have to fucking sleep in it," she said, twisting her face in disgust.

"I don't think there's anything more we can do, Sandra," he sighed, flexing the muscles in his back and running his hand along the back of his neck.

"We might as well get back to the party," he added, stepping back from the room.

"What's the hurry," she whispered, wrapping her arms around his back and pressing her lower body against his buttocks.

"Jimmy's unconscious. There's no one here to disturb us. Why don't we have a quick fuck before we go back to the party," she said, pushing her breasts against his back and peppering soft kisses along the back of his neck.

"I've missed this," she smiled, lowering her hand and squeezing his cock.

"Christ, Sandra," he gasped, shuffling nervously on his feet and craning his neck to look over his shoulder. "What the fuck are you doing," he snorted, turning quickly on his heels and giving her a look of disapproval.

"Are you fucking mad," he blurted, grabbing her hand and pulling her onto the landing, the sound of floorboards creaking under their weight only adding to his panic.

"He's the mad one," she retorted, pointing a finger at Jimmy. "I just want a fuck," she laughed.

"We both know that Jimmy's mad and extremely violent, because he's just put a man in hospital for fucking his wife," he responded, lowering his voice an octave, glancing into the bedroom and checking on Jimmy's semi-unconscious status, the relief that he hadn't moved forcing a nervous sigh and a reminder for caution.

"And you want me to fuck you knowing that he's just a few feet away," he added, shuffling his feet nervously on the floor and wiping a layer of sweat from his brow.

"I think it might be safer if we both go back to the party," he sighed, waiting anxiously for an answer he didn't expect to hear.

Sandra was hot. She was dirty. She was impatient. She wanted fucked.

"Will a blow-job change your mind," she smiled, ignoring his retreating gestures and lowering to the floor on her knees, the fire of passion sweeping away the need for caution, a wanting woman driven by irresistible urges, a woman craving for fulfilment, an impatient woman desperate to feel the awesome muscle stretching and filling her body again.

She had his cock in her mouth, long before her knees had touched the floor.

"It usually does," she whispered, flashing her eyes with erotic intent, easing him in and easing him out, the confidence and expectation in her voice flirting with danger.

"And so, does this," she smiled, loosening the buttons on her blouse and wrapping her breasts around the thick girth, letting him feel the heat of her tits sliding up and down his cock and her tongue sweeping in circles around the bulbous head.

"I thought you were in a hurry to get back to the party," she grinned, wiggling her tongue in the single eye and looking up from the floor to see his reaction.

"I knew a blow-job would change your mind," she smiled, easing the gruesome limb back into her mouth.

"Okay, but we'd better be careful," he whispered, glancing nervously into the bedroom. "I think It might be safer if we fuck on the landing," he croaked, placing his hand on her head and moving his hips in a gesture of oral stimulation.

"I don't care where we fuck," she grunted, a familiar wetness gathering between her thighs, sucking him in and blowing him out with a well-practiced skill.

"I would fuck you in the street, if I had to," she mocked, sweeping her tongue over the smooth helmet before easing him into her hungry mouth.

"But it's a lot more exciting when it's in front of your husband," she grinned, bobbing her head up and down, easing him in and easing him out, giving his balls a gentle squeeze before dragging her teeth over the loose foreskin on the way back.

"Keep quiet. He might wake up if he hears your voice," he cautioned, never once taking his eyes off the drunk asleep on the bed.

"I promise to be quiet. If you promise to fuck me from the back," she croaked, letting his cock slip from her mouth and lifting from the floor.

"I need to see his face while you're fucking me," she insisted, gripping the handrail with both hands, bending over and opening her legs, the floorboards creaking in quiet protest as she shuffled her feet on the floor.

"It's dark in the bedroom, but I can still see Jimmy's eyes staring up at the ceiling," she said, a thin smile lifting the corners of her mouth.

"He's either unconscious or he's dead," she sniggered. "But who gives a fuck about Jimmy. He's nothing but the fucking arsehole," she blurted, glancing back over her shoulder and flashing her eyes.

"Put it in," she said, brushing hair from her face and opening her legs.

"Christ, Sandra. I'm not sure. This is dangerous. If Jimmy wakes up hell fucking kill us," he sighed, the guilt and betrayal and the crippling uncertainty of what they were about to do, filling his head with haunting images of Jimmy's violent temper.

The faceless coward in the fast car lying in a hospital bed with a broken jaw and no teeth, trying to eat his food through a straw. The very same man who had probably saved his life.

'You'll be sorry when Jimmy finds out you've been shagging his wife.' A virtuous voice whispered a word of warning from somewhere in the dark recesses of his mind.

Fuck Jimmy, he's nothing but a fucking arsehole.... She's gagging for it.... Give her a damn good fucking. A sinful voice quickly replied.

"Don't worry about Jimmy. He'll not wake up. He's had far too much to drink," Sandra said, interrupting his thoughts.

"Let me put it in," she whispered, lowering her hand between her legs and wrapping her fingers around the throbbing limb. "Oh yes," she breathed, guiding his cock between the slipper flaps and folds and easing the swollen muscle inside her body.

"What a cock," she gasped, as he moved inside her body, easing in and easing out, pushing in and pulling out, stretching and filling her entrance with hard flesh.

"Fuck, that's big," she blurted, pursing her lips and twisting her face. "It's nearly splitting me apart," she gasped, opening her legs wider and gripping the handrail tighter.

"But don't you dare stop," she smiled, shuffling her feet on the floor and pushing back to meet the force, embracing the awesome length and formidable girth, easing him in and easing him out in a steady momentum of give and take.

"That's so fucking good," she whispered, glancing back over her shoulder and searching his face for reassurance, smiling at his nervousness and listening to the smacking noise of skin hitting skin and the sloppy wet noises echoing off the stairwell walls as he entered and retreated from her body.

"There's not a better sound, than two people fucking," she grunted, wiggling her bottom and pushing back, feeling the length reaching depths that hadn't been reached before.

"Fuck. Fuck. What a Fuck. What a cock," she cursed, whispered moans and whimpering cries of encouragement growing louder and louder as he penetrated the depths of her inner core.

"You're making too much noise, Sandra" he hissed, narrowing his eyes and distorting his face, as if this physical gesture would help to calm the situation.
"Keep quiet or you'll wake Jimmy," he added, a sudden movement on the bed and a throaty gurgling noise stopping him in his tracks, like a burglar caught in the act.
"Keep still. Don't say a word," he whispered, covering her mouth with his hand and choking back a lump in his throat. "I heard a noise coming from the bedroom," he croaked, his eyes wide open in panic and his heart beat increasing by the second.
"It's gone quiet again," he sighed, removing his hand from her mouth and never once taking his eyes off Jimmy.
"Wed better keep still until we know for sure," he whispered, breathing in air through his nose and nervously chewing the inside of his mouth, watching and waiting, praying that Jimmy wouldn't wake up and jump from the bed in a violent rage.
"We need to finish what we started. I'm too close to an orgasm," she whispered, breaking his mental turmoil. "I promise to be quiet," she smiled, turning on her heels and resuming her position against the handrail.
Under the haunting sound of the timber banister squeaking in an overture of painful noises and the old floorboards moaning and groaning under their feet, they fucked each other in a steady rhythm of give and take.

"Oh, that's good," she whispered, wriggling and swaying her hips, rocking back and forward and pushing back, making sure she was getting it all inside.

"Faster. Fuck me, faster," she whispered, looking back over her shoulder and twisting her face in a euphoric mask of pleasure. "Harder. Fuck me harder," she insisted, moans and groans growing into agonising cries and filthy curses turning into words of endearment.

"I'm coming. I'm coming," she hissed, a wanting woman reaching the heights of euphoric bliss, hovering on the summit of no return, the floodgates of passion exploding inside her body and taking her over the orgasmic cliff.

"Oh. Fuck. Oh. Fuck. Ahhh....Fuck," she gasped, gripping the handrail with both hands as if her life depended on her never letting go. "Arrrggghhh," she hissed through gritted teeth, the heat of passion spilling in rivers down her thighs, a knee trembling orgasm celebrated in breathless whispers of silence.

They slipped back into Mary Boyd's house, relatively unnoticed.

Some of the guests were in the kitchen drinking and eating the remains of the buffet. Those who had drunk too much had fallen asleep on the sofa and a few people were showing off their dancing skills on the living-room floor.

"I'm wondering if we should have checked on Jimmy, just to make sure he was okay, before we left the house," he whispered, in Sandra's ear.

"I don't think that would have been a good idea. What would we have done if he'd woken up? Anyway, who gives a fuck about Jimmy," she replied. "Get me a drink, I'm going to the bathroom to freshen up," she added, grabbing her handbag and disappearing through a door.

"Is everything okay with Jimmy. What took you so long?" Frank asked, the questions interrupting the glass touching his lips.

"Yes. he's okay. He's sleeping like a baby," he replied, sipping his drink. "Its heavy going dragging a drunken man around the estate," he added, unconvincingly, scanning the buffet table, hoping to avoid further questions.

"I hope you put him face down on the bed and not on his back?" Frank continued.

"Yes. I did," he answered, biting on a curled-up sandwich just as Sandra came back into the room.

"Don't worry, Frank. Jimmy's fine. He just needs to sleep it off," she smiled, raising her glass in the way of a toast. "Happy New Year."

It was just after five in the morning when he crawled into bed. And after the tireless session with Sandra and his bloodstream fuelled with alcohol it only took a couple of minute before he was fast asleep.

He wasn't sure whether it was the calling of nature or the telephone ringing that woke him from his

sleep, but there was more urgency to empty his bladder than to answer the phone.
"Fucking telephone," he cursed, taking the stairs two at a time, ignoring the hammer banging inside his head and the painful ring of the telephone as he headed for the toilet.
The telephone was still ringing when he came out of the toilet, so he picked it up.
"Hello?" he barked into the mouthpiece, blinking his eyes into focus and glancing at his watch, the timepiece informing him that he had only been in bed for a couple of hours.
There was an eerie silence at the other end of the phone, so he repeated the question.
"Hello whose there?" he grunted.
"Mark, it's me, Frank," he answered, the restraint in his voice fading into the mouthpiece.
"I'm with Sandra at the Queen Elizabeth Hospital, in Gateshead," he croaked, choking back a lump in his throat. "Jimmy's dead, Mark....He died in his sleep last night."
There was a deathly silence hanging over the phone before Frank eventually broke the silence.
"Sandra found Jimmy dead when she got home. The paramedics said that he must have fallen asleep on his back and died in his own vomit," he sighed, pausing to gather his thoughts.
"The police are asking a lot of questions. They've spoken to Sandra to establish if there were any suspicious circumstances surrounding his death. They also want to talk to you, because they know

that you and Sandra were the last two people to see him alive."

"Christ," he thought, struggling to think through the miasma of alcohol and sleep deprivation and his mind filling with irrational speculation.

"Did Sandra kill Jimmy while he slept," a cautious voice inside his head asked. *"Christ. We didn't check on him before we left the house. What if Jimmy was already dead, while he was fucking Sandra."*

"What have I done," he sighed, dropping the phone into the cradle and wiping stinging tears from his eyes, his mind plagued with guilt and betrayal and a resounding nausea lying in the pit of his stomach.

"I should have listened to Frank and put him face down on the bed," he thought, climbing the stairs and crashing on the bed, staring up at the ceiling and searching the heavens for forgiveness.

"Poor Jimmy," he sobbed, biting the inside of his mouth until he tasted blood, hoping this gesture of self-pity would be a fitting punishment for his deceit.

In the black gloom, he closed his eyes, hoping he could hide from the world.

He slowly fell into a troubled sleep......The sleep of the guilty.

Tartan Blanket (circa-1968)

From the day, their mother and father informed family and friends that their daughter, Victoria had been diagnosed with terminal cancer, it took less than four months before her battle against the disease finally ended and her life slipped slowly away.

In the last few days of her life her body had been reduced from a nine-stone beautiful young woman to a weak and helpless skeletal frame. With skin hanging like soft paper tissue from frail bones, she was unrecognisable and resembled a woman more than twice her age.

Ellen Brand told friends and relatives that Victoria was in so much pain and suffering that when her life ended, it was a welcome relief.

After the funeral, Ellen fought with her own recovery. But after too many sleepless nights, too many pills and too many severe bouts of depression leading up to, and after her daughter's death, she eventually lost the fight and spent the rest of her life lost to pills and despair.

Eddie Brand was no stranger to death. He had seen enough during his National Service.

He had endured the pain, the sorrow and the anger when the life of a friend or loved one is unexpectedly taken away. He was also aware that when it happens we always look for someone to blame, and that someone is usually that devout man in heaven.

But even after losing too many friends in World War II and spending too many sleepless nights drinking and cursing at a bible, he wasn't prepared for the loss of a child.

If he had remembered about the heater not working in his father's Rover 90, he would have worn a leather jacket over his thin cotton shirt.
"It's freezing in here," he grunted, looking at his father and rubbing his hands up and down his arms.
"Is it. I don't feel cold," Eddie replied, his shirt unbuttoned at the front and his sleeves rolled up to his elbows, the badly scratched tattoo of a scorpion on his left arm, a permanent reminder of a heavy drinking session during his National Service days.
"I must remember to get the heater fixed," he grinned, flicking his cigarette ash through a small gap in the side window.
If the truth were known his resilience was probably the reason why he hadn't replaced the thermostat in the car. But nothing seemed to bother his father. Even the deformity in his left arm didn't prevent him from becoming a tailor.
It was quite bizarre to think that Eddie had gone through World War II relatively unscathed. But when the war ended, Eddie and six other troops were driving through France in an army vehicle when the driver – who was apparently drunk at the time – collided with an obstacle at the side of the road.
After losing control of the steering wheel the vehicle turned over and landed in a ditch. The six soldiers

were thrown from the back of the vehicle and other than a few cuts and bruises they were relatively okay. Eddie was less fortunate. After falling under the weight of the vehicle his left arm was crushed beneath one of the wheels. Medics told him that the soft ground probably saved him from losing his arm. The one with the tattoo.

After driving for almost twenty-minutes neither of them had spoken a word. But with the age divide and nothing in common, conversations between fathers and teenage sons were always at a premium.

But although they didn't talk much, he still had a lot of respect for his mother and father, knowing how difficult it was during their upbringing, providing food and clothing for him, his brother Frank and his two sister's Victoria and Eve.

His parents were both humble people from working class backgrounds. They had no proper education and in those pre-war days they were expected to leave school at an early age to earn money to support their own parent's modest wages. After leaving school at fourteen his father worked as a trainee tailor and his mother worked as a seamstress.

Married at nineteen, by the time Ellen Brand was in her mid-twenties she had given birth to four children. With six mouths to feed Eddie and Ellen, worked tirelessly through the night, making suits or altering clothes for friends and neighbours, desperately trying to earn a little extra cash to supplement their modest income.

They made all their regular day-to-day clothing and made sure their children always looked smart and respectable. They even made their school uniforms from left over material that they had suspiciously acquired from previous jobs.

And they always made sure their names were written inside.

"How's the job going?" Eddie enquired, through a cloud of cigarette smoke, the sudden break in silence, forcing a stammered reply from his son.

"It's.... Its, okay."

"I hope you're sticking in at college," his father asked.

"You must have a good boss, letting you take a day off work each week to attend Newcastle College," he added.

"Yes," he answered to both questions.

"You're training to be an architect?" Eddie said, with pride in his voice.

"Building surveyor," he quickly replied.

"Same thing.... I tell everyone you're an architect."

"Are they paying you enough?" his father boldly asked.

"Good enough, considering what my friends are earning," he answered, hoping this would be the last of his father's interrogation.

It wasn't.

"When you're going through an apprenticeship period, you're expected to do all the menial tasks at work. But make sure they don't give you all the shitty jobs to do," Eddie said, pulling on his cigarette.

"Fucking shitty jobs.... Don't let him give you all the shitty jobs," he thought, wondering how his father would react if he told him about a recent job his boss had asked him to do.

Apparently, someone using the men's toilet felt it necessary to smear the walls of one of the toilet cubicles with human excrement, and the only way they were going to catch the perpetrator was to hide someone inside the toilet and observe the comings and goings of everyone using the facilities.

The humorous remark of the boss telling him they were looking for someone who didn't bite their finger nails, did little to help the mindless hours and boring days sitting on a wooden stool inside a cleaner's cupboard, peeking through a grille in the door like some kind of perverted voyeur, waiting for the 'phantom crapper' to decorate one of the toilet cubicles.

A week had passed. There were lots of visitors in and out of the toilet. There were lots of bladders emptied and plenty of bowel movements, but unfortunately no desecrated toilets.

It was late one Friday afternoon when the sound of heels tapping across the ceramic floor tiles broke the boredom. He peered through the grille in the door. He couldn't believe his eyes. Nicola Thompson from the admin office, walked into a toilet cubicle and closed the door.

A few minutes later the door opened, and she was gone.

He slipped out of the cupboard and opened the toilet door. The walls of the cubicle were smeared with human faeces and a signature of brown hand marks decorated the inside of the toilet door.
He went back to the cleaner's cupboard, filled a bucket with hot water, grabbed a cloth and a bottle of disinfectant and returned to the cubicle.
It took less than ten-minutes to clean the cubicle and return to the sanctuary of the cupboard.
He never asked her why.....Only a psychiatrist could tell her that.
"Is that another new shirt you're wearing? I hope you've written your name inside," his father chuckled, blowing smoke against the windscreen.
"Oh Fuck," he cursed silently. *Not the story about writing their names inside their clothing.*
He knew that if he didn't change the subject quickly he was going to hear the story for the millionth time. But he couldn't stop thinking about Nicola Thompson desecrating the toilet cubicle and he had no intention of betraying her dark obsession to his father.
"I knew you would do well son," he smiled, tapping his fingers across the steering wheel, a thin smile lifting the corners of his mouth.
"Did I ever tell you the story about when you were all growing up and you wondered why I had written your names inside your clothing," he said, with the guidance and composure of a Nursery School teacher.
"I did it because I knew it would encourage you to strive for better things in life," he said, with the

conviction of a politician, searching his memory for infamous quotes.
"If your names on the outside of a building, you are considered to be a rich man. If your names on the inside of a building you are known to be a working-class man. But if your name is on the inside of your clothing, you will always be classed as a poor man."
There was a long silence before Eddie spoke again.
"From the day we are born, we travel on the conveyor belt of routine. Working Class. Middle Class. Upper Class. Rich and Poor. All striving for better things in life. The only thing in common is that we all fall off the end, smelling of piss."
"So, you must have thought about what I said, otherwise you wouldn't have become an architect. Who knows, one day you might be the next Christopher Robin," he smiled, winking proudly and lifting his shoulders. "You never know, son. You never know," he chimed.
He was about to correct his father's mistake, but fearing it might grow into an extended debate, which he wasn't in the mood for, he just sighed and waited for the anecdote that always followed.
"There are only two things that matter in life, son. Sex and money," Eddie announced, pulling on his cigarette. "This is not a rehearsal son. Get as much as you can before you die," he added, searching his memory for the name of his wife's sister.
"Look at your aunt Gloria, poor sod," Eddie sighed. "It's only been six months since we put her in the ground and she's already forgotten. She had no life

with that bastard she married. He spent his money like a drunken sailor. And If he wasn't spending it on drink, he was throwing it away in the betting shop," he barked, lowering his voice an octave and repeating his words of advice. "Get as much as you can son."

For a man who didn't have a driving licence, Eddie Brand handled a car extremely well.

If you were to ask him why he had never taken a driving test he would be the first to tell you that driving licences are for people who lack the confidence and need a certificate to tell them they are competent behind a wheel.

The country roads had a thin covering of black ice and required Eddies deep concentration, so the rest of the journey fell silent until they reached Bishop Auckland.

Eileen Brand waved a welcoming hand through her living-room window, when the car pulled to a halt outside her dreary council house.

"Come inside, Eddie," she invited, raising both hands and wiggling her fingers. "And bring that handsome young man with you," she added, a cheerful smile lighting up her face.

"I've made you and Mark a brew and something to eat," she offered, spinning on her heels and heading towards the kitchen.

"Where's Malcolm?" he enquired, glancing in the living room and lighting two cigarettes.

"Where do you think," Eileen cursed, taking a cigarette from his outstretched hand.

"He's in bed pissed. Your brothers always pissed," she barked. "I married the wrong fucking brother," she mocked, covering her mouth with her hand in the way of an apology when she realised her outburst of inappropriate language might have embarrassed Eddie's son.

"You handsome, young architect," she smiled, flashing her eyes and brushing her fingers through his hair, hoping that this playful gesture would recompense for her careless oversight.

"Building surveyor," he replied, catching a glimpse of her huge breasts and sitting quickly on a stool to hide an untimely erection beneath the kitchen table.

"How's Ellen coping with the loss of Victoria?" Eileen enquired, pouring tea into cups and placing a plate of ham sandwiches on the kitchen table.

"She's devastated. We all are. I just hope she feels better tomorrow....Once the funerals over," Eddie said, biting his teeth into a ham sandwich.

"Cancer and only in her early-twenties," Eileen sighed. "She's only a child for Christ sake," she barked, staring at the reminder of her Catholic faith hanging on the wall, as if the man on the cross would give her the answer.

"You know we'll have to stop using these," Eileen said, pulling on her cigarette. "They're not good for you," she added, drawing smoke into her lungs and wagging a finger at Eddies son. "You're too smart and far too handsome to start smoking," she smiled, brushing her hand gently against the side of his face.

"I wished I was nineteen again and know what I know now," she sighed.
"I can't afford to smoke," he replied, lifting the hot cup to his mouth and thinking back to the night he was smoking cigarettes and fucking Sandra Boyd, while her husband Jimmy, lay dead in his bed.
"I'd better go and check on my drunken brother," Eddie volunteered, scraping his stool across the kitchen floor. "We might have to sober him up for the drive back to Gateshead," he sighed, before disappearing through the door and heading up the stairs.
"It must be more than a year since I last saw you," Eileen smiled. "You've grown into a fine young man. Your mothers proud of you. She never stops talking about you when we're on the phone," she added, humming a tune inside her head and fussing around the kitchen sink.
"Thanks," he uttered, catching fleeting glances of her huge tits bouncing inside a white blouse and her shapely bottom wiggling enticingly beneath a snug pair of cotton trousers.
"You don't have to thank me," she smiled, washing and drying dishes, clinking cups and rattling plates into cupboards, lifting and lowering and bending over, every movement laden with suggestive implication.
"Can I help you with anything?" he asked, watching the fabric stretching over her shapely bottom when she lowered to her knees and creeping inside the crack of her bottom when she stood up.

'Christ no wonder I'm getting hard. Does she need to bend over that often. Or is she teasing him, he thought, his hand flirting with the growing muscle inside his pants and his head swimming in a sea of hormonal chaos.

Ripping her blouse off...Her big tits spilling into his hand...Fondling one and squeezing the other...Burying his face between her cleavage...Feasting on one nipple and biting the other....Breathing in her sex until she begged him to fuck her.

"That'll have to do," she sighed, turning quickly on her heels, the unexpected gesture breaking his lustful thoughts.

"Will Malcolm be okay for the drive back to Gateshead?" he asked, sneaking another glimpse of her shapely breasts and discreetly lowering his hand beneath the kitchen table, moving the growing nuisance from its uncomfortable angle inside his pants.

After living with a drunk for most of her married life, who spent most of their income on alcohol, Eileen had given up worrying about her husband. And with a tired face hidden beneath too much makeup and short blonde hair showing evidence of dark roots, it was clear that Eileen had also given up on her own self-esteem.

But with a cute little bottom and a pair of tits that could stop traffic, she was always going to get his undivided attention.

"Fuck Malcolm," she barked. "He can stay here for all I care. I'm sick of his drinking and I'm fed up with him constantly being drunk. The only time he wants sex is when he's pissed. But because he's pissed all the time, he can't get it up," she added, sighing into her cup and lighting a cigarette.

"Malcolm thinks a woman's place is in the kitchen," she frowned, blowing a stream of white smoke at the ceiling. "But I've been told that men who say women belong in the kitchen, usually don't know what to do in the bedroom," she said, forcing a laugh that quickly faded.

"I've gone too long without love or sex. If it wasn't for my phallic friend in my bedroom drawer, I think I would have left him a long time ago," she sighed, placing a comforting hand on his shoulder and frowning when she caught sight of her wedding ring.

"I'm sorry about the outburst," she said, crushing her cigarette in an ash tray and raising an eyebrow. "I hope I'm not corrupting your young mind with too much information," she giggled. "I know your mother wouldn't be pleased if she found out that I've been discussing my troubled sex life with her precious son."

With her solo practices now embedded in his memory files and knowing he would have to stand up at some point with an obvious lump inside his jeans, he waited until the moment was right, lowered his hand and made another quick adjustment.

"Here he is." Eddie grunted. "Black coffee Eileen," he insisted, ushering Malcolm into the kitchen and sitting him on a stool.

“I don’t think we’ve got enough time or coffee to sober him up,” Eddie sighed, glancing at his watch and looking out the window. “It’s getting dark outside and the roads will be icy,” he added, lighting a cigarette and taking the coffee cup from his brother’s hand.

“We can’t sit around here waiting for Malcolm to sober up,” he said, taking his brothers arm and lifting him off the stool. “He’ll have to sleep it off in the car.”

“I don’t want that drunk in the back of the car with me,” Eileen barked, picking up a small suitcase with their pre-packed clothes for the funeral.

“Don’t panic,” Eddie replied. “Malcolm can sit in the front with me. If he needs to vomit or use the bathroom, I’d rather have him in the front, where I can keep an eye on him.”

“You’ll need to wear something warm, Eileen. The heater doesn’t work. Mark said it was cold in the car on the way here,” he grinned. “I don’t feel the cold,” he added, with a smug smile.

After slipping a woollen sweater over her head, Eileen opened a cupboard door and removed a large tartan blanket. “This should keep us warm in the back seat,” she smiled, lowering her eyes and catching a glimpse of the impressive bulge inside his jeans.

With his shirt sleeves rolled up to his elbows and a cigarette dangling from his mouth, Eddie scraped a thin layer of ice from the windscreen, while Mark poured Malcolm into the front seat of the car and Eileen put their luggage into the boot.

After too many turns of the ignition key and a few frustrated curses from the driver, the old Rover 90 eventually fired into action.

Under the veil of a darkening sky they headed back to Gateshead.

"Put this over you, Mark" Eileen whispered, the promise of playful entertainment dancing behind furtive eyes. "It'll keep us warm," she smiled, shuffling on the seat and covering their legs with the tartan blanket.

Eddie didn't talk too much during the journey, he just puffed on his cigarette and concentrated on the driving. And apart from the occasional grunt from the drunk in the front seat, the inside of the car was reasonably quiet.

"The roads are slippery," Eddie confirmed, pulling on his cigarette, the headlights beaming into the night sky and lighting up the country roads. "I think it's going to snow," he sighed, glancing in the rear-view mirror and muttering curses and apologies under his breath.

"Take your time. There's no hurry," Mark said, blinking his eyes and trying to focus in the darkness, just making out the silhouette of his father's proud face in the rear-view mirror and the dashboard lighting up the fine hairs on his disfigured arm.

The man who didn't have a driving licence. The man with a scorpion tattooed on his arm that looked more like a lobster. The man who thought one of the most highly acclaimed architects in history was called Christopher Robin.

"I hope it's not snowing tomorrow," Eileen chirped in, shuffling on the seat in a gesture of movement, pulling the blanket up and resting her head against his arm.

"No not at the funeral," Eddie croaked, gripping the steering wheel with both hands and pulling the car out of a slight skid, the untimely swerve shifting Eileen in her seat.

"Wow," he gasped, feeling her weighty breasts flattening against his arm and whispers of warm breath blowing intermittently against the side of his face.

Her eyes were closed. She looked as if she was sleeping. But with her big tits pressing against his arm, he had no intention of wakening her up, he thought, slipping his hand under the blanket and giving his stirring limb a gentle tug, his fertile imagination creating images of Eileen flaunting her body over the kitchen sink.

She must have known what she was doing. Was it deliberate? He thought. *Christ some of her bending positions with her legs apart were bordering on the erotic.*

A soft purring whisper and a slight movement in the seat, interrupted his lustful reverie.

He quickly moved his hand from his groin and glanced at Eileen. Her eyes were still closed.

"Sorry," his father said, raising his hand in the way of an apology, when the car collided with a pot hole in the road, throwing the car one way and then the other.

The sudden movement didn't wake Eileen, but her weight had shifted again and even though the warmth of her breasts pushing against his arm held his interest, what concerned him most was that her hand had moved onto his thigh and her fingers were almost touching his penis.

'It was dangerous. It was risky. It was exciting,' he thought, his imagination flirting with opportunity and intimate pursuit, an adventurous mind rejoicing in the endless possibilities of surreptitious foreplay, until a distressing thought brought him back to reality.

'What happens when she wakes up and discovers that her hand is touching his penis? She might think I've put it there while she slept. And if he had, what else had he been up to in the darkness. Christ, she might think I'm a pervert.'

He decided to move her hand.

Holding his breath and twisting his face with nervous apprehension, he carefully lowered his hand beneath the obscurity of the blanket, ignoring the staining lump inside his pants and weaving his feather light fingers with the skill of a watchmaker beneath her hand.

"It's starting to snow," Eddie announced, the windscreen wipers squeaking in quiet protest across the glass and the volume in his voice awakening Eileen from her sleep.

"It's snowing," Eileen, echoed, blinking her eyes into focus, the acquaintance of hands and the intimacy of touch beneath the blanket, lifting the corners of her mouth.

"Just as well you brought that warm blanket with you," Eddie chuckled, through a throaty cough before dropping his cigarette through a gap in the window and glancing in the rear-view mirror.
'In more ways than one,' he silently mouthed from the back seat, keeping his eyes focused on the reflection of his father's face in the mirror, when he felt her hand moving with flirtatious intent beneath the blanket.
'It's nothing more than a little bit of playful flirting.' he thought, opening his legs and lifting his bottom slightly from the seat, responding to the invitation of touch.
"Help me," she whispered, fiddling impatiently with the zip on his jeans and pointing a finger at the metal fastening, lifting her shoulders in defeat and making silent gestures with her hand.
"We've got to get the heater fixed," he said, glancing at the reflection in the rear-view mirror, making sure there were no suspicious looks from his father before lowering the zip with agonising slowness. "I'll help you to fix the new thermostat," he added, coughing into his hand as the material surrendered to the metal fastening.
Without waiting for an invitation, she slipped her hand inside the tight fabric, feeling the firmness of youth growing beneath the warm confines of his briefs, hissing her frustration through tight lips when she was unable to liberate the throbbing limb from its dark enclosure.

He nodded his head again, held his breath and lifted his buttocks slightly from the vinyl seat, slipped his hands into the waist and slid his pants over his thighs, never once taking his eyes off the driver or the drunk snoring next to him.

"Wow," she gasped, feeling the gruesome length and formidable girth throbbing in her hand, the accidental outburst breaking the silence and getting the drivers attention.

"What was that Eileen...? Did you say something?" Eddie asked, blinking his eyes in the darkness and looking back through the rear-view mirror.

"Oh, I was just wondering if Malcolm was okay," she lied, with an easy calm, smiling at Eddies reflection in the mirror and tightening her grip on the gruesome limb, beneath the blanket.

"He's okay. He's sleeping like a baby," Eddie confirmed, through a cloud of white smoke.

"Would you like a cigarette?" Eddie offered, raising the packet in his hand.

"No thanks," she replied, the acquaintance of touch flirting with the promise of expectation and the ache between her legs overcoming the need for a cigarette.

"Later," she added, closing her fingers in a tight fist around the girth and working the length back and forth, slow and deliberate, gripping the meaty flesh on the down stroke, feeling his pubic hair brushing against her hand, holding it for a moment before easing her grip on the way back, pulling the loose foreskin over the smooth head and feeling a sticky deposit oozing from the open eye.

"Are we nearly there," Eileen asked, using her voice to disguise any suspicious noises, pulling and tugging, thrusting and pulling, back and forth, increasing the pace, faster and faster, euphoric mutterings letting her know that his release was only seconds away.
"Not far now," Eddie announced, pointing a finger at the brightly lit signpost with one arrow pointing to Newcastle and another pointing to Gateshead.
"I'm looking forward to seeing Ellen, although I wished it could have been under different circumstances," Eileen replied, working his cock back and forth.
"We talk on the phone a lot, but I haven't seen her for almost a year," she added, raising her voice an octave, trying to mute any signs of mischief going on in the back of the car.
"It's been too long," she uttered, as his balls exploded, spewing out a phenomenal quantity of milky white cargo in four repetitive bursts, coating her hand, smearing his stomach and decorating the tartan blanket.
Eddie helped his brother to the front door. Mark carried Eileen's case and his deflated appendage. Eileen carried the soiled tartan blanket containing his fertile seed.
After a friendly hug at the door and an exchange of comforting words and condolences, Ellen Brand ushered Malcolm and Eileen into the warmth of her living-room.

"I've put you and Malcolm in Frank and Mark's room," Ellen said, forcing a smile that quickly faded. "Two single beds.... I hope that's okay," she added, in a whispered apology.

"Couldn't be better," Eileen uttered, under her breath.

"Frank's stopping at a friend's house. Mark can sleep downstairs on the sofa," Ellen said, removing a handkerchief that she always kept under her sleeve and wiping a tear from the corner of her eye.

"I'll take you to your room. After you've hung your clothes up, we can eat," Ellen offered, an outstretched hand forcing another question.

"Let me carry that blanket for you."

"No!" Eileen snorted, in a raised voice. "I can manage," she insisted, forcing a smile and lowering her voice, before pulling the stained blanket against her chest.

It was pouring with rain on the day of Victoria's funeral.

Surrounded by a sea of headstones, blackened through the passage of time, family and friends gathered around the open grave to say goodbye to Victoria Brand.

Ignoring the rain battering against his face the minister opened his bible.

"Our father which art in heaven....," voices croaked through sobs, sniffles and tears as the coffin was lowered into the ground by four burly men holding thick ropes.

Under a veil of black umbrellas, family and friends said their final goodbye to Victoria.

As the mourners slowly melted away in a steady tide of grief and the gravediggers shovelled the earth back into the hole, Eileen and Mark linked arms with Ellen and Eddie and Malcolm followed slowly on their heels, heading towards a black limousine waiting patiently at the main gates of the cemetery.

"These fucking graves are getting a bit too close to the dual-carriageway," Eddie chuckled, pulling on a cigarette and pausing occasionally to read the names on a headstone.

"They'd better keep room for me," Eddie added, through a cloud of cigarette smoke.

"I've told her to burn me. There not putting me in a fucking hole," Malcolm replied, removing a flask of whisky from his pocket and lifting it to his mouth.

Ellen made a long shushing noise in quiet protest. Eileen just smiled. Mark wasn't listening. His mind was on other things.

"It's been good seeing you again, Ellen, although I wish it had been under different circumstances, Eileen said, shaking her head from side-to-side and forcing a smile. We should get together more often. When you're ready, of course" she added, as the funeral car pulled away from the cemetery.

"When Mark passes his driving test, he can drive you to Bishop Auckland," she smiled, giving his hand a gentle squeeze and crossing and uncrossing her legs, trying to hide her emotions and trying to calm the familiar wetness gathering inside her knickers.

"I'll do anything you ask if you promise to let me rip your knickers off and fuck you in the back seat of this funeral car," he thought, the warmth of her hand and their moment of intimate foreplay in the back seat of his father's car, stirring the sleeping muscle inside his pants.

After a small buffet for family and friends at the local British Legion Club, Ellen, Eileen, Mark and his sister Eve, walked the short distance back to the house.

"We'll not see Eddie or Malcolm until the pubs call last orders," Eileen sighed.

"How's that friend of yours getting on Mark?" Eileen enquired. "I can't remember his name. The one who moved to Ipswich with his mother."

"Andy Dobson," he replied. "He's doing well. He's got a good job and he lives with his girlfriend, in a two-bedroom flat in Ipswich.

There was a long silence before his mother chirped in.

"I heard a rumour that his mother, Ruth, married a schoolteacher just a few months ago."

The news about Ruth getting married had left him speechless. It felt like a lead weight had suddenly dropped into the pit of his stomach. He choked back a lump in his throat, glanced at his watch and quickened the pace.

It was after midnight when Malcolm and Eddie eventually staggered back from the pub.

After climbing the stairs and an unnecessary clashing of doors and a few curses from Eileen, the house fell silent.

Alluring images of Eileen's tight little bottom, big tits and the phallic friend she kept in her bedroom, quickly gathered a space inside his head. So, with enough material for masturbation, he stretched out on the sofa and removed the swollen muscle from his briefs.

It was quick. It was powerful. It was messy. It was the perfect anaesthetic for an uncomfortable night on the sofa.

A warm hand touching his arm and a whispered voice broke him from his sleep.

In the flickering shadows of the glowing coal fire there was no mistaking the familiar silhouette of Eileen, wearing nothing but a pyjama top and a pair of white panties.

"I can't sleep with his snoring," she whispered, pursing her bottom lip in an innocent but seductive provocation, smiling into his eyes and unbuttoning her pyjama top, brushing it from her shoulders and letting it pool at her feet.

"What if he wakes up and you're not there," he croaked, catching a glimpse of the dark shadow of pubic hair hidden beneath her white knickers.

"You can't wake Malcolm when he's pissed. Trust me he won't bother us tonight" she smiled, optimism flashing in her eyes and a nagging pulse between her legs, slipping out of her panties and sliding on the sofa, catching a glimpse of the scrunched-up paper tissues abandoned on the floor.

"But, what if he does wake up. And what happens if he comes looking for you?" he sighed, chaos and uncertainty rattling around inside his head, the acquaintance of her hand clutching his growing attachment and the heat of her breath against his neck brushing away the clouds of doubt and bringing him back to reality.

"I hope you've still got some fuel left inside those tanks," she grinned, throwing the paper tissue into the fire, the promise of suggestion lifting the corners of her mouth.

"I'll soon find out," she said, flashing her eyes with lustful intent, lowering her head and peppering soft kisses of light affection over his stomach, tasting the salty evidence of his earlier eruption on his warm skin, coming to a halt when she felt the whispery curls of pubic hair and his throbbing limb, brushing against the side of her face.

"It's so big," she gasped, wrapping her fingers around the girth, pulling and tugging and dragging her long fingernails over his scrotum, pulling the fine hairs covering the rugged skin and cradling both testicles in her hand.

"They feel full," she smiled, letting go of his balls and easing him into her mouth, working the long shaft with a well-practiced skill, breathing him and blowing him out, licking and sucking and sweeping over the bulbous head, dancing around the rim and pushing the tip of her tongue into the small eye, savouring the taste of his youthful seed.

"I want you to fuck me," she whispered, letting him slip from her mouth, hormonal chaos teasing her

senses and a surge of adrenalin rushing through her veins, fuelling the fire of passion between her legs.
"It's been too long. I need to feel a man inside me," she sighed, shifting her weight on the sofa and hovering above his thighs, feeling the threatening force of nature throbbing against her bottom, a woman with urgent needs giving in to the hiatus of a sexual drought.
"Let me put it in," she said, urgency responding to suggestion, lifting her bottom slightly from his thighs, lowering her hand and easing the fleshy column inside her body.
"Ahhh, Fuck," she hissed, twisting her face in a distorted mask of pleasure and digging her finger nails into his arms, shuffling on the sofa and opening her legs, gestures of movement and breathless moans and groans turning into painful cries.
"Keep still. Let me do the work," she volunteered, shifting her weight and moving her hips in a slow seductive rhythm, lifting and lowering, easing him in and easing him out, wriggling her bottom and taking him deep inside her body, whimpering through a euphoric moan when she felt the length and girth breaching the limits of the vaginal vault.
"That's better. It's been a while, I've almost forgotten what to do," she mocked, lifting and lowering over his cock, bouncing and wriggling and thrusting her body with promiscuous intent, her pendulous tits swinging carelessly in front of his face, and a euphoric smile lifting the corners of her mouth.

"Fuck, that's good," she breathed, thrashing her head from side to side, frustrated sighs chasing breathless gasps, a wanting woman hungry for physical fulfilment, a needy woman launching into a tireless marathon of physical endurance, wriggling and twisting, bouncing and thrusting, lifting and lowering in a synchronised motion of give and take, easing him in and easing him out in a commentary of filthy curses, then letting him slip from her body in a chorus of frustrated sighs.

"The springs on the sofa are making too much noise," she sighed, brushing hair from her face and cursing under her breath, the urgency in her voice and the quickness in her step, brushing away the need for caution.

"It'll be better on the floor," she whispered, rolling off the sofa and lying on the floor in front of the fire, the dying red embers just enough to capture the alluring images of her dark hairy bush against her milky white thighs.

"Fuck me," she whispered, opening her legs and brushing wet hair from her face.

With a single thrust of his hips he was inside her body, flexing his buttocks and thrusting his hips, pushing through the forest of pubic hair and parting the slippery flaps and folds, moving back and forth, pushing in and pulling out, ignoring the threadbare carpet beneath his knees and her pleading cries for calm, when he quickened the pace.

"You're very good," she breathed, wrapping her long legs around his waist and digging her feet into his lower back, moving her hips in a slow rhythm of give and take, moaning when she felt the length reaching the depths of her inner core and groaning when she felt the girth bruising the walls of the vaginal vault.

"Fuck me. Make me come," she cursed, tightening her grip, and moving back and forth to persuasive urges.

"You're making too much noise," he cautioned, his heart banging like a drum inside his chest and carpet burns torturing his knees, ignoring her outburst and responding to her urgent commands, fucking fast and fucking hard, pushing in and pulling out, deeper and deeper, thrusting and grinding, pounding and hammering, letting her feel the unforgiving force of a perpetual fucking machine stretching her entrance and filling her body, letting her rejoice in the euphoric mutterings of a woman reaching climax.

"Ah. Fuck. Oh. Fuck. Oh. Ah....Fuck...Fuck," she hissed, through gritted teeth, the rapture of euphoric release reverberating inside her bruised and battered body, in a climax of earth-moving proportions, tingling her feet, curling her toes and shaking her legs, sweeping through her chest and face and rattling her teeth, a whiplash of orgasm exploding inside her vulva and stealing the last breath of air from her lungs.

"Wow," she gasped, through a breathless wheeze and a contented smile, a woman lost in the overwhelming heat of passion, waiting for calm and the climax to melt away, unable to hide the post-orgasmic flush colouring her face.

"You need to finish," she whispered, turning over and kneeling on all fours, looking back over her shoulder and opening her legs.

"What was that," Eileen, gasped, the sound of a creaking door and a whisper of movement in the shadows, interrupting their moment of passion.

"I think someone was at the living-room door," she croaked, blinking her eyes into focus and speaking in conspiratorial whispers.

"Didn't you hear it," she nervously asked, slipping into her knickers, the fading echoes of hurried footfalls disappearing up the stairs, sweeping away any doubt she might have had.

"No. I didn't hear anything. Are you sure?" he sighed, choking back a nervous lump in his throat and reaching for his pants.

"Did you see who it was?" he asked, his eyes vacant, his throat dry and the hairs standing up on the back of his neck.

"No," she replied, hunching her shoulders and staring at the living-room door. "It couldn't have been Malcolm. If it was he would be beating the shit out of both of us," she sighed, slipping into her pyjama top.

"Christ. I hope....I hope it was my sister Eve and not my mother or father," he mumbled, through a nervous stammer.

The tension at the breakfast table was unbearable.

There didn't appear to be any suspicious signs coming from his mother or father and Eve was her usual buoyant self, talking too fast and laughing too loud, fluttering around the kitchen and absorbing all the energy inside the room.

The suspense of not knowing who was at the living-room door had left him with a cold sweat and a feeling of nausea. But the incident didn't seem to bother Eileen. She carried on a deep conversation with his mother, smiling and talking as if nothing had happened.

"Did you and Malcolm sleep well, Eileen?" Ellen enquired, pouring tea into cups, the question breaking the crippling anxiety.

"As soon as my head hit the pillow," Eileen lied, forcing a smile and lifting a cup to her mouth.

"You need something to eat before you go, Mark," his mother insisted, an unexpected smile lifting the corners of her mouth.

"Yes," his father chirped in. "You need to keep your strength up son," he winked.

'Christ' he thought. *'Do they both know or is it just his paranoid mind playing with innocent words.*

He wasn't surprised to see his brother Frank, casually reading a newspaper and sporting a black eye, when he walked into the house. But he was surprised when he announced that he intended to join Malcolm and Eileen on their journey back to Bishop Auckland.

"Have you been in trouble again?" his father asked, pointing a finger at his bruised eye.

"Nothing I couldn't handle," Frank replied, without looking up from his newspaper.

With the build of a middleweight boxer Frank Brand was no stranger to the occasional brawl. When he was in his late teens he was, streetwise and mature well-beyond his years.

But at times he was impulsive and if he was ever pushed into a corner he could be reckless and violent. And with his contempt for authority and discipline, most people were surprised when he said he was joining the British Armed Forces.

Eddie and Malcolm carried the stale smell of cigarettes and alcohol to the car.

Frank carried his black eye and newspaper.

Mark carried Eileen's small case and a look of disappointment.

Eileen carried her smile and the cleaned-of-all-mischief tartan blanket.

Any thoughts they might have had about a repeat performance in the back seat of the car were quickly eroded when Frank sat in the front passenger seat and Malcolm ended up in the back with him and Eileen.

Under a claustrophobic cloud of cigarette smoke and the smell of stale alcohol and sweat, Eddie turned the key in the ignition and after a couple of spluttered protests from the engine and a familiar curse from the driver, the old engine roared into life.

Frank had acquired the ability of being able to talk to his father and read the newspaper at the same time. But if the truth were known, it was probably nothing more than a pretence for the inevitable stories of their childhood.

With the skill of a magician, Malcolm removed a half-bottle of whisky from the inside of his jacket pocket and after a few gulps of the golden liquid he fell asleep against the door.

"Drunk," Eileen, sighed, frowning in disgust and shuffling across the seat.

"It's cold. You'll have to remember to get the heater fixed, Eddie," she said, spreading the tartan blanket over their legs and resting her head against his arm.

The comforting warmth of her body and a light fragrance of perfume teasing his nostrils and her more than ample breasts brushing against his arm was enough to wake the sleeping monster inside his pants.

But even without the benefit that darkness always brings and Malcolm sleeping next to Eileen, they both knew there would be no opportunities for mischief.

They hadn't travelled very far when he felt her fingers creeping slowly over his thigh....

Double Room (circa-1970)

After the death of Victoria, and his brother Frank away most of the time with the British Armed Forces and his younger sister Eve in those unbearable teenage years, living at home with his parents was never going to be the same.

So, when Gary Fowler offered him the opportunity to move into his flat, it didn't take him long to make up his mind.

In the beginning their loyalty and friendship towards each other worked quite well, but over time, with one glass half-empty and one glass half-full and two different personalities, in only six-months of living together, the cracks were beginning to show.

But although they had given up sharing a flat, they remained good friends, especially when Gary sustains major injuries in a head-on car accident.

It took most of the day and all his energy to help Gary move his belongings out of the flat they had shared for the last six-months and into his new home with Stella Mason.

He was tired and exhausted, and he wasn't in the mood for going out. But with only a couple of cigarettes left in the packet, he knew he would have to visit the off-licence at the end of the street.

"Fuck me. It's after eight," he cursed, glancing at his watch and grabbing his leather jacket from a chair. *"I'd better get a move on,"* he thought, picking up his wallet from a table and taking the stairs two at a time, trying to remember if Laura Beckett closed her shop at eight or nine o'clock.

"Fucking rain," he cursed, running from the storm, pulling the zip up on his jacket and brushing water from his face, quickening the pace and cursing again when he saw the lights inside the shop fading into darkness.

"Hello," he barked, tapping his fingers on the door and brushing his hand across the murky glass. "Laura. It's me, Mark Brand," he croaked, blinking his eyes and peering into the darkness, the shadowy figure of a woman climbing a step ladder behind the counter, wearing a short skirt and flashes of white thighs blossoming from a pair of knee length leather boots, keeping his interest for a while, until she recognised the familiar face looking through the glass.

"We're closed," she mouthed, pointing a finger at the sign on the door, narrowing her eyes and staring out through the misty glass.

"Please let me in. I just want a packet of cigarettes," he sighed, pushing his face against the wet glass and placing the palms of his hands together in that common sign for prayer or begging, pursing his lips and mimicking a smoking gesture with two fingers.

"You frightened me. I nearly fell off the ladder," she said, in a breathless whisper, brushing hair from her face and smoothing her skirt over her hips, the fluorescent lamps pinging and buzzing in unison and bringing the shop back to life.

"Thanks Laura. I owe you one," he smiled, stepping into the warmth of the shop and shaking water from his jacket onto the vinyl floor.

"I couldn't leave you in the rain," she replied, with a hint of amusement. "And I wouldn't do it for anyone else," she added, a thin smile showing a small gap between her two front teeth.

"I know your brand," she announced, picking a pack of twenty cigarettes from the fixture.

"I was just about to pour myself a drink before taking a shower. If you follow me into the kitchen I've got a spare umbrella you can borrow. It's a little girlish, but it'll keep you dry," she smiled, turning the lights off inside the shop and heading through a door into the kitchen.

In all the time, he had known Laura Beckett, he couldn't remember ever seeing her with a man, which he thought was strange, because although she wasn't stunningly attractive, for a woman in her early-forties, she had great personality and a fantastic body.

"I drink alone far too often, so if you're not in a hurry...." she said, cursing under her breath, the presumptuous invitation slipping from her mouth before she realised what she'd said.

"You're welcome to join me," she invited, hiding her embarrassment behind a smile and placing a bottle of vodka and two glasses on the kitchen table.

"I'm just going to take a shower," she smiled, picking up a yellow umbrella from a recess beneath the stairs. "I said it was a little girlish," she laughed, her smile persuasive, her eyes optimistic and her voice hopeful.

"If you're not here and the umbrellas gone when I return, I'll understand," she said, forcing a smile that quickly faded. "I won't be long," she said, flashing her eyes and choking back a frustrated sigh, the thought of spending another lonely night in bed with her fingers and phallic friend her only companion, forcing another shameless offer.

"It's Russian vodka."

The top was still on the bottle of vodka when she walked back into the kitchen, brushing wet hair from her face and wearing a flimsy white bathrobe tied loosely at the waist.

"I've been in the shower for ten minutes and the glasses are still empty," she smiled, playing with a silver cross hanging from a chain around her neck.

"I didn't want to start without you," he said, lifting the bottle and almost filling her glass.

"That's how I like them," she mockingly replied, pushing her tongue between the small gap in her front teeth. "The bigger the better," she added, flashing her eyes and ignoring the commotion between her legs.

During two very large vodka's, Laura did most of the talking, although most of the conversation was about her dull and lonely social life, due to the endless nocturnal hours working in the shop.

He smiled and nodded his head a couple of times trying to look interested, but his eyes were fixed on the growing nipples hardening beneath the fabric

and below the table there was a familiar stirring inside his pants.
She was frustrated and impatient. He was hard and ready. Any meaningless small-talk and any thoughts or attempts at foreplay were quickly brushed aside in the emerging heat of passion, the promise of expectation and the overwhelming desire to fuck, fuelling the fire between her thighs.
She was wet. Too wet. It had been too long.
She was on her knees before her bathrobe hit the floor, fumbling impatiently with the zip on his trousers, frustration and arousal forcing a string of filthy curses, a triumphant sigh lighting up her face when his zip surrendered, and his pants fell to the floor.
"Wow. Oh, my goodness," she smiled, wrapping her fingers around the gruesome limb and easing him into her mouth, running her tongue up and down the length and sweeping over the bulbous head, wiggling her tongue inside the open eye, easing him in and easing him out, cradling his balls in her hand and sucking one into her mouth, looking up from the floor to see his reaction, a persuasive whisper and a motioning gesture getting her back on her feet.
"I want to fuck you from the back," he insisted, almost throwing her across the kitchen table, the sound of her hands slapping against the timber surface spooking a cat that had been sleeping in a basket beneath the stairs.
"Gently," she gasped, opening her legs as the cat disappeared through a small flap in the door.

"I don't do gentle," he smiled, peeling back the slippery flaps and folds and easing inside her body an inch at a time, feeling the swollen muscle growing in length and thickening in girth as it completed its journey inside the vaginal vault.

In a commentary of verbal filth, he fucked her across the kitchen table like a man possessed, strokes long, deep and aggressive, powerful and urgent, in and out, hard and fast, plunging into her depths, letting her feel the energy of his tireless libido, letting her feel his endless stamina of youth.

"Oh, Fuck. Oh, God," she blasphemed, sucking in air through her nose, the length battering and bruising her body with an unforgiving force and the girth almost splitting her apart.

"Take it easy. It hurts," she cried, through tight lips and gritted teeth, looking back over her shoulder, pleading for gentleness and begging for calm, the sound of table legs squeaking in helpless protest, letting him know that if he didn't slow down the table was going to collapse.

But with her shapely bottom perched invitingly in the air, her legs wide open and his cock sliding seamlessly inside her body and her tits squashed flat against the table, he had given up worrying about a tired piece of furniture.

He fucked her fast. He fucked her hard, balls deep inside her bruised entrance, moving his hips back and forth in a tireless momentum of give and take, easing in and easing out, pushing in and pulling out, a physical and merciless demonstration of table-top sex, a wanting woman left slumped over the table in a pool of perspiration, the euphoria of a knee-trembling orgasm sucking the last breath of air from her body.

"I need to lay down," she gasped, brushing wet hair from her face and gripping the table for support, sucking in air through her nose and trying to calm the heart banging like a drum inside her chest, waiting for the euphoric tremors to melt away.

"Let's finish in the bedroom," he said, taking her arm, in a persuasive gesture of movement.

"Finish," she gasped, forcing a smile. "I'm not sure if I can take anymore. My legs are shaking. I can hardly walk," she said, in a breathless whisper, reaching the top of the stairs in a gasping wheeze and rolling on the bed before she passed out.

But after the performance in the kitchen, she didn't really care about her legs.

Laura had experienced an awakening and she was going to make up for lost time.

As soon as she had him between the sheets, she didn't care if she never walked straight again.

With a single thrust of his hips he was inside her body, pushing in and pulling out, fucking hard and fucking fast, banging her body without mercy, letting her feel the energy of youth and the brutal force of a tireless fucking machine.

"Fuck, that's good," she cursed, pushing back to meet the force and wriggling her hips to the persuasion of movement, the bed bouncing, the headboard banging against the wall and the springs squeaking in a rhythm of give and take.

"Oh. Yes. Oh. Ah," she groaned, through a chorus of euphoric mutterings, twisting her face and whimpering through a pleasurable cry when she felt the meaty length reaching the limits of the vaginal vault and brushing against the cervix.

"Fuck. Oh, Fuck," she gasped, the euphoria of sexual combustion and the inevitable waves of convulsions, beginning their irreversible tidal surge.

"I'm coming. I'm fucking coming," she screamed, thrashing her head from side to side and arching her back off the bed, tightening her legs and curling her toes, coming through a running commentary of orgasmic filth and a sea of vaginal fluids spilling down his cock.

"You'll have to run out of cigarettes more often," she smiled, breathing in short gasps of air through her nose and blowing out through her mouth, settling into silence, waiting for calm and the euphoric tremors to melt away.

No words were needed as he headed down the stairs. The glint in her eyes and the smile on her face were all signs that Laura Beckett had slept alone far too often.

"Fucking rain," he cursed stepping out into the dark street, ignoring a shrieking cat showing sharp teeth before disappearing through the flap in the door, pulling up the zip on his jacket and opening the yellow umbrella.

"Fucking kids," he cursed, looking up at the broken street lights and sprinting like an athlete down the dark street, brushing water from his face and blinking his eyes into focus, cursing the kids again and crossing the road between two parked cars.

He didn't see the black BMW speeding up the road without lights, but he certainly felt the force of the impact against his right leg and the inevitable flight over the car bonnet before crashing to the ground in a pool of water.

"I'm sorry," a woman said, apologetically, stepping from the car and helping him to his feet.

"I didn't see you. Its, so dark," she sighed, stooping to pick up the umbrella.

"That's why cars have lights," he retorted, limping to the safety of the footpath.

Curtains started to move in windows of nearby houses as curious neighbours peeked out.

"Let's get out of the rain," she said, taking his arm and opening the car door.

"Are you injured?" she asked, shuffling nervously in her handbag and cursing under her breath until she found her cigarettes.

"Aren't you supposed to offer the wounded a cigarette?" he said, forcing a smile.

"Yes…Yes. Of course," she said, pulling another cigarette from the pack.

"I hope you're not going to call the police?" she enquired, pursing her bottom lip and exaggerating puppy-dog-eyes. "I've just come from a sales conference at the Five Bridges Hotel, a couple of

streets away," she said, pointing a finger in the wrong direction. "I've had a lot to drink, so the last thing I want to see is a copper," she added.
"No police," he said, clutching his thigh and stretching out in the comfort of the front seat.
"Thanks," she uttered, pulling on her cigarette and blowing smoke through a small gap in the window.
"I think I'd better take you home and have a look at that wound," she smiled, handing him the umbrella.
"Couldn't you get one in black?" she mocked, raising a quizzical eyebrow.
"I like to carry the yellow one on dark nights, just in case I happen to bump into idiots driving without lights," he retorted.
"Touché," she snorted, turning the key in the ignition, a subservient smile growing into a girlish-giggle, the type of giggle that most teenagers reserve for their first date.
It only took five minutes to reach his flat, but it was just enough time to find out that her name was Amanda King, with big tits, figure hugging curves and a wedding ring on her left hand.
"Are you capable of climbing the stairs," she offered, her voice betraying a hint of sarcasm, placing a comforting arm around his waist, before climbing the stairs to his flat.
"That certainly helps," he croaked, the soft whisper of nylon stockings brushing over feminine thighs, taking his mind off his injury and bringing a smile to his face.

"I can offer you a drink, but I can't give you one of these," he said, exaggerating a limp and dropping a crushed packet of cigarettes on the coffee table.
"You look in pain. It might be more serious than you think," she said, sipping her drink and handing him a cigarette.
"let me have a look…Don't be shy. Drop your pants," she smiled.
"Shy," he laughed, putting his drink on the table and dropping his trousers to the floor, an impressive bulge inside his briefs, catching her eye.
"That looks swollen," she teased, running her hand over the bruise on his thigh. "Sit on the sofa. You need some therapeutic treatment," she smiled, flashing her eyes and lowering to the floor on her knees.
"It's very swollen," she smiled, pulling his briefs over his thighs and curling her fingers around the thick girth, looking up from the floor and easing the fleshy limb inside her mouth.
"Fuck," she blurted, moving her head in a seductive rhythm of pleasure, sucking him in and spitting him out, licking and probing and swallowing deep, gasping and gagging and sucking in air through her nose, when she felt the bulbous head touching the back of her throat.
"My knees are sore. And my jaws aching," she sighed, lifting up from the floor.
"Haven't you got a comfortable bed," she smiled, unzipping her dress and letting it fall to the floor, the capture of black stockings and suspenders and the

unmistakable shape of a camel-toe, bulging beneath her knickers, getting him back on his feet.
"Wow. I want to....I want to," he stuttered, choking back a lump in his throat.
"Fuck me," she finished for him, flashing her eyes and twisting the gold wedding ring around her finger, her smile widening, and her words breathed in a seductive whisper.
"Take me to the bedroom."
He waited until Amanda had turned the lights on her car before driving away from his flat.
"I need to eat something," he thought, opening the fridge door and staring blankly at the flickering light, as if he was expecting some kind of delicacy to jump out.
There wasn't much to offer. A piece of tired looking cheese, the wilted leftovers of a half-eaten take-away and some unrecognizable thing that had acquired a green covering.
'Such was the life of a sleepless bachelor,' he thought, nibbling at the remains of the previous night's take-away and taking a bottle of malt whiskey from the drinks cabinet.
"It's been a busy day," he thought, pouring a large measure of whiskey into a glass and slumping on the sofa by the fire
"Helping Gary Fowler to move into his new flat. Two hours of sex with Laura Beckett and an hour with Amanda King. No wonder I'm feeling tired," he sighed, yawning into his hand and picking up a book from a table.

"Masters and Johnson. Human Sexual Response," he sighed, reading the inscription on the inside cover for the millionth time and choking back a lump in his throat.

'To my dearest Mark.... You will always be in my thoughts. All my love Ruth'

Below the inscription, he had written a code of conduct based on the information he had gathered from the book.

Be pleasant and courteous - show her kindness and understanding – gain her trust and respect - be patient - be sympathetic – explore and stimulate the erogenous zones during the arousal stage – ensure she reaches increased stimulation during the plateau stage – be thoughtful and caring during the resolution stage – when her body moves into the orgasmic phase, bring her to orgasm before you.

It was almost two in the morning when he put the half empty bottle back into the cabinet and stumbled unsteadily into bed.

He hated Monday mornings. It signalled the week-end was over and ahead of him were five working days.

'The two cups of black coffee and four Paracetamol tablets hadn't helped to ease the pain, so the drive to Lancashire with a thunderous hangover and an aching leg, would take a little longer than normal,' he thought, yawning into his hand and glancing at his watch, the timepiece informing him it was almost six in the morning.

His employer, Mather, Simmons and Logan - an established firm of architects and building surveyors - had just been awarded a lucrative contract with a Multi-National Banking Organisation who had recently acquired over five-hundred properties in the Lancashire area. Most of the acquisitions were in the city centres or on the outskirts of Manchester and Liverpool. The conditions of the contract involved the re-signing and re-branding the bank's new asset, incorporating their new corporate name, image and logo.

The contract period was expected to be somewhere in the region of three years.

"Fucking rain," he cursed, dropping through the gears and pulling onto the A1 motorway.

"Fucking Amanda King," he sighed, clutching his right thigh and making a mental note to look out for mad women driving cars without lights.

"Fucking boring motorways," he blurted, fiddling with the buttons on the radio and scanning the stations, pausing when he heard, 'The Beatles' singing, 'Let it Be.'

"Not far to go. I must have been driving for more than two hours," he thought, opening a window and yawning into a clenched fist, a green motorway sign, with a white arrow pointing left to Manchester, signalling his departure from the A1 motorway.

"Christ, I might be doing this for the next three years," he sighed, dropping through the gears and pulling off the motorway, another sign directing him to Stockport.

"Book a hotel with a double-room near Manchester city centre," George Logan had told him. *And nothing too expensive. If you tell the landlord that we might be residents for the next three years, he might offer you a discount"* he added, the authority in his voice letting him know who was in charge.

"Fucking cheapskates. People with fucking power," he sighed, lighting a cigarette and blowing smoke against the murky windscreen.

"I think I'm fucking lost," he cursed, brushing away condensation from the windscreen and looking for a familiar road sign, turning off one road and into another, driving aimlessly through traffic until he came to a set of traffic lights.

"I've never seen so many road signs," he thought, pulling to a halt at a red light and looking up at a maze of arrows all pointing in different directions, cursing when the lights turned to green and he had to pull away.

"That looks promising," he thought, a red bricked Victorian building about fifty yards up the road with a red neon sign above the door catching his eye and forcing him to make a quick manoeuvre into another line of traffic.

After a few honking horns and finger gestures from disapproving motorists, he pulled into the car park, stepped out of the car and walked into the premises.

'The Royal Belvedere Arms Hotel,' had a warm and informal atmosphere.

White painted walls and a myriad of horizontal and vertical black stained beams decorated the main entrance foyer and lounge and a range of antique tables and chairs were strategically placed over colourful rugs and hardwood floors.

A wide staircase from the bar led up to the bedrooms on the upper floors and in a small recess at the end of the bar a log burning fire crackled on an open grate.

Behind the bar a mahogany cabinet displayed an assortment of golfing paraphernalia and several photographs of men, smiling and holding silver trophies above their heads.

Apart from the melodic chimes from an ornate clock on the wall behind the bar and a middle-aged man with a bald head and a huge stomach, watching a game of golf on a television screen opposite the bar, the place was quiet.

He lit a cigarette and cleared his throat to get the landlords attention.

"Yes sir," the landlord smiled, never once taking his eyes from the television. "What can I get you?" he added, his heavy-lidded eyes taking a temporary detour from the screen.

"Have you got a double-room for...?"

"Yes," the landlord replied, interrupting his question and turning quickly on his heels, picking up a glass from a shelf and holding it under the Lambs Navy Rum optic.

"Double-Rum," he smiled, placing the glass of dark rum on the counter and shaking his head at the television screen. "I could have hit the ball straighter than that," he sighed, punching his fingers into the cash register and ringing up the price of the drink.

"Do you play," the landlord asked, pointing a finger at the television.
"No…No. I…I don't," he stammered, staring at the drink on the counter and then at the landlord's outstretched hand, the misunderstanding forcing him to reach inside his wallet.
"Just what I needed after a long drive," he smiled, handing him a one-pound note and draining the contents of the glass, any attempt at building a conversation with the landlord, lost in an outburst of laughter when the ball landed in a bunker on the fourth.
"I'd better ask him again," he thought, pulling on his cigarette and making sure he overstated his diction and gave longevity to the syllables Bed and Room.
"Have. You. Got. A. Double-BED-ROOM. I. Can. Have. For. The. Next. Five-Nights?
"I'm sorry about the misunderstanding," the landlord said, forcing a smile that quickly faded. "You have a very strong North-East accent," he added pointing a finger at his mouth which wasn't really necessary.
"Please accept my apologies," he added, offering his hand in the way of introduction.
Charles Henderson was only in his mid-fifties, but he had the look of a man ten-years older.
"You might need a permanent room for the next three-years," Charles smiled, the thought of a regular income taking his mind off the golf and giving him an urgency in his step.

"I'll show you to your room, Mr. Brand" he volunteered, picking up his suitcase and heading for the stairs.
"The bedrooms are on the first-floor," he said, gripping the handrail and climbing the stairs.
"I'll give you one of the better rooms, overlooking the street," he offered, puffing and panting and sucking in air through his nose. "They're bigger and they all have en-suite showers," he smiled, gasping for breath and pointing a finger at a door when they reached the top of the stairs.
"The negotiation on the standard price of the room over three years should put a smile on George Logan's face," he thought, lighting a cigarette and transferring the contents of his suitcase into a wardrobe.
"Four o'clock," he muttered, glancing at his watch, the decision to either sit in his room, watch the golf with Charles Henderson, or go for a walk and see what the streets had to offer was an easy one to make.
"There's certainly plenty of local pubs," he thought, walking aimlessly through a myriad of endless streets for an hour until he discovered a large whitewashed building at the junction of Denby Lane and Manchester Road.
'The Poco-a-Poco Club,' the sign above the door informed him.
"This looks promising. And it's not too far from the hotel," he thought, peering through the tinted glass doors, blinking his eyes into focus and catching a glimpse of

faceless people cleaning floors and arranging tables for the evening's entertainment.

It was just after five o'clock when he arrived back at The Royal Belvedere Arms Hotel.

A group of smartly dressed businessmen all wearing dark suits and identical blue ties with a yellow golfing motif and all making a lot of noise at the bar, wasn't something he expected to see so early in the evening.

"They've started early," he muttered under his breath, ignoring the commotion and pulling up a stool at the opposite end of the bar, lighting a cigarette and caching sight of a beautiful woman serving drinks behind the bar.

"What a gorgeous pair of tits and what a fantastic arse," he thought, her shapely breasts bouncing inside a pink blouse and her curvy bottom poured into a pair of white trousers, a hint of bare flesh above her waist just enough to make your imagination run wild with torment.

The businessmen crowded her space, challenging each other for position at the bar, flashing bulging wallets and throwing money on the counter as if it was wedding confetti, ordering champagne and boasting about their earnings and expensive cars.

"Fucking arseholes," he thought, pulling on his cigarette at the end of the bar and frowning at a group of men making fools of themselves with their futile attempts of seduction.

"I'll be back in a minute," she informed the suits, catching sight of the stranger at the end of the bar, crushing her cigarette into an ashtray and lifting off her stool.

"I've got a customer waiting to be served," she added, gliding across the room in a whisper of movement, her hips swaying with alluring fascination and her breasts bouncing with the capture of movement.

"What can I get you?" she asked, with a seductive confidence, brushing away a loose strand of hair that had fallen over her face, a heart-melting smile flirting with the most striking blue eyes he had ever seen.

'You can take your panties off and sit on my face until it turns blue.' he was tempted to say, stealing a glimpse of her tits through a small gap in her blouse, before ordering a beer.

'Surely this is not the woman who shares a bed each night with Charles Henderson, he thought, staring wide-eyed at the vision of beauty, images of her nakedness finding a place inside his head and stirring the sleeping limb inside his pants.

"Double Rum for this gentleman," Charles Henderson announced, in a burst of snorting laughter, the friendly hand on his shoulder, interrupting his lustful thoughts.

"Have you met my beautiful Beverley and my golfing friends?" he chuckled, his huge stomach wobbling in unison with each word, pausing momentarily to take in air and regain his composure before telling the story about the misunderstanding over a double-room.

The suits laughed hysterically. Their laughter a little too loud and a little too forced.

Perfect Timing (circa-1971)

If only he had gone straight to the Cavendish Club on Friday night, he wouldn't have had the police knocking at his door and he would certainly be in a better frame of mind for the long drive to Stockport.

He was beginning to regret his act of chivalry.

The Bay Horse public house in Gateshead, was a place you generally called into for a quick drink on the way to somewhere else. It was a dirty, sleazy place and so were the clientele.

The smell from the toilets and a fog of cigarette smoke hung permanently in the air and the carpets were so old and threadbare if you stood in one place for too long, your shoes stuck to the floor.

The glass had barely touched his lips when a young girl walked onto the dance floor and removed all her clothes. Under the hypnotic spell of Norman Greenbaum singing *'Spirit in the Sky,'* she danced with a carefree confidence, floating in a dreamy trance around the floor, oblivious to the world around her.

The unexpected exhibition quickly attracted an audience of curious eyes.

Testosterone loaded males with bulging eyes and bulging pants gathered around the dance floor like a pack of hungry wolves, their voices laden with crude suggestion, willing the girl to open her body and give them a solo performance.

A guttural voice behind him interrupted the glass touching his lips.

"She's a loon mate."
"She's a what," he questioned, turning quickly on his heels to see a short middle-aged man with a covering of perspiration on his chest and unsightly sweat marks under both arms, grinning hideously behind the bar.
"A fucking loon," he repeated, circling a finger at his temple. "The wheels spinning but the hamster's dead," he smiled, his bulging eyes crawling shamelessly over her naked body.
"Nice pair of tits though," he snorted, shifting position and craning his neck, anxious not to miss a second of the erotic performance.
He took an instant dislike to the lecherous pervert who felt it necessary to scratch his balls as he continued to question him about the girl.
"I don't understand. What do you mean. Does she have mental problems?"
"She's certainly got a problem," he grinned, wiping a layer of sweat from his brow and crushing a cigarette into an overflowing ashtray.
"Why are you so concerned," he added, leaning over the counter until their faces were almost touching, his cheesy smile showing yellow stained teeth and his breath smelling of cigarettes and the inside of a sewer.
"This is not the first time she's stripped naked and given a performance," he sniggered, a cigarette dancing between two nicotine stained fingers.
"Apparently, she exposes herself in other pubs in the area," he smiled, putting his hand inside his trouser

pocket just as the young girl bent over and opened her legs.

His next question interrupted the pervert's hand playing inside his pants.

"Who is she, and why doesn't anyone stop her?"

"Stop her," he croaked. "Why would anyone want to stop her? It's just getting interesting," he laughed, pulling on his cigarette and shuffling his feet behind the bar, trying to get a better view and making it obvious that he wasn't in the mood for exchanging words of sympathy. A depraved audience of cowardly predators circled the dance floor like vultures around a carcass. Some of them were chanting obscenities. Some were whistling and jeering. Others were making crude suggestions and a man with his cock in his hand was encouraging her to perform oral sex.

He finished his drink and glanced at his watch, the timepiece reminding him that he should be heading to the Cavendish Club.

After giving the barman a look he reserved for perverts and fools, he pushed his way through the throng of predatory filth. After picking up her clothes from the floor and lifting her into his arms, he headed out the door, an onslaught of verbal abuse and angry gestures, following in his wake.

"What's your name and where do you live?" he asked, putting her in the back of his car and waiting patiently for an answer, but she just stared into the distance as if he wasn't there.

"If you don't tell me where you live, I'll have to take you to the police station," he sighed, the mere mention of the police, getting a quick response.
Apart from an ambient light above the entrance door, the vicarage was in darkness.
"It's like something from a Dracula film," he thought, the tyres crunching in quiet protest over the long gravel drive, the headlights lighting up the eerie grounds and a forest of tall trees casting haunting shadows over the sinister looking house.
"Can I help you?" a voice asked, through a small gap in the door.
"My names Mark Brand," he announced, blinking his eyes into focus and looking through the gap, catching sight of a nose and a mouth.
"Your daughters in the car," he added, pointing a finger at a shadowy figure inside his car.
"Just a moment," a voice replied, the ominous sound of deadlocks disengaging and chains rattling in frames, forcing him to step back from the door.
"I'm Alistair Bainbridge. I'm the vicar of St Andrews Methodist Church," said a tall man wearing a tweed jacket and sporting a white dog-collar.
"Let me take her inside. I hope she hasn't been in trouble again," he sighed, the discourteous movement of the door closing behind him, letting him know that Alistair Bainbridge had nothing more to say.
"A thank you would have been enough," he muttered to himself, glancing in the rear-view mirror as he drove away from the house, a little surprised to see an

elderly woman at the door and Alistair Bainbridge writing something on a notepad.

The following day a police officer arrived at his door and questioned him about the events at the Bay Horse on Friday night. Alistair Bainbridge had reported the incident to the police and had given them the make and registration details of his car.

The officer told him that he wasn't under arrest but asked him if he would come to the police station and make a statement, so they could complete their report.

After moving into the flow of traffic without indicating, the sound of a car horn behind him was enough to remind him that George Logan was travelling with him today and he realised that if he wanted to get them both to Stockport in one piece, he would have to push Alistair Bainbridge and the police at the back of his mind.

The rain hammering against the windscreen and the poor visibility made the driving more demanding and required his deep concentration. He was also aware that the ache at the back of his neck was the prelude to a thunderous headache.

Fortunately, he had travelled the route so often he could almost set the car on auto-pilot.

The week ahead looked promising, both for work commitments and for sociable events.

On their working agenda, he had to survey a couple of buildings in Manchester city centre and George

Logan had to attend a client progress meeting in Liverpool.
On their social agenda, Charles Henderson and Beverley Jackson had invited them both out for dinner, to celebrate his birthday.
"We're almost there and it decides to stop raining," he sighed, humming along to James Taylor singing *'Fire and Rain.'* dropping through the gears and pulling off the motorway.
It was only six-thirty in the evening and the hotel bar was already filling with locals and strangers, some were catching a quick drink before heading to Old Trafford to watch the match and others were sitting on stools at the bar, content to watch the game on the television.
"They're playing Newcastle United, so we'd better keep a low profile. The last thing we need is a confrontation with Manchester United supporters." George whispered, handing him a drink and trying to disguise his North-East accent.
"Come on the reds," growled a drunken supporter, waving a red scarf above his head as he headed for the door.
"Come on the black and whites," he muttered under his breath, raising his glass in salute to the stranger and catching sight of Beverley Jackson gliding down the stairs in a whisper of movement, a figure hugging black dress and long slender legs growing from a pair of towering black heels, taking his breath away and turning heads in the room.

Bruno Dante greeted his guests in the entrance foyer of the Bella Roma restaurant.

After hugging and kissing everyone on both cheeks and making a fuss and commotion as if they were all Hollywood celebrities, he welcomed them into his humble establishment.

"The best table in the house," Bruno announced, snapping his fingers and skipping across the floor, a waiter with a bottle of champagne following quickly on his heels.

"Compliments of the house," Bruno smiled, pouring wine into fluted glasses, a couple of waitresses moving anxiously around the table, moving chairs and clinking cutlery, forcing smiles and handing out menus.

"Happy Birthday, Charles," Beverley toasted, smiling and raising her glass.

"Happy Birthday," voices echoed in unison across the table, the sound of chinking glasses and spirited voices, momentarily interrupted by a waitress delivering food to the table.

A taxi dropped them back at 'The Royal Belvedere Arms Hotel,' just after eleven.

"Keep our guests entertained. I won't be long, Charles" Beverley said, before disappearing into the kitchen and returning with a smile and a bottle of champagne in each hand.

"Champagne for everyone," Beverley announced, pouring wine into glasses.

Compliments followed compliments, flirtatious smiles exchanged under a surreptitious veil of stolen glances, pledges and promises and truth and lies smothered under the sound of popping champagne corks, spirited voices and the cacophony of George and Charles, giggling and laughing like a couple of teenagers, telling dirty jokes and making suggestive innuendos.

"This is a good one," George said, in a high voice, holding his hands about ten-inches apart and attempting to tell a joke about a man with a large penis, but with too much alcohol and a touch of memory loss, he missed the punch line and launched into a fit of laughter.

"Mark can tell that joke better than me," he giggled, pointing a finger at his friend and shamelessly announcing that he was hung like a horse.

"Is that a fact?" she whispered in his ear, dipping a finger into her wine and sucking the liquid from her finger with flirtatious suggestion, a mischievous smile curling the corners of her mouth.

"I always thought you were a bit of a dark horse," she teased, the sound of the telephone ringing, interrupting the sexually charged atmosphere hanging between them.

"I'll get that," Charles volunteered, lifting quickly off his stool and picking up the phone behind the bar.

"It was the landlord from the Red Bull," he said, dropping the phone into the cradle and running his hand over the back of his neck.

"What did he want?" Beverley asked.

"He's with some members of the golfing club. They're discussing the next tournament in Spain," he said, forcing a smile that quickly faded.
"I know its late, but I'm the secretary of the golfing society, so it's important that I'm there to approve the financial implications," he said, kissing her on the cheek and draining the contents of his glass.
"I'll take George with me. I won't be long," he said, slipping into his jacket and heading out the door.
"Happy Birthday," Beverley sighed, rolling her eyes and lifting her glass in mocking salute. "It looks like the birthday celebrations have come to an end," she added, lifting off her stool and pressing a button on a black and chrome box behind the bar.
"In the wee small hours of the morning," Sinatra sang, his soothing voice filling the room with intimate and flirtatious suggestion.
"It doesn't have to end. Listen to Frank. The whole world might be fast asleep, but the nights still young," he smiled, placing his hand over hers, the intimacy of touch fuelling the fire of passion between her legs.
"Charles and George won't be back for a while," she smiled, flashing her eyes and pursing her lips with seductive persuasion. "So why don't we have another drink and you can seduce me," she added, pulling up a stool next to his and pouring wine into glasses.
"That's an invitation I can't refuse," he replied, brushing his hand across her face, tracing the outline of her mouth and full red lips, the kind of lips that

pleaded for gentle kisses and offered a passionate response.

"You're making me tingle," she whispered, faces coming together and noses touching, lips meeting and tongues sweeping over teeth, duelling in a sea of saliva and alcohol, two mouths feasting on the heat of each other's breath, two lovers flirting in an intimate dance of promise and expectation.

"Take my hands," she invited, shuffling on her stool and slipping her shoes off her feet, flashing her eyes with lustful intent and leaning back precariously on the stool, a promiscuous smile lifting the corners of her mouth.

"A little bit of foot stimulation to start with," she offered, running her feet up and down his legs and wiggling her toes playfully between his inner thighs, finding the growing lump inside his pants and pressing her foot against the fleshy muscle, the acquaintance of touch providing the ultimate tease.

"I thought that might get you hard," she smiled, removing her foot from his groin, the playful pursuit of his genitalia momentarily interrupted by a compelling urge and an overwhelming need for sexual interaction.

"I've been hard from the first day I met you," he replied, pulling her into his arms and peppering her neck with soft and meaningful kisses, blowing warm air into her ear and fondling her breasts, feeling them rising and falling in his hands, the heat of passion stimulating genitalia and heightening expectation.

"You certainly know how to seduce a woman," she smiled, impulsive urges responding to the acquaintance of touch, wrapping her arms around his neck and pushing her breasts against his body, letting him feel the weight and the firmness of her nipples pressing against his chest.

"You're making me tingle again," she said, brushing hair from her face and flashing her eyes with flirtatious intent, lowering her hand and squeezing the throbbing muscle inside his pants.

"Wow. It feels very hard. And big," she gasped, lustful thoughts filling her head with the promise of endless hours of bed rattling sex.

His masterful touch...His taste...His hard flesh inside her mouth...His big cock stretching and filling her entrance...A frenzied fuck and a breath-taking orgasm sucking the last breath of air from her lungs.

"What was that," she croaked, the ominous sound of the old building settling into silence breaking the erotic thoughts playing inside her head.

"Don't panic," he whispered, giving her hand a gentle squeeze and smiling into her eyes. "It's just the heating system and the wind shaking the window frames."

There was a great deal of nervous apprehension at the true reality of what they were about to undertake, knowing that Charles and George could bust through the door at any minute.

But with their brains operating much slower than the speed of hormonal chaos, and increasing heart beats firing a surge of blood into genitalia, any thoughts of caution were lost in the pulsing flesh throbbing between her fingers.

"We'd better do something about that," she smiled, urgency stimulating arousal, lust and desire overflowing with expectation, caution and danger sweeping away in the heat of passion, lifting off the stool and lowering to the floor on her knees.

"There will be other times when we'll be alone with no one to disturb us," she said, looking up from the floor and flashing her eyes with the promise of oral stimulation.

"So, until then….Let me take care of you," she smiled, pulling his trousers over his thighs and slipping her hand inside his briefs, wrapping her long-painted fingers around the girth and lifting the weighty limb from the dark confines of the fabric.

"Wow," she gasped, blinking her eyes and staring in admiration at the impossible object bobbing and swaying in front of her eyes, her stomach fluttering with excitement and a familiar wetness pooling between her thighs.

"It must be over nine-inches long and it's as thick as a woman's wrist. The last time she'd seen anything so obscene, it was hanging from a horse." she thought, images of hours of bed rattling sex, finding their way back inside her head.

She couldn't believe her eyes. She stared in disbelief. She wanted it.

"Just relax," she smiled, blowing soft kisses between his inner thighs, one hand caressing his balls and the other hand working the length back and forth, pulling the foreskin over the bulbous head and dragging a finger nail over the dark blue vein running along the side of the fleshy column.

"It's huge," she whispered, pressing her thumb against a blue vein, feeling the pulse and the surge of blood rushing through the shaft, tugging and pulling the length with sensitive and calculated strokes, an urgent desire to taste his flesh dancing behind a flirtatious smile.

"Let's see what it tastes like. If I can get it in," she smiled, the warm melting pleasure of her mouth and the pulse of her lips, bringing a smile to his face and gasps of appreciation hissing between tight lips.

"You taste so good," she whispered, easing him in and easing him out, sweeping her tongue in a slow seductive dance around the swollen head, sucking in air through her nose and swallowing as much flesh that her mouth would comfortably accept, flashing her eyes and looking up from the floor to see his reaction.

"And so, delicious," she added, sucking him in and spitting him out, bobbing her head up and down working the shaft in a steady rhythm of pleasure, nipping the sensitive membrane playfully between her teeth, giving the sensitive glans a little extra attention before removing a clear drop of sticky fluid from the unblinking eye.

"My legs are aching. I'll have to stand up," she sighed, shuffling uncomfortably on the timber floor and letting the swollen limb slip from her mouth.

"Don't worry. I haven't finished with you yet. I just need to get my legs working again," she smiled, the warmth of her mouth and the acquaintance of her hand stroking his cock, removing the anxiety and turning his frustration into reassuring expectation.

"Is that better," she breathed, closing her fingers around the thick appendage and working the length back and forth, tugging and pulling, faster and faster, blinking her eyes into focus and watching the foreskin playing hide and seek with the bulbous head.

"I think you're ready," she smiled, easing him into her mouth, sucking him in and spitting him out, holding his balls in tender capture and dragging her teeth along the swollen shaft, easing him in and easing him out, euphoric muttering and a sticky substance on her tongue, signalling his fast-approaching climax.

"I'm coming…I'm coming," he hissed, a photograph of Charles Henderson looking out from the golfing cabinet behind the bar, smiling and holding a silver trophy above his head, momentarily interrupting his concentration.

"Let it all come," she smiled, the warmth of her mouth sucking his cock with eager enthusiasm and her hand caressing his balls, taking his mind off the photograph and bringing him back to reality.

"Here I come. Here I fucking come," he announced, hissing through tight lips and clenched teeth, the fluids of passion erupting from his testicles with an unforgiving force, spilling inside her mouth and splashing the back of her throat, showering her teeth and filling her mouth with a copious amount of his sticky mess.

She sucked and swallowed. She coughed and spluttered. She choked and gagged on the fleshy muscle breaching the back of her throat and threatening to stop her breathing.

"Fuck," she gasped, pulling the gruesome limb from her mouth and wiping strings of sperm and saliva from her chin, a final surge of his messy offering spilling recklessly over her tits, decorating her hair and showering her face with the syrup of sex.

"I won't be a moment," she whispered, lighting a cigarette and lifting off her stool.

"I'm just going to the bathroom to repair my makeup and remove any signs of mischief," she smiled, slipping into her shoes and disappearing into the shadows.

"That's what I call perfect timing," Beverley whispered, sitting back on her stool at the bar, the familiar laughter of two drunken men crashing through the front door, signalling the return of Charles and George.

"I think I've had too much to drink," Charles giggled, holding George Logan's arm for support and staggering unsteadily on his feet.

"Sorry we're late. I was going to ring you, but I thought you might have gone to bed," Charles slurred, taking one step forward and two steps back.

"You said you wouldn't be long, so we had another bottle of champagne," Beverley replied, blowing smoke above her head. "Mark's been telling me all about his job and a little bit about living in the North East," she lied, lifting her drink to her mouth, the darkness of the room masking the hot flush colouring her cheeks.

"I've discovered a lot about Mark Brand tonight," she said, forcing an innocent smile.

They talked for a little while, mainly about Charles and George's fleeting visit to the Red Bull and an imminent golfing tournament somewhere in the Mediterranean.

With the conversation fading into meaningless trivia and their bodies giving in to sleep, they left the dying log fire and headed off to bed.

Persuasive Approval (circa-1971)

"Meeting Beverley Jackson for the first time after their impulsive moment of intimacy when Charles and George left them alone in the hotel and went to visit the landlord of the Red Bull, was always going to be a little uncomfortable," he thought, stepping out of the car and walking into the hotel reception.

He wasn't surprised to find the place deserted, but he always arrived at the same time on a Monday morning, so he knew Charles and Beverly would be expecting him.

He pulled up a stool at the end of the bar and lit a cigarette, the intake of nicotine easing the anxiety and giving him a moment to reflect on the events over the week-end.

"Fucking Karen Ashton. Fucking Jeff Calder," he sighed, cursing under his breath at his stupidity. *A night that promised hours of steamy sex, ending in a night in the cells at Gateshead Police Station.*

It was an offer they couldn't refuse when they left the Cavendish club and Karen shamelessly announced that she was up for a threesome.

After parking the car in a quiet country lane and removing their clothes, the heated copulation quickly gathered speed.

Three naked people fucking in the darkness, through a chorus of grunts and groans and squeaking car springs, the intimate give and take momentarily interrupted by a call of nature.

"I need to pee," Karen announced, gathering her clothes from the floor.
"I won't be long," she smiled, stepping from the car and heading for the privacy of the bushes.
In the crippling silence, they waited for almost twenty minutes, smoking cigarettes and brushing condensation from the windows, staring aimlessly into the darkness, watching and waiting.... No sign of Karen.
"I'd better go and look for her," Jeff volunteered, pulling on his briefs and stepping from the car, the glare of a torch shining in his face and an unexpected voice laden with mocking amusement, stopping him in his tracks.
"Well-Well-Well and what have we got here?" a policeman chuckled. "Come and have a look at this, Tom" he smiled, waving a hand to his colleague.
"They look like a couple of nice boys," he grinned, shining his torch and peering inside the car.
"It's not something you see every day. Two naked men in the back seat of a car in a quiet country lane," Tom sniggered, lighting a cigarette and making an unnecessary comment about needing a puff.
"It's not what you think," Jeff and Mark barked in unison, the echoes of mocking innuendo feeding their panic, fumbling nervously in the darkness, cursing and swearing and searching the floor for clothes.
"We're not...We're not," Jeff sighed, slipping into his shirt and pulling up his pants, trying to proclaim their innocence, searching for mitigating words in

their defence, like homophobic, straight men and this will all be revealed when Karen gets back to the car. But Karen had spotted the two police officers questioning her two companions and she had no intention of having a confrontation with the law.
"I don't think we've got time to wait for your friend, Karen," one of the policemen said, with mocking tease, pulling on his cigarette and making a sarcastic comment about Jeff's sexual orientation.
"Fuck you, arsehole," Jeff barked, sending another message with a couple of fingers.
"A gay man with a temper," the copper laughed. "Well let's see if a night in the cells calms you down," he grinned, bundling them both in the back seat of the police car, the voice of a police controller crackling through the radio in Echoes, Bravo's and Foxtrot's, that two men have been arrested for indecent exposure in a public place, feeding his panic and throwing his mind into chaotic turmoil.
The courtroom…The Trial...The Judge…The Sentence...The newspapers…His Family…His Friends, he sighed, the ominous sound of a creaking door opening in the floor behind the bar and the familiar figure emerging from the dark abyss of the cellar, interrupting his thoughts and bringing him back to reality.

"Is that you Mark," Beverley smiled. "I'm sorry I wasn't there to meet you. I had to get a few things from the cellar," she added, struggling to push a crate of alcohol through a hatch in the floor.

"Let me help you with that," he said, lifting quickly off his stool, taking a crate with one hand and helping her up with the other.
"Thanks," she smiled, letting go of his hand. "I know I shouldn't be climbing ladders at my age, but my cellar man hasn't come in today and Charles has gone to Spain for a few days to play golf," she sighed, pulling up a stool at the bar.
"How are you. Have you got a busy week ahead of you?" she asked, pouring coffee into cups, the small-talk breaking the nervous silence hanging between them.
"I'm fine," he answered, sipping his coffee and shuffling uncomfortably on his stool.
"Some days are busier than others," he added, lighting two cigarettes and searching his mind for something appropriate to say.
"Thanks," she smiled, taking a cigarette from his outstretched hand.
"Let's sit on the sofa in front of the fire," she said, brushing hair from her face and picking up their cups from the bar.
"Charles flew to Spain, yesterday. He won't be back until Thursday," she smiled, settling on the sofa, sipping her coffee and blowing smoke above her head.
"I'm taking you out for dinner tonight and when we get back to the hotel I want you to make love to me," she smiled, the audacious invitation getting his undivided attention and removing the uneasiness hanging inside the room.

"If you insist," he smiled, running his fingers through her hair, the mood and the conversation changing into fleeting compliments and sincere words of endearment.

"I've missed you. I go to sleep thinking about you and I wake up thinking about you," he smiled, kissing her neck and nibbling her ear.

"Thanks, but you don't have to seduce me again. You're on a promise, remember," she giggled, flashing her eyes and sipping her coffee.

"I'll have to go. I've got things to prepare. We can talk over dinner tonight," she smiled, lifting from the sofa and giving his hand a gentle squeeze.

"She never mentioned the name of the restaurant," he thought, sitting on a stool at the end of the bar, lighting a cigarette and adjusting his tie in the mirror.

"I don't think she'd be brazen enough to go to the Bella Roma restaurant without Charles," he pondered, a voice behind him interrupting his hands playing with his tie.

"Sorry I'm late," she smiled, sweeping gracefully across the floor on towering heels, a red satin dress clinging to every curve like a second skin, swaying her hips and bottom in a tantalising way that seems to come naturally to a beautiful woman wearing heels.

"I forgive you," he replied, a voice inside his head and a movement inside his pants urging him to rip her dress off and fuck her on the floor until she couldn't breathe.

"You look beautiful," was all he said.

Bruno Dante greeted his two guests in the entrance foyer of the Bella Roma restaurant.
"Mrs Jackson, how beautiful you look tonight," he smiled, kissing her on both cheeks, his well-rehearsed bow and persuasive Italian demeanour, always gaining her approval.
"Bella Donna…Bella Donna," Bruno chimed, casting a suspicious eye at her companion.
"This is my friend Mark. He was our guest at Charles's birthday," Beverley announced.
"Let me show you and your friend to your table, Mrs Jackson," Bruno said, avoiding the formality of a handshake, the insincerity in his voice and the disapproving look on his face making him feel like he was being marched to the gallows.
"Your favourite table, Mrs Jackson," Bruno smiled, pulling out a chair. "Please allow me," he offered, leaning over the table and lighting her cigarette.
"Let me know when you're ready to order," he added, skipping away through a myriad of tables and chairs to attend to a group of people waiting in reception.
"Sorry about Bruno. I'm always with Charles when he sees me, so it's understandable that he doesn't approve of seeing me with another man," she sighed, sipping her wine and blowing smoke above her head.
"I've been with Charles for almost ten years," she said, brushing hair from her face and shuffling uncomfortably in her chair.

"We first met when I was on holiday in Majorca. Charles was there playing golf with some friends. He bought me a drink at the hotel bar and asked me to dance. He was charming and a perfect gentleman. Later that evening he asked me if I'd like to have dinner with him the following day," she sighed, hiding her sadness behind a smile.

"The rest is history," she frowned, stubbing her cigarette into an ashtray.

"I like Charles and I do value his friendship," he replied, echoes of guilt and betrayal rattling around inside his head. "I don't know what he'd do if he ever found out that I've been sleeping with you," he added, lighting a cigarette and searching her eyes for reassurance.

"There's something I need to tell you," she said, lowering her voice to a surreptitious whisper and glancing over her shoulder.

"Charles can't get an erection," she casually announced. "It's something to do with his diabetes. We haven't had sexual intercourse for the last four years," she confessed, pouring wine into glasses and lighting a cigarette.

"Most nights I lie in bed imagining what it would be like to have a physical relationship again. I'm still young. I have needs," she sighed, an impish smile lifting the corners of her mouth.

"You don't have to worry about Charles," she said. "He knows about us. I told him. I also asked him if I can sleep with you," she said, with shameless ease

and rather matter-of-fact, the boldness of her statement, forcing him to gasp into his glass.
"You asked him.... What!?" he barked, picking up a serviette from the table and wiping dribbles of wine from his chin, lowering his voice to a whisper when he realised his outburst was attracting the attention of other diners.
"You asked him if you could sleep with me?" he repeated, running his hand across the back of his neck and staring at the floor, hoping it would open up and swallow him alive.
"Charles understands that everyone has needs. He just wants to make me happy," she said, reassuringly. "And he also values your friendship," she added, with casual ease, flashing her eyes and raising her glass as if proposing a toast.
"Are you ready to order?" she asked, changing the conversation and lifting the mood. "You need to keep your strength up," she smiled, raising her hand at one of the waters.
"And don't forget you're on a promise, so don't drink too much," she whispered, brushing hair from her face and casually flicking her ash into a tray.

"If we want to avoid suspicious eyes and gossiping tongues, it might be safer if you go straight to your room until the staff have left, and I've locked the premises," she whispered, stepping from the taxi outside the Royal Belvedere Arms Hotel.
"Thirty minutes should be enough time to let the staff go and lock the premises," he thought, closing the door to

his room and heading down the stairs, the soft soothing voice of Roberta Flack, filtering through the overhead speakers and the two glasses of wine on the bar, with a smearing of red lipstick on one of the glasses, signalling that Beverley wasn't too far away.

"The First Time Ever I Saw Your Face," he hummed, sitting on a stool at the bar, smoking a cigarette and sipping his wine, glancing at the clock on a wall behind the bar and watching the hands approaching midnight, a movement at the top of the stairs, interrupting the song playing inside his head.

"I hope I haven't kept you waiting. I just nipped back to my room to change into something more comfortable," she smiled, twirling on her toes in a black silk robe and towering heels.

"I hope you approve," she whispered, flashing her eyes and posing like a model at the top of the stairs.

"It was certainly worth the wait," he smiled, the promise of hours of steamy entertainment, lifting the corners of his mouth and stirring the sleeping monster inside his pants.

"Is that all I get," she mockingly replied, lifting an eyebrow and brushing hair from her face, opening the black silk robe and like unveiling a statue, brushing it from her shoulders and letting it fall to the floor.

"I've got something for you," she teased, floating on air down the stairs, swaying her hips and flaunting her Marilyn Monroe curves to perfection.

"Let's take our drinks into the lounge," she insisted, taking his hand and skipping across the floor, the curves and contours of perfection caught in the shadowy silhouettes from the open fire, the fleeting images revealing all her naked beauty.

"I told you there would be times when we would be alone," she smiled, wrapping her arms around his neck and pulling him into a crushing kiss, letting him feel the heat of her breasts flattening against his chest and the warm melting pleasure of her tongue slipping inside his mouth.

"We've got plenty of time. We don't have to hurry. Charles won't be back for a few days," she smiled, breaking away from the kiss, the acquaintance of touch fuelling the fire of passion between her legs, the promise and expectation washing away the need for caution and any thoughts about valued friendships evaporating in the fire.

"Can you handle three days of sex?" he smiled, pulling her into his arms and brushing his fingers gently over her face, tracing her ears and her nose, lowering his hands and exploring the sculptured curves of her waist and shapely bottom, fondling her breasts and pulling her nipples, squeezing her bottom and pulling the cheeks apart, slipping a finger along the dark valley and probing the anal opening, two people converging in a physical exchange of intimate pursuit, two lovers embarking on a journey of sexual discovery.

"I'll certainly give it a try," she smiled, breathing in the scent of arousal and the promise of coital engagement, breathing in the excitement and the aroma of sex.

"But I need to get you out of these," she whispered, opening the buttons on his shirt and unbuckling his belt, slipping her hands into the waist and pulling his pants and briefs over his thighs, staring in admiration at the swollen object peeking through his shirt.
"It's been a long time since I made love on the floor," she whispered, her head swimming in a sea of hormonal chaos and a warm liquid heat manifesting between her legs.
"Let's have some fun on the floor before we go to bed," she smiled, wrapping her fingers around the long thick column and leading him onto a rug in front of the fire.
"Providing I don't get too many carpet burns," he laughed, dropping to his knees in an intimate union of sixty-nine, with his bottom hovering above her head and his hairy testicles swinging just above her face.
"Fuck the carpet burns," he smiled, slipping his hands between her thighs and opening her legs, a well-practiced tongue embarking on a journey of irresistible need, marking a warm wet trail over her stomach and slipping the tip of his tongue into her naval, pushing his nose through the forest of pubic hair and peppering soft kisses between her inner thighs, sweeping his tongue over her vulva and feasting on the moist flaps and folds, bathing and nibbling the soft frills and petals around the urethra, breathing in the musty odours of sex and pressing his chin against the pubic bone, wiggling his tongue

in sensuous circles over the soft tissues and coaxing the clitoris pearl from the sanctuary of its protective hood.

"Fuck. That's good," she gasped, sucking in air through her nose, moans and groans and involuntary movements responding to the intimacy of oral stimulation, arching her back off the floor and brushing her fingers through his hair, pulling his head down against her warm entrance, the warmth of his tongue sweeping over the swollen hood and teasing the clitoris, propelling her senses into overload and filling her head with persuasive thoughts.

"Oh, yes," she whimpered, gripping the fleshy limb in her hand and working it back and forth, pulling the tight foreskin over the bulbous head and then stretching it down the length, sweeping her tongue over the hairy scrotum and sucking one of his testicles into her mouth, holding it in gentle capture between her teeth before letting it slip from her mouth.

"Oh, fucking yes," she cursed, urgent cries of encouragement and pelvic movements responding to the acquaintance of an eager finger parting the outer lips of her labia and sliding inside her body.

"Don't stop," she begged. "More fingers. More tongue," she pleaded, a second finger twisting and curling inside the vaginal vault and his tongue bathing the clitoris, bringing her to the edge of euphoric release.

"I'm going to come," she announced, grabbing his buttocks with both hands and digging her fingernails into the soft flesh, lifting her hips and pushing her vulva hard against his face, letting him smell the heat of passion, letting him taste the fluids of arousal, letting him breathe in the aroma of sex.

"Oh. Yes," she moaned, euphoric mutterings and filthy curses spilling from a helpless mouth. "I'm coming. I'm coming," she screamed, thrashing her head from side to side.

"Fuck. Fuck. Fuck" she cursed. "I'm coming. I'm coming," she grunted. "Ah. Ah. Oh. Ahhhhhhhhhh," she hissed, through clenched teeth and tight lips, the heat of passion exploding in a powerful surge of euphoric bliss, tingling her feet and shaking her legs, the aftershock of a momentous orgasm sucking the last breath of air from her mouth.

"Wow!" she gasped, sucking in air and brushing away a few strands of wet hair hanging over her face. "I'm absolutely drained. I can hardly breathe. I think I'm going to need some help getting up," she sighed, shuffling awkwardly on her knees.

"Help me onto the sofa," she smiled, reaching out and taking his outstretched hand.

"I'm getting too old to have sex on the floor," she sighed, crashing on the sofa, waiting for her heartbeat to calm and her legs to stop shaking.

"If you're going to fuck me, you're going to have to carry me up the stairs," she smiled, lifting off the sofa and taking his hand.

"No. Not in your room," she insisted, interrupting the urgency in his step. "I've got a double bed in my room. It'll be more fun," she smiled, flashing her eyes and pointing a finger in the opposite direction.
"Follow me," she giggled, grabbing his swollen appendage and skipping along the corridor, swaying her hips and wriggling her bottom with alluring effect, a smile and a curling finger beckoning him into the room.
"Make yourself comfortable. I'm just going to freshen up," she smiled, disappearing into the en-suite bathroom in the corner of the room, a four-poster bed and mirrored wardrobes running the entire length of the wall, offering hours of steamy sex and furtive observation.
"Do you like my bed?" she asked, wrapping her arms around his neck and pushing him onto the bed, the headboard banging against the wall and the mattress creaking under their weight.
"I do like the bed. And the mirrored wardrobes," he smiled, heart beats racing and pulses throbbing, the promise of endless sex fuelling the fire of passion, two hungry mouths crashing together in a pulsating kiss, eager tongues invading mouths, duelling in a battle and dancing to a salsa, sweeping over teeth in a mutual exchange of oral fluids.
"I thought you'd like the mirrors," she smiled, flashing her eyes and brushing hair from her face, the invitation of surreptitious amusement lifting the corners of her mouth.

"If you make me come again, I'll let you watch me sucking your cock in the mirror," she grinned, urgent gestures responding to the promise of oral stimulation, a tangle of hands moving to impulsive urges, touching and feeling, probing and searching, two people embracing in a courtship of intimate enquiry, two lovers suffocating in the heat of passion.

"Get on your back," she said, shifting her weight on the bed and pushing her warm tits against his chest, sliding over his stomach and resting her bottom on his muscular thighs.

"You can watch in the mirror," she smiled, cupping her weighty breasts in each hand and lowering them over the gruesome limb, pushing her tits together and wrapping them around his cock, sliding up and down the length in a slow seductive tempo, watching the smooth head appearing and disappearing beneath a shroud of foreskin and the unblinking eye opening and closing with the capture of movement.

"Keep watching," she smiled, letting his cock slip from her cleavage, shuffling on her knees and straddling over his body in an intimate alignment of north and south, with her bottom perched just above his face and her vagina and anus open and inviting.

"Fuck," he snorted, craning his neck in the mirror, making sure he didn't miss any of the erotic performance, the warmth melting pleasure of her tongue sweeping around the ridge of the bulbous helmet and wiggling inside the small eye, getting a responsive gasp of approval.

"Is that good," she whispered, wrapping her fingers around the swollen limb, feeling the pulse between her fingers and the surge of blood racing through the web of blue veins, glancing in the mirror and easing him into her mouth, sucking him in and spitting him out, dragging her teeth over the sensitive membrane and feasting on the seminal fluids oozing from the myopic eye.

"I'm wet. I want you inside me," she pleaded, shuffling on the bed with her knees on each side of his hips and her hands outstretched on the mattress, flashing her eyes and hovering over him like a prowling lioness scenting prey, the hard muscle pressing against her bottom, lifting the corners of her mouth and bringing a smile to her face.

"Let me put it in," she volunteered, reaching back with her hand and wrapping her fingers around the fleshy column, the unexpected ringing of the telephone and a blanket of silence descending on the room, interrupting their moment of passion.

"I have to get that. It'll be Charles," she sighed, lifting her shoulders in submissive frustration and cursing at the phone.

"Talk about bad timing. If I didn't know he was in Spain, I'd be checking to see if he was hiding inside the wardrobes," she said, forcing a laugh that quickly faded.

"I don't know why he rings me every night," she frowned, pausing momentarily to regain her composure, before rolling off the bed and picking up the phone.

"Hello," she whispered into the mouthpiece.... "Oh, hi," she answered, pointing a finger at the phone, pursing her lips and silently mouthing *'Charles.'*

"Are you having a good time? What's the weather like in Spain?" she asked, brushing hair from her face and yawning into her hand. "Don't forget to wear your hat. You don't want to get sunstroke again," she replied, picking up the phone and walking towards the bed, a precarious smile lifting the corners of her mouth.

"Good. I thought you wouldn't forget about your hat," she added, sitting on the edge of the bed and flashing her eyes with hungry pursuit.

"No. I'm just about to go to bed," she said, wrapping her fingers around his cock and working the length up and down with shameless amusement…." Yes, we had dinner at the Bella Roma. Bruno sends his best wishes," she added.... "No. I'm alone in my bedroom," she lied.... "No, he didn't.... No, we haven't.... He's got a meeting first thing in the morning, so he decided to have an early night," she lied again...." Okay, enjoy the golf. I'll see you in a few days," she said, dropping the telephone into the cradle and gasping a sigh of relief.

"He'd better not interrupt us tomorrow night," she whispered, falling on the bed and opening her legs, the sight of an open vagina peeking through a forest of pubic hair and the promise of another night of sex, getting him back on his feet.

"I'm overheating. I can't wait. Let me get on top," she smiled, shuffling on the bed and straddling over his thighs, lifting her bottom slightly and lowering her hand, wrapping her fingers around the fleshy muscle, feeling the weight and the pulse between her fingers, before easing the massive limb inside her body.

"Fuck that's good," she cursed, bodies connecting and hips moving to persuasive urges, lifting and lowering in a mutual exchange of give and take, up and down, joining and separating, easing him in and easing him out, lifting and dropping, thrusting and grinding, hard and fast, soft and slow, nine-and-a-half-inches of hard flesh stretching her burning entrance and bruising the fleshy folds, reaching the limits of the vaginal vault and banging against the cervix.

"It's been too long," she sighed, brushing wet hair from her face and wiping a layer of perspiration from her brow, lifting and lowering, easing him in and easing him out, moving her hips to impulsive movements, two lovers fucking to a commentary of filthy curses and a brief exchange of compliments, moans and groans and gasps and cries, smothered under the sound of squeaking bedsprings and the headboard banging against the wall.

"Oh. Yes," she cried, arching her back and shaking her head from side to side, lifting and lowering over the perilous limb, easing him in and easing him out, each thrust pushing her closer and closer towards the edge.

Ahhhh. I'm....I'm.... cuuminng!" Fuck! Fuck! Fuck! she screamed, hissing through gritted teeth and twisting her face in a euphoric mask of pleasure, the fluids of passion spilling from her vulva and pooling between her thighs, the overwhelming release of a knee trembling orgasm lost in the echoes of euphoric cries, squeaking bedsprings and the headboard banging against the wall.

"I'm not sure if I can manage another two days of this," she gasped, letting him slip from her body and resting her head on his chest, breathless pants and wheezing sighs stumbling over choking gasps for air.

"You'll feel better once you've had a good night's sleep," he smiled, ignoring her pleas for calm, lowering his hand and easing the gruesome limb back inside her body, lifting her up and lowering her down the slippery shaft, pushing in and pulling out, sweeping his hands over her bottom and pulling the cheeks apart, the intimacy of a finger probing her anal opening, increasing the blood flow to vital organs and bringing him to climax.

"Ahhh. Fucckkk," he gasped, the liquid passion erupting from his balls and shooting from the shaft with the force of a volcano, streams of emotional lava splashing against the inner walls of the vaginal vault and coating the mouth of the cervix, the last reserves of seminal fluid spilling from his body in a choking chorus of moans and groans and euphoric cries of pleasure.

"I'm exhausted," she gasped, letting his softening organ slip from her body and falling on the bed, their bond of intimacy broken in trailing strings of seminal fluids.

“I need a cigarette,” she smiled, lifting off the bed and picking up her cigarettes from the bedside table, the scratch marks of passion clearly visible on her buttocks and lower back.

“Why didn’t you tell Charles that we were having sex? he asked, taking a cigarette from her outstretched hand. “I thought he didn’t object,” he added, pulling on his cigarette and pointing a finger at the incriminating evidence on her bottom.

“He’ll know when he discovers those scratch marks on your arse,” he smiled, blowing smoke at the ceiling.

“I was going to tell him, but I had my mind on other things and I didn’t want to prolong the call,” she replied, craning her neck in the mirror and twirling on her toes.

“He won’t see them. He’s always in bed before me,” she sighed, sitting on the edge of the bed and reaching for his hand.

“Make sure you cut your nails tomorrow,” she smiled, the welcoming surge of nicotine flowing through her bloodstream, ending the conversation and bringing her back to reality.

“I’ll have to take a shower. It’s getting late. I won’t have time in the morning,” she said, lifting off the bed and skipping across the floor to the bathroom, an invitation laden with flirtatious suggestion following in her wake.

“There’s room for two. If you’d like to join me,” she smiled, curling her finger and flashing her eyes with lustful intent.

"There's certainly enough room for sex," he smiled, stepping under the shower head and reaching for the bottle of shampoo.

"You need to see a sex therapist. If you don't calm down I'll turn the cold tap on," she laughed, brushing soapy water from her face.

"I thought you were my sex therapist," he smiled, gripping the cheeks of her bottom with both hands and peppering her neck with warm kisses of affection.

"No more scratch marks on my bottom," she smiled, brushing water from her face, the familiar movement of hard flesh pressing against her thigh and a finger probing her anal opening, fuelling the fire of passion between her legs.

"You're insatiable," she smiled, turning on her heels and leaning against the wall with her hands flat against the tiles, arching her back and opening her legs.

"There's nothing to compare to that invigorating feeling you get when you fuck a woman covered from head to toe in soapy water. He wasn't sure if it was the slippery movement of hands sweeping over body parts or the assistance it offered when attempting to penetrate a tight opening," he thought, picking up the bottle of shampoo and spilling the coloured liquid over her bottom.

"I've heard that fucking in the shower keeps you young," he smiled, sliding his hands between the soapy groove and pulling her cheeks apart, probing the sphincter and slipping a finger into the dark orifice, the intimacy of a moving finger invading the dark shrine, gaining her approval and lifting the corners of her mouth.

"I like that," she smiled, looking over her shoulder and flashing her eyes, the invitation for anal penetration breathed in pleading whispers of caution.

"Be gentle with me," she begged, shuffling her feet on the floor and opening her legs, lowering her hand and guiding the swollen limb between the cheeks of her bottom.

"Oh fuck," she cursed, as he eased the swollen muscle inside her bottom, nine-and-a-half-inches of hard flesh stretching the rectal pocket and bruising the sphincter.

"That hurts," she gasped, brushing wet hair from her face and gritting her teeth, sucking in air and shuffling her feet, reaching back with her hand and gripping his arm, her pleas for tenderness echoing off the walls inside the steamy enclosure.

"That's better. Slow and gentle," she urged, discomfort surrendering to pleasure, wriggling her hips and pushing back to meet the force, balls deep inside the dark abyss, the sphincter muscles tightening around the girth, easing in and easing out in a steady rhythm of give and take.

"Fuck," she cursed, sucking in gasps of air through her nose and losing her grip on the wall.

"I think my legs are about to give way. I can't breathe. I need a moment" she pleaded, a deep sigh of relief hissing between tight lips, as he eased the blockage from her bottom.

"Let's finish in the bedroom," he said, the uncompromising gesture getting a hesitant reply.

"You're a machine," she sighed, stepping from the shower and following on his heels.

He was inside her body the moment they hit the mattress.

"Oh yes," she cried, wriggling and swaying her hips in a mutual rhythm of give and take, easing in and easing out, pushing in and pulling out, all the way in and all the way out, body-to-body, flesh-to-flesh, thrusting and banging, grinding and penetrating, stretching the inner walls of the vaginal vault, fucking like a wild stallion in heat.

"I'm coming," she croaked. "Fuck. Fuck," she gasped. "I'm coming. I'm fucking coming. Ohhhhh," she cried, pushing her hips back and driving him deeper, feeling the bulbous head battering the cervix, the heat of passion and the combustion of coital union spinning her head into sensory overload, the overwhelming release of a teeth-clenching orgasm, sucking the last breath of air from her throat.

"Fuck," he hissed, his legs stiffening and his balls tightening inside the scrotum, seminal fluids shooting up the shaft and spilling with a force inside her body, the fluids of passion washing the inner walls of the vaginal vault and flooding the dome of the cervix, easing in and easing out in a chorus of moans and groans and euphoric cries, until his balls were empty, and his softening penis had slipped from her body.

"I'm absolutely drained. I can't breathe," she gasped, falling on the bed, the knee-trembling orgasm and the brutal invasion of her bottom, leaving her drained of energy and almost incapable of speech.

"I'll have to get some sleep," she muttered, pulling the bed sheets over her battered and bruised body, blinking her eyes and staring at the clock on the bedside table, the timepiece reminding her that the early morning staff would be arriving for work in less than two hours.

November Rain (circa-1972)

Cursing at the workmen for digging up the street below his bedroom window with a pneumatic drill for most of the morning, did little to ease the thunderous hangover banging inside his head.

"I hope I'm not disturbing you," Charles Henderson said, stepping into his room and removing a handkerchief from his jacket pocket. "I've been knocking at the door, but you probably didn't hear me with all the noise in the street," he said, forcing a smile and wiping a layer of perspiration from his forehead.

"The council engineer said the road works should be finished by the end of the day," he smiled, shuffling his feet on the floor and fiddling nervously with his shirt collar, a question lifting the corners of his mouth.

"Mark, my good friend....I need a massive favour from you," he smiled, running his hand over the back of his neck and lowering his voice to a furtive whisper.

"I've got a little problem and I need your help," Charles said, glancing nervously over his shoulder and scanning the room like a spy being pursued by the KGB.

"You know I've arranged this surprise retirement party for one of my golfing friends, Alan Purvis," he said, narrowing his eyes as if deep in thought.

"I did....I did give you an invitation for tonight," he stammered, searching his pockets for an invitation that wasn't there.

"It's going to be held in the dining room. Any time after seven will be fine. Make sure you avoid Alan when he arrives. Alan thinks he's just coming here to have a drink with a couple of friends," he smiled, hesitating to clear his head and gather his thoughts.

"You said you wanted a favour from me?" he prompted Charles, the question interrupting his hands searching inside pockets.

"Oh...Yes," Charles replied, removing his hands from his pockets.

"I've booked three strippers for Alan's retirement party," he casually announced. "I'm fully booked, so I was wondering if you would let them use your room to get dressed," he said, a questioning eye waiting anxiously for an answer.

"You want me to let three strippers use my room to get dressed," he repeated, shaking his head and cursing at the noise in the street.

"Thanks. I knew you wouldn't object," Charles said, forcing a smile and heading for the door, the confidence and enthusiasm in his voice following in his wake.

"The strippers said that if I give them some more cash, they would perform extras," he grinned, exaggerating a wink and rubbing his thumb and index finger together in that universal sign for money. "I'll see you later. As soon as the girls arrive,

I'll bring them to your room," he added, stepping from the room and closing the door behind him.

"He sounded just like a hooker's pimp," he grinned, stepping from the shower and removing a suit and shirt from the wardrobe. *"If I wasn't fucking Beverley I would have told him to sling his hook,"* he thought, slipping into his new mohair suit and glancing in the mirror, an impeccably groomed and handsome man looking back with a conceited nod of approval.
"I'll have a couple of drinks to celebrate Alan Purvis's retirement, and then I'm off to the Poco-a-Poco Club," he thought, the heavy hand of Charles Henderson banging on his bedroom door interrupting his fingers fumbling with his tie.
"Come in Charles. The doors open," he invited, splashing a generous amount of after shave over his face.
"It's only me with the girls," Charles announced, puffing and panting and wiping a layer of perspiration from his brow.
"This is my friend, Mark. He's agreed to let you use his room to get changed," Charles said, forcing a smile and stammering nervously with introductions, their names unimportant and their virtue less.
"Hi Mark," they smiled, ignoring the protocols of invitation, skipping across the floor on towering heels and claiming the bed.
"Nice suit. You must have a date tonight," one of the girls giggled. "If you're still here when the shows finished, we'll give you a freebee for letting his use

your room," she smiled, handing out cigarettes and opening her bag.
"You're making him nervous," said the older woman, who appeared to be in charge of the act. "Give him a drink and a cigarette," she added, pulling two bottles of red wine and an assortment of vibrators and rubber dildos from her bag.
"I'll see you all later. I've got things to prepare, before my guests arrive," Charles said, slipping out of the room, the gaiety of flirtatious laughter and wine being poured into glasses, interrupting his cowardly departure.
The three women had a streetwise confidence. Shameless and cool and every word prefaced with innuendo and obscenities. But they were extremely polite, respectful and humorous, so he made small talk and accepted their hospitality, always aware of the damage red wine can do to a silver-grey mohair suit.
"Thanks for helping me out with the girls, Mark," Charles said, greeting him with a smile and a friendly hand, at the function room door.
"Someone's been busy," he said, lighting a cigarette and casting an eye over a long table at the back of the room, with an assortment of hot a cold food for the guests.
"Beverley and a couple of the staff did most of it," Charles admitted, guiding him to a seat, facing a small stage assembled at the front of the room.
"I'm responsible for that," Charles chuckled, sitting on a seat next to him and pointing a finger at a white

banner with bold red letters reading 'FUCK THE BUILDING TRADE' hanging across the front of the stage, a clear sign that Alan Purvis had worked long enough.

"You'll be pleased to hear that the council engineers have finished the road repairs," Charles announced, the appearance of the strippers arriving on stage, interrupting the small-talk and getting his undivided attention.

"Who wants some of this," one of the girls said, skipping across the stage with a phallic object in her hand and moving it in and out of her mouth with shameless suggestion.

"What's the other one up to," Charles, croaked, reaching for his handkerchief and wiping a layer of perspiration from his forehead.

"She's sitting on a chair and she's got something in her hand," Charles said, answering his own question, holding his breath and craning his neck to get a better view.

"I think It's a string with something attached," he grinned, as she opened her legs and pulled a long string from her vagina, the place erupting into hysterical laughter and repeating chants of 'Bravo,' when they discovered it was the ingredients of a full English breakfast.

"This one looks dangerous," Charles, smiled, as the older woman arrived on stage wearing lethal heels and sporting a huge strap-on penis.

"Would anyone like to join me on the stage," she offered, flashing her eyes and stroking the gruesome object with suggestive meaning, the lowering of heads and negative reaction from her audience, lifting the corners of her mouth in dismissive condemnation.

"You're all cowards," she smiled, walking to the centre of the stage and placing an empty wine bottle on the floor.

"That bottle looks familiar, he thought, her invitation for someone to hold the bottle, interrupting his thoughts and getting Alan Purvis on his feet.

"Hold the bottle tight, Alan," she grinned. "You can look but you can't touch," she mockingly added, opening her legs and squatting over the phallic target.

"I think Alan's done this before," she smiled, easing the rigid column inside her body to a chorus of lecherous men with bulging pants and loaded with testosterone.

LOWER! LOWER! LOWER, they chanted, breaking into a resounding applause when the bottle disappeared inside her body.

"I want you to give Alan a night to remember," Charles said, opening a bulging wallet and pushing a handful of notes into the older woman's hand.

Through a fanfare of echoing wolf-whistles and a resounding chorus of, 'OFF! OFF! OFF, the three women sat Alan on a chair, removed his jacket and pulled his trouser down to his ankles.

He had seen enough. He finished his drink and looked at his watch. It was time to go.

It was just after eleven when he stepped from the taxi, the black clouds hanging overhead and the ominous rumbles of thunder, suggesting that rain wasn't too far away.

He made a mental note about the damage rain can do to a new mohair suit before glancing at the bill-board by the door. *'The Poco-a-Poco-Club – Tonight's Entertainment Presents - The Black Abbotts Band with supporting comedian and impersonator - Ray Bishop.'*

The club was cavernous with a mezzanine level dividing the place into two areas.

A bar and lounge area with casual seating took up most of the upper level and the lower level comprised mainly of a stage and a myriad of tables and chairs for people to eat and watch the entertainment.

Overhead spot-lights lit up the stage where the resident band sang a range of melodies from *'Sergeant Pepper's Lonely-Hearts Club Band.'*

The evening's entertainment always followed the same format. The night would begin at eight o'clock with the band playing at intervals and introducing the various acts. After midnight, the resident DJ took over, playing records until the club closed at two in the morning.

The Poco-a-Poco Club attracted a diverse range of people from all over Lancashire.

Young and old, single, married or divorced, all populated the club on a regular basis, some of them looking for love and long-term commitment, others just after a good night out.

After midnight, men with unfashionable taste in everything would swagger about trying to look cool and women wearing skimpy outfits that covered flesh but hid little, flashed their eyes at every man in the room.
But the outcome was always predictable. At about ten minutes to two o'clock in the morning just when the club was about to close, desperate men would circle the dance floor like a pack of hungry lions, looking for an antelope with a limp.
He stood for a while, watching the band through a claustrophobic fog of cigarette smoke, proudly showing off his new mohair suit, cursing under his breath and pulling up a stool at the bar when he realised no one was paying him any attention.
"She's nice," he thought, lighting a cigarette and casting an eye over a beautiful young woman serving drinks behind the bar, a figure hugging black skirt stretching over shapely curves and her dark eyes dancing behind a flirtatious smile.
"No engagement ring or wedding ring," he thought, watching her bottom rolling inside her skirt as she glided across the floor with provocative suggestion, the evidence of no knicker line and her huge breasts bouncing beneath a white cotton blouse getting his undivided attention and stirring the sleeping muscle inside his pants.
"Not more fucking golfers," he sighed, catching sight of five smartly dressed business men at the opposite end of the bar, laughing and flirting and flashing bundles of money, buying her drinks and offering

her cigarettes, trying their best to get between her legs.

"At least tell us your name," one of the men asked, blowing smoke from a fat cigar and handing her a piece of folded paper.

"Kath Evans," she replied. "And that's all you need to know," she added, placing the piece of paper behind the bar and catching sight of a handsome young man in a grey mohair suit sitting on a stool at the end of the bar.

"What can I get you?" she smiled, showing perfect white teeth and brushing a whisper of hair that had fallen over her face.

'You can tell that pack of hungry wolves to fuck off and then you can sit on my face.'

"Pint of bitter," he said, returning her smile and brushing the erotic thoughts from his mind.

"Will you join me," he added, reaching for his wallet and catching a glimpse of her tits peeking through a gap in her blouse.

"Thanks for the offer, but I've already got too many drinks," she said, pointing a finger at a row of drinks at the end of the bar.

"Later maybe," she said, placing his drink on the bar and taking money from his outstretched hand, a hint of promise lifting the corners of her mouth.

"Later definitely," she smiled, skipping across the floor, picking up her drink and another piece of folded paper on the bar.

"I told you my name and that's all you're going to get," she said to one of the suits, crumpling the piece of paper in her hand and dropping it into an ashtray.

'What's going on with this silly paper chase. And what the fuck are they writing on the pieces of paper, he thought, lighting a cigarette and brushing away an imaginary mark on his new suit.

"It looks like they're here for the night. I'm going to have to work hard if I want to find out if she's wearing any knickers," he thought, pulling on his cigarette, the lights dimming and a single spotlight shining on a fat man wearing a white linen suit and holding a microphone in his hand, taking his mind off men with bulging pants and any further pursuit of Kath Evans.

"My names Ray Bishop," he announced, his dyed black hair and thin moustache giving him the appearance of a hooker's pimp.

"Let's start with a dirty joke and see what kind of an audience we've got in tonight," he smiled, stretching the boundaries with his cocky attitude and filthy humour, some of the people clapping their hands like a bunch of circus seals, others shuffling uncomfortably in their seats and frowning in disapproval.

"I little bit of both," Ray sighed, running his hand across the back of his neck.

"I'll tell a couple of clean joke until you've all had time to get pissed," he said, in a theatrical voice.

"I went out last night and got really hammered. I woke up next to a fat ugly woman who was snoring and farting.... At least I got home alright."

'I was driving home from work the other night and called into the local pub for a quick pint.
I got talking to a stranger at the bar and he told me he was the local window cleaner.'
I didn't take him long before he began to brag about his sexual conquests.
'I've shagged every woman in Belmont Drive, apart from one,' he said with pride.
I jumped into my car and drove to the nearest store and bought a beautiful bouquet of flowers and the biggest box of chocolates I could find.
As I pulled into Belmont Drive, I could see my wife looking out through the front window.
I burst through the front door and handed her the flowers and the chocolates, telling her that from now on things were going to change."
"What the hell's come over you?" She asked
"Well my love, I was having a drink with our window cleaner and he told me that he had shagged every woman in our street, apart from one."
"Apart from one," she repeated..."That'll be that stuck-up-cow from number eleven."

"Thank you. Thank you," Ray acknowledged his audience with a courteous bow.
"I've got plenty more like that," he smiled, lifting his hands in the air, trying to calm the deafening

applause and the repeating chants of *More. More. More.* echoing inside the room.

"I've seen better. The people in this audience needs to get out more often," he thought, turning on his stool and giving Kath Evans his best smile, a sudden commotion at the end of the bar interrupting the cheers and chants and his flirtatious pursuit of the attractive barmaid.

"Keep away from the disturbance. Come over here, Kath," he said, getting off his stool and waving his hand in an urgent gesture of movement.

"What's happening. Why are they arguing?" he asked, removing two cigarettes from the pack and giving her enough time to regain her composure.

"The tall man with the attractive woman is demanding an apology from one of the men at the end of the bar, after he made an inappropriate comment about his wife's bottom," Kath replied, taking a cigarette from his outstretched hand.

"Here's Freddie. He'll sought it out," she sighed, a well-built doorman with an unshaven face and tattoos on both hands, skipping across the floor with the speed of a gazelle.

"What's going on here?" Freddie asked, his calming smile lacking a full set of teeth and his steely eyes darting around like a caged rat, carefully registering everyone in the room.

"It's nothing," one of the suits replied, puffing on a fat cigar. "I said she had a fat arse and she has," he sniggered, the four men with him laughing out loud and nodding their heads in approval. "You can go

now," he grinned, waving a dismissive hand at Freddie and blowing smoke in his face.
"I think it's time you fucking left," Freddie barked, grabbing him by the arm and opening an exit door.
"Fuck off and don't come back," he growled, pushing him into the street.
"You'd better be careful. There's five of us," he shouted, waving a clenched fist in the air, the bravado and defiance in his demeanour, fading into defeating recoil when his four friends followed him through the side door and into the street.
"It was getting a little bit heated. The bouncer arrived just in time," he said, holding her hand and hiding his delight behind a comforting smile.
"I'm pleased to see them go," Kath sighed, a thin smile lifting the corners of her mouth.
"I'll have that drink now, if it's still on offer," she smiled, letting go of his hand.
"Here's to Freddie," she smiled, raising her glass in the way of a toast, the calm inside the room bringing them back to reality and providing the opportunity to flirt and find out more about each other.
Although the night looked promising, he was still consumed with curiosity.
"I'm interested to know what the men in suits were writing on the pieces of paper," he boldly enquired, lifting his drink to his mouth. "All of them ended up in the ashtray, so I know you didn't approve," he smiled, handing her a cigarette.
"Oh that," she casually replied, taking the cigarette from his outstretched hand.

"They were giving me their telephone numbers and asking me for a date," she laughed, shrugging her shoulders and brushing hair from her face. "They were all wearing wedding rings and anyway none of them were my type."
"And what type would that be?" he asked, lighting her cigarette and smiling into her eyes, the impatient voice of someone at the end of the bar demanding drinks, momentarily interrupting their flirtatious interlude.
"I won't be a moment," she smiled, resting her cigarette in an ashtray and skipping across the floor to serve the man at the end of the bar.
"It's getting late. I'd better give her my best leg-opener line," he thought, lifting off his stool and heading into the reception foyer to find someone with a pen and a piece of paper.
"Sorry about the interruption. Where were we," Kath smiled, sipping her drink and catching sight of a piece of folded paper on the counter.
"This looks familiar. I don't think this one will end up in the ashtray, like the others," she smiled, disappearing into a small recess behind the bar, opening the piece of paper and reading the note.
'Can I take you home tonight – I'm hung like a donkey.'
"What," she gasped. "Ha," she laughed, the boldness of his inquiry lifting the corners of her mouth and getting a hurried reply.
'I finish around two o'clock.'

Oblivious to the weather or the disapproving looks from others waiting in the taxi queue, they kissed each other with a suffocating passion, like two reunited lovers after a long separation.

"Beech Terrace," Kath informed the driver, climbing into the back seat of the taxi, hormonal chaos swimming inside her head and a familiar wetness gathering between her thighs, pushing her to the limits of emotional overload.

"Number seventeen," she added, mouths crashing together and tongues sweeping over teeth, impatient hands searching in the darkness, touching and fondling, probing and groping, the sexually charged intimacy steaming the windows and lifting the corners of her mouth.

"I'm curious," she whispered, blinking her eyes and slipping her hand inside his pants. "Christ, you weren't kidding," she smiled, lifting the weighty column from the warm confines of his briefs.

"It's starting to rain," the driver muttered, pulling to a halt at a red light, the noise of squeaking wipers brushing water across the glass, breaking the silence and the flirtatious interaction in the back seat of his taxi.

"You'd better have a brolly because the weather man said it's going to rain for the next three days," he sighed, pulling away from the lights and adjusting his rear-view mirror, trying to get a better view of the shameless action in the back seat.

"I know it's in here somewhere," she sighed, rummaging impatiently through an overflowing handbag, cursing and swearing and ignoring the embarrassment of a loose tampon falling to the ground.

"Here it is," she said, breathing a sigh of relief when she found what she was looking for.

"Let's get out of the rain," she added, sliding the key in the door lock with metallic urgency, the adrenaline rush kicking into overload and the heat of passion pooling between her legs.

She was wet and impatient. He was hard and ready. Two strangers, drowning in a sea of hormonal chaos, two sexually charged lovers moving to persuasive urges in a turbulence of urgent enquiry, fondling and groping in a mutual engagement of give and take, tongues dancing over teeth in a prolonged marathon of oral endurance, twisting and twirling, claiming mouths and exchanging saliva, feasting on the heat of each other's breath.

"I want this," she moaned, her heart banging like a drum inside her chest and a visceral rush of adrenaline flooding vital organs, lowering her hand and squeezing the swollen limb inside his pants, the acquaintance of touch heightening expectation and the promise of primal interaction screaming from every nerve in her body for this man to get between her legs and fuck her until she begged for mercy.

There would be no time for foreplay. They both knew what they wanted.

No conditions. No promises. None of those complicated things that get in the way of a good fuck.

"Let's go to my bedroom," she smiled, taking his hand and skipping up the stairs.
"You can hang your suit on the back of that chair. It kooks expensive," she smiled, kicking her shoes off her feet and throwing her blouse, skirt and bra on the floor.
"She never said anything about children," he thought, blinking his eyes in the darkness, a photograph of a child in a picture frame on the bedside table momentarily interrupting his urgency to remove his pants.
"I'd better not hang around just in case there's an angry husband," he sighed, the invitation of her legs spread apart on the bed and an open vagina peeking through a dark bush of pubic hair, taking his mind off matrimonial issues and bringing him back to reality.
"That feels good," she breathed, need responding to impulsive urges, moving her hips to the persuasion of touch, the intimate caress of his hands fondling and squeezing her breasts and the warmth of his mouth sucking and biting her nipples, teasing her senses and flooding her head in a sea of euphoric sensation.
"Fuck," she cried, the heat of passion flooding her thighs and a familiar ache between her legs demanding attention, a tangle of hands embarking on a journey of sexual discovery, caressing and stroking, fondling and probing, the acquaintance of nine-and-a-half-inches brushing against her thigh, getting her onto her knees.

LICK ME." she pleaded, grabbing his hair and pulling his head down between her legs, the warm melting pleasure of his mouth bathing the urethra and a well-practiced tongue sweeping over the hood of the clitoris, pushing her towards the edge of euphoric bliss.

"SUCK ME," she whispered, shuffling on her knees in an orientation of north and south, two hungry mouths moving with heightened intensity and almost suffocating in each other's sex, sucking and blowing in a mutual exchange of give and take, the acquaintance of his tongue sweeping over the swollen hood and teasing the clitoris from the sanctuary of its sticky lair, gaining her approval and lifting the corners of her mouth.

"EAT ME," she begged, arching her back and keeping his head pressed hard against her burning heat, his warm tongue embarking on a mission of oral stimulation, dipping in and dipping out, sucking and blowing and slipping between the moist flaps and folds, blowing warm air over her vulva and brushing his face through the dark bush of pubic hair, feeling the silky hairs slipping between his lips, breathing in the smell of urine and the musky odours of sex, smothering his face in her vagina, feasting on the warm secretions between her legs and drinking in the raw fluids oozing from her inner heat.

"You're so good," she gasped, cradling his balls in one hand and gripping the swollen shaft with the other, working him hard and working him fast, pulling and tugging, dragging the tight foreskin down the length and pulling back slowly over the bulging helmet, the pulse between her fingers and a familiar ache between her thighs, getting her back on her knees.

"I'm not sure if I'll get all this in my mouth," she smiled, sweeping her tongue over the tender membrane and removing a drop of emotional fluid from the single eye, feasting on the saltiness of arousal and dragging her teeth over the bulbous head, easing him in and easing him out, sucking and blowing and taking him deep, easing him out in trailing strings of saliva and choking gasps for air.

"Move over to the edge of the bed," he insisted, the mattress squeaking under their weight as he rolled off the bed and she followed his instructions and moved to the edge.

"Give me your legs," he smiled, holding her ankles and lifting her legs in the air. "This might hurt," he grinned, gripping his cock in his hand and shuffling his feet on the floor, spreading her legs and opening her body, nine-and-a-half-inches of swollen flesh pushing through the pubic jungle, stretching the petals and folds and sliding inside her body.

"Oh. Fuck. That does hurt," she cursed, hissing and grunting through clenched teeth, thrusting her hips and pushing back to meet the force, the fearsome length and impossible girth bruising the flaps and folds and stretching the walls of the vaginal vault.

"More, cock" she begged, genitalia embracing genitalia in a mutual engagement of give and take, pushing in and pulling out, back and forth, forward and back, sliding in and slipping out, wriggling her hips and pushing back in a slow rhythm of intimate persuasion, an urgent gesture of need, lifting the corners of her mouth.

"Faster. Fuck me faster," she urged, easing him in and easing him out, pushing in and pulling out, in and out, back and forth, entering and retreating in a mutual engagement of involuntary movements and a brief exchange of promises and filth.

"Fuck me harder," she begged, brushing hair from her face and blinking stinging sweat from her eyes. "Fucking hurt me, she pleaded, gripping her legs with both hands and pulling her knees to her face.

"You want me to hurt you," he repeated, clenching his buttocks and thrusting his hips, moving inside her body like a man possessed.

"You want me to fuck you faster," he grunted, entering and retreating, in and out back and forth, skin smacking against skin, genitalia embracing genitalia, rivers of sweat running down his face and pooling on her tits, the energy, the turbulent friction and the power of hormonal combustion driving them both into a wild and reckless frenzy.

He fucked her, and she fucked him, two strangers fucking in a synchronised motion of give and take, two people fucking well beyond their stamina, two strangers fucking at the speed of a hammer drill, a fanfare of squeaking bedsprings and a chorus of moans and groans and euphoric cries spilling from a helpless mouth and propelling her into emotional overload.

"YES. YES. YES," she screamed, sucking in air through her nose and gripping his arm, a well-oiled machine changing through the gears, his foot on the accelerator pedal and his tireless stamina going at full throttle, pushing hard and pushing fast, easing in and easing out, thrusting and grinding, sliding in and slipping out, banging and pumping, stretching and filling her inner core with an unforgiving force.

"I'm losing my grip," he grunted, shuffling his feet on the floor and tightening his grip on her legs, flexing his buttocks and thrusting his hips, pushing in and pulling out, strokes long, deep, powerful and urgent, the sloppy wet sounds of nine-and-a-half inches entering and retreating from the vaginal vault and the fluids of passion spilling over her thighs, teasing her senses and moving her closer to the edge of euphoric release.

"Turn over. I want to fuck you from the back," he insisted, lowering her legs and pulling the swollen muscle from her body.

"You're very persuasive," she smiled, shuffling on the bed and kneeling on all fours, gripping the headboard with both hands and opening her legs.

"Oh, yes," she gasped, twisting her face and gritting her teeth as he eased the gruesome limb inside her body, pushing in and pulling out, all the way in and all the way out, sliding in and sliding out, thrusting and grinding, banging hard and plunging deep, hard and fast, moving in and out with primitive and merciless restraint, like a dog fucking a bitch in heat.

"That's good," she moaned, impulsive gestures responding to persuasive urges, swivelling her hips and pushing back, swaying and wriggling, rocking forward and pushing back, easing him in and easing him out, making sure she had every inch inside her body.

"I'm coming," she announced, letting go of the headboard, smothering her face in a pillow and gripping the bedsheet with both hands, euphoric cries and a blast of crude obscenities, guiding her on the way to climax.

"Ah. Fuck. Ah. Fuck. Ah. fuck. Ahhhhhh," she gasped, moaning and groaning through a chorus of orgasmic grunts and an outpouring of liquid passion spilling down her thighs, an earth-shattering orgasm rattling her teeth and curling her toes, the tremors of euphoric release sucking the last breath of air from her lungs.

"You need to finish," she whispered, blinking her eyes and looking back over her shoulder, sucking in gasps of air through her nose and brushing wet hair from her face.

"I'm nearly there," he blurted, a tireless fucking machine grunting out his pleasure with ruthless determination, banging and thrusting, penetrating deep, pushing in and pulling out, in and out, back and forth, hard and fast, asserting his primal need for possession and domination, a masterful and unforgiving assault on her burning orifice, a demonstration of supremacy over submissiveness

and a sustained exhibition of carnal lust and unrefined need.
"I'm coming. I'm coming" he shouted, the climax vocal and powerful, a copious amount of his seminal cargo spewing from the open eye, shooting in progressive spurts inside her body, splashing the walls of the vaginal arena and flooding the neck of the cervix, the final fluids of passion draining from his balls and his softening penis slipping from her body.
"I'm exhausted," she gasped, falling on the bed and brushing hair from her face, puffing and panting and sucking in air through her nose, trying to come down from the heights of euphoric release, settling into silence and waiting for calm, waiting for the euphoric tremors to melt away, two lovers obeying the rules of exhaustion, two strangers giving into sleep…
He wasn't sure if he had heard a noise, a movement or a voice, but something in the darkness of the room, interrupted his sleep.
"Who's there," he croaked, blinking his eyes and looking at his watch, the sound of Kath Evans, snoring quietly in the bed, reminding him of his sexual exploits a few hours earlier.
"Is there someone there," he repeated, yawning into his hand, the shuffle of tiny feet and the haunting silhouette of a child peeking through a gap in the bedroom door, feeding his panic and getting him on his feet.
He woke Kath. It was time to go.

"Its six o'clock. I'll have to get back to my hotel. I've got an early morning meeting with an architect and then I'm heading back to Newcastle," he lied, forcing a smile and gathering his clothes from the floor.

"I'll be back next week. I'll see you in The Poco-a-Poco Club," he said, slipping into his shirt, gathering his suit jacket from the back of a chair and heading out the door.

"That looks ominous," he thought, closing the front door and lighting a cigarette, a blanket of clouds obscuring the possibility of any early morning light and a faint rumble of thunder in the distance, reminding him of the damage rain can do to his new mohair suit.

"Fucking weather," he sighed, sheltering under a small canopy above the front door, making a mental note of his options and contemplating his strategy for protecting his suit from the rain.

No point in seeking refuge with Kath and her child. No telephone. No taxi. 'An umbrella,' he thought...No. If she had one she would probably hit him over the head with it, and anyway he was in no mood for parental small talk.

"No more options," he sighed, pulling on his cigarette and looking up into the dark sky.

'If I hurry, I might just make it to the bus stop.' he thought, walking quickly down a long narrow street of post-war terraced houses, lit only by a watery orange glow of street lights on both sides of the road, quickening his step and cursing under his breath when it started to rain.

"Fucking rain," he muttered, dropping his wet cigarette in a stream of water at the side of the road, fastening the buttons on his jacket and sprinting like an athlete from the storm.
"Fucking public transport," he cursed, skipping between pools of water and ignoring the whipping sound of a loose shoelace striking the pavement, cursing the rain, cursing Kath Evans, cursing himself, wishing he had gone back for the umbrella.
"At last," he sighed, pausing to catch his breath at the side of the road, brushing water from his face and stepping back from the curb to protect his new suit from speeding vehicles, throwing up water from the side of the road.
"Fucking traffic. I could be here all fucking day," he cursed, the sound of wailing sirens and blue flashing lights from an ambulance weaving between cars, slowing the flow of traffic and giving him enough time to safely cross the road.
"I need to get back to the hotel. My shirt feels wet," he thought, stepping into the refuge of a bus shelter and bending on one knee to fasten his shoe lace, the sound of a double-decker bus pulling up at the stop, breaking his thoughts and getting him back on his feet.
"If my shirts wet, my suit must be drenched," he sighed, cursing silently at the rain and checking his suit for damages, making a mental note to take it to the dry-cleaners as soon as he gets back to the North East.
"I need a shower and a cigarette," he muttered under his breath, Ignoring the shameful phallic objects

defacing the bus shelter walls and the queue of impatient people shaking umbrellas and stamping their feet.

"I'll sit at the back of the bus. It's only a fifteen-minute journey," he muttered, sitting between three other people on one of the bench seats at the back of the bus.

"She's attractive," he thought, casting an eye over a teenager, sitting opposite, with firm breasts and long legs disappearing beneath a mini-skirt, breaching all the rules of decency, but guaranteeing to keep his attention during the short journey.

"If I was sitting next to her and it wasn't so fucking quiet, I would be trying to get her telephone number," he thought, the unforgiving hour and that early morning absent look, sending out a clear warning that nobody was in the mood for conversation.

'It must be the new mohair suit,' he proudly thought, heads turning and curious eyes staring in his direction. *'At last someone's taking notice.'*

"Hold tight," the bus conductor cautioned, swaying unsteadily with the motion of the bus, rocking from side to side and the wheels fighting with pot-holes in the road.

"Fares please," he croaked, juggling a matchstick inside his mouth and making it twist and turn between two front teeth sticking out at an angle at the front of his mouth.

"Try and have the right change ready," he said, in a nasal voice, pulling a dirty handkerchief from his trouser pocket and emptying the contents of his nose into the filthy cloth.

"Fares please," he repeated, pushing the dirty rag back into his pocket and holding out his hand, his nicotine stained fingers betraying his weakness for cheap unfiltered cigarettes and his jaundice face the colour of a hangover piss.

'I suppose his blind mother must love him. he thought, the conductors outstretched hand prompting him to reach inside his pockets and grab a handful of coins.

'If there was ever a competition for eating an apple through a letter box he would certainly win first prize,' he grinned, forcing a smile at the repulsive man and opening his clenched fist, the haunting image of silver and copper coins and both hands covered in blood, taking the smile off his face.

"Where's that come from. I must have cut my hand," he thought, shuffling uncomfortably on the seat and searching for a wound that wasn't there.

"It looks like I've been cleaning a slaughterhouse floor," he sighed, staring in horror and disbelief at the red stained coins in his bloody hands.

"You must have cut yourself," the dirty man said, removing the matchstick from his mouth and pushing it behind his ear.

"I'll clean them on my handkerchief," he said, pulling the dirty rag from his pocket and casually removing a few coins from his blood-covered hand.

"There. Good as new," he grinned, dropping the coins into his leather bag and recovering the matchstick from behind his ear, skipping up the aisle and whistling a tune through his two front teeth.

"I must have cut my hand when I closed Kath's front door," he thought, surreptitious glances, and suspicious eyes, interrupting his thoughts and bringing him back to reality.

"They're all staring at me, but I don't think it's the suit," he thought, the furtive smile curling the corners of the teenager's mouth, shamelessly informing him that his passion for cunnilingus during a monthly menstrual cycle, hadn't gone unnoticed.

"No. Surely not," he sighed, a hemorrhage of memory clearing the fog.... *'The Tampon....Kath Evans must have started her period during their night of passion. It was always dark and, in his urgency, to get away, he never got the chance to look in a mirror.'*

'Christ,' he thought, choking back a lump in his throat. 'My face...If there's blood on my hands.... There's got to be blood on...My face.'

"Ah fuck," he cursed, lowering his face in his hands, the reality and the madness, torturing his mind and feeding his panic.

"This is embarrassing," he sighed, finding himself in that uncomfortable situation of not knowing where to look, peeking through the narrow gaps between his fingers and gazing into the nightmare, a woman with a child shuffling nervously on her seat, avoiding any eye contact with the scary man with the red face.

"Thank fuck for that," he croaked, the sound of a bell signalling the bus was coming to a stop, getting him quickly on his feet.

"The bus stops fifty-yards past the hotel. I'm wet enough" he thought, ignoring safety protocol and leaping from the moving vehicle, his footfalls splashing in pools of water on the pavement and his legs almost buckling beneath him before coming to a halt.

'Fucking rain...Fucking public transport...Fucking periods...How on earth do women still live after bleeding every month without a fucking blood transfusion,' he sighed, leaning forward with both hands, clutching his knees and sucking in air through his nose, his head hanging in humble despair and his dignity in the gutter.

"Nearly there," he grunted, jogging along the footpath and brushing water from his face, the cold November rain thrashing with an unforgiving force against his back, blinking his eyes and searching inside his pocket for his key, quickening the pace in his step as he approached 'The Royal Belvedere Arms Hotel.'

"At last," he gasped, slipping the key into the lock, the heavy oak door creaking on rusty hinges and opening just enough to avoid the bell chimes hanging overhead.

"That's the easy part," he muttered silently, sucking in air and squeezing through the narrow gap in the door, cursing under his breath when a button sprung free from his jacket and fell to the floor.

"Can anything else happen to this fucking suit," he sighed, bending down on one knee and picking up the button from the floor.

The entrance foyer was deserted but the smell of bacon and eggs and the humming of an electric floor sweeper, informed him that the early morning staff weren't too far away.

"I'd better move fast. I don't want to bump into Beverley Jackson" he thought, holding his hands across his face and taking the stairs two at a time, making sure he avoided the treads at the top of the stairs that always creaked.

"Morning," greeted one of the cleaning staff, pushing a floor sweeper across the landing, her early morning greeting smothered under the bedroom door slamming in her face.

"What a fucking mess," he cursed, standing at the hand basin and staring in the mirror, a crimson tide of menstrual blood coating his teeth and decorating his face like a circus clown and his wrinkled mohair suit hanging from his body, like a wet rag.

"No wonder they were all staring at me," he sighed, squeezing toothpaste onto a brush and splashing hot water over his face, grabbing the scented soap and scrubbing his finger nails with a brush, the memories and the haunting images, disappearing down the plughole in a whirlpool of red water.

He hung his wet suit on a coat hanger, grabbed a towel and headed for the shower.

If Only (circa-1973-1975)

The forty-five-minute drive to the seaside village of Newton-by-the-Sea council offices each day wasn't something he looked forward to, but the increase in salary and the positive signs for promotion far outweighed the negatives, so the decision to accept the job was an easy one to make.

At the interview, he said that the position offered him a diverse challenge and an opportunity to gain new skills in a multi-disciplinary department, but in reality, it was all about the money.

"I think the weather forecaster was right when he said we might get snow before Christmas," he thought, lighting a cigarette and cursing under his breath for not getting the heater fixed in the car.

"It's cold," he sighed, pulling into the staff car-park and adjusting his tie in the rear-view mirror, a DJ announcing a new band called Slade and the gravelly voice of Noddy Holder singing, *'Merry Xmas Everybody,'* blasting from the radio, taking his mind off the weather and the broken heater.

"They're good," he thought, tapping his fingers across the steering wheel. *'So here it is merry Christmas,'* he sang, stepping from the car and crossing the road, wondering if that song would ever become a Christmas classic and making a mental note to find a garage in the village and get the thermostat replaced.

Newton-by-the-Sea Planning, Building Control and Engineering, the neon-sign above the door read, the modern statement out of character with the architecture of the double-fronted three-storey Victorian building.

"That's better," he smiled, warming his hands on a radiator, a tall pine tree decorated with baubles and coloured lights and streamers draped across ceilings and walls with glossy images of Santa Clause and Rudolph pinned to office doors, greeting him inside the entrance foyer.

"Hello. Can I help you?" asked an attractive girl in her late teens, with innocent blue eyes, who looked as if she had just fallen from the top of the Christmas tree.

"If you follow me, Mr Brand, I'll take you upstairs to see Mr. Thomas," she volunteered, a slight lisp in her voice only adding to her innocence and charm.

"My names Claire Simpson," she smiled, brushing a whisper of hair from her face and climbing the stairs, the fleeting images of firm breasts bouncing beneath a white blouse and a shapely bottom poured into a pair of tight denim jeans, keeping his interest during the short journey to the first-floor.

Hugh Thomas had the look and attitude of a man who was desperately counting the days to early retirement. He was a large fat man in his mid-fifties with heavy lidded eyes, huge bushy eye-brows and a forest of unsightly hairs growing from his nose and ears.

Hugh Thomas would never admit that he was an alcoholic or a heavy smoker, but the bottle of whiskey and several cartons of cigarettes that he always kept in his desk drawer, confirmed his unwillingness to accept the truth.

His deputy, Richard Lee was a much younger man in his mid-thirties. With jet-black hair and a chin stained with a permanent five-o'clock shadow, his body language spoke of a person waiting impatiently for Hugh Thomas to take early retirement and allow him to take over the ship.

"Welcome to the team, Mark," Hugh announced, offering his hand and pulling on a cigarette, a throaty cough and a wheezing gasp, letting him know that if he didn't quit smoking and lose a few pounds, his early retirement date might be closer than he thinks.

"Claire will show you around the offices and introduce you to the other members of staff," he smiled, his lecherous eyes crawling shamelessly over her breasts.

"I'll talk to you later, once you've settled in," Hugh said, refocussing his eyes and stubbing his cigarette into an overflowing ashtray on his desk.

After slipping in and out of offices and meeting members of staff on all three-floors for most of the morning, it was a welcoming relief when Claire said that there was only one more room on the ground-floor to show him.

"This is the File Store. It's not easy to access, because of the tree" she smiled, pointing a finger at a hand painted door, hidden behind the beacon of festivity, in a recess below the stairs.

"Do you like our Christmas tree?" she proudly smiled, squeezing her hand inside her tight denim jeans and searching inside a pocket for the key.
"It's very impress," he said, taking the key from her hand and opening the heavy door.
"It's dark in here. Watch your step," Claire said cautiously, flicking a switch next to the door and brushing away feathery cobwebs above her head.
"I don't like coming in here. It's creepy," she frowned, fluorescent lamps pinging and buzzing in unison before flooding the room with light. "The File Store holds every council application on Planning, Building Control and Engineering," Claire innocently confirmed. "There are only two keys for quality and security reasons," she added. "One is held by the Chief Administration Officer and the other by Richard Lee's personal assistant, Emma Charlton.

The cup of coffee had barely touched his lips when an attractive young woman entered the room and approached his desk.
"Hello. I'm Emma Charlton," she smiled, the offer of her hand in greeting and a fleeting glance of her breasts through a gap in her blouse, getting him quickly on his feet.
"Hello," he repeated, stealing another glance at her tits, hoping she was going to offer him a blow-job and a quick fuck over the desk, checking his silk tie for coffee stains before taking her outstretched hand.
"I just need to get some information to put on your personnel file, conditions of employment, holiday

entitlement welfare etc," she smiled, playing carelessly with a silver chain around her neck. "It won't take long. If you're too busy, I can come back later today."

"No, let's get it over with. I'm all yours," he smiled, pulling up a chair and staring into her sleepy eyes, listening to her soft comforting voice and the enchanting capture of nylon brushing over her thighs as she shifted her weight in the chair and crossed her legs.

"She's a little plump around her thighs and bottom and she appears to be self-conscious about her arse being a little on the big side," he thought, taking a quick tour over her curvy figure, cursing at his stupidity when he realised that her increased weight was due to the inevitable changes her body was making during the early stages of pregnancy.

"Just a couple of more questions and a signature and that's it," she smiled, cradling a pen in the corner of her mouth and sweeping her tongue over the phallic end with flirtatious suggestion, a familiar stirring inside his pants and erotic thoughts gathering inside his head.

"I wonder what kind of underwear she might be wearing. Was she shaved or neatly trimmed. What would she look like bent over his desk with her plump arse perched submissively in the air and his cock buried balls deep inside her body. Would she plead for calm or would she beg him to fuck her like a dog in the street," he thought, discreetly lowering his hand beneath the desk and

making a quick adjustment to the untimely growth inside his pants.

"Fire away," he said, returning her smile and nodding his head at some of the questions, some of his answers accompanied with a little light-hearted humour and playful innuendo, the familiarity and flirtatious suggestion, lifting the corners of her mouth and making her shuffle in her chair.

"This is a typical building file," she confirmed, dragging her chair across the floor, moving closer and handing him the file, the acquaintance of her hand and the authority in her voice interrupting his erotic thoughts.

"The index at the front gives you all the relevant sections," she smiled, the intoxicating smell of perfume and the warmth of her breath blowing in soft whispers against the side of his face, filling his head with corrupt thoughts and stimulating another movement inside his pants.

"That'll do for now. Sorry to disturb you on your first day. I'll let you get back to work," she smiled, brushing a whisper of hair from her face and lifting off the chair.

"If there's anything you need, just let me know," she said, a thin smile and an outstretched hand, getting him back on his feet.

"That was painless," he said, taking her hand and holding it just a moment longer than she would have expected, the flirtatious suggestion gaining her approval and fuelling the fire between her legs.

The festive season always brought out the best in everyone. Most people laughed and smiled a little more than they had done over the entire year. Everybody was in a better mood and pretended to be people they weren't.

It was a time for the giving and the receiving of gifts. It was also a time for social gatherings.

Too much alcohol and too much flirting during the Christmas party often left a regrettable stigma the following day, especially amongst those who lived a little too dangerously.

After a couple of hours in the local Fisherman's Arms, some of the staff went home and others filtered back to the office party.

'I Wish it Could Be Christmas Everyday,' people chanted, moving their feet and waving their arms above their heads, showing off their skills on the dance floor.

"You know it's getting close to Christmas when you hear Wizard on the radio," the DJ announced, turning up the volume and singing along with the band. *'When the kids start singing and the band begins to play.'*

"Claire Simpson looks like an angel," he thought, lighting a cigarette and sipping his drink, watching her skipping around the dance floor, swaying her hips and wriggling her cute little bottom with flirtatious suggestion, a young engineer with no natural rhythm following her around the dance floor, trying his best to charm his way into her pants.

"You can't blame the young boy for trying. I think we'd all like to get Claire Simpson between the sheets," he thought, brushing away a loose thread from his grey mohair suit, grateful to his local dry cleaners for bringing his suit back to life, the haunting images of the night at Kath Evans flat and the bus journey back to the hotel with his hands and face covered in blood, forever embedded in his mind.

"The buffets open," the DJ announced, the mere suggestion of food getting most people onto their feet and brushing away the haunting memories of Kath Evans from his mind.

"Don't panic. Form a queue. There's plenty for everybody," he added, a feeding frenzy of impatient people pushing and shoving, juggling with paper plates overflowing with food, gathering in circles or just sitting on chairs, all devouring their food like starving people.

"Emma Charlton looks nice. I wonder who she's talking to," he thought, catching sight of a young attractive girl and an older woman in her late-forties sipping wine and nibbling food from the buffet table, laughing and giggling and flirting with everyone in the room.

"I'm curious. I'll go and join them," he thought, picking up his drink and weaving his way across the dance floor, a friendly smile and a questioning eye looking for introductions.

"Hello Emma. I hope I'm not interrupting you, but you and your two sisters seem to be having such a good time, I thought I'd join you," he smiled, the mere mention of youth, lifting the corners of the older woman's mouth and bringing a smile to her face.

"I'm Jane Anderson," she announced, flashing her eyes and sipping her wine. "I'm the post woman," she added. "I've been delivering the post to the council offices for the last ten years," she said with pride, brushing hair from her face and lifting her glass in salute.

"This is my younger sister, Debbie," Emma said, the unexpected introduction and his outstretched hand, interrupting a song playing inside her head.

"I don't remember seeing you in the pub?" he enquired, letting go of her hand, a sip of wine giving her a moment to gather her thoughts.

"No," she smiled, showing perfect white teeth and brushing a whisper of hair that had fallen over her face. "I'm on my lunch break. I only get an hour," she sighed, nibbling a sandwich and glancing at her watch.

During the brief conversation, he discovered that Emma Charlton had been married for just over a year. Debbie was single and worked in a chemist shop, in the village. She lived with her mother in a flat above an auto-repair garage that her mother owned. Jane Anderson said she was happily married, but her wandering eyes and flirtatious behaviour, told a different story.

With alcohol fuelling confidence and flirtatious innuendo joining the conversation, he worked his charm, filling their heads with intelligent conversation and occasionally making them laugh, watching their body language and searching their eyes, gaining their trust with endless compliments and well-rehearsed words of endearment, stealing their hearts and trying his best to get into their pants.

"I have to get back to work," Debbie announced, her dark eyes and soft voice betraying a hint of sadness.

"I've enjoyed the party. I must remember to take a day's holiday next year," she said, searching inside a bag.

"This is my mother's business card," she smiled, flashing her eyes and handing him the card.

He looked vague.

"You said your car needs a new thermostat," she prompted, pointing a finger at the name on the card.

"That's my mother....June Chambers....She owns an auto-repair garage in the village. Give her a ring. Her numbers on the card," she smiled, waving her hand and heading out the door.

"I'll call your mother first thing in the morning," he smiled, tucking the business card safely inside his jacket pocket and taking Emma Charlton's empty glass from her hand, a confident smile lifting the corners of his mouth.

"Let's have another drink and you can tell me all about Newton-by-the-Sea."

"So, what does your husband do for a living?" he asked, handing her a glass of wine, the question nothing more than a pretence to keep the conversation going and to find if he's picking her up, after the party.

"He's a joiner," she replied, brushing hair from her face and fiddling with the buttons on her blouse. "He works for a small builder in North Shields. It's their Christmas party today. It's nothing fancy. A drink in every pub in the town until they can't stand up and a taxi home at midnight," she said, forcing a smile.

"At least I don't have to worry about a jealous husband," he thought, glancing at his watch, a blanket of darkness shrouding the windows and his timepiece letting him know that if he wanted to get inside her pants, he'd better move fast.

Those with inescapable parental commitments and those suffering from the humiliation of romantic rejection had already left the party. Others were still drinking or scavenging at the left-over lifeless crumbs of what used to be the buffet. Some people had fallen asleep and others had simply passed out in convenient chairs.

A teenage girl with the birth of a hickey blossoming on her neck straddled a young man on a stool, unaware that the cheeks of her bottom were creeping precariously above the waist of her pants. A couple wriggling on the dance floor made no attempt to follow the rhythm of the music and someone had pinned a photocopied image of a naked bottom on the stationery cupboard door… No doubt a subject for discussion in the New Year.

The door to Richard Lee's office had been locked from the inside and Hugh Thomas's secretary hadn't been seen for almost two hours, although the unmistakable sound of two people groaning out their pleasure in a mutual exchange of give and take was a clear sign that the deputy was getting an early Christmas present.

"Keep your eyes on the stairs and let me know if you hear anyone coming," Emma whispered, squeezing through a forest of pine needles and sliding the key into the lock.

"Fucking Christmas tree," she silently cursed, narrowing her eyes and twisting her face, hoping the cellar door wouldn't make a noise, cursing under her breath when the heavy door creaked on its hinges.

"The doors open. Come inside. Quickly," she prompted, guiding him into the eerie darkness and closing the door behind them, breathing a deep sigh of relief, knowing that the dead-lock would ensure they wouldn't be disturbed.

"Wed better not put the lights on, there's a high-level window in the corner of the room that can be seen from the side street," she whispered, the stairs creaking in quiet protest as they slowly descended into the dark abyss of the cellar, the ensuing silence thick with expectation of what was to come.

They both knew what they were there for. They both wanted the same thing. There would be no time for romance. No ceremony. No foreplay.

"What was that. I thought I heard a noise," she gasped, choking back a nervous lump in her throat and sucking in air through her nose, the haunting sound of the old heating system hissing and blowing and the pulsing beat of the music filtering through the floors above, momentarily interrupting their lustful pursuit.

"This is dangerous," she whispered, blinking her eyes in the darkness and glancing at the window in the corner of the room, hormonal chaos fuelling the fire of passion between her legs and a familiar wetness gathering inside her knickers, brushing away the need for caution.

"But It's also exciting," she breathed, faces colliding and mouths crashing together, heart beats racing and pulses throbbing, blood flooding vital organs and stimulating genitalia, impatient hands searching in the darkness, impulsive urges and involuntary gestures responding to the persuasion of touch, fondling and groping, probing and scratching, two people driven by lust and expectation, two lovers embarking on a journey of betrayal and infidelity.

"Let's get these out," he grunted, slipping his hands inside her blouse and unclipping her bra, the acquaintance of two milky white breasts tumbling out into his cool hands, stirring the fleshy muscle inside his pants.

"They're hot," he smiled, kneading the soft flesh between his fingers and thumbs, feeling the warmth and the weight filling his hands, feeling the nipples growing to a lengthy firmness and pressing like studs against the palms of his hands, squeezing and pulling, biting and sucking, the painful pleasure breathed in a chorus of moans and groans and breathless whispers of approval.

"I'm hot all over," she breathed, the persuasion of movement and the intimacy of touch heightening expectation and wetting her thighs, a growing lump inside his pants pressing against her leg and moving in a simulation of coital engagement, gaining her approval and lifting the corners of her mouth in a tenacious proposal.

"I want to feel that in my hand," she said, primal response flirting with curiosity, blinking her eyes and shuffling her feet on the floor, lowering her hands and pulling his pants over his thighs and down his legs, the acquaintance of nine-and-a-half-inches throbbing in her hand momentarily interrupting her lustful enquiry.

"Wow," she gasped, wrapping her fingers around the thick girth, a familiar wetness pooling between her legs and the urgent desire for penetration bringing her quickly back to reality.

"It's huge," she whispered, gripping the swollen muscle firmly in her hand, the persuasion of touch and the promise of intimate engagement inviting capture, working him hard and working him fast, tugging and pulling, up and down, back and forth, gripping the length and squeezing the girth, rejoicing in the pulse between her fingers.

"That feels good," she groaned, feeling his hand stroking her inner thighs and an eager finger slipping inside her knickers, searching through a thick bush of pubic hair and parting the moist flaps and folds, working his fingers in lazy circles over the swollen hood, stimulating the clitoris and teasing the urethra, two lovers drowning in a sea of hormonal chaos, two people desperate for one thing.

"I'm getting wet. I can't wait any longer," she sighed, turning quickly on her heels, modesty melting away in the heat of passion, shuffling and wiggling her hips, sliding her knickers down her legs and letting them drop to the floor.

"I want you to fuck me," she pleaded, stepping over the flimsy piece of fabric, pulling her skirt up to her waist and opening her legs, leaning forward and gripping the metal frames with both hands.

"I'll put it in," she said, with uncompromising determination, brushing hair from her face and looking back over her shoulder, reaching back with her hand and guiding him in.

"Oh. Ah. That's big," she gasped, shuffling her feet on the floor and easing the swollen limb inside her body, nine-and-a-half-inches of hard flesh reaching the limits and stretching the boundaries of her inner core, the deep penetration stinging her eyes and twisting her face in a euphoric mask of pleasure.

"Oh Yes. That's good," she moaned, moving her hips in a mutual exchange of give and take, hard thighs banging against soft buttocks, skin smacking against skin, genitalia embracing genitalia, joining and separating, in and out, back and forth, hard and fast, entering and retreating, thrusting and grinding, breaching and violating, using and abusing, fucking hard and fucking fast, a tireless exhibition of two people fucking like a couple of dogs in the street.

"Fuck me. Fuck me," she pleaded, painful cries of encouragement and a commentary of filthy curses turning into pledges and promises, and words of endearment, moans and groans and euphoric mutterings, smothered under a fanfare of squeaking metal frames and paper files dropping to the concrete floor.

"I'm coming. Fuck me Faster. Harder," she begged, looking back over her shoulder and brushing wet hair from her face, compelling urges and impulsive movements stimulating genitalia and taking her closer to the euphoric edge.

"Ah. Ah. Oh. Oh, Fuck. I'm....I'm coming," she gasped, shuddering and shaking and gripping the metal frames with both hands, moans and groans growing into a crescendo of euphoric release, a knee-trembling orgasm sucking the last breath of air from her body.

"Wow. That was certainly worth the risk," she gasped, sucking in air through her nose and letting go of the metal frames, reaching back with her hand and pulling him free from her burning interior.

"You need to come," she breathed, lowering to the floor on her knees and wrapping her fingers around the meaty column, working the length with vigorous determination, up and down, pulling and tugging, stretching the loose foreskin over the bulbous head, moans and groans and euphoric mutterings signalling his approaching climax.

"I'm nearly there," he announced. "Be careful. We don't want any signs of mischief on our clothes," he said, the gesture for caution bringing a smile to her face and a shameless reply.

"It won't. My mouth will take care of that," she casually answered, sweeping her tongue in playful circles around the ridge of the helmet and feasting on the sticky substance oozing from the small eye, easing him in and easing him out, sucking and blowing and swallowing deep, the announcement of his approaching climax, lifting the corners of her mouth in a gesture of persuasive approval.

"Let it come," she urged, closing her mouth over the smooth head, easing him in and easing him out, tugging and pulling and cradling his balls in her hand, emotional fluids shooting from the open eye and splashing inside her mouth, the unforgiving mess gathering at the back of her throat and threatening to stop her breathing.

"I can't breathe," she gasped, sucking in air through her nose and easing the swollen limb from her mouth, a gulp and a swallow confirming her promise to protect their clothing.

"I need to look presentable before we go back to the party," she sighed, shuffling inside her hand bag and pulling out a compact mirror.

"Thanks. It's better than nothing," she smiled, the offer of his cigarette lighter giving her just enough light to make some creative repairs to her hair and lipstick.

Claire Simpson viewed the world through smiling eyes. And like most teenage girls her values in life depended on only four things. Shopping. Clubbing. Music and Boys.

So, when she accepted his invitation to dinner, at the Italian restaurant, in the town centre, he was a little surprised when she consented with a few conditions.

"My parents have gone to Edinburgh for a few days to visit my grandmother, so before I do anything, I must go home to feed my dog," she declared, rather matter-of-fact, tilting her head to one side, pursing her bottom lip and mimicking puppy-dog-eyes.

"After I've showered and changed we can have a quick game of pool at the local Leisure Centre," she said, an innocent smile showing perfect white teeth.

"Can you play pool, Mark?" she asked, hiding the presumptuous request behind a smile.

"Can I play pool?" he answered, the mere mention of her parents going to Edinburgh for a few days, lifting the corners of his mouth and prompting a quick response.

"It's only my favourite game," he lied, pulling the car to a halt, outside her parent's house.

"His names Roxy. He's our blind dog," she announced, closing the front door behind them and smiling lovingly into his dark brown eyes.

"I'm sorry. I wasn't aware that one of your parents was blind," he sighed, bending on one knee and stroking the dogs head. "Will your parents not need his help when they're in Edinburgh?" he asked, the question lifting the corners of her mouth in an innocent smile.

"No," she giggled, pulling a funny face and rolling her eyes. "Roxy can't see…. Roxy's blind."

"You shower and get changed," he offered, forcing a smile and frowning at his stupidity. "While you're doing that, I'll feed Roxy and then we can go," he added, the acquaintance of a wet tongue licking his face, getting him back on his feet.

Apart from a couple of spotty faced teenagers wearing t-shirts that looked like they hadn't seen a hot iron for quite some time, the Leisure Centre was relatively quiet.

"If you set up a pool table, I'll go and get some drinks," he smiled, pointing a finger at the end of the room, making sure he selected a table at a safe distance from the wrinkled t-shirts.

"I can see you've done this before," he smiled, handing her a glass of wine and watching her gathering the balls from the table and placing them in a triangle.

"You look like a seasoned professional," he laughed, taking a pool cue from a rack on the wall and catching a glimpse of her shapely bottom, the tight fabric hugging every contour and curve and leaving nothing to the imagination.

"Ladies first," she announced, in a girlish giggle, placing the white ball on its spot, shuffling her feet and bending over the table, her choice of underwear and a panty line blossoming beneath the tight fabric, keeping his interest for a while.

Were they White…? Were they Red…? Or were they Black…? he thought, lowering his hand and discreetly moving the stirring limb inside his pants.
"I surrender. You win," he declared, forcing a smile and glancing at his watch.
"Let's go and get something to eat," he said, returning the pool cues to the rack.
"Ok," she smiled, triumphantly, brushing hair from her face and unashamedly pulling a wedgie from her bottom.
"It's getting cold. I should have brought a warm coat" she sighed, rubbing her hands together and shuffling uncomfortably on the vinyl seat.
"It'll soon warm up," he smiled, turning the key in the ignition, knowing that the new thermostat that June Chambers recently fitted, would soon be warming the interior of the car.
"Have you been to this restaurant before," he asked, ignoring the double yellow lines at the side of the road and pulling the car to a halt outside the Italian restaurant.
"No," she answered, stepping from the car, a modest smile lifting the corners of her mouth. "This is my first time in a restaurant," she added, taking his hand and fumbling nervously with a silver chain around her neck.
A smartly dressed waiter with dyed black hair, a courteous smile and a spurious Italian accent brought the wine list and menu to the table.
"I'm a little nervous. You'll have to help me," she whispered across the table, opening a menu and

staring at a list of culinary delights that she didn't understand.

"Let me go through the menu with you," he offered, the sincerity in his voice and his attention to deal with trivial issues of etiquette, removing the anxiety and lifting the mood.

"It's so romantic," she smiled, flashing her eyes and humming to the classical music filtering through overhead speakers, the arrival of the waiter delivering a bottle of wine to the table and the sound of a popping cork, interrupting the romantic interlude.

"I've never had Champagne before," she said, flashing her eyes and taking a long-stemmed glass from his hand.

"Beautiful women should always drink Champagne," he smiled, raising his glass in salute.

"To a beautiful young woman," he toasted, smiling into her innocent eyes and flirting at any opportunity, the endless compliments and words of endearment, a cunning pretence to gaining her trust, stealing her heart and finding out the colour of her knickers.

"You say nice things," she smiled, lifting the glass to her mouth, the romantic atmosphere of the restaurant and too much alcohol fuelling a surge of Dutch courage, adolescent pride and the subject of virtue lifting the corners of her mouth in a conspiratorial whisper.

She told him she was a virgin. She told him something he already knew.

"Have you missed me, Roxy?" she smiled, stepping into her house and closing the front door, dropping on her knees and hugging the dog with playful affection.

"I think the panting tongue and the wagging tail answers your question," he said, bending on one knee and making a fuss over the dog, the friendly greeting and comforting words nothing more than a surreptitious charade to gain precious brownie points.

"I'll put some music on," she said, opening the lid of the record player and carefully placing a selection of black vinyl discs on the chrome support, the static and crackle giving way to the soothing voice of Art Garfunkel singing *'Bridge Over Troubled Water.'*

"Come and get warm in front of the fire," she said, humming along to the music and warming her hands on the fire, a brief exchange of light-hearted small-talk, fading in breathless whispers and apprehensive sighs, two people swimming in a sea of hormonal chaos, two lovers embarking on a journey of sexual discovery.

"I've had a wonderful night," she smiled, flashing her eyes and brushing hair from her face. "Would you like a cup of coffee?" she asked, moving away from the fire, a persuasive hand and responsive reply, interrupting the skip in her step.

"No thanks. But I will have a kiss," he smiled, pulling her into his arms and peppering her neck with soft welcoming kisses of light affection, the fragrance of perfume and the aroma of youth teasing his senses and wakening the sleeping monster inside his pants.

"You've got juicy lips," she smiled, wrapping her arms around his neck, mouths crashing together and tongues flirting in a gesture of romantic unity, probing and sweeping over teeth, twisting and twirling in a sensuous ballet of give and take, the flirtatious enquiry heightening expectation and fuelling the fire between her legs, a heart melting kiss stealing her heart and stealing his way into her pants.

"No," she sighed, moving his hand from her breast, and sitting on the sofa, a wash of uncertainty flooding her eyes and an innocent smile betraying her inexperience.

In his pursuit of human sexual response experience had told him that 'No' can actually mean, NO! Definitely not, and don't try that again. But he was also aware that 'No' can sometimes mean 'No,' but give me a little more time because I'm thinking about it. Nevertheless, he knew that if he wanted to get between her legs, he would have to be extremely patient.

"I'm sorry. I know I'm moving too fast, but you're a beautiful woman," he smiled, sitting on the sofa and holding her hand, gaining her trust and making her feel special, the soothing voices of Simon and Garfunkel easing the tension and lifting the mood.

"It's not your fault. I want to. I'm just nervous," she smiled, shuffling along the sofa, the embrace spontaneous, the kiss soft, gentle and passionate, the warmth of his mouth and the flirtatious pursuit of his lips, embarking on a sensuous trail over her nose, ears and forehead, teasing her senses and corrupting her mind.

"You make me tingle all over," she whispered, a young woman swimming in an ocean of mixed emotions, her breathing ragged and unsteady and her eyes vague and confused, indecision and uncertainty flirting with curiosity and excitement, impulsive urges responding to the intimacy of touch, a heart beating like a drum inside her chest and the static of arousal dancing between her legs.

"Just relax. I'll be gentle. You can stop me at any time," he smiled, trying to gain her trust and lift her confidence.

"I promise," he added, unbuttoning her blouse and unclipping her bra, his feather-light fingers embarking on a mysterious journey over virtuous skin, cupping her breasts and squeezing them gently in his hands, sweeping his tongue in sensuous circles over her small nipples and holding them in playful capture between his teeth.

"I'm okay. You have a sensuous touch. It makes me feel good," she breathed, a submissive whisper of approval responding to the intimacy of touch, a familiar wetness gathering inside her panties and the place between her legs getting hotter and hotter, euphoric pulses teasing her senses and tingling her toes, her modesty melting away in the heat of passion.

"The sofas uncomfortable. The floor looks better," he smiled, the springs squeaking under their weight as

they slid off the leather sofa and joined Roxy on the floor.
"There's nothing wrong with the sofa. I'm onto you," she smiled, a beating heart welcoming the embrace with renewed enthusiasm, impulsive urges responding to the persuasion of touch, softness pushing against hardness in a mutual gesture of give and take, impatient hands sweeping over curves in a courtship of touch and feel, the heat of passion wetting her knickers and teasing her thighs, pulses racing and heart beats gathering speed, moans and groans chasing breathless whispers in a mutual chorus of vocal persuasion.
"I'm not nervous anymore. I won't stop you," she whispered, the innocence of youth yielding to temptation, a young virgin surrendering to the phenomenon of human sexual response, shuffling on the floor and opening her legs, offering her body in submissive capture, proclaiming her enthusiasm and her willingness to engage in sexual intercourse.
"Let's take these off," he whispered, reaching inside the waist of her jeans and pulling them down her legs. *"I knew they'd be red,"* he thought, smiling into her eyes and slipping his fingers inside her red panties, any thoughts of modesty or indecision melting away over her milky white thighs.
"Are you okay?" he smiled, the captivating vision of porcelain beauty and the images of purity and perfection silhouetted in the glow of the fire, keeping his interest long enough to make a quick adjustment inside his pants.

"I'm fine. But you look a little uncomfortable," she smiled, twisting the chain around her neck and catching a glimpse of the growing lump inside his pants.

"I can't control that. It's got a mind of its own," he laughed, blinking his eyes into focus and taking a quick tour over her firm young body. "You're absolutely gorgeous," he whispered, gazing at her small white breasts and watching her nipples blossoming from dark areolas, noting her toned stomach and cute little belly button and the neat butterfly folds peeking out through a whisper of silky pubic hair.

"Just relax. I promise to be gentle," he smiled, the warmth of his mouth and talented tongue, embarking on a virtuous journey, sweeping in playful circles over her stomach and bathing her naval, stimulating her senses and wetting her thighs.

"Wow. That feels so good," she whispered, responding to the soul warming sexual union, moving her hips in a simulation of coital foreplay, breathless whispers of approval spilling between tight lips, a young woman swimming in a sea of hormonal chaos, lost in the heat of passion and longing for physical contact, impulsive urges driven by desire and need, lifting her bottom off the floor in a gesture of persuasive movement, pulling his head down between her legs and smothering his face in her private place of intimacy.

"You smell nice," he whispered, a jubilant smile tugging at the corners of his mouth, rejoicing in the power of surrender, victorious in the thrill of sexual conquest, basking in her beauty and innocence and breathing in the aroma of sex, the odours of virtue and the essence of youth teasing his nostrils and stirring the muscle inside his pants.

"I could eat you," he smiled, sweeping his hands over undiscovered curves, caressing precious yielding textures and touching unchartered virgin flesh, his eager fingers dancing in melodic pulses over her inner thighs, parting the flaps and folds and teasing the clitoris from the sanctuary of the swollen hood.

"Oh, yes," she gasped. "Eat me," she pleaded, the warmth of his mouth and eager tongue dancing and swirling between her inner thighs and edging closer and closer to the sexual arena, heightening expectation and fuelling the fire between her legs.

"Does that feel good," he whispered, pressing his chin against the pubic bone and blowing a whisper of warm air over the virgin folds, sweeping his tongue over the urethra and bathing her clitoris in a wash of oral fluids, the petals of virtue opening like a flower in bloom, a persuasive gesture and a whispered invitation, welcoming his finger inside.

"That certainly confirms her purity," he thought, the sacred barrier of virtue interrupting the eager pursuit of his finger and forcing him into a quick retreat.

"Don't say I didn't warn you," she said, forcing a smile and shuffling nervously on the floor, a heart beating frantically inside her chest and a choking lump inside her throat threatening to stop her breathing, the true reality of knowing it was about to happen, stinging her eyes and flooding her head with uncertainty, any thoughts of ending the initiation, swept away in an urgent gesture of movement and his pants dropping to the floor.

"Oh," she gasped, a young woman seduced by an invitation of intimate enquiry, blinking her eyes into focus and staring in disbelief at the gruesome muscle bobbing and swaying in front of her face.

"What do you want me to do?" she asked, her innocent eyes tracing his with consenting apprehension and a reserved compliance of impending uncertainty, watching and waiting, as if seeking his permission to respond to intimate foreplay.

"There's no rules or conditions. Just follow your instincts," he smiled, brushing his fingers through her hair, lifting her chin and kissing her gently on the lips, the acquaintance of her hand brushing over his genitals, confirming her intent to respond to instinctive urges.

"It feels big," she breathed, frustration and hesitation flirting with curiosity, flashing her eyes and wrapping her fingers around the thick girth, moving her hand to the persuasion of touch, pulling and tugging, squeezing and releasing, exploring and touching, stoking and learning, the pulse between her fingers and the ache between her legs lifting the corners of her mouth in a welcoming smile and an invitation they'd both been waiting for.

"Make love to me," she whispered, opening her legs and brushing away the principles of virtue, a welcoming smile and a gesture of persuasive movement, letting him know that she wanted him inside her body.

"Oh. Ah," she gasped, a breathless sigh and a begging-him-to-be-gentle whisper hissing between tight lips, nine-and-a-half-inches of hard muscle stretching the delicate flaps and folds and easing inside her body, the acquaintance of a thin membrane brushing against the bulbous head, momentarily interrupting their moment of pleasure.

"Are you okay?" he asked, the engagement of intimate connection, held momentarily in captured silence and a subtle exchange of reassuring words and persuasive gestures.

"It won't hurt," he said, pushing in slowly until the hymen yielded to the force, smiling into her eyes and easing the swollen limb from her body, waiting for her lost membrane to dissipate and letting her get used to the unfamiliar object breaching her body, the fluids of her former purity, spilling down his cock and decorating his thighs.

"I'm ready," she confidently announced, blowing a whisper of hair from her face, the sound of another record dropping onto the turntable and Freddie Mercury's fingers dancing over black and white keys, interrupting the brief moment of virtuous silence and waking Roxy from his sleep.

"It's okay. I'm still here," she whispered, smiling lovingly into his lifeless eyes. "Go back to sleep," she said, stroking his ears and easing his head back to the floor.

'Open your eyes, look up to the skies and see....'

"Hold me. Kiss me," she pleaded, an untried body welcoming the strange object inside her most sacred place, the lubricating warmth of coital connection and a courtship of genitalia moving in a mutual exchange of give and take, heightening expectation and easing the pain.

"It doesn't hurt anymore. It feels good," she smiled, rejoicing in the euphoric sensation, the influence of persuasion and the promise of coital expectation, responding to the intimacy of union, easing in and easing out, a couple of inches at a time, breaking and entering, in and out, soft and slow, easing out and prolonging the moment, taking her to heights she could only have imagined, and then bringing her slowly back from the edge.

Sent shivers down my spine, body's aching all the time....

"You're too precious. I would never hurt you," he said, lifting her legs and wrapping them around his back, flexing his buttocks and thrusting his hips in a turbulent rhythm of give and take, hardness slapping against softness, in and out, back and forth, deeper and deeper, all the way in and all the way out, banging and thrusting, penetrating deep, stretching and filling her body with hard flesh, her pleading cries for calm lost in the echoes of Freddie's invitation.

Scaramouche, Scaramouche, will you do the fandango?
Thunderbolts and lightening, very, very frightening....

"I'm overheating. Give me a moment to catch my breath," she sighed, sucking in air through her nose, an innocent face glowing in the heat of passion and a cocktail of emotions swimming inside her head in a blend of dance and song, a heart fluttering in time with the melodic beat and her virtue lingering on the precipice of an exotic place somewhere in heaven.

"Be gentle," she whispered, every nerve in her body alive with euphoric sensation, waves of abdominal contractions combusting in the emerging heat of passion between her legs, a young woman responding to the euphoria of impending release, genitalia embracing genitalia in an orchestration of mutual engagement, impulsive urges and suggestive movements gaining momentum in a persuasive invitation of give and take, arching her back and thrusting her hips, bucking and pushing, rolling with the rhythm and rocking with the momentum, holding his flesh in tender capture inside her body.

Easy come, easy go, will you let me go?
Bismilla! No, we will not let you go....

"I'm reaching climax. Come with me," he grunted, a subtle key change from major to minor, the tempo gathering speed in a concerto of sweeping arpeggios, a rock aria of sharps and flats, an opera of perfect harmony, the melodious interaction adding unity to the intimacy and the seduction of vocal persuasion orchestrating the rhythm of copulation, a union of genitalia and pubic bones, pushing together in a seductive rhythm of give and take, easing in and easing out, giving and taking and entering and retreating, a chorus of moans and groans and persuasive gestures, signalling he was only seconds away from impact.

"Ah, Fuck," he cursed, the explosion of liquid passion erupting like an active volcano, a warm sea of seminal solution spilling from the open eye, flooding the vaginal vault in a tidal wave of liquid passion and coating the mouth of the cervix.

"Can you feel me inside you. Can you feel the heat? Come for me," he urged, the engine still running and his reserves empty, the strings of passion inevitably subsiding, the chords fading and the opus easing into a calming coda, a compelling finale of seduction lost in a chorus of euphoric cries and an announcement of imminent release.

'Let him go.' Bishmillah! We will not let you go....
Never, never, never let me go. Ah....
No, no, no, no, no, no, no....

"Yes, yes, yes, yes....Oh. Oh. Ah…Fuck…Ahhh," she screamed, choking back a lump in her throat and sucking in air through tight lips, her dignity lost in the heat of passion and a euphoric sensation manifesting between her legs.

"I'm coming," she gasped. "Ah. Oh...Ahhhh," she hissed, brushing hair from her face and twisting her face in a contorted mask of pleasure, arching her back off the floor and tightening her legs, thrusting her hips and pushing back, impulsive urges and persuasive gestures responding to the intimacy of coital union, moans and groans rejoicing in the symphony of touch and the sonata of euphoria stinging her eyes, curling her toes and shaking her legs, a momentous orgasm smothered under a chorus of harmonic melodies and a perpetual overture of resonating percussions.

'Nothing really matters....'
'Any way the wind blows.'

It felt more like a hanging than a disciplinary hearing, especially when he was told Councillor Martin Keane was a cold-hearted individual who thought the term 'Going Clubbing' meant taking a boat out to the 'Farne Islands' and bashing grey seals over the head with a baseball bat.
Nevertheless, he thought it prudent to bring his CV up to date before the hearing.
'Fucking weather,' he sighed, lighting a cigarette and looking out onto the grey suburban street below, watching a woman pushing a child in a buggy and fighting with an umbrella against the wind, cursing

into the heavens when a wheel collided with a road cobble and fell off.

'Poor sod. If the circumstances had been different, I would have gone to her rescue. But I've got enough to worry about today,' he thought, pacing the floor and looking at his watch for the millionth time, his job and his future, hanging by a thread.

'Fucking June Chambers. Fucking Martin Keane,' he sighed, pulling on his cigarette and choking back a lump in his throat, searching inside the dark room of his subconscious and flicking through the memory files of deceit and betrayal, the consequences of his actions and the outcome of the hearing, today, hanging in the air with haunting uncertainty.

'He didn't know how much Martin Keane knew. But if it was just about getting caught fucking June Chamber's in the show-house, he might just get away with it,' he thought, sipping his coffee and skipping through a list of potential candidates, who might be on his agenda.

'He certainly wouldn't know about the night of the Christmas party when he fucked Emma Charlton in the cellar and neither would he know about their impulsive meetings in the file store during the day and the hurried sex that followed,' he thought, the convincing appraisal lifting the corners of his mouth and increasing his confidence.

The sex with Debbie Chambers, in the back of his car was certainly risky, especially when her sister, Emma went on maternity leave. In the winter months, their meetings were always infrequent and rather casual, but when the warm summer nights arrived they became a little more daring.

They fucked on the grass. They fucked over the bonnet of the car. They had screaming knee-trembling sex up against a tree. And even when Debbie told him she was getting engaged, their time together slowly diminished but never really ended.

Claire Simpson continued her love for clubbing and shopping, but after losing her virginity she had now added sex and orgasms to her list of teenage interests.

'I think I'm in trouble if Hugh Thomas ever finds out about Lucy Hamilton,' he sighed, draining the last of the coffee in the cup and lighting another cigarette.

In the final stages of a year-out after finishing school and about to take a degree in Architecture and Town Planning at Newcastle University, out of friendship and loyalty to her father, Hugh Thomas offered her a job in the office for a period of six weeks.

Lucy Hamilton was too old to be a girl and too young to be a woman, but she had a fresh-faced cheeky innocence that he instantly found appealing. However, after spending a couple of nights at his flat he quickly discovered that she was nothing more than a complicated and self-centred, nose-in-the-air individual with plenty of attitude. Nevertheless, when Lucy Hamilton started to fuck, it was almost impossible to get her to stop. And with a chain of metal braces filling her mouth, the cock-sucking little vixen's ability to give fellatio, was always a mind-blowing experience.

"I'm only human. It's just sex. We all need it," he sighed, brushing his hand over the misty window and removing a layer of condensation from the glass. "Some need more than others," he smiled, catching sight of Jane Anderson heading up the footpath in the pouring rain, their intimate rendezvous later today, inevitably broken by circumstances beyond his control.

'They might be wrong about Martin Keane. He might be a sexual compulsive. Who knows he might have dipped his toe in the water a few times himself,' he thought, dropping his cigarette into an ashtray and glancing at his watch.

"Not long now. I'll soon find out," he sighed, sitting down and standing up, wishing the time away, wishing he had been more responsible, wishing he was somewhere else.

If only he hadn't taken his car to June Chambers auto-repair garage to get a new thermostat.

If only she hadn't encouraged his flirtatious advances. If only that chemistry thing hadn't sparked between them. If only he didn't have an attraction for older women, especially those who looked sexy in dirty overalls. If only he hadn't taken her to the show-house.

It seemed a good idea at the time. It offered a combination of excitement, exhilaration and danger, and there was always that thrill of doing it in a semi-public place.

In his remit as project manager he had access to all the houses on the riverside residential site. So, what better opportunity would they have? The two of them locked inside the show-house, fucking on the living room floor, like two dogs on heat.

"Christ, it must have been embarrassing for Martin Keane during his tour of the new houses on the riverside estate development, although the delegation of residents viewing the new show-house, seemed rather amused," he thought.

If only....If only, he sighed, the mantra kept repeating inside his head, the haunting reality of familiar faces gathering outside the meeting room door, feeding his panic and getting him on his feet.

"I'm Councillor Martin Keane. I'm chairing this meeting today," he announced, waiting patiently for people to settle into chairs and take a cup of coffee from a tray.

"The meeting, today, is a serious matter of unprofessional conduct by a member of staff," he added, sipping his coffee and opening a file.

"Mark Brand, is represented by Hugh Thomas and Richard Lee, from Planning, Building Control and Engineering," he declared, forcing a smile and pointing a finger at the accused.

"Johnathon Younger is here to represent the trade union and Paula Harman is here from administration and personnel," he confirmed, sipping his coffee and writing notes on a pad.

"Paula Harman," he gasped, choking back a lump in his throat and loosening his tie.

"I'd forgotten about her," he sighed, the crimson colour on her face, confirming that she hadn't forgotten

about their reckless night of sex during the local elections, almost a year ago.

"She looks nervous. She must have crossed and uncrossed her legs a dozen times. She's very attractive," he thought, watching her playing with the buttons on her blouse and shuffling uncomfortably in her chair, her smile flirtatious and her shapely breasts a work of art.

"The night of the local elections. What an unforgettable night that was," he smiled, thoughts and images of Councillor Martin Keane retaining his seat in the council elections for the third year running and the heat of passion that followed inside the pre-fabricated building, still fresh in his mind.

'Even before the ballet box had swallowed up the first vote he was flirting with chance and looking for any opportunity to get into her pants.

"I'm a happily married woman. You can look but you can't touch," she told him, raising her left hand and flaunting her wedding ring.

Her gesture of fidelity and loyalty to her husband didn't last long. He recalled, a brief exchange of flirtatious compliments laden with sexual innuendo, removing the pretence of innocence and fuelling the fire of passion between her legs.

It was almost ten o'clock when Paula closed the Polling Station and allowed the other staff to drift away.

He wanted to take things slow. He wanted to steal her heart in a progressive courtship of flirtatious pursuit and heightening expectation, before getting between her legs.

But Paula had no intentions of going through the preliminaries of foreplay and there would be no time for pretence or refinement. Paula just wanted a good fucking.

"We don't want observers," she smiled, turning the key in the lock and flicking the light switch on the wall, any thoughts of fidelity or loyalty to her husband fading in the darkness and the ensuing silence hanging between them.

"It's not the most romantic place, but it'll have to do," she sighed, "It's certainly my first time in a Polling Station," she confessed, grabbing his hand and leading him into a small kitchen at the rear of the pre-fabricated building.

"Let's get these off," she breathed, flashing her eyes and fumbling in the darkness with the belt buckle and zip, urgency and expectation flirting with frustrated sighs, before dropping his pants to the floor.

"Wow. What a huge cock," she gasped, sucking in air through her nose and blinking her eyes in the darkness, the acquaintance of nine-and-a-half-inches filling her hand, wetting her thighs and lifting the corners of her mouth in a gesture of persuasive intent.

"I'd better get naked. We don't want to waste that," she smiled, shuffling and wiggling her hips and letting her knickers drop to the floor. "Fuck me from the back," she whispered, stepping over her knickers and pulling her skirt up to her waist, leaning over the kitchen sink and opening her legs.

Paula had a husband to go home to. Her invitation came with two conditions.

She wanted fucked and it had to be quick.

"Oh, yes," she gasped, the length and girth easing inside her body in a carnal connection of intimate engagement

and a mutual commitment of give and take, thrusting and pushing, grinding and banging, hard merciless strokes pounding her body into submission, in and out, hard and fast, moving back and forth like a well-oiled machine and a perpetual piston of endless endurance, entering and retreating without remorse, pushing in and pulling out, stretching her tight entrance and filling her body with hard flesh.

"Fuck, that's good. You're a fucking machine," she hissed, through a commentary of curses and obscenities, wriggling her hips and pushing back to meet the force, moans and groans and breathless pants responding to the heat of passion gathering between her legs.

"Ah, fuck. Ah fuck," she cried, leaning forward and trying to find purchase on the worktop, careless hands sweeping plates and cups across the surface, euphoric mutterings smothered under the echoes of filth and broken crockery crashing to the floor.

"I'm coming. I'm coming, she announced, thrashing her head from side to side and moving her hips to the promise of euphoric release, a knee-trembling orgasm lasting long enough to capture a generous amount of his seminal cargo inside her body.

"Let's get this over with. We've all got better things to do," Martin Keane said, tapping a spoon against his coffee cup and bringing the meeting to order, the authority in his voice interrupting his thoughts and clearing the erotic images from his mind.

Martin Keane was at the Farne Islands. He had his baseball bat. He wasn't taking any prisoners.

"The date. The venue. The accused. The names of the residents, otherwise known as the witnesses, are all detailed in my statement," he said, removing a pair of spectacles from his jacket pocket and opening a file.

"My recommendations on this man's future are very clear," he said, clearing his throat and staring across the table, the embarrassing events inside the show house unfolding in an outburst of threatening accusation, dripping like acid off his tongue, the carotid arteries and jugular veins pulsing in his neck, betraying the seriousness of the situation.

"When I walked into the show-house with a group of people from the resident's association, I didn't expect to see two people fucking like rabbits on the living-room floor," he barked.

"And during the day….I can still see the look of surprise on their faces. What a fucking mess," he sighed, rolling his eyes and throwing his pen across the table in disgust.

"You've gone too far young man," he shouted, pointing a finger and punching the table with a closed fist. "It's all over the fucking village," he yelled, lifting from his chair and pacing back and forth across the floor.

"I've had a lot to explain to members of the council and certainly too many apologies to make," he sighed, pausing to clear his throat and regain his composure.

"The Herald and Post have asked the Chief Executive for comments because they intend to run the story in their newspaper," he sighed, sitting back in his chair and sipping his coffee.

"The Chief Executive. The newspapers. I'm in serious trouble," he thought, choking back a lump in his throat and lifting his shoulders in defeat, the reality and the magnitude of the situation hanging in the air with crippling uncertainty and inevitable consequences.

"Jonathon Younger. What a waste of time and union subscriptions. He rarely spoke in his defence," he thought, watching his head nodding up and down like one of those toy dogs in the back of a car window, agreeing with everything the councillor said, the pen and note pad in his hand nothing more than a pretence of alliance to his valued member.

Paula Harman ignored any eye contact as she gathered her notes from the table and Hugh Thomas reached inside a drawer and opened a packet of cigarettes, unaware that he already had one burning in the ashtray. Richard Lee, fiddled with his tie, while the union man scribbled a smiley face on a note pad.

"I need a fucking miracle," he sighed, his future hanging by a thread and his eager eyes scanning the room for sympathetic support, the shameful lowering of heads and surreptitious gestures of contempt, a painful reminder that he was nothing more than an abandoned stranger.

"The meetings over. Thanks for your time" Martin Kean announced, sipping the last of his coffee and lifting to his feet.

"The minutes of the meeting will be circulated in a couple of days," he added, grabbing his file and a handful of papers from the table before disappearing through a door, the energy, the anxiety, the arrogance, the union man and Paula Harman, following in his wake.
"He has a fiery reputation, but I've never seen Martin Keane so outraged," Hugh said, picking up the phone and asking his secretary to bring in three cups of coffee, the sound of the phone dropping into the cradle and a choking emphysema wheeze, breaking the unnerving silence and the miasma of uncertainty hanging inside the room.
"You got a right battering in there. How do you feel?" Richard Lee asked, making small-talk and handing out cigarettes.
"I've had better days. I'm certainly not expecting a Christmas card from Martin Keane," he replied, taking a cigarette from his outstretched hand, the light-hearted humour replaced by a fog of smoke and fingers tapping impatiently across the desk, three tongue-tied men blowing smoke above their heads and staring at the wall like three strangers on a train, waiting for the coffee to arrive.
"I had hoped that during the meeting I could convince Martin Keane that you were a trustworthy and honourable man, who was just caught up in a moment of reckless intimacy, but unfortunately compromise and forgiveness is not part of his vocabulary," Hugh said, shuffling in his seat and pulling on his cigarette.

"What the hell were you thinking about, fucking that woman in the show-house during the day. You knew the risks. Did you not think about the consequences of getting caught?

I've been informed that the woman was Emma Charlton's mother, but I really don't want to know," he added, sighing into his hands and lighting another cigarette from the one he was already smoking.

"I'm sorry. You're in deep trouble. You've gone too far. I can't help you," he sighed, brushing cigarette ash from his jacket and opening a file.

"I've also had a complaint from Peter Crosby, the manager at the Leisure Centre," he added, shaking his head and rolling his eyes in disbelief.

"One of his security staff caught you and the post woman, Jane Anderson on his closed-circuit television camera, having sex in your car, near the woodland next to the Leisure Centre car- park. And furthermore, Peter has told me it happens quite regularly," he sighed, pulling on his cigarette and blowing smoke across the table.

"The post woman. The fucking post woman!" he barked, crushing an empty cigarette box in his clenched fist and throwing it into a waste bin, leaning over and casually taking a new pack of twenty from the desk drawer.

A gentle tap on the office door announcing the arrival of his secretary with the coffee interrupted any further details concerning his sexual liaisons with Jane Anderson.

"Come in," Hugh croaked, through a bout of coughing and wheezing, aware that with all the emotional stress it could be the beginning of an angina attack.
"I'm getting hot," Hugh sighed, removing his tie and wiping a layer of perspiration from his brow. "I'd better take my medication," he added, removing a small oral spray from his jacket pocket and squirting the spray under his yellow stained tongue.
"That'll kick in in a couple of minutes," he smiled, slipping the plastic container back into his pocket and calmly reaching for his cigarettes.
Richard Lee cleared his throat and raised his voice to assert his authority.
"Mark, we understand that Emma Charlton's husband has discovered that someone in the office has been...," he paused momentarily, raising both hands and curling his fingers to emphasise the quotation marks...."Shagging his wife," he sighed, pausing again to gather his thoughts. "Emma Charlton's nursing a black eye from a very angry and hurt husband and furthermore, rumours are circulating around the office, that you are the guilty shagger."
"Christ Mark, It's all or nothing with you. You're like some kind of sex predator. Your contract of employment doesn't include sex as an occupational perk," he added, sipping his coffee and wiping biscuit crumbs from the corner of his mouth.

"I was going to suggest that you see a sex therapist, but you'd probably end up sleeping with her," he said, forcing a smile that quickly faded.

"I need a drink to calm my nerves," he sighed, reaching into his desk draw and removing a bottle of whiskey. "Purely medicinal. Doctor's orders," he smiled, stubbing his cigarette butt into an overflowing ashtray and pouring a generous measure into his cup, the thought of his friend's niece raising a questioning eye.

"With all the rumours going around, I had to think twice about letting my friend's niece, Lucy Hamilton work in the office," he sighed, lighting another cigarette and rubbing his hand across the back of his neck, as if deep in thought.

"Fortunately, for all concerned she was only here for a short time, so thankfully that innocent child was saved from your clutches,"

With his options thinning by the second, he had given up any thoughts of trying to proclaim his innocence and because there was enough assurance and volume in Hugh's voice, he considered it unwise to interrupt his flow.

He said nothing in response.

"You were in the wrong place at the wrong time. If it had been any other councillor but Martin Keane, you might have gotten away with it," he sighed, regaining his composure and clearing his throat to speak.

"The Chief executive rang me before the meeting. I'm sorry. It wasn't good news," he said, fiddling with his tie and shaking his head from side to side. "I told him you were a valued member of staff and you were ashamed and sorry for what happened. But I'm afraid he wasn't moved," he sighed.

He said as Chief Executive he has an obligation to protect the reputation of the council and therefore its best for all concerned if you tender your resignation with immediate effect.

"I'll give you a good reference and I'll also make sure you get everything you're entitled to under the conditions of your contract," Hugh said, lifting from his chair and offering his hand.

"Good luck, Mark," he added, the smell of whiskey and the pungent smell of cigarettes, lingering in the air long after he had left the room.

"I'm unemployed. At least my CVs up to date. I'll have to visit the Job Centre tomorrow," he thought, waving a friendly hand at Claire Simpson as he headed out the door.

"She's worth coming back for," he smiled, opening the car door and looking up into the sky, a blanket of black clouds gathering overhead and a faint rumble of thunder in the distance, suggesting that rain wasn't too far away.

"Fucking rain. I suppose it's appropriate weather to end a miserable day," he cursed, climbing into the car and lighting a cigarette, the anxiety of the day lost in the intake of nicotine and the sound of tyres squealing across tarmac surfaces.

Wind of Change (circa-1975)

Whitehall Primary School was in the last week of a mid-term break and with only a few members of staff on the premises and no obstructions from interfering children, it should make his survey a lot easier to complete.

The tyres crunched in the deep snow and the windscreen wipers squeaked across the windscreen as he manoeuvred the car carefully through a pair of black metal gates, before pulling to a halt in the school car park.

He waited until Lou Reed had finished singing *'Perfect Day'* before stepping from the car.

After pressing a button on the door intercom panel to announce his arrival, he brushed snow from his hair and took shelter under a small canopy above the door.

The minutes passed with agonising slowness as he waited in the cold for the door to open.

"Fucking weather," he cursed, lighting a cigarette, the brief interlude giving him a moment to think about his recent holiday on the sunshine island of Tenerife.

When a friend suggested spending a couple of weeks relaxing on a sun-soaked beach, rather than face the bitter winter weather in the UK, it didn't take him long to pack a suitcase.

They soaked up the sun by the pool during the day and fucked at night.

Then he met Fiona.

It was a flirtatious acquaintance embroiled under a haze of clandestine confusion and a fleeting extravaganza of impossible circumstances.

But it was a holiday narrative that he would always cherish with furtive amusement.

A meeting of eyes and a brief conversation at the hotel reception was all it took.

It was almost four in the morning when they eventually got back to the hotel.

Even before the lift doors had opened, Fiona was pooling between her legs and he was sporting a noticeable lump inside his pants. And with pulse rates accelerating at the speed of sound and both overcome with an urgent desire to get between the sheets, by the time they reached his room they were almost sprinting.

For the next two hours, he fucked her, and she fucked him. The sex was raw, hungry and extremely physical, exploring and penetrating every orifice in a mutual gesture of give and take, a knee-trembling climax leaving them swimming in a pool of perspiration and both drained of energy.

The sun was beginning to rise when Fiona staggered unsteadily from his room, her dignity and her knickers abandoned on the bedroom floor.

"I've got plenty of knickers," she sighed, ignoring the flimsy garment on the floor and heading out the door, her heels clicking along the corridor and her legs sliding apart like Bambi's on the ice, as she headed for the lift.

"Something smells nice," he thought, the early morning aroma of fried food, drifting up from the restaurant, reminding him that sleep would have to wait until after breakfast.

"I need food, sleep and a shower. In that order," he muttered to himself, slipping into a t-shirt and shorts and tucking the abandoned panties inside his pocket, closing the door behind him and heading to the restaurant on the ground-floor.

After filling a plate with a mixture of fried food that would make any heart surgeon frown in disgust, he was surprised to see Fiona sitting at a table, having breakfast.

He muttered a friendly greeting, before pulling up a chair, at her table.

In the ensuing silence hanging over the table, she glanced around the room at all the empty tables, shuffled nervously in her chair and forced a smile.

He thought the re-acquaintance of her knickers might break the apprehension.

It didn't.

She just stared in horror and disbelief at the flimsy underwear that he had placed on the table in front of her, forced another smile and kept her eye on the floor manager.

"You left them in my room," he smiled, pushing her knickers across the table.

"Or shall I keep them, and you can collect them later?" he added, sipping his coffee and pushing the garment back into his pocket, her virtue and modesty fading by the second.

"It was a great night," he said, lighting a cigarette and launching into a detailed narrative of their reckless night of sex in his bedroom, the intimate details of her ability to give oral sex, interrupting the coffee cup touching her lips.

An unexpected hand on his shoulder caught him by surprise and interrupted the shadier details emerging about the anal sex over the balcony.

"I see you've met my twin sister Lorna," Fiona smiled, removing her hand from his shoulder and pulling up a chair at the table.

"What. Who," he gasped, turning in his chair and blinking his eyes, choking back a lump in his throat and twisting his face in a comical mask of uncertainty, the reality and the nausea of humiliation, dropping like a lead weight in the pit his stomach and the contents of his breakfast threatening to make an appearance.

"Can I help you?" a voice enquired, the volume and seriousness of the question, interrupting his holiday reverie.

"Yes," he replied, turning quickly on his heels and catching sight of a fat man with wire rimmed glasses perched on the end of his nose, peeking suspiciously through a small gap in the door.

"My name's Mark Brand. I'm a building surveyor. I've made arrangements to carry out a survey for the building improvements," he said, the heat of his breath evaporating in a cloud of white mist above his head.

"I have a nine o'clock appointment with a Mrs Julie Reid," he confirmed, pulling his glove back and checking the time on his watch.
"Yes. Julie informed me about the appointment. I thought you might have cancelled, due to the severe weather," he grinned, opening the door and ignoring his outstretched hand.
"Put that cigarette out and come inside," he invited, the authority in his voice and the persuasive hand gesture, more of a command than an invitation.
"I'm sorry but my secretary, Julie Reid can't get in to work today. She lives in the country. All the roads are blocked," he sighed, cleaning his spectacles with a handkerchief and pointing a finger of disapproval at his shoes, bleeding snow on the vinyl floor.
"After you've wiped your feet, I'll take you to see Caroline Spencer. She's one of the teachers at the school. Caroline will show you around the premises," he volunteered, fiddling with a plastic card hanging from a silver chain around his neck, revealing his name and photograph.
"My name's Mathew Grainger," he announced, in a refined 'I'm-In-Charge voice,' smiling with pride and lifting the card. "I'm the Head of School," he added, extending his hand.
"Put that cigarette out. Wipe your feet. He thinks he's talking to one of the kids," he thought, a friendly smile and a welcoming handshake from Caroline Spencer, removing any thoughts of the arrogant fat man in silly spectacles and wearing a cheap suit.

"The snow didn't prevent you from getting into work. I assume you don't live in the country," he smiled, letting go of her hand, the slightest touch from a beautiful woman with dark eyes, firm breasts, a slender figure and insanely long legs blossoming from a pair of heels and finishing somewhere under her arms, was enough to spark a swelling inside his pants.

"I do. I live in Northumberland. My father drove me to work today. He's got a four-wheel drive," she smiled, brushing hair from her face and picking up a handful of keys from the desk.

"If you follow me I'll open the classrooms and show you around the school," she said, disappearing through a door, the sound of clicking heels and the fragrance of expensive perfume following in her wake.

The feasibility study and the endless meetings with The Headmaster. The Chair of School Governor's and members of the delegated Parents Group proved to be more extensive than he had thought, but the architectural fees were very attractive, so his employers didn't complain about his time or his input, providing he satisfied their client's objectives.

He made any excuse to carry out a survey or arrange a meeting at the school, although most of the meetings and surveys were nothing more than a cunning charade to see Caroline Spencer.

And even though their acquaintances were sometimes only brief, it wasn't long before he worked his charm and she eventually agreed to have dinner with him.

It wasn't going to be easy getting Caroline into bed. After their first date, he realised that if he wanted to get between her legs, he would have to be extremely patient.

Even after their fourth date things hadn't improved. The routine was always predictable and frustrating. Dinner and a bottle of wine at her favourite restaurant, followed by a few drinks and then back to his flat. Classical music to soften the mood, followed by lots of kissing, plenty of heavy breathing and brief exchanges of foreplay.

And although she appeared to be sexually aroused at his advances, when it came to sexual intercourse, she always managed to control her emotions.

At first, he was a little frustrated with her denial, but there were positive signs and he knew it was only a matter of time before she would surrender to the natural forces of human sexual response and let him get between her legs.

"My mother and father always go on a winter cruise to the Caribbean, this time of the year," she casually announced. "They usually go for a month. Sometimes two. I don't mind. It means I've got the house to myself," she smiled, the car tyres crunching in the fresh snow and the windscreen wipers squeaking a painful tune across the glass, as she manoeuvred the car through a large set of black metal gates.

"Wow. What a house," he gasped. "I'm getting an erection," he teased, blinking his eyes and brushing his hand across the murky glass, a bothersome thought nagging inside his head.

My father worked in a hospital and my mother worked for a firm of lawyers. She told him. A fucking hospital porter and a clerk in an office.... I fucking don't think so.

"My father was The Head of Paediatric Neurology in one of the largest hospitals in New York and then he worked for a short time in Boston and Chicago before returning to the UK and living in Northumberland," she said, rather matter-of-fact.

"My mother was a barrister," she calmly added. "Before she retired, she worked at The Royal Courts of Justice, in London. They still occasionally travel around the world to attend and chair lectures, and they've both written books on their respective professions," she concluded, circling a white marble water feature of a gracious biblical lady holding a child, before pulling the car to a halt in front of the magnificent house.

'This house is huge. Who cleans it. Do you have servants? He enquired, admiring a montage of oil paintings covering the wall of a hardwood timber staircase leading to the first floor.

"The cleaners come in early in the morning and sometimes later in the afternoon,' she replied, brushing hair from her face and fiddling with an earring. 'I'll just get a bottle of champagne from the fridge in the kitchen. We can take it to the swimming pool," she added, motioning with her hand towards a set of double doors.

"Swimming pool?" he echoed, following on her heels through the double doors leading into a spacious glazed atrium at the rear of the property, the leisure facilities boasting a generous sized swimming pool, a Sauna, Jacuzzi and two shower rooms located at one end of the pool.

"There's more to see through here," she smiled, opening another door and gaining access to a number of self-contained rooms, offering fitness and gymnasium facilities, a television and recreation room and a bar with a full-size snooker table.

"This might interest you if you're keen on gardening," she smiled, a set of French doors from the swimming pool, providing access to a huge paved veranda and a red gravel footpath leading down to two tennis courts and a timber pavilion, bordered by an extensive forest of mature trees.

"That's enough of the tour," she smiled, popping a cork and pouring wine into two glasses.

"Cheers," she toasted, raising her glass. "It's time to relax and have some fun," she added, flashing her eyes, the estate agent's enthusiasm lost in the clinking of wine glasses and the intimacy of touch.

The kiss was warm and meaningful, his early morning whiskers brushing against her skin and the warmth of the embrace, heightening arousal and fuelling the fire between her legs.

"It's time for a swim," she smiled, breaking from the kiss, pulling a funny face and rolling her eyes, when he said he hadn't brought a swimming costume.
"Neither have I," she giggled, flashing her eyes with mischievous intent, removing her clothes and dropping them in a heap by the side of the pool.
"If you're shy, you can keep your briefs on," she mocked, spinning on her toes and flaunting her naked body with flirtatious suggestion, before diving into the pool.
"Come in. I'm naked," she smiled, brushing water from her face and bobbing up and down in the water with playful amusement.
"You'd better still have that erection," she teased, the mere mention of his growing appendage and the fleeting images of her tits playing hide and seek beneath the water, getting him on his feet.
"Fuck me, I've been trying to get between her legs for the last couple of months and now she's naked and flaunting her body with potential and suggestive implications. No point questioning the 'Wind of Change,' he thought, slipping out of his pants and diving into the pool.
"I've had an erection all day. But not like this one," he grinned, mouths crashing together and tongues duelling in an intimate battle of oral endurance, the exchange of chemistry electric, the promise of expectation overwhelming, the haunting images of her nakedness beneath the water and her breasts floating invitingly on the surface firing a surge of blood into his penis and leaving him with a

formidable growth pulsing and swaying beneath the water.

"Good answer," she smiled, wrapping her arms around his neck, the embrace warm and passionate, the sensation of touch and the pulse between her legs responding to the hard muscle pressing against her thigh and a finger probing her anus.

"I like that," she whispered, glancing over her shoulder. "But I prefer that big thing brushing against my thighs," she smiled, flashing her eyes and lowering her hand beneath the water.

"Wow. That's impressive. That's what I call an erection," she smiled, brushing water from her face, the unexpected acquaintance of nine-and-a-half-inches, filling her hand forcing a startled gasp and a gesture of persuasive engagement.

"Don't move," she said. "I'm Jacques Cousteau. I'm going in pursuit of hidden treasure," she playfully teased, holding his waist with both hands and taking a deep intake of breath, before submerging below the water.

"Wow. A blow-jobs under water. What happened to Miss Prude," he thought, blinking his eyes and watching her head bobbing up and down with eager enthusiasm.

"Help me up. I need a drink," she smiled, brushing water from her face and wrapping her arms around his neck in a breathless gesture of assistance.

"You can have a drink when I'm finished with you," he said, pulling her out the water and laying her on her back on the side of the pool. "This'll take your mind of alcohol," he added, opening her legs and pushing his face against her pubic bush, breathing in the musky odours of sex and blowing warm air over her vulva, his warm wet tongue embarking on an oral mission of intimate courtship, following the familiar path of expectation, mapping a sensuous route over her inner thighs, wiggling and swirling his tongue in a creative dance of coital persuasion, up one thigh and down the other, brushing his chin against the soft skin of her inner thighs, letting her feel the fine bristles on his chin and the warmth of his tongue sweeping over the urethra and teasing the clitoris from the sanctuary of the hood.

"Oh yes. That's good," she moaned, hormonal chaos stimulating arousal and fuelling the fire of passion between her legs, persuasive cries of encouragement increasing in volume when he slid two fingers seamlessly inside her inner heat, followed by a third and then a forth.

"Do you like to feel me fucking you with my fingers," he grunted, fisting and sliding, pushing in and pulling out, twisting and turning, opening and closing, stretching the limits of her tight opening with vigorous determination, easing out slowly under pleading cries for calm and a chorus of euphoric mutterings.

"I want you to fuck me in the water, from the back, against the side of the pool," she insisted, the urgency in her voice letting him know she was desperate to feel him inside her body.

"That's an invitation I can't refuse," he smiled, pulling his fingers from her vagina and lifting her back into the water.
"Oh. Yes," she gasped, as he eased the gruesome limb inside her body, wrapping her legs around his waist and digging her heels into his buttocks, moans and groans and whispers of encouragement hissing between tight lips.
"I can feel you inside me. Its feels good. I want more," she pleaded, moving her hips to the persuasion of give and take, easing him in and easing him out, back and forth, faster and faster, deeper and deeper, fucking fast and fucking hard, lifting and lowering, penetrating the depths of her inner core, in an unforgiving display of coital conviction, the probing enquiry of nine-and-a-half- inches, stretching the walls of the vaginal vault and curling the corners of her mouth in an uncompromising gesture of positional change.
"Put me down and fuck me from the back," she whispered, easing the meaty flesh from her body, lowering her legs and shuffling her feet on the tiled floor.
"That was timely. My legs were giving way," he gasped, turning her around to face the wall.
"I thought so. We can't have that" she smiled, gripping the side of the pool, leaning forward and opening her legs.
"Let me put it in," she volunteered, lowering her hand beneath the water and easing him inside her body, the intimate engagement of genitalia joined

together in a mutual exchange of give and take, easing in and easing out, entering and retreating, pushing in and pulling out, the carnal union of two people lost in the heat of passion, groaning out their pleasure in a chorus of moans and groans and euphoric cries of encouragement.

"Yes. Yes. Faster. Faster," she urged, sucking in air through her nose and moving back and forth to impulsive urges, two people swimming in a sea of hormonal chaos, fucking each other with merciless conviction, a tsunami of waves crashing against the side of the pool, two lovers riding the waves of a perfect storm, a turbulent sea of euphoric contractions and a running commentary of orgasmic mutterings, chasing the inevitable waves of climax, breathless gasps and euphoric cries of pleasure, resonating off the walls in a blast of emotional filth.

"Fuck. I'm coming...Fuck. Fuck. I'm coming...I'm coming. Oh. Fuck. Ahhhhhhh," she cried, the echoes of a knee-trembling release, dancing across the water in a verbal outpouring of surrender and euphoric fulfilment, choking gasps for air and a chorus of orgasmic cries, stinging her eyes and sucking the last breath of air from her mouth.

"I can't move my legs. You'll have to help me out of the water," she breathed, the gruesome muscle swaying beneath the water and brushing against her thigh, reminding her that she still had a duty to perform.

"If you give me a moment to catch my breath, I'll see if Jacques Cousteau is still diving for treasure."

Keep on Running (circa-1976)

If you were looking for a woman with style and sophistication, the place to visit was the Bridge Hotel wine-bar between the hours of 6 p.m. and 8 p.m.

Positioned high on an embankment with panoramic views over the River Tyne, the wine-bar attracted a diverse range of corporate, stylish and beautiful people, eager to unwind, flirt and get up to mischief, or just go straight for the desirable option of committing adultery.

This particular time frame was their playground and they played life to the full.

A gaggle of smartly dressed men, smoking fat cigars and drinking champagne, stood in a corner of the room, discussing the world of global finance. One of them pointed a finger at the business page of a broadsheet newspaper, cursing at the Chinese for something only he knew, words like fiscal market indexes, commodities and bond yields and world trading and banking, spilling naturally from his lips.

But it was nothing more than a theatrical charade for their real purpose in life, because once they had left their corporate domain, they could do whatever they wanted.

If the truth were known most of them just wanted a fuck and get back to making money.

It was just after seven when he walked through the door.

"This looks promising," he thought, pulling up a stool at the end of the bar and ordering a drink, watching

the men in expensive suits and smoking cigars, trying to impress each other with meaningless predictions, mathematical statistics and endless corporate nonsense.

With the boredom of accountancy, fading into insignificance, he scanned the room looking for anyone who wasn't wearing a suit or looked like a banker or accountant.

"That's more like it," he smiled, catching sight of a beautiful woman, sitting on a stool at the opposite end of the bar, sipping a cocktail and smoking a long black cigarette, deep in conversation with a smartly dressed man.

"He's punching above his weight," he grinned, pulling on his cigarette and sipping his drink, watching with interest as the fast talking, over-confident Don Juan, worked his charm, trying his best to get into her knickers.

"She appears nervous and uncomfortable," he thought, a long split up the side of her skirt, revealing a hint of black stockings and suspenders, keeping his interest during a heated exchange of words, the determination in her voice and gestures of disapproval, hinting that Don Juan's time was slowly running out.

The cocksure Casanova was heading out the door, when a waitress delivered a bottle of wine to her table, compliments of the man at the end of the bar, the gesture acknowledged with a friendly smile and providing the opportunity for introductions.

Stephanie Monroe was a beautiful and confident woman, who was probably in her late-thirties, although she looked and acted much younger.

"Thanks for coming to my rescue. He was making me feel a little uncomfortable with his suggestive innuendo and wandering hands. And he smelled of garlic," she sighed, lifting her shoulders and twisting her face in disgust.

"I'll try and keep the innuendo to a minimum and I promise to keep my hands in my pockets," he smiled, glad that he'd chosen a sandwich rather than the left-over Currie in his fridge.

"You have an adorable accent. Is it French?" he enquired, lighting a cigarette and sipping his wine, waiting patiently for an answer while she shuffled inside a handbag.

"Yes. I was born in Strasbourg. I lived there with my parents until I was in my late teens," she smiled, lighting a long black cigarette.

"I moved to London to attend the Royal Academy of Performing Arts. I wanted to be an actress," she smiled, flashing her eyes and lifting her shoulders in resignation.

"It's a ruthless business. The only success I had was a couple of TV commercials and an extra in a BBC drama," she sighed, blowing smoke above her head.

"My husband didn't approve. When we lived in London we struggled to make ends meet, but we managed, and we were reasonably happy. It wasn't until we moved to Newcastle, when things began to change," she sighed, the seductive French nuance, stirring a movement inside his pants and lifting the corners of his mouth with a couple of questions he usually avoided.

"Yes. I was married for eight-years, until I discovered he was having an affair with another woman. I've got a six-year-old daughter and I've been separated for almost a year," she sighed, sipping her wine and brushing hair from her face, pausing to gather her thoughts before answering his other question.

"His name is Ronnie Monroe," she hissed, sipping her wine and blowing smoke into the air, above her head.

"A fucking crook…A fucking gangster…A fucking drug dealer…A fucking arsehole, a man with a violent temper and a reputation for being a hard-man in the West End," she barked, crushing her cigarette into an ashtray.

"Let's not talk any more about marriage and unfaithful husbands," she sighed, forcing a smile that quickly faded. "I think I've had enough to drink," she said, glancing at her watch and slipping her cigarettes into a handbag.

"Would you like to come back to my flat?" she asked, shuffling on her stool, the boldness of her enquiry breaking the uneasiness hanging between them and getting him on his feet.

"Put this card in the machine and punch the code on the keypad," she smiled, the movement of a security barrier allowing access to a private car park beneath a residential apartment block, in an exclusive part of West Jesmond.

"It gives you peace of mind," she smiled, stepping into a lift and pressing a button on a stainless-steel panel. "And it keeps the riff-raff out," she added, checking the status of her lip gloss in the full-length mirror while she waited for the lift to stop at the penthouse suites on the top floor.

"This is certainly impressive. She said he was a crook and a drug dealer. He must have been dealing in a big way to afford this. And they say crime doesn't pay," he thought, a delightful tableau of fine art painting hanging on pastel painted walls and a tasteful arrangement of classical furniture strategically placed over polished hardwood floors, keeping his interest, as she pressed a chrome button on a Bose music system.

"I hope you like my choice of music," she smiled, a soft serenade of violins filtering through concealed speakers and filling the room with the promise of intimate liaison.

"Who doesn't like Beethoven," he smiled, lighting a cigarette and glancing out the window.

"The panoramic views over the city skyline are rather spectacular," she said, opening the sliding doors to the balcony.

"I'll let you take in the views. I won't be long," she smiled, skipping across the living-room floor and disappearing through a closed door.

'Fuck me. We must be high up. I can almost see the football ground from here,' he thought, blinking his eyes and looking down from the balcony, the endless red stream of tail-lights from the slow-moving traffic,

winding through the dark city streets below, confirming his thoughts.
'I'd better keep away from the balcony. They would have to scrape you off the pavement, if you fell from this height,' he muttered to himself, stepping back and blowing plumes of white smoke into the dark sky, the haunting reminder of Stephanie's estranged relationship with her husband and homicidal maniac, Ronnie Munroe following in its wake.
"I hope you like Champagne?" a soft voice asked, interrupting his thoughts.
"What," he croaked, turning quickly on his heels and choking back a lump in his throat.
"Yes. Thanks," he smiled, crushing his cigarette in an ashtray and taking a long-stemmed glass from her hand, a fleeting glance at her choice of dress, lifting the corners of his mouth in a gesture of approval.
"It's not every day you're offered a glass of Champagne from a beautiful woman wearing a white Basque, white lace panties and stockings and suspenders," he smiled, lifting his glass to his mouth and staring shamelessly at her breasts, any thoughts of her violent husband swept away in a familiar movement inside his pants.
"I like the fingerless gloves," he casually added, lowering his hand and making a quick adjustment to the untimely lump.
"Is that all you like," she smiled, flashing her eyes and raising her glass in salute.
"What about this," she giggled, twirling on towering heels and flaunting her body like an underwear

model posing for a photograph, the white panties exposing a dark bush of pubic hair and the alluring image of a bulging vulva nestling beneath the fabric, making the ultimate revelation of her mysterious secrets, all the more intriguing.

"Not bad," he casually offered, pushing his eyes back into their sockets and making another adjustment inside his pants.

"Pas mal. Pas mal" she repeated, clipping him playfully across the head, the mere hint of her French accent bringing a smile to his face and another rush of blood to his penis.

"I've got a surprise for the bedroom. I just need to get it from the fridge," she said, flashing her eyes with flirtatious suggestion, her smile widening and her heels clicking across the hardwood floor.

"I hope you like the taste of lemon," she said, placing a bottle of wine and a carton of yogurt on a table next to the bed, the surreptitious suggestion of a bottle of wine and lemon flavoured yogurt, offering hours of playful entertainment.

"Keep the gloves on.... And the heels," he grinned, kicking his shoes off his feet and throwing his shirt and pants in a heap on the floor, a photograph of a child next to the bed, catching his eye and interrupting the urgency in his step.

"It's my daughter, Michelle. Don't worry we won't be disturbed. She spends the week-ends with her father," she smiled, flashing her eyes and throwing her panties in his face.

"So you can fuck me for the next three days," she smiled, falling on the bed, lips crashing together, pulses racing and heart beats gathering speed, hormonal chaos fuelling a visceral surge of adrenaline, bleeding through veins and into vital organs, two strangers driven by lust and expectation, genitalia pressing together in a mutual simulation of coital foreplay, a tangle of hands sweeping over curves with lustful intent, his feather-light fingers burning a warm trail over her vulva before slipping between the moist flaps and folds and teasing the clitoris from its shrouded hood.

"That feels good," she gasped, sucking in air through her nose and moving her hips to the persuasion of touch, her heart beat banging like a drum inside her chest and her breathing ragged and urgent, the persuasive movement of nine-and-a-half-inches, brushing against her thigh and lifting the corners of her mouth in a gesture of urgent enquiry.

"Wow. That's dangerous," she smiled, lowering her hand over his stomach and wrapping her fingers around the gruesome column, feeling the flesh pulsing between her fingers and a familiar wetness gathering between her legs.

"It's massive," she gasped, stroking the length and gripping the girth, the promise of coital connection dancing behind her eyes.

"It's so long and so thick," she whispered, the enormity of nine-and-a-half-inches, filling her lace covered hand and a familiar sticky substance oozing from the open eye, bringing a smile to her face and a persuasive gesture of movement.

"Let me get over you," she volunteered, flashing her eyes and shuffling on the bed in an orientation of sixty-nine, the image of her bottom hovering just above his face and the aroma of sex teasing his nostrils, getting his undivided attention.

"Permet de se faire plaisir," she smiled, flashing her eyes and reaching over to the bedside table, a glass of wine and the carton of yogurt, joining the foreplay, the playful recipe curling the corners of her mouth with furtive suggestion.

"Let's indulge in some therapeutic foreplay," she grinned, spilling wine over his stomach and watching it pool in his naval, smiling into his eyes and pouring a generous amount of yogurt from the container over his swollen limb and hairy testicles.

"I think I need a bigger carton," she giggled, gripping the meaty girth and moving her hand up and down the slippery shaft, pulling the foreskin back and smearing the bulbous head with yogurt, lowering her hand and giving his oval testicles a gentle squeeze, before looking back over her shoulder to see his reaction.

"Pas mal," she mockingly teased, hormonal chaos flirting with the power of persuasion and the promise of coital expectation, dancing behind a flirtatious smile.

"You're hard to please," she sighed, brushing hair from her face and increasing the movement of her hand when he didn't respond to the question.

"Let's see if this meets with your approval," she smiled, pursing her lips and sucking wine from his naval, a hungry mouth and eager tongue embarking a mission of oral pursuit, peppering soft kisses up and down his legs and sweeping her tongue in a flirtatious dance between his thighs, scraping a finger nail over the scrotum and sucking one of his testicles into her mouth, holding it in playful capture between her teeth, before easing it out in wet strings of saliva and trailing threads of yogurt.

"Yogurt and cock. Delicious," she smiled, dipping her long fingers into the container and coating the swollen limb with the sticky mess, flashing her eyes and easing the gruesome limb back into her mouth, easing him in and easing him out, sucking him in and blowing him out, sweeping her tongue in a playful dance around the rim of the bulbous crown, feasting on a recipe of yogurt and wine and the taste of seminal fluids, oozing from the unblinking eye.

"Very tasty," she smiled, licking yogurt from her fingers and brushing hair from her face.

"Have you had enough. Do you want me to stop?" she mockingly teased, the warmth of her mouth sweeping in playful circles around the smooth head, getting an urgent response.

"Don't stop," he croaked, as she sucked him in and swallowed him deep, easing him in and easing him out through a chorus of moans and groans and gestures of approval, euphoric mutterings and responsive movements, signalling an approaching climax.

"Don't come. Not yet," she whispered, letting him slip from her mouth and shifting her weight on the bed, momentarily smothering his face with her bottom before rolling onto her back and opening her legs.

"Play with me," she said, flashing her eyes and spreading a generous coating of yogurt over her vulva, the acquaintance of touch and his early morning stubble brushing over her inner thighs, greeted with a startled gasp and a breathless word of encouragement.

"Touch me," she pleaded, arching her back and spreading her legs, opening her body and giving him intimate access to her inner heat, a wanting woman overwhelmed with desire and a vulva pleading for attention, lifting the corners of her mouth in a plea for oral stimulation.

"Suck me," she insisted, pulling his head down into the sexual arena and smothering his face in her sex, pulling his hair and moving her hips to the persuasion of touch, the warmth of his mouth and well-practiced tongue, bathing the urethra and flirting with the clitoral jewel, teasing her senses and curling her toes in a welcoming gesture of approval.

"Play with me. Touch me. Suck me," he repeated. "You're very demanding" he added, lifting her thighs, pulling the cheeks apart and opening her bottom, gliding a wet finger along the perineum valley, teasing and probing her dark place of intimacy, smiling into her eyes and sliding a slippery finger inside her anal passage.

"Do you like this?" he whispered, holding it momentarily inside her bottom, before easing it out slowly and slipping two fingers inside her vagina, curling and probing the inner walls of the vaginal vault, the intimate pursuit of his fingers searching for the g-spot, lifting the corners of her mouth in a pleading cry for penetration.

"No more games. I'm wet and ready," she smiled, a woman overwhelmed with emotional need and hormonal chaos fuelling the fire of passion between her legs, impatient gestures and frustrated sighs stumbling over a nuance of persuasive words.

"Je veux que tu me baises…I want you to fuck me," she said, flashing her eyes with flirtatious intent, the uncompromising demands of a temptress, bringing a smile to his face and moving his lips, in a responsive reply.

"Only if you promise to keep talking dirty in that seductive voice," he grinned, lifting her legs in the air and resting her feet on his shoulders, her legs open and inviting and her lethal heels hovering precariously on either side of his face.

"I promise," she smiled. "Maintenant metre ce coq interieur de moi," she pleaded, blinking her eyes and gritting her teeth, as he manoeuvred into position.

"Oh, oui. Oh, yes. Oh, putain," she gasped, hissing through tight lips and brushing hair from her face, as he eased the swollen limb inside her body, stretching the sticky flaps and folds and filling the vaginal vault with nine-and-a-half-inches of swollen flesh.

"Yogurt and vagina," he teased, thrusting his hips in a turbulent commitment of perpetual movement, entering and retreating, pushing in and pulling out, all the way in and all the way out, easing in and easing out, thrusting and grinding, fucking fast, fucking slow and fucking hard, the tireless marathon, stealing her dignity and the air from her lungs.

"Ce un coq. What a cock. What a fuck. I can hardly breathe," she whispered, sucking in air through her nose and pulling the gruesome limb from her burning vault.

"Give me a moment to catch my breath," she sighed, choking back a lump in her throat and brushing yogurt from her hair and face, the kiss somewhat unexpected, but nevertheless meaningful, the taste of yogurt and the familiar smell of her own sex on his lips, a tasteful reminder of their oral union.

"No mercy. Turn over," he grinned. "You can breathe when I'm finished with you," he teased.

"You're very persuasive," she smiled, shifting her weight on the bed and kneeling on all-fours with her hands flat on the mattress and her shapely bottom perched submissively in the air.

"Sois gentil, she whispered, clenching her teeth and looking back over her shoulder, blinking her eyes and curling her toes, as the perilous object, slid inside her body.

"Oh, yes," she moaned, easing him in and easing him out, wriggling her bottom and moving her hips back and forth in a mutual exchange of give and take, the capture of trailing strings of yogurt mixed with vaginal fluids smearing her vagina and hanging from his cock, lifting the corners of his mouth, in an uncompromising gesture of playful intent.

"I don't do gentle. Let me know when you want me to stop," he said in mocking jest, his stamina in overdrive and his libido in overload, a tireless piston fuelled with testosterone, moving inside her body without sympathy or compromise, her cries for tenderness lost in his urgent desire to fuck her until she begged for mercy.

"You're very good at this," she hissed, turning her head and looking back, watching the beads of sweat running down his face and dropping onto her back, feeling his hard thighs smacking against her bottom each time he entered and retreated from her body.

"This is the best fuck I've ever had," she gasped, gripping the bedsheets with both hands, swivelling her hips and pushing back, easing him in and easing him out, genitalia embracing genitalia in an intimate gesture of give and take, pushing in and pulling out, back and forth, thrusting and pushing, balls deep inside her slippery opening, probing and penetrating and reaching the limits of the vaginal vault, the acquaintance of the head brushing against the cervix, stinging her eyes and fuelling the fire of passion between her legs.

"FUCK ME. BAISE-MOI!" she cried. "FASTER. HARDER!" she urged, the euphoria of approaching climax flooding vital organs and curling her toes, a commentary of euphoric muttering and persuasive

gestures of impending release, lifting the corners of her mouth in a euphoric announcement.
"I'm coming...I'm fucking coming," she screamed, thrashing her head from side to side and sucking in air through her nose, a knee-trembling, breath-taking orgasm, flooding her thighs and sucking the last gasp of air from her throat.
"Come inside me. Please come inside me," she pleaded, brushing wet hair from her face and looking back over her shoulder.
"Venir a l'interieur de moi," she repeated, the persuasion of vocal expression increasing momentum and bringing his balls to boiling point, the energy sapping eruption fast and powerful, spilling inside her body in progressive bursts, streams of emotional ballast and trailing strings of yogurt glistening on her bottom and smearing her thighs.

He had only been in the bathroom for a few minutes. The time it takes to empty a bladder and clean yogurt from his hands and face. So, when he walked back into the bedroom, he was surprised to see Stephanie holding a telephone to her ear and dialling a number.
"Who could she be ringing at this time in the morning," he thought, glancing at his watch and sitting on the end of the bed, acrylic nails tapping impatiently across the bedside table, keeping his interest, while he gathered his clothes from the floor.
"Hello Ronnie. It's me Stephanie. I hope I'm disturbing you," she barked into the phone.

"I thought you ought to know that I've just been fucked to death by a handsome young man with a massive cock," she snapped, the crippling silence at the other end of the phone giving her enough time to add a few crude remarks into the mouthpiece.

"And this time I didn't have to fake an orgasm," she laughed hysterically, the violent threats of a maniac echoing through the earpiece, momentarily interrupting his search for clothing.

"Are you...I don't think so...Well fuck you too...You're not man enough...Go fuck yourself," she shouted, dropping the phone into the cradle, the mere mention of her husband's name, feeding his panic and getting him back on his feet.

He wanted to tell her what he thought about her verbal assault on a man who she had earlier referred to as a violent maniac, but the lack of intuitive rational that panic sometimes induces, left him stammering in helpless retreat.

"Christ was that....Was it....Please tell me it wasn't," he mumbled, shaking his head from side to side, the knots of dread tightening inside his stomach and a lump in his throat, threatening to stop him breathing.

"Ronnie," she answered for him. "Yes, it was," she laughed, falling flat on the bed and reaching for her cigarettes.

"Fucking arsehole. That'll teach the two-timing bastard," she sighed, lighting a long black cigarette and blowing smoke at the ceiling.

"What the fuck was that all about?" he barked, giving her a look, he reserved for fools and pointing a finger at the telephone.
"Where…Where does he live?" he nervously stuttered, his urgency to get dressed increasing by the second, pulling his pants up with one hand and buttoned his shirt with the other.
"In Gosforth…Not far from here…About a mile," she casually replied.
"In Gosforth…A fucking mile away," he repeated, choking back a lump in his throat and brushing beads of sweat from his brow, the fear of a confrontation with a violent maniac, sending a cold chill of nausea down his spine.
"What the fuck were you thinking about calling him at this time in the morning, just to tell him you were getting fucked," he muttered under his breath, the sound of a car engine in the street below, feeding his panic and throwing him into nervous recoil.
"I could hear him shouting down the telephone....What did he say to you?"
"Ronnie said he's going to kill you," she said with shameless ease, flashing her eyes and flicking her cigarette ash into a tray by the bed.
"Fuck me. This maniac wants to kill me. He only lives a mile away. He could already be in his car heading this way," he thought, visions of a mad man in a speeding car and a movement in his bowels, reminding him of the urgency to get away.
The echoes of threat were still reverberating around the room when he left the apartment. *"Fucking mad*

woman," he cursed, avoiding the lift and taking the stairs, two at a time scanning the car park for homicidal maniacs, before opening the door and climbing into his car.

"Fucking mad women. Fucking violent husbands," he cursed, turning the ignition and pressing his foot on the accelerator pedal, the tyres screeching over concrete surfaces and his eyes glued to the rear-view mirror, cursing again under his breath, before speeding away through the anger and fatigue.

Smoke and Shadows (circa-1976)

"Fucking Stephanie Monroe...Fucking mad woman...Fucking violent husbands," he cursed, yawning into a clenched fist and making a mental note to cross 'The Bridge Hotel' off his list of social venues.

"What the...," he gasped, the sudden impact of the car mounting the pavement and crashing into a row of metal railings at a bus stop, waking him from an untimely sleep, the natural reaction to grab the steering wheel after the event, offering little to prevent or cushion the blow from the impact.

"That hurt," he croaked, choking back a lump in his throat and sucking in air through his nose, trying to calm the racing heart beat banging like a drum inside his chest and the excruciating pain in his head, after being thrown like a rag doll against the car windscreen.

"Fuck," he cursed, blinking his eyes and looking in the rear-view mirror, trying to focus through the cobwebs of nausea and the shards of broken glass from the shattered windscreen, covering his face and hair like sparkling diamonds.

"What a fucking mess," he sighed, brushing away the pieces of glass and tracing a finger over an open wound spitting blood from his forehead.

"That'll need a few stiches," he thought, lighting a cigarette and stepping from the car to examine the damage.

"What a Fucking idiot," he muttered to himself, cursing under his breath at his stupidity, a fleeting glance at his watch reminding him that things could have been more serious.

If he had been travelling this route an hour later the bus stop would have been littered with people on their way to work. And if the car had of mounted the pavement instead of colliding with the barrier, someone could have been seriously injured.

"Christ," he gasped, pulling on his cigarette, the rush of nicotine in his bloodstream clearing his head and bringing him back to reality.

"I could have been facing manslaughter charges…I could be in prison…I could be spending the night in hospital, or even the hospital morgue," he thought, making a mental note to drive more carefully and start wearing his seat belt, before examining the car.

The impact of the wheels hitting the high kerb had slowed the car enough to cushion the blow, just before hitting the metal railings and surprisingly the front of the car, didn't appear to have sustained too much damage.

"The radiators leaking water and there's no windscreen. But I might just make it home," he thought, glancing at his watch, a yellow glow on the horizon, signalling the beginning of a new day.

"The last thing I need to see at this time in the morning is a police car," he sighed, dropping his cigarette on the ground and pushing the car back onto the road.

The journey home was painfully slow, but the early morning bird-song and the welcoming cool breeze

on his face, swept away the haunting images of his close encounter with death and helped to ease the nagging pain inside his head.
The taxi drive to Newcastle Royal Victoria Hospital, took less than fifteen minutes.
"Mr Brand," a nurse with a look of someone who had a craving for carbohydrates, called out from a consulting room door.
"My names Susan Owen," she said, nibbling a chocolate biscuit and sipping a cup of coffee.
"That looks painful. let me have a look," she smiled, sitting him in a chair and examining the cut on his forehead.
"It's a deep wound, Mr Brand. But I think we can save you," she said in playful jest, picking a shard of glass from his hair and dropping it into a waste bin.
"A few stitches and you'll be on your way home," she confirmed, brushing hair from her face and reaching for her chocolate biscuit.
After a couple of glasses of red wine and a restless night's sleep punctuated by disturbing dreams of becoming the latest statistic in a long list of road accident victims, he was shaved and showered before seven o'clock the following morning.
June Chamber's was having breakfast when the telephone rang.
After giving her a brief summary of the accident and the subsequent damages to his car, she said she would arrange for a breakdown vehicle to bring it to her garage in Newton-by-the-Sea.

Between slurps of coffee and a conversation laden with innuendo and flirtatious phone sex, followed by a description of the recent addition to her dressing-up-wardrobe and some new phallic toys, she made him an offer he couldn't refuse.

After a few minor body repairs, a new windscreen and radiator and a solo demonstration with her new phallic toys, followed by two hours of bed rattling, steamy sex, he was heading back to Gateshead.

A peaceful evening with Caroline Spencer in her favourite Italian restaurant, was a welcoming relief after the bizarre night at Stephanie Monroe's flat.

It had certainly been an anxious two weeks of constantly looking over his shoulder and staring into the eyes of faceless strangers, jumping nervously whenever someone knocked at the door or a car, unexpectedly backfired in the street.

The facial wounds from the road accident had now healed and the last thing he needed was a question and answer confrontation with Caroline, so he thought it prudent not to mention his close encounter with death.

"I've missed you. I've been away on a training course in Birmingham for the last two weeks," he lied, smiling into her eyes, as a waiter placed a bottle of wine on the table.

"I suspect you've been busy at the school now the children are back," he added, pouring wine into glasses and picking up a menu from the table.

"I've handed in my notice at the school," she casually announced. "I'm changing careers. I'm going to work as a probation officer at HMP-Durham," she smiled, raising her glass in the way of a toast.
"It was a big decision to make, but I needed a change," she smiled, gathering her thoughts and continuing with a long and uninteresting summary about her decision to leave teaching and a brief outline of her new job in the prison service.
"I trust your parents are having a good time. Have you heard from them?" he asked, the unexpected question interrupting the boredom of work.
"Yes. They rang me yesterday. They're in the Bahamas," she answered, brushing hair from her face and sipping her wine.
"Did you tell them we had sex in the pool and then helped ourselves to a bottle of vintage wine," he laughed, lifting his glass to his mouth.
"I most certainly did not," she giggled, slapping him playfully across the head, the mere mention of their intimate liaison in her parent's swimming pool, fuelling the heat of passion between her legs, any further discussion about career moves fading away in the echoes of flirtatious laughter.
If only he'd telephoned a service engineer when the pilot light kept going out on the central heating boiler, they wouldn't be going back to a cold house.
"Sorry about the heating," he offered, removing the front casing on the boiler and fiddling with the pilot light.

"Try to get it going. I'm freezing," she sighed, chattering her teeth and rubbing her hands up and down her arms.

"Look how cold I am," she giggled, pointing a finger at two erect nipples, making an appearance through her blouse.

"I'm trying my best, but I don't think it's going to ignite," he answered, stealing a glance at her tits and cursing at the boiler, until he remembered that he still had hot water from the emersion heater

"I've got an idea," he smiled, taking a bottle of wine from the fridge and a couple of glasses from a cupboard.

"Follow me," he smiled, sprinting up the stairs to the bathroom and making a mental note to ring a service engineer first thing in the morning.

"Get naked," he smiled, pouring wine into glasses and pointing a finger at the water coming from the tap.

"It's hot. Get in. It'll warm you up while I put some music on" he said, disappearing into a bedroom.

"David Bowie. Space Oddity. It's your favourite," he shivered, dropping his clothes on the floor and climbing into the bath.

Ground control to Major Tom....

"How do you know I liked David Bowie?" she enquired, lifting a questioning eyebrow and brushing hair from her face.

Take your protein pills and put your helmet on….

"I had a look through your record collection after our swim in your parents swimming pool," he said, smiling into her eyes and pulling her into his arms.

Commencing countdown, engines on….

"I'll have to keep an eye on you. You'll be going through my underwear drawer next," she smiled, flashing her eyes and wrapping her arms around his neck, lips melting together in a smouldering kiss and tongues sweeping over teeth, impatient hands touching and feeling and fondling and groping in a mutual exchange of give and take, the heat of passion warming her heart and tingling the place between her legs.

And I'm floating in a most peculiar way….

"I'm warm and wet…. I'm hot and ready…. If you want me," she whispered, hormonal chaos teasing her senses and a familiar ache between her legs pleading for attention, a young woman craving for intimate contact, a wanting woman overwhelmed with emotional need, a young woman accepting that her body was now his and he could do whatever he wanted with it.

TEN.

She followed his instructions, stood up in the bath and turned to face the wall.

NINE.

"You're very demanding," she smiled, brushing wet hair from her face and taking a deep intake of breath, leaning forward and placing her hands flat against the tiled wall, arching her back and opening her legs.

EIGHT.

"A little lubricant always helps," he teased, pouring liquid from a container, soaping her curvy bottom and the bush of pubic hair around the vaginal opening, a choking gasp and a thrust of his hips and he was inside her body, pushing in and pulling out, easing in and easing out, genitalia embracing genitalia in an intimate connection of give and take, the welcoming suction of her inner walls stretching to accommodate nine-and-a-half-inches of swollen flesh, twisting her face in a comical mask of pleasure and lifting the corners of her mouth in a gesture of persuasive encouragement.

SEVEN.

"Fuck me. Put it all in. Hurt me," she urged, through a commentary of filth and breathless moans and groans, two people groaning out their pleasure in a frenzied rhythm of give and take, pushing in and pulling out, in and out, grinding and banging, thrusting and pounding, the sound of hard masculine skin smacking urgently against soft feminine skin and the sloppy wet sounds of coital interaction, echoing off the walls inside the room.

SIX.

"You're an animal. A wild man. A man with a big cock, who knows how to use it. A man who knows what a woman wants," she gasped, choking back a lump in her throat, impulsive gestures responding to persuasive urges, thrusting her hips and pushing back, easing him in and easing him out, all the way in and all the way out, making sure she had every inch inside her body.

FIVE.

"I don't think I can keep this up much longer. My hands and feet are slipping in the soap," she sighed, craning her neck and looking back over her shoulder.

FOUR.

"Okay. Let's finish in the bedroom. I'll bring the wine," he smiled, easing the fleshy limb from her body and helping her out of the bath.

THREE.

"The beds freezing. Cuddle me. Warm me up," she pleaded, shivering and moving closer, the welcoming embrace of his comforting arms and his hands sweeping over cold skin, more of a spontaneous exchange of body heat than an intimate gesture of sexual response.

TWO.

It was physical. It was wild. It was vocal. A progressive interaction of genitalia colliding in a union of coital connection, easing in and easing out, entering and retreating, pushing in and pulling out, in a merciless demonstration of give and take, moans and groans chasing shallow gasps and breathless pants, spasms following spasms and muscle contractions reaching every nerve, hormonal chaos teasing her senses and wetting her thighs, a wanting woman warming to the heat of passion.

ONE.

"You're a sex-machine," she panted and sighed. "A tireless fucking machine," she moaned and groaned. "Fuck, that's good. Give me more," she gasped and cried. "You're reaching all the right places," she whispered, brushing hair from her face and gripping the bed sheet with both hands, arching her back and thrusting her hips, sucking in air through her nose and flashing her eyes, impulsive gestures and euphoric cries, signalling that 'blast off' was only seconds away.

LIFTOFF.

"YES. YES....AH YES. AH FUCK…AH FUCK. FUCK ME....FASTER! FASTER! YES. YES….I'M COMING....I'M COMING…Ahhhhhhh," she screamed, shaking and shuddering and thrashing her head from side to side, groaning out her pleasure through a fanfare of squeaking bedsprings, and the continuous clack-clack-clacking of the headboard, banging against the party wall.

"I'm exhausted. You certainly know how to warm a bed up," she gasped, sucking in air through her nose and reaching for her glass of wine.

"I hope I didn't wake your neighbours," she smiled, flashing her eyes and pointing a finger at the bedroom wall.

"You were very vocal," he answered, mindful of a similar situation when his elderly and religious neighbours thought they were witnessing a murder and almost called the police.

"I don't think we'll hear from them. They both have hearing aids," he sighed, pointing a finger at his ear, that wasn't really necessary.

"If they ask me about the noise, I'll just tell them I was moving furniture around," he smiled, sipping his wine and lighting two cigarettes.

"At this time in the morning," she laughed, lifting the glass to her mouth and draining the last of her wine.

"Thanks," she smiled, taking a cigarette from his outstretched hand and placing the empty glass on the floor by the bed.

"I'm tired," she said, yawning into her hand and settling into silence, pulling on her cigarette and staring at the ceiling, watching spirals of white smoke drifting aimlessly across the room before disappearing through a small gap in the window.

He wasn't sure whether it was the urgency in her voice or the claustrophobic fog of black smoke choking the room, that woke him from his sleep.

"The beds on fire," she screamed, blinking her eyes and trying to focus in the darkness, the haunting sight of the duvet glowing in a sea of burning embers feeding her panic and forcing another urgent cry.

"The fucking beds on fire," she cursed, rolling off the bed and onto the floor, the deafening sound of shattering glass and her painful cries for help, getting him quickly on his feet.

"Are you hurt?" he barked, choking back a lump in his throat and shuffling his feet on the floor, blinking his eyes and searching blindly through the smoke and shadows.

"I'll be with you in a minute," he added, gathering the burning duvet in his hands, sprinting across the landing and dropping it into the bath.

"Let me have a look," he sighed, stepping over small fragments of broken glass on the floor and lifting her carefully onto the bed.
"Fucking wine glass," he cursed, stepping on a shard of glass and piercing his foot.
"It's a deep wound. I think it needs stiches. I'll have to take you to hospital," he sighed, limping around the room and gathering her clothes from the floor.
He wasn't surprised to find the Accident and Emergency Room inside Newcastle Royal Victoria Hospital, littered with sobering drunks, but he was surprised and a little embarrassed when Susan Owen greeted him in the waiting room.
"Bring Caroline into the examination room," she invited, lowering her eyes and raising an eyebrow. "Are you injured too? You seem to have a limp," she enquired.
"No....No. I'm fine," he answered, choking back a lump in his throat and forcing a smile, relieved that she hadn't recognised him.
"It's a deep cut. How did it happen?" she asked, removing particles of glass from Caroline's wound, half listening to his unconvincing account of the unfortunate accident, smiling occasionally at his impetuous humour, scowling the next at his brazen arrogance.
"Just finishing off and you can be on your way," the nurse smiled, closing the wound in a seamless row of stitches and wrapping a dressing around her thigh.
"Thank you, nurse," he smiled, placing a comforting hand around Caroline's waist and searching inside

his jacket pocket for his car keys, the unexpected voice of Susan Owen following him out the door.
"Drive carefully Mr Brand."

Ignoring the Signs (circa-1978)

As soon as you walked through the door, the unmistakable aroma of weed and the familiar smell of infidelity, left you in no doubt that you had just entered the Cavendish Club.

As usual the place was full of desperate people, some of them searching for everlasting love, others just after a one-night stand.

The events over the last few days had certainly left him depressed and emotionally drained.

The day started badly and progressively got worse.

It began with an early morning telephone call from Stella Mason, informing him that his friend, Gary Fowler had been rushed to hospital after sustaining serious injuries in a road accident.

She said that Gary was in an induced coma fighting for his life, and although he was showing some signs of recovery, the doctors confirmed that the damages to his spinal cord were so severe, that he might never walk again.

The afternoon didn't get any better. Too many cigarettes and too much alcohol, pacing the floor, picking up the phone and putting it down, trying to build up the courage to phone Caroline Spencer.

He must have lifted the phone a dozen times before dropping it back into the cradle.

He knew that if he made the call her father would have probably answered and given the regrettable circumstances he wouldn't expect the conversation to be sociable.

The more he thought about the unfortunate incident in his bedroom, he was beginning to accept the fact that he wouldn't see Caroline again.
(He was wrong. They would eventually meet up again in 1985, although the circumstances would be very different and a little embarrassing.)
After spending the last hour sitting on a stool at the bar, drowning his sorrows in alcohol and wrestling with his conscience, he felt as if his heart and his life had suddenly come to a milestone he would like to forget.
Staring through the bottom of another empty glass, aware that there aren't many things in life that can beat alcohol in a crisis, he lit a cigarette and ordered another drink.
"You look like someone who's just lost his puppy," a familiar voice said, the reflection in the mirror behind the bar, throwing back an image of his good friend, Heather Chapman.
"A dog gives you unconditional love. Not like the human race," he sighed, pulling up another stool at the bar, and ordering another drink.
If he ever wanted to spend the rest of his life with a woman who came with all the attributes, then Heather Chapman would be at the top of his list.
Twice married and twice divorced. A free spirited 'life and soul of the party,' type of woman, enjoying life and making the most of her single status, obsessed with sex and drifting between her many lovers without feeling any obligation to make any one of them a permanent fixture in her life.

No baggage. No conditions. No commitments. No longevity. After finding a new direction in her life, she had no regrets and made no apologies for any of her actions. She dated whoever she wanted and slept with whoever grabbed her fancy.

Heather Chapman's sympathetic voice and comforting smile always came with an invitation.

The sea front car-park above the cliffs of Tynemouth beach was a place he often took female friends for sex, although at two in the morning, he was surprised to find it full.

"Fucking cars…Everybody shagging," he sighed, pulling on his cigarette and blowing smoke through the open window.

"It doesn't look like anybody's in a hurry to leave. Christ, we could be here all fucking night," he thought, blinking his eyes into focus and scanning the car-park, watching and waiting, listening for the sound of an engine or a headlight beam.

"Yes," he remembered, rolling the window down and dropping his cigarette onto the ground, a smug smile lifting the corners of his mouth.

'There's a small gap in the barrier fence at the end of the car park that leads to a small dirt track above the cliffs. But remember it's very close to the cliff edge,' said a cautious voice inside his head.

"I know a private place, Heather," he smiled, turning the steering wheel and putting the car into reverse, the tyres spinning over gravel and used condoms and the headlights beaming intrusively into the windows of other cars.

"It's at the very end of the car park," he confirmed, smiling at the shadowy silhouettes of couples engaged in various stages of copulation.

"Is it safe?" she asked. "I hope you know what you're doing," she smiled, lighting a cigarette and staring into the darkness.

"Of course, it's safe," he said unconvincingly, ignoring the warning sign and turning the headlights onto full beam.

"Trust me," he smiled, navigating the car through the narrow gap in the fence and over a grassy terrain, the headlight lighting up the dark sky and the suspension protesting against the uneven ground.

"Just a little further," he muttered, brushing his hand over the murky glass and blinking his eyes into focus, making sure he avoided the rocks and the muddy area, just above the cliffs.

When Heather Chapman performed fellatio, you knew you had just been given the best blow-job of your life. A well-practiced technique, never hurried, slow and meaningful and always performed with sensuous ease. A prolonged and flirtatious engagement of oral stimulation, executed with precision and persuasive meaning, a mind-blowing performance to remember.

"Just relax. This'll take your mind off things," she whispered, easing him into her warm mouth and working the shaft with the skill and finesse of an artist, easing him in and easing him out, swallowing the length down to the root and blowing him out in whispers of warm air, sweeping her tongue in lazy circles around the swollen head and teasing the small eye with flirtatious suggestion.

"I thought that might help. Now let's see what a fuck can do," she smiled, flashing her eyes and brushing hair from her face, climbing into the back seat of the car and shuffling on the seat, removing her blouse and bra and slipping out of her skirt and knickers.

There were times when Heathers fitness and compulsive needs proved to be more of a marathon of endurance, rather than a quick fuck in the back seat of a car.

"Let me get on top," she whispered, shifting her weight on the seat and straddling his thighs.

"I can fuck better, when I'm on top," she added, placing both knees on each side of his hips with his back pressed hard against the cool vinyl seat and her pendulous tits swinging in front of his face.

"You'll soon forget about your troubles," she smiled, bouncing up and down, lifting and lowering, easing him in and easing him out, all the way in and all the way out, in and out, up and down, wriggling and twisting, grinding and thrusting, fucking through a running commentary of filthy curses and choking gasps of approval.

"Oh yes," she whispered. "What a big cock," she groaned. "What a great fuck," she added, lifting and lowering, easing him in and easing him out, the heat of passion manifesting between her legs and rivers of sweat gathering in pools of pleasure on the vinyl seat, curling the corners of her mouth in a gesture of persuasive approval.

"You're making me wet," she moaned, holding him in pubic capture between her legs, squeezing his cock in a vice-like grip and prolonging the moment, moans and groans and euphoric cries of pleasure smothered under the perpetual echoes of shameful filth resonating inside the metal enclosure.

OH, MY GOD! OH, GOD! FUCK ME! FUCK ME FASTER! FUCK ME HARDER! FUCK THE ARSE OFF THIS COCK SUCKING BITCH, she screamed, her dignity evaporating in the heat of passion, her pleas for Gods help accompanied by a shameful outburst of sinful language, never gaining his approval.

"What was that," she gasped, shifting her weight in the seat, the persuasion in her voice momentarily interrupting their moment of passion.

"I thought I heard something. It sounded like a creaking noise," she added, brushing condensation from the glass and pressing her forehead against the steamy window.

"Did you not hear anything?" she asked, blinking her eyes and trying to focus in the darkness.

"FUCK!" she cursed, brushing hair from her face and choking back a lump in her throat.

"The fucking cars moving down the embankment," she screamed, letting his cock slip from her body and jumping up from the seat in a panic.

He couldn't remember the last time he moved so fast.

"I need to get to the steering wheel. Move out of the way and let me get past," he shouted, grabbing her arm and pushing her aside, jumping up from the back seat and trying to squeeze his body through the tight gap between the two front seats.

"Fuck. No," he cursed, one hand searching frantically for the handbrake and the other hand trying to grab the steering wheel.

"Please let the tide be out...Please not in the fucking sea." the mantra repeated inside his head, as the car gathered momentum, rocking and swaying with the uneven terrain and throwing them against the doors and windscreen, like a couple of rag-dolls.

"Brace yourself, Heather" he shouted, as the wheels collided with a solid object, throwing it sideways and into an unrelenting roll down the embankment, a deafening explosion of broken glass raining down inside the vehicle and cutting into flesh, painful cries smothered under the screeching sound of metal ripping apart, just before the car crashed onto the sandy beach.

"Thank fuck for that. What a result," he sighed, lifting his head from the steering wheel and brushing shards of glass and debris from his bruised and battered body, the welcoming sound of the ocean crashing on the shore interrupting the pleading mantra of tidal waters playing inside his head.

"Heather. Where are you?" he croaked, choking back a lump in his throat and staring into the claustrophobic darkness, the familiar smell of engine

oil and petrol spilling from the car, suddenly feeding his panic.
"Fuck me. You can't survive all that and end up being burnt alive," he thought, blinking his eyes into focus and searching through the mangled wreck, peering over the front seats and catching sight of Heathers bruised and battered body lying naked on the floor.
"Heather. Can you hear me. We've got to get out of here," he barked, a rush of adrenaline to his heart and lungs giving him a renewed surge of energy, banging his foot repeatedly against the rear door until it eventually broke free from its hold.
"I've got you. You're going to be okay," he whispered, sucking in air through his nose and pulling her limp body through a small gap in the door.
"I need to get you away from the car," he sighed, ignoring the broken glass torturing his knees and pulling her to a safe distance from the wreckage, mindful to grab his pants on the way.
It would have been a moment to rejoice, if the fuel tank hadn't exploded, sending a mass of metal fragments flying into orbit, in a halo of orange and yellow flames.
"That should interrupt the lovers in the car park," he thought, a flock of seagulls squawking in protest above his head, sweeping and diving in the thermal slipstream along the cliff face, bringing him back to reality and lifting the corners of his mouth in a pleading cry.

"Help...Help," he shouted, blinking his eyes and staring up at the cliff top, choking back a lump in his throat and waving his arms above his head.
"They've seen us Heather," he sighed, pointing a finger at the car headlights shining over the cliff edge, the white glow casting shadowy silhouettes of disturbed lovers standing in a line at the top of the embankment, trying to get a glimpse of the tragedy that had just occurred.
It seemed like a lifetime waiting for the emergency services to arrive. Watching and waiting, shivering in the cold sea breeze and pacing nervously back and forth, listening to Heathers painful cries and staring up at the faceless shadows looking down from the top of the embankment.
"Where's the fucking ambulance," he cursed, slipping into his pants and making a mental note never to ignore warning signs again, the welcoming noise of wailing sirens and a carnival of flashing blue lights above the cliff top breaking his thoughts and drowning out Heathers painful cries.
It took less than ten minutes for the ambulance to reach Newcastle Royal Victoria Hospital.
Heather was rushed into the emergency room to be examined by a doctor, while a nurse attended to his minor cuts and bruises.
"What a fucking mess," he sighed, the comfort of the hospital waiting room giving him time to focus on the reality of another near-death encounter.
'You shouldn't have ignored the warning sign. You were lucky the tide was out. You could have ended up

swimming with the fishes. You could both be in the hospital morgue,' said a familiar voice, somewhere inside his head.

He sighed into his hands, knowing how fortunate he was to walk away from the accident without serious injury. Apart from a slight ache in his right leg and a few minor cuts to his face, knees and feet he was relatively okay.

Heather wasn't so lucky. She was badly hurt in the accident.

His guilty conscience got the better of him. He decided to feign a limp.

"It appears to be getting lighter outside," he sighed, the dark sky beyond the windows turning into a light shade of grey, and the sound of birdsong, in the distance, signalling the beginning of a new day.

He looked at his watch but there was nothing attached to his wrist. *"It's probably in the wreckage,"* he thought, turning his head and glancing at the clock on a white painted wall behind the reception desk.

"Six o'clock," he muttered quietly to himself, picking up a dog-eared glossy magazine with a photograph of a woman wearing a skimpy bikini.

"Nice tits and a great arse," he thought, a squeaking door and the sound of heavy footfalls marching into the waiting room breaking his lustful reverie.

"What," snapped the nurse, sweeping her tongue across her teeth and removing evidence of chocolate from her mouth, forcing a smile and raising both eyebrows at the familiar figure sitting in a chair.

"Not you again," she barked, raising another eyebrow and scowling with disapproval at the magazine in his hand.

"Mark Brand. If I'm not mistaken," she added, shaking her head in disbelief, the mere mention of his name interrupting her early morning food orgy.

"What is it now, or should I say, who is the victim now?" she asked, discretely slipping the chocolate bar back into her pocket.

He was exhausted, and he certainly wasn't in the mood for another lecture from Susan Owen.

"How is she," he sighed, lifting his shoulders in defeat and throwing the magazine on a table.

"How is she," she repeated, shaking her head and reaching inside her pocket.

"Heathers very poorly," she said, biting on the chocolate bar and squeezing his hand, the warmth of her touch and her chocolate coated words unexpectedly sympathetic.

"The doctors are presently examining her injuries. When they've finished, I'll take you to the ward and you can have a few minutes with her in private," she said, exaggerating a wink and pointing a finger at the floor. "Providing that limp of yours improves."

Even after the nurse had cleaned the dried blood from her battered and bruised body and dressed her wounds, Heather still looked dreadful.

"Hi. It's me. Mark. How are you," he croaked, pulling up a chair at the side of her bed and holding her hand, forcing a smile and choking back a lump in

his throat, trying to find some comforting words that would ease the excruciating anxiety.
"I'm so sorry," he sighed. "When you're better, I'll make it up to you. I promise" he offered, kissing her bandaged forehead and giving her hand a gentle squeeze.
"Don't worry about me. Are you okay?" she whispered, pointing a finger at the cuts and bruises on his face.
"My leg aches a little," he said, touching his thigh and feigning pain, the swishing noise of the privacy curtain being pulled along a rail and the authority in Susan Owens voice announcing that his visiting time was over, interrupting his shameful charade.
"I'll see you later," he smiled, lifting to his feet and leaning over the bed, holding the kiss long enough until the nurse looked away.
"I've just had a thought," he whispered in her ear, looking nervously over his shoulder, the question bringing an unexpected smile to her swollen lips.
"With everything that's happened...I wondered if you had remembered to remove Trap 2."
"Don't worry, I've taken care of him," was all she said.
Heather Chapman sustained a broken collar-bone, a broken arm, three broken ribs and several deep cuts and bruises to her face and upper body.
The headlines in that nights evening newspaper read, *'Love on the Rocks.'*

A Question of Gender (circa-1980)

If someone had told him that one day he would fuck a middle-aged woman with a broken leg, who would then persuade him to join a swinger's club and participate in group sex in a room full of faceless strangers, he would have said they were on drugs or completely mad.

But there he was leaving the Cavendish Club with a fifty-year old woman with a leg in a plaster cast, swinging on crutches and holding his arm as if her life depended on it, heading to his car through a chorus of wheezes and gasps and filthy curses.

From the moment, he walked into the club, Sarah Davison made her intentions very clear.

A flirtatious acquaintance and the price of a drink at the bar was all it took. Without shame or decorum Sarah asked him if he'd ever fucked a drunken woman with a broken leg.

Bold brazen and cheap, too much makeup and too much mascara, a skirt, too short and explosive tits spilling out of a blouse with too many buttons undone. For a woman who looked like she made a living from porn, Sarah Davison was still sexy enough to stir a movement inside his pants.

The directions to her home were a little vague and her finger pointing West was even less convincing. Nevertheless, he started the car and headed East towards Ellington Village.

After a week of blistering temperatures souring into the high-seventies, the humidity of the early morning promised to be no different.

"It's a warm night," he said, trying to break the silence and build a conversation. "How's the leg?" he added, waiting for a reply that never came.

"Cigarette," he offered, swerving the car and pressing his foot hard on the brake, thinking she might have fallen asleep.

"Bloody cats," he muttered, blowing smoke through a small gap in the window.

"Yes, it's a warm night. My leg hurts, and I didn't see a cat. I wasn't sleeping," she smiled, taking a cigarette from his outstretched hand.

"You'll wish you hadn't kept me awake because whenever I'm drunk, all I talk about is my husband and his infidelity," she sighed, lighting her cigarette and blowing smoke against the windscreen.

"Husband," he barked, easing his foot off the accelerator pedal.

"Don't worry. He's six feet under. He died from a massive heart attack a couple of years ago," she said, brushing hair from her face and searching inside a bag, the sobering moment giving her time to gather her thoughts.

"He was a two-faced bastard," she barked, dropping her cigarette out the window and pulling another one from the packet.

"He never hid the fact that he had other women in his life. In fact, he made it obvious to everyone, including me, that he was leading a double life with

a woman half his fucking age," she growled, lighting the cigarette.
"He was a monster. A cruel and unforgiving man," she confessed, her speech slightly slurred.
"If I ever questioned him about the other women he would physically beat me. Most people weren't aware of his violent temper because he always made sure the bruises were in places that weren't on show," she sobbed, wiping her eyes with a paper tissue.
Listening to Sarah vent her anger made him a little uncomfortable and there were times when he found it difficult to concentrate on driving the car. He didn't really care about her husband's infidelity or her failed marriage, but with a guaranteed fuck on offer he just kept his eyes on the road and said nothing.
"Fucking bastard," she cursed, removing a compact mirror from her handbag and checking her bruised mascara, knowing she might have said too much and was probably boring the pants off him, but mindful that she had also promised him a fuck.
She repaired her face and continued.
"I hated him so much there were times when I wished he was dead," she said, an unexpected smile lifting the corners of her mouth.
"I have to confess on the morning I discovered he was dead it was an amazing relief. In fact, I celebrated the occasion with a glass of wine before calling the emergency services," she sighed, flashing her eyes and pulling on her cigarette.

"I actually considered not going to his funeral because I knew I would have to present a sad persona to his family and friends, and no doubt some of his faceless mistresses."

It was a question he immediately regretted asking, but the words had already left his mouth.

"Do I ever think of him," she laughed, rolling her eyes and twisting her face with furtive amusement.

"Only when I'm cutting sausages," she replied, with mocking sarcasm.

"We need to make a slight detour before we go to my house," she smiled, the authority in her voice interrupting any further conversation about infidelity or death.

"Take the next left at this junction," she added, giving his thigh a gentle squeeze, as he changed down through the gears and pulled into a small car park next to the main entrance of Ellington Methodist Church.

"It's something I have to do," she sighed, taking her crutches from the back seat of the car.

"This won't take long. I promise," she smiled, brushing hair from her face and hobbling unsteadily on her feet.

"This way. Follow me," she insisted, the metal gates to the cemetery, creaking on rusty hinges.

In the warm morning air and under the bright glow of a full moon, he followed on her heels, weaving through a sea of headstones, eventually stopping when they came to a grave with her husband's name engraved on a low piece of white marble.

"He often said that he had to get oral stimulation from his other women because I wouldn't suck-him-off," she whispered, under a chorus of chirping crickets.

"Well, Robert Davison. I hope you're fucking watching," she cursed, dropping her crutches to the ground and lifting her leg onto the gravel stones, ignoring the decomposing wreath of a loved one crushed beneath her plaster cast.

"Stand behind the headstone," she motioned, with a sweeping hand, flashing her eyes and hovering precariously with both feet on the grave.

"Take your cock out," she said, in a surreptitious whisper and a persuasive gesture.

"What's that," he croaked, glancing nervously over his shoulders, the untimely hooting of an owl somewhere in the darkness, momentarily interrupting his hand fumbling with his belt buckle and zip.

"Fucking owl," he cursed, lowering his pants to his knees and unfolding the gruesome piece of flesh from the warm confines of his briefs, the long white column bobbing and swaying in the moonlight, casting sinister shadows over the dead and forgotten.

"Fuck me," she gasped. "Another monster in my life," she smiled, her eyes widening and her lips parting as she eased him into her warm mouth.

"I hope you've got that registered as a dangerous weapon" she mockingly teased, sucking the swollen limb with eagerness on the way in and dragging her teeth over the length on the way out, easing him in

and easing him out, never once taking her eyes off her husband's headstone.
The blow-job was given with the well-practiced skill and creative longevity that you would expect from a scorned and bitter woman, although the running commentary of filth at her husband's headstone wasn't really necessary.
"I don't want to finish you here. Take me home," she said, letting him slip from her mouth.
The untimely death of her husband and the final resolution of his business affairs must have left Sarah Davison financially at ease. The five-bedroom detached house on a small residential estate in the leafy hamlet of Ellington village was truly outstanding.
It was never going to be easy. The plaster cast was always going to make it awkward and complicated. Just removing her clothes and getting her into bed was a libido deflating task.
"Let me help you onto the bed. I'll have to fuck you from the back," he casually announced, lifting her up until she was kneeling precariously on the end of the bed with her arms supporting her weight and both hands flat on the mattress.
"What a fucking nightmare," she sighed, half on the floor and half on the bed, one leg straight and one leg bent, a guiding hand reaching back and easing the fleshy limb between the slippery flaps and folds.
The entry from the rear was unexpectedly effortless, the penetration powerful and deep and the carnal connection compelling and possessive.

"Let me know if it hurts," he said, unconvincingly, moving his hips back and forth with ruthless determination, a brutal and uncompromising demonstration of persuasive interaction, a responsive expression of unquenchable virility, battering her broken body into painful submission, a tireless and unforgiving bed rattling fuck, given with no concern or respect for her condition.
She screamed. She pleaded. She cursed. She panted. She moaned and groaned, through a running commentary of euphoric cries and filthy curses, the crucial point of climax explosive, his balls erupting and the dam breaking, the sweating mass of a mature woman swimming in a sea of euphoric bliss, the outpouring of communal fluids wet, sticky, messy, sustained and momentous, a tit wobbling, toe-curling, leg-shaking release, sucking the last breath of air from her lungs.

Sarah's persistent snoring kept him awake most of the night, but it was the sound of a car pulling onto the driveway that got him on his feet.
"What the fuck does he want," he thought, peering through a small gap in the curtains, blinking his eyes and trying to focus in the darkness, the shadowy silhouette of a uniformed man stepping from a police car and walking towards the front door of the house, feeding his panic.
"Wake up Sarah," he grunted, pulling the duvet back and shaking her arm.

"There's a copper at your door," he cursed, his voice melodramatic and a little too high.
"What's the police doing here," he sighed, lowering his voice an octave and pacing nervously across the room, a touch of OCD forcing him to straighten a tilted picture frame hanging on the wall, before peering through the curtains again and waiting for a knock at the door that never came.
"Don't worry," she sighed, blinking her eyes and catching a glimpse of her naked body.
"It's only 'Speed' coming home from his shift," she added, pulling the duvet back, decency demanding that she cover up her middle-aged spread and an unsightly caesarean scar.
"My leg hurts, you animal," she sighed, ignoring his anxiety, leaning over the bed and turning the table light on, yawning into her hand and checking the time on the clock.
"Speed....Who the fuck is Speed?" he barked, his head spinning in utter confusion and his heart beat increasing by the second.
"That's his nickname. We live together," she said, with casual ease, the ominous sound of heavy footfalls, thudding across the living room floor, twisting his face with anger and a question waiting at the back of his throat.
"What do you mean. We live together?" he barked, choking back a lump in his throat and gathering his clothes from the bedroom floor.
"This could get fucking nasty," he thought, pulling up his pants and slipping into his shoes, scanning the

room for opening windows, just in case he needed to make a quick exit.

"Relax, Mark. Trust me. Speed's not a jealous or violent man," she said, defensively, smiling through a long throaty yawn.

"A fucking copper, who takes fucking speed, is not something I find amusing," he sighed, sitting on the edge of the bed, fastening his shoe laces and slipping into his shirt, watching and waiting through the nausea of disquiet filling the room.

A polite voice echoing up the stairs, broke the crippling silence.

"Sarah, sweetheart...I'm making coffee. Would you like me to bring you one up?"

"He wants to know if you want coffee," he gasped, turning his head and staring into her eyes, his facial expression steadfast and uncompromising, waving a threatening finger and moving his head from side-to-side, signalling that her answer should definitely be no.

"Yes please, Speed.... And will you bring one up for my friend, Mark?" she answered, in a calm voice with no emotion.

"How does Mark take his coffee?" he enquired, his voice fading into silence as he waited anxiously for confirmation.

"He wants to know how I like my fucking coffee," he repeated, sighing into his hands and choking back a lump in his throat. *"Laced with a dozen paracetamol tablets, if I was a betting man,"* he muttered silently.

"Well, how do you like it?" Sarah teased, smiling at his nervousness, her face smeared with black mascara and red lipstick, casually patting a hand on the pillow and adjusting her weight on the bed.

He stood up. He sighed. He sat back down, before lowering his voice to a furtive whisper.

"What the fucks going on," he cursed, running his hand across the back of his neck.

"He must know I've been shagging his woman and all he wants to do is make me fucking coffee?"

"Relax. He just wants to know how you like your coffee," she giggled, rolling her eyes and twisting her face in a gesture of playful amusement.

"Strong and black with no sugar," he sighed, the haunting sound of footfalls echoing up the creaking stairs with agonising slowness, interrupting the brief moment of laughter and getting him back on his feet.

"I'm ready for you. Come and get it" he muttered under his breath, the cold reality of confrontation hanging in the air, clenching and unclenching his fists and scanning the room for a weapon, catching sight of Sarah's crutches lying on the floor next to the bed.

"Copper or no copper," he thought, staring at the door, watching and waiting, the cold chill of fear washing over him, the hairs standing on the back of his neck and goose pimples growing on every part of his body.

"Fuck me," he croaked, his brain radiating assertive hostility and his mind conjuring images of a violent man with the build of a gladiator, carrying an axe with only one thing on his mind.

"Come in," Sarah invited, sitting up in bed and pulling the duvet up, covering the scratch marks on her tits and a couple of large hickeys, developing on her inner thighs.

"Speed, this is my friend Mark," she announced, with a thin smile and a sweeping hand. "We met last night in the Cavendish Club. He's been a complete gentleman."

There was an eerie silence for a few seconds with both men locked in eye-to-eye contact until the short skinny man with enormous ears and big feet, eventually placed the coffee cups on the bedside table and offered a friendly hand.

Speed left the room to take a shower. He breathed a sigh of relief. Sarah confessed.

"My relationship with Speed is sexually compliant," she smiled, brushing hair from her face and sipping her coffee.

"We have no secrets or hidden agendas. We both have other sexual partners, and we both like to indulge in group-swapping. Swinging, we like to call it, or social interaction with like-minded people who want to engage in sexual activities with other couples. We are both committed swingers," she smiled, flashing her eyes and lifting her cup to her mouth.

"We are members of a private swinger's club in Sunderland, 'The Brandling Club.' Have you heard of it?" she enquired, taking a tissue from a box on the bedside table and removing a smearing of red lipstick from the rim of her cup.

"No, I can't say I have," he replied, sipping his coffee and catching a whiff of his fingers, the bitter smell reminding him of an old pair of shoes.

"Then I must take you there one evening, as my guest. You'll enjoy it. I know my female friends would enjoy you," she said, a persuasive smile lifting the corners of her mouth.

"Emily would like to meet you. She's a nymphomaniac who loves to fuck well-endowed men, while her husband looks on. Her deep throat techniques are legendary," she giggled.

"You must promise to come one night," she offered, pulling the duvet back and exposing a mass of middle-aged flesh.

"I'll ring you," she smiled, narrowing her eyes and shifting her weight on the bed, lying on her side with her head resting on one elbow, waiting patiently for an answer.

"Sorry about the leg," he said, avoiding the question and casting an eye over her plump white body, the uncanny image bearing a remarkable likeness to one of Ruben's nudes.

"Fuck the leg, although I think your bedroom acrobatics might have loosened the plaster cast," she laughed.

"I'm a sexually neglected widow," she sighed, pursing her bottom lip and feigning puppy dog eyes.

"I would do it all over again, if I had the chance," she said, an impudent smile lifting the corners of her mouth with persuasive intent.

"So, can I ring you and arrange a threesome. In about two weeks. When my plaster cast is removed?" she brazenly asked, the shameless invitation making him cough into his cup.
The precarious act of copulating with women while husbands and strangers or even weirdos looked on with voyeuristic intrigue certainly had a dark appeal, he thought, the surreptitious invitation to swing with her nymphomaniac friend Emily, enough to inspire an impetuous decision.
"How can I refuse such an offer," he replied with a noncommittal shrug of his shoulders, catching a glimpse of her stained knickers lying on the floor, glancing at his watch and placing his empty cup on the bedside table.

"Rosebud," Sarah announced, confirming the password into a stainless-steel voice box on a black painted door.
"Hello Sarah," said a security man, peering through a viewer in the door, the sound of a deadlock disengaging from its housing giving them access into the Brandling Club.
A female receptionist dressed in a white tunic with eye-watering tits, long legs and a permanent smile, welcomed Sarah and her guests at reception.
"Sarah Davison," greeted a fat man in his mid-fifties with a young attractive woman in her early-twenties, both wrapped in nothing but a towel.
"It's always good to see you," he smiled, kissing Sarah on both cheeks and giving Speed an

overpowering bear hug, casting a cautious eye at their guest before extending his hand.

"Harold," he offered, holding the handshake long enough to introduce the young gold-digger, hanging on his arm.

"I'm the owner of the club. And this is Tina" he smiled, pointing a finger at the beautiful model-like-creature standing next to him.

"Mark," he politely responded, pulling his hand away from his sweaty palm and staring wide eyed at the sex goddess, young enough to be his daughter.

"I've made some changes to the club, since the last time you were here. Let me give you and your guest a quick tour of the facilities," Harold volunteered, punching a code number into a security-controlled door. "Follow me," he smiled, the dreamy serenade of Haydn's violin string quartet filtering through overhead speakers, as they walked along a dimly lit corridor.

"The rooms are self-explanatory," he said, pointing a finger at the brass nameplates on the doors, the signs indicative of the sexual interaction inside each room.

Dark Room. Sauna. Fun Room. Bondage Room. Massage Room. Spanking Room. Porn Room.

"Please note that some of the doors are equipped with peep-holes," he smiled. "They offer intimate examination for those with voyeuristic curiosity," he added, looking through one of the holes.

"That rooms my favourite," Sarah said, flashing her eyes and pointing a finger at a door.

"We must visit the 'Dark Room' or the 'Grope Room' as some like to call it. You can't imagine what goes in there," she smiled, giving his hand a gentle squeeze.
"This is 'The Social Room,' often referred to as 'The Playground of Sin. It's where most people spend their time," Harold smiled, opening another door.
"You didn't tell me Michelangelo was a member," he said, in playful amusement, casting an eye over a tableau of phallic symbols and images of men and women in different stages of copulation decorating the walls and the ceiling of a circular swimming pool.
"Art doesn't do anything for me. I like the real thing," she said, brushing hair from her face. "That's what I like. That's what turns me on," she smiled, flashing her eyes and pointing a finger at a middle-aged man with a forest of grey hair on his chest, fucking a woman from the rear as she casually practiced the art of fellatio on a younger man sitting on the side of the pool.
"And that," she added, a gaggle of men and women, actively engaged in various stages of sexual arousal, groping and fondling in a circular hot-tub in a recess at the end of the room.
"Welcome to the playground of sin," Harold smiled. "Have fun," he added, removing their towels and placing them on a chair next to the door.
"Rules of the house," Harold grinned, "Everyone must take a shower," he added, smacking Tina's naked bottom with one hand and scratching his balls with the other.

"I've no objection to the rules," he muttered under his breath, staring shamefully at her shapely breasts and curvy bottom, only breaking his gaze to blink and breathe.

"She's a breath-taking beauty. What's she doing with him? She could have any man she wanted. She could have me," he thought, lowering his hands and making a quick adjustment to the untimely awakening inside his pants.

"We'll join you in the shower room," Harold said, picking up the towels from the chair and heading towards a door at the side of the pool.

"I'm coming. Wait for me," Tina smiled, skipping across the floor like an angel, swaying her hips like a cat-walk model and flaunting her hour-glass figure to perfection.

"You'll be coming if I find you in the Dark Room," he thought, following on the heels of Sarah and Speed.

Just standing next to Tina in the shower was enough to give you a sexual experience.

"How's the leg, Sarah?" Harold enquired. "You had a plaster cast on the last time we met. Broken leg, wasn't it? I hope it didn't affect your love life," he grinned, picking up a container and soaping his balls with a sponge.

"You know me. I would never let a plaster cast get in the way of a good fuck," she smiled, pouring shampoo from a bottle and soaping her hair, listening to Mark's best leg-opener lines and smiling at his futile attempts to control his emotions.

"What a stunning figure. What a beautiful pair of tits. What a fantastic arse," he thought, wondering why this iconic beauty wasn't on the front cover of every celebrity magazine.

"Shampoo," he offered, handing Tina the container.

"Just let me know if you need any help with the shampoo," he jested, watching the streams of soapy water cascading over her shapely breasts, spilling over impossible curves and disappearing between the cheeks of her bottom.

"I'll let you know," she winked, lowering her hands and running her fingers through her pubic bush, the petals of the most delicate little flower, peeking through the soapy shroud and promising hours of flirtatious entertainment.

"I'm not sure if there's enough shampoo in the bottle," she playfully mocked, handing him the container and glancing at the gruesome appendage hanging in a curve over his left thigh.

"Christ. I'm getting a lazy on" he thought, hoping that in the vaporous atmosphere of the shower the untimely swelling had gone unnoticed.

"Don't ask questions and don't ask anyone their names," Sarah whispered, as they left the shower room and headed for the hot-tub. "It's another rule of the club," she confirmed, lifting her shoulders and forcing a smile.

"If they offer their name, that's fine. Just be aware that most people who come here insist on discretion and confidentiality," she added, a mischievous smile lifting the corners of her mouth.

"You can fuck them. But don't ask questions," she grinned, flashing her eyes and climbing into the hot-tub.

"That's my friend Emily. The one surrounded by men," Sarah whispered, nodding her head in a gesture of furtive direction.

"She'll be over here before you can blink an eye," she smiled, brushing water from her face and waving a welcoming hand at her friend.

"Welcome to the Brandling Club, Mark," Emily whispered, gazing into his eyes and running her fingers through his hair.

"Sarah was right. She said you were handsome. She's told me all about you," she smiled, flashing her eyes and brushing hair from her face.

"And I know she's told you all about me," she added, lowering her hands beneath the water in a gesture of flirtatious enquiry.

"Fuck me, Sarah wasn't exaggerating about that," she giggled, wrapping her fingers around the fleshy muscle and squeezing his balls.

"I like a man with a big cock," she teased, tugging and pulling beneath the water, feeling the swollen limb growing rapidly in her hand.

"And a cute little arse," she added, sliding a finger between the cheeks of his bottom and probing his anus.

"The Dark Room," someone shouted, the eager invitation getting a triumphant cheer from everyone fondling and groping inside the hot-tub.

"It was a woman's voice. It didn't sound like Tina. It was probably Emily. But who gives a fuck. Once I get them in the Dark Room, I can fuck them both," he thought, following quickly on the heels of Emily and Tina, like some kind of predatory stalker.

"The firmness of youth," he thought, staring at Tina's shapely little bottom, lifting and lowering with every step.

"The maturity of an older woman," he smiled, shifting his eyes to Emily and catching sight of a couple of cellulite marks on her bottom and thighs, the crimson flush colouring her buttocks, betraying her fondness for spanking.

"You can't see a thing in here," Sarah, smiled. "Most people just navigate by touch and feel. It's a lot of fun," she giggled, taking his hand as they entered the Dark Room.

Under the soothing aria of *Nessun dorma,* a dozen or more naked bodies, all eager to engage in coital interaction, moved slowly and precariously inside the room.

"Be careful who you touch and what you feel," she laughed, blinking her eyes and pushing her way through a tangle of heated bodies.

"Don't say I didn't warn you," she added, invisible hands groping and fondling in the darkness, touching and squeezing, probing and sucking, faceless people leaving soft sounds of pleasure, hidden beneath a surreptitious veil of mystery.

"I thought I'd join you and Mark," Emily whispered, slipping her hand around his waist.

"I've already examined the goods in the hot-tub and now I want to see if it works," she giggled, lowering to the floor on her knees.

"You're not getting him all to yourself," Sarah whispered, lowering to the floor and wrapping her fingers around the fleshy limb.

"Wow. A fucking threesome," he muttered, the sensuous feeling of being consumed by two hot mouths gaining his approval and firing a surge of blood into his swollen muscle.

"No teeth, Sarah," he jested, as she sucked the meaty length with eager enthusiasm, easing him in and easing him out, running her tongue over the scrotum and licking his balls.

"Sarah's got the front door covered. It looks like I'll just have to use the back door," Emily giggled, grabbing his buttocks and pulling the cheeks apart, slipping her tongue inside the hairy crack and rimming his anus.

"I'll have to get up. My knees are sore," Sarah sighed, letting his cock slip from her mouth.

"Me too," Emily added, giving his bottom a parting kiss before lifting from the floor.

"Don't go too far. I'll be back for more," Emily announced, disappearing into the claustrophobic darkness like a sexual junkie, searching for cock.

"Where the fucks Tina?" he sighed, searching blindly through a veil of darkness, like a phantom stalker going in pursuit of the breath-taking beauty.

"I can hear her voice. She's not too far away," he thought, the promise of a fuck or even a blow-job

heightening expectation and quickening the pace in his step.

"It's coming from somewhere over there," he muttered under his breath, blinking his eyes and pushing through a sea of overheated bodies, the acquaintance of a warm hand stopping him in his tracks and lifting the corners of his mouth in a gesture of furtive enquiry.

"Is that you Tina?" he whispered, breathing a sigh of relief and running his fingers through her short blonde hair, the thrill of discovery bringing a smile to his face.

"I've been looking everywhere for you," he added, the warmth of her mouth moving south over his stomach and her fingers curling around the long thick muscle, letting him know the moment was real.

"Oh yes," he gasped, one of her hands cradling his balls and the other hand working his cock back and forth with increasing determination, fisting and pulling, tugging and stroking, running her tongue along the fleshy limb and swirling and dancing around the bulbous head, easing him in and easing him out, sucking his manhood from the root to the head and feasting hungrily on the sticky fluids oozing from the small eye.

"That's so fucking good, Tina," he cursed, putting his hands on her head and moving his hips, as the music moved into a crescendo. "Don't stop. I'm almost there," he urged, persuasive gestures, moans and groans and euphoric cries of pleasure lost in the spirited overture.

"I'm coming. I'm fucking coming," he gasped, his balls exploding and a sea of seminal fluids firing up his shaft, the release powerful and unforgiving, the sticky mess spilling in endless bursts inside her mouth.

The thought of another flirtatious liaison with Tina was the only reason he went back to the Brandling Club, one more time with Sarah and Speed.

The evening followed the same routine. Lots of tangled bodies fondling and groping in a commentary of persuasive gestures and a vocal exchange of orgasmic mutterings, the true reality of gender lost in the dark obsession of conspiratorial uncertainty.

The experience was certainly liberating, and the spontaneous sexual indulgence was also erotic and stimulating, but the sexual interaction with virtual strangers and the uncertainty of gender, always made him feel a little uncomfortable.

There was a slight tone of disappointment in Sarah's voice when he rang to explain his reason for not going back to The Brandling Club.

She sniggered into the mouthpiece when he mentioned gender.

What she said next, left him speechless.

She said she was surprised that he wasn't aware that Speed was bisexual and most of the other members of the club were either bisexual or homosexual.

There was nothing more he could say. His mouth was dry and wordless. He choked back a lump in his throat and dropped the phone into the cradle in humiliating retreat.

The brashness of her statement had his head swimming in a sea of utter confusion and his subconscious tracing through a paradox of fragmented hypothesis.

"Fuck no," he thought, reaching for his cigarettes, conflicting scenarios flashing across the memory screen inside his head, the haunting vision of faceless people performing sexual acts under a veil of anonymity inside the dark room, filling his head with absurd thoughts.

"No! Oh, shit. No!" he thought. *Surely Not....No Fucking Way....Not a Chance....They were all women who....Weren't they....It was Tina who....It must have been Tina...He remembered feeling her short hair.*

"Fuck me," he gulped, lighting his cigarette, the reckless assumptions of sexual orientation and the taboo and the uncertainty of gender feeding his panic.

Were they searching for anything, or were they looking for someone in particular. Surely, I couldn't have been touched by....No....No....No Fucking Way, the mantra kept repeating, inside his head.

He Looked Familiar (circa-1982)

When Brenda Morton entered a room, her tits came first, and the rest followed.

"Come inside," she invited, flashing her eyes and taking a quick tour over the smart young man old enough to be her son.

"I was expecting someone older," she said, raising an eyebrow and forcing a smile, a swoop of waves falling over her shoulders, in that 1940's Lauren Bacall style.

"Please take that age thing as a compliment," she smiled, brushing hair from her face and lighting a cigarette.

"Everyone looks so young these days, unless it's just me getting older," she sighed, rolling her eyes and playing with a silver pendant hanging on a chain around her neck.

"Follow me into the living-room," she said, blowing smoke above her head and swaying her hips in a graceful walk, a waist squeezing belt showing shapely curves and black seamed stockings growing from a pair of towering heels.

"My mother-in-law…Grace," she offered, pointing a finger at a frail old woman sitting in a wheelchair in a spacious conservatory at the rear of the house, the back of her head just visible above the top of the chair.

"She's ninety-four," she sighed, opening a door and stepping into the conservatory, her heels clicking on the ceramic floor tiles. "Hello Grace. I've got some business to attend to. I'll just make you comfortable," she said, adjusting her pillow and pulling a woollen blanket over her blue-veined hands.

"I won't be long," she smiled, pulling a paper tissue from a box and wiping traces of saliva from the corners of her mouth.

No movement. No reaction. No signs that she even knew they were there.

It was difficult to tell whether Grace was sleeping, or her life had already ended.

"The dining-room will give us some privacy to discuss the building proposals," she smiled, opening a door from the living-room and settling into comfortable chairs at a polished table, a bottle of wine and two glasses on a silver tray, a little unexpected.

"I want to give my mother-in-law the privacy and dignity she deserves," she said, brushing a tear from her eye and pouring wine into two glasses.

"I know it's a little early," she smiled, brushing a whisper of hair from her face and ignoring his protest for half a glass.

"We require a ground-floor extension at the rear of the house with provision for a bedroom and an accessible bathroom for a wheelchair user," she said, shifting her weight in the chair, leaning over and pulling a piece of paper from a drawer.

"My husband has made a rough sketch," she smiled, regaining her posture in the chair and smoothing out a folded piece of paper on the table.

"He thought it might help. But he's not an architect," she sighed, lifting her glass to her mouth, a huge pair of tits and a dangerous cleavage spilling out of a white silk blouse.

"You're the professional. I'll leave it up to you," she added, sipping her wine and fondling with the buttons on her blouse, flashing her eyes and nodding her head as she listened to his briefing on the design and building proposals.

"It's going to take me about an hour to survey the house," he said, quickly refocusing his eyes when he realised he was talking to her tits, glancing at his watch and picking up his tape measure and file notes from the table.

"If you have no objection....Mrs Morton....I'll get started on the survey."

"I can see I'm in good hands," she whispered, flashing her eyes and sipping her wine.

"Please call me Brenda. And you must let me know if I can hold something for you," she smiled, brushing hair from her face and giving his hand a gentle squeeze

A door from the kitchen led into a delightful landscaped garden at the rear of the house.

"Cigarette," she offered, interrupting his inspection of the drainage system, the brief interlude for a smoke giving him time to admire the beautiful arrangement of shrubs bordering a manicured lawn and a cluster of mature trees at the bottom of the garden.

"I'm afraid some of the shrubs will have to be removed," he sighed, stretching a tape measure across the ground and pointing a finger at the proposed building line.
"That's okay. I'll get my gardener to dig them up and replant them at the bottom of the garden," she said, shrugging her shoulders and pulling on her cigarette, a flirtatious gesture lifting the corners of her mouth.
"I've got another bush that needs some special care and attention," she smiled, dropping her cigarette into a drain and walking back into the house.
"Is it just flirtatious innuendo, or is she hitting on me" he thought, pulling the tape measure across the living-room floor, with Brenda following on his heels like a bothersome fly, a glass of wine in one hand and a cigarette in the other, her life story unfolding in his wake.
"I'll just take a couple of measurements in here," he said, stepping from the living-room and into a brightly lit entrance hall, a framed photograph of a man and woman on a small table next to a grandfather clock, keeping his interest, while Brenda disappeared into the kitchen to get another bottle of wine.
'She's younger, but it's definitely Brenda. The man must be her husband. 'He looks familiar,' he thought, pausing to study the photograph and scanning his memory files for familiar faces, trying to remember where he had seen him.

"I've got all the information I need," he confirmed, glancing at his watch and picking up his jacket and survey notes from the table.

"If there's nothing more I'll...."

"There is," she said, grabbing him by the arm and guiding him back into the living-room.

"I can't let you go without giving you something to eat," she smiled, pointing a finger at a plate of sandwiches and a bottle of Pinot Grigio, waiting on a coffee table in front of a sofa.

"Come and sit down," she invited, patting a hand on the sofa, smiling into his eyes and pouring wine into glasses.

"Cheers," she toasted, raising her glass and handing him a cigarette.

"Let's not talk about buildings. I think it's time to change the subject," she whispered, lighting her cigarette and picking up a photograph album from the floor.

"Let me show you some of my photographs," she smiled, shuffling up close on the sofa, letting him feel the heat of her breasts pushing against his arm, her body language seductive and her voice laden with flirtatious suggestion.

"Okay," he answered, biting into a sandwich and lifting his glass to his mouth, the closeness meaningful and deliberate, the intimacy and familiarity a little unexpected.

"I'll not bore you with the wedding photographs," she said, skipping randomly over a dozen pages, cursing at some old photographs and laughing at others.

"These are more interesting," she said, smiling at a holiday photograph.

"What do you think," she smiled, the promiscuous outfit of tight-fitting white shorts and a pair of knee-length leather boots, putting a smile on his face and getting his undivided attention.

"You look fantastic in those white shorts," he offered, the unexpected compliment boosting her ego and flushing her face.

"Do you think so," she smiled, brushing her fingers through her hair and pouring wine into glasses, her smile widening and her confidence growing.

"That was taken on my thirtieth-birthday," she said, closing her eyes and counting back the years inside her head.

"Almost twenty-two years ago," she lied into her glass, turning quickly on the sofa and catching a glimpse of the promising bulge inside his pants.

"Wait a second," she blurted, a sudden flash of memory breaking the nostalgic interlude.

"I think I've still got those white shorts in my bedroom wardrobe," she announced, flashing her eyes and lifting off the sofa.

"Come upstairs with me," she insisted, taking his wine glass from his hand, placing it on the table and pulling him to his feet.

"They're in here somewhere," she smiled, opening the wardrobe door and searching impatiently inside a drawer, breathing a deep sigh of relief when she found the white shorts.

"Turn around and close your eyes," she giggled, kicking her heels across the floor and shuffling her feet, clothes riding up and buttons coming undone.

"I'm nearly there," she whispered, wriggling her hips and sliding her skirt to her feet, deep intakes of breaths and frustrated sighs joining a commentary of undignified curses.

"I'm ready. You can turn around now," she said, humming a tune inside her head and playing with the silver chain around her neck.

"Well. What do you think?" she smiled, twisting and turning with both hands on her hips, craning her neck and admiring her bottom in the full-length mirror.

"After all these years, they still fit," she whispered, performing a theatrical pirouette in the mirror, the white fabric clinging to her arse like a second skin, stretching over plump cheeks and disappearing into the long crack of her bottom.

"I told you so. I can hardly believe I can still get into them," she said, forcing a smile and spinning on her heels, a bulging vulva and a discerning camel-toe imprinted in the tight fabric and a forest of pubic hair spilling from both side of her shorts, leaving nothing to the imagination.

"Well. Do you like what you see?" she smiled, sweeping her tongue over her top lip with flirtatious suggestion, wrapping her arms around his neck and kissing his mouth.

"Well that's a good sign," she smiled, feeling the growing limb inside his pants, pressing against her thigh.

"Yes. I do," he muttered, the familiar movement a reminder that even in her mid-fifties, Brenda Morton was still sexy enough to get him hard.

"Yes, I do. Yes, I do. Is that all I get. What about. You look fantastic," she smiled, lifting her eyes in contempt and sitting him on the edge of the bed, the smouldering heat of passion burning between her thighs and the inviting camel-toe almost touching his face.

"It'll do for now," he grinned, proximity and expectation reacting to impulsive urges, slipping his finger into the deep groove, sweeping over the fleshy lips and teasing the clitoris, feeling the warmth and the wetness seeping through the cotton fabric, lowering his head and breathing in the smell of mature sex.

"I need to pee," she announced, taking his hand, the shameless invitation to follow her into the bathroom somewhat unexpected, but nevertheless an offer he couldn't refuse.

"Too much wine," she said, the urgency to pee brushing away any thought for modesty.

"Fucking shorts," she cursed, shuffling her feet on the floor and wriggling her hips.

"I didn't expect to be taking them off so quickly," she sighed, sucking in air through her nose, before pulling the white shorts to her ankles.

"Just made it," she gasped, flashing her eyes and pissing like a horse into the white ceramic bowl, a thin smile lifting the corners of her mouth with flirtatious intent.

"Come a little closer," she smiled, brushing hair from her face and catching a glimpse of the bulge inside his pants.

"I need to examine the goods," she teased, shifting her weight on the toilet seat and pulling his pants to the floor.

"Wow. I wasn't expecting that," she gasped, lifting the heavy object from his briefs and gazing in admiration at the semi-erect piece of flesh hanging like a fire hose in front of her face.

"It's huge…Can I keep it," she smiled, flashing her eyes and wrapping her fingers around the meaty shaft, feeling the gruesome muscle growing rapidly in her hand.

"This is the first time I've sucked a cock and had a piss at the same time," she laughed, digging her manicured nails into his buttocks, pulling him forward and taking him into her mouth.

"But there's always a first time for everything," she smiled, sucking the length from the tip to the root, easing him in and easing him out, sweeping her tongue in playful circles around the bulbous helmet, dipping into the single eye and feasting on the sticky essence of youth, blinking her eyes and removing a thin stream of saliva, drooping from the bell-end to her lips.

"It's been too long. I need to feel a man inside me," she whispered, letting him slip from her mouth and lifting from the ceramic pan, a discernible clitoris the size of a finger nail peeking through a forest of pubic hair, keeping his interest while she struggled with her shorts.

"Give me a moment," she sighed, sucking in air through her nose, irritating sighs and filthy curses, joining a pantomime of undignified twists and frustrated turns.

"Nearly done," she gasped, two hands working with the skill of a contortionist, eventually squeezing her middle-aged flesh back into her shorts.

He was heading for the bedroom when he felt his shirt being pulled.

"Not that way," she whispered, brushing hair from her face and wiping a smear of lipstick from the corner of his mouth.

"In the living-room," she insisted, taking his hand and skipping down the stairs with the eagerness of a teenager, glancing into the conservatory, no surprise to find her mother-in-law still sleeping, probably unaware that they had even been out of the room.

"I can't believe I'm doing this," she smiled, an adventurous heart beating with the promise of coital intimacy and a conventional exterior concealing a furtive passion hidden too long by a reserved upbringing.

"I want you to fuck me here...In the living-room…In front of my mother-in-law," she insisted, a refined lady changing into a sluttish wanton nymph, a desperate woman with an overwhelming desire to fuck, a flirtatious smile and persuasive words already forming on her lips, her dignity left on the bathroom floor.

"It's risky. I'm a little nervous," she smiled, a familiar wetness gathering inside her shorts and the pulse between her legs, teasing her senses and lifting the corners of her mouth in a gesture of persuasive intent.

"But it's also exciting," she breathed, lips meeting and mouths crashing together in a smouldering kiss, the acquaintance of tongues embarking on a trail of sexual promise, snaking between lips and flirting over teeth, impatient hands responding to the movement of touch, sweeping over curves and gripping the cheeks of her bottom, pulling her close and letting her feel the swollen limb, pressing urgently against her body.

"That feels hard and big," she smiled, the influence of suggestion and the promise of coital union fuelling the fire of passion between her legs, persuasive movements and a flirtatious smile lifting the corners of her mouth in a gesture of oral pursuit.

"Don't move," she grinned, flashing her eyes and lowering to the floor on her knees, pulling his pants and briefs to the floor and curling her long-painted fingers around the thick girth, working the length back and forth with feline calculation, tugging and pulling and fisting and thrusting, taking him into her mouth, easing him in and easing him out, sucking him in and blowing him out in trailing strings of saliva and choking gasps for air.

"It's too big. I can hardly breathe," she gasped, sucking in air through her nose and pulling the blockage from her mouth.

"My jaws aching," she sighed, lifting from the floor and glancing into the conservatory, no surprise to find her mother-in-law still sleeping, oblivious to the unfolding exhibition going on around her.

"Bless her," she whispered, brushing hair from her face and flashing her eyes in a gesture of mischievous intent.

"I don't think we need to worry about making too much noise," she smiled, removing her blouse and bra, two massive breasts the size of grapefruits, tumbling out into his hands.

"Fuck me. What a huge pair of tits," he gasped, feeling the weight and the abundance of soft flesh spilling between his fingers, nipping and twisting both nipples between his finger and thumb, the heat of passion manifesting between her thighs and the promise of intimate union forcing a collection of uncompromising demands.

"I need to feel you inside me. I want you to fuck me over the sofa." she said, shuffling and wriggling her hips, the white shorts abandoned on the floor, leaning over the back of the leather sofa with her plump bottom perched in submissive invitation.

"Wow. This is so exciting. So risky. So dirty," she smiled, spreading her legs and opening her body, craning her neck and looking back over her shoulder, brushing a curtain of hair hanging over her face, lowering her hand between her legs and navigating the swaying column towards her moist opening.

"Let me put it in," she whispered, easing him inside her wet entrance, nine-and-a-half inches of potent flesh pushing through the pubic jungle and sliding between the sticky flaps and folds, easing in and easing out, wriggling her hips and swaying her bottom in a provocative dance of intimate seduction.

"Fuck me. Put it all in. Every inch. Fuck me hard. Hurt me," she pleaded, thrusting her hips to the persuasion of carnal connection, hard masculine flesh smacking against soft feminine flesh, a union of genitalia slapping and squelching in a mutual interaction of urgent give and take.

"I'll fucking hurt you," he responded, plunging in and pulling out, strokes long, deep, powerful and urgent, buttocks clenching and relaxing, thrusting and grinding in a coital demonstration of reckless lust and unrefined need, fucking like a wild man on a mission to abuse and torture her body, claiming her openings in a ferocious assault, moving from one orifice to the other, every cavity fully explored and exploited, moans and groans and painful cries giving way to pleasure, the summit of impending release hanging on her lips.

"Oh yes...Oh, fucking yes...Ohh," she snorted, through tight lips and gritted teeth, a sexually undernourished woman melting into orgasmic bliss, euphoric mutterings and persuasive gestures brushing away any last hope of respectability.

"MY FUCKING GOD!!" she screamed, a final blast of undignified filth spilling from her mouth. "Oh…Fuck. I'm….COMING!....Ahhhh....Ohhhh," she cried, the echoes of filth smothered in the soft fabric of the sofa, an earth-shattering orgasm shaking her legs, curling her toes and sucking the last breath of air from her mouth.

"FUCK. YES, he hissed, fucking like a randy bull, his balls erupting in a raging inferno, his hot syrup of life shooting from the single eye and washing the walls of the vaginal vault in an endless rain of emotional fluids.

After retrieving her shoes and skirt from the bedroom and collecting her dignity from the bathroom, a refined and elegant woman walked back into the living-room, glanced into the conservatory, casually lit two cigarettes and poured wine into two glasses.

"I haven't had sex for the last five-years," she boldly confessed, her voice almost apologetic, as if seeking his forgiveness for her shameless actions.

"My husband lost interest in sex on his sixtieth-birthday. That's the last time he fucked me" she said, forcing a smile that quickly faded.

"Even before he lost interest, sex was confrontational, hurried and very disappointing," she sighed, lifting the glass to her mouth and finishing the last of her wine.

"I look forward to our next appointment." she smiled, showing him into the entrance hall, the

reflection in a mirror hanging on the wall a haunting reminder of the age divide.
They could have easily been taken for mother and son.
"You've got my telephone number," she said, flashing her eyes and opening the front door.
"It'll take about four weeks to prepare the drawings," he said, glancing at the photograph on the table, the melodic chimes from the grandfather clock interrupting the question waiting at the back of his throat.

A month later. And a nagging toothache. He rang Brenda.
He put as much cheer into his voice when he tried to arrange another meeting to discuss the design proposals and the estimated building costs for the project, the giggles and the flirtatious innuendo at the other end of the phone, hinting that Brenda was already on her second bottle of wine and had no intention of talking about buildings.
"I'm looking forward to seeing you again," she slurred into the mouthpiece, her business mind running through the conditions of contract.
"If I give you a little extra fee for your professional services, will you promise to give me a good workout between the sheets? "
After two hours of sweaty mattress action and succumbing to two teeth-grinding orgasms, Brenda was still trembling from the aftershocks when she led him to the front door.

He paused in the entrance hall and asked her about the man in the photograph.
"He's my husband, Philip Morton. He's a Dentist. Do you know him?"

The gruesome picture of a mouth full of decaying teeth and bleeding gums hanging on the wall, did nothing to ease the anxiety and pain when he took a seat in the Dentist waiting room.
"Dentists waiting rooms are so depressing," he thought, thumbing through an old copy of a 'Horse and Hounds' magazine and shuffling nervously in his seat, crossing and uncrossing his legs for the millionth time and brushing a light covering of perspiration from his brow.
But it wasn't just the toothache that was making him nervous. There was something more sinister plaguing his mind.
It had suddenly hit him when he was driving home from Brenda's house.
'My husbands a Dentist....Philip Morton....Do you know him? she asked.
"Do I know him. Do I fucking know him? Yes, I fucking know him," the mantra kept repeating inside his head.
He was flying to Malaga the next day and a toothache in Spain was the last thing he needed, so when the pain became too unbearable he had no alternative but to make the call.
Brenda was thrilled to hear his voice again, although she was disappointed when he skipped the flirtatious

telephone sex and a little surprised to hear that her husband was his dentist.

"You've got nothing to worry about," she said, with the confidence of a barrister.

"His dental practice keeps him too busy. It was Philip who suggested that I meet the architect and discuss the design and building costs.

Philip doesn't even know your name," she confirmed, ending the call with an invitation he couldn't refuse.

Philip Morton had been running his dental practice from an old terraced house in Gateshead for almost forty-years. After probing around inside too many disgusting mouths, he was now looking forward to his retirement.

Always pleasant and courteous Philip Morton greeted his next patient with a reassuring smile that was probably meant to put him at ease.

It didn't.

After a brief consultation, he was leaning back in the dentist chair, with his mouth wide open and a bright light shining into his eyes.

"One of your teeth needs an urgent filling," Philip confirmed, smiling with assurance and writing something on a card.

"This won't hurt, just a little numbing of the gum before I drill out the decayed areas," he said, raising the lamp a little and whistling cheerfully to Bizet's *'Chanson-du Toreador.'*

"You can stay in the chair for a few minutes until were ready," he smiled, giving instructions to a young girl in a white tunic moving busily around the room, filling water beakers and preparing metal filling.

"Open wide," Philip said. "This won't take long," he added, the nauseating smell and the haunting noise of the drill grinding into a tooth, curling his toes and making him shuffle nervously in the chair.

"Nearly done," he smiled, blinking his eyes and staring into his open mouth, his grey bushy eyebrows and unsightly nasal hair, unflattering in the light.

'I wonder what he'd do if he knew he had just left his wife lying in his bed like a wet rag.

"Fuck me," he thought, choking back a lump in his throat, memories of a classic film finding its way inside his head.

'The Perfect Murder.' his subconscious reminded him.

'A dentist discovers that his wife is having an affair with one of his patients. The dentist carefully conceals the heart drug 'Digitalis' into a filling coated with a time-releasing gel. After a few hours, it dissolves into the bloodstream causing cardiac arrest and finally death.'

"I note from our records that your last visit was almost two years ago. And I understand you've had this toothache for a few weeks," Philip confirmed, the question interrupting the film playing inside his head and bringing him back to reality.

"You mustn't put off the inevitable, Mr Brand," he smiled, adjusting the lamp above his head and removing the protective gown.

"Your teeth are far too important to neglect them," he added, as the young girl in the white tunic handed him a beaker of water and a paper tissue.

'I fucking know that. I've had to put up with this excruciating pain for weeks now because I've been fucking your wife's brains out.'

"I've been busy," was all he could manage through a numbed mouth and aching jaw.

Painful Visit (circa-1984)

"Fucking Dentists. Fucking Philip Morton," he cursed, exercising his jaw and picking bits of metal fillings from under his tongue.

'Fucking Human Race. Fucking Fate,' he sighed, lighting a cigarette and pulling the car to a halt outside Gary Fowler's house, the wheelchair access ramp and handrail supports leading up to the front door, a chilling reminder of a young man paralysed from the waist down.

'Poor Sod. Sitting alone on his birthday, his wheelchair his only companion,' he thought. 'Fucking women. Fucking loyalty,' he cursed, 'Stella Mason with aspirations stretching far beyond the care and wellbeing of a broken man, long gone.'

"The girls are late," he thought, glancing at his watch and pulling on his cigarette, the brief interlude giving him time to forget about his toothache and think about his friend and the injuries he had sustained in the head-on car crash.

The physiotherapy and rehabilitation and the months travelling to and from the hospital to help with Gary's psychological recovery. The regular meetings with the hospital consultants and the endless meetings with the local council, helping to arrange accessible accommodation, mobility aids and specialist equipment that would help to improve his quality of life.

The information from the doctors and specialists were at best conflicting.
The doctors said that the human body has a natural healing process and will eventually make some recovery, but the damages to his spinal cord were so severe it had left him incapable of any significant movement below the waist.
The consultants and specialists said that although spinal cord injuries affect erections, orgasms and ejaculation, medical research had identified that paralysed men still produce testosterone and have sensory functions, erogenous zones and feel sexually aroused in the conventional way. And because the human body will find other ways of functioning, some men who have lost all genital sensation might still be capable of orgasm through stimulation of other parts of the body.
After six months of therapeutic and physical exercise it was reassuring to see that Gary was showing signs of improvement. Except for a slight numbness in his left arm his upper body was unaffected, and with a little assistance he quickly acquired the confidence to move around in a wheelchair. It was also reassuring for everyone helping with his recovery when he announced that it was time to stop feeling sorry for himself and get on with the rest of his life.

"That must be them," he smiled, stubbing his cigarette in the ashtray and glancing in the rear-view mirror, the sound of a car horn and flashing

headlights, signalling that Janice Barton and Linda Graham had arrived for their next client.
"Sorry for being late," Janice announced, stepping from a car in skyscraper, 'fuck-me-hard heels and wearing a skirt that could easily have been mistaken for a wide-belt.
"We were held up in a traffic jam," Linda added, her arms draped in gold bangles and her tits bouncing beneath a scrap of cloth no bigger than a handkerchief.
"How's the toothache?" Janice enquired, forcing a smile and handing out cigarettes.
"I'll live," he casually replied, taking a cigarette from her outstretched hand.
"I don't intend hanging around too long, so I'll give you this now," he offered, handing Janice an envelope with their fee.
"I've got to get back and pack a suitcase. I'm flying to Spain tomorrow," he added, lighting
their cigarettes.
Both in their late-twenties, Janice and Linda had spent most of their late teens working as 'strippers' in North East Working Men's Clubs, but the money wasn't that good, and the competition was ruthless.
If you weren't prepared to give the booking agent a blow-job, you didn't get work.
They tried working the streets, but after too many rough fucks in smelly back alleys, too many blow-jobs in dirty secluded doorways and too many black eyes and no cash, for the sake of their health they

decided it would be safer to register with an escort agency.

With their virtue for rent, Janice and Linda traded sex to strangers.

'Fucking-for-money in a safe and controlled environment was less of a risk and gave them potential earnings of almost ten times that of an average office job.

The girls were street-wise and astute business women. They were also aware that age brings with it the inevitable demands of gravity. So, before things started to head south they had the forethought to put all their hard-earned cash into useful and meaningful investments.

Working seven-days-a-week in their well-practiced profession, Janice and Linda had acquired about twenty regular clients who they entertained at least once a month.

Married. Single. Working-Class. Professional. Lawyers. Policemen. Politicians. Men of the cloth, the occasional celebrity and those suffering from erectile dysfunction, were all accepted without question.

Their terms and conditions of engagement were not exhaustive, but dirty unkempt men and those requesting bondage, severe pain, sadism and torture were immediately rejected.

No credit cards. No refunds. No deliveries taken in the back door.

After leaving their corporate image of respectability and a world of suburban boredom, dressed in their expensive Italian suits and loaded with testosterone, the alpha males entered a new dimension. A furtive playground of sin, hidden under a veil of mischievous fantasies and dark conspiratorial undercurrents, fuelling their enigmatic obsessions and stimulating their suppressed libidos.

Most of their clients were commissioned on a one-to-one basis, but there were some wealthy businessmen who were willing to pay a lot more, especially if it involved a lesbian act or something more sinister. Something with an unconventional agenda.

Their best customers were those men who were married and were just after a quick fuck or a blow-job, especially those who were doing it for the first time.

They weren't sure if it was their guilty conscience that prevented them from getting an erection, but it was certainly good for business because they kept coming back until the familiarity relaxed them enough to accomplish the deed.

One wealthy client paid handsomely for his moment of voyeuristic stimulation.

There was no physical contact involved. All they had to do was to dress up in a French maid's outfit and wear stockings and suspenders and skip around the bedroom with a feather duster, bending over and orchestrating their bodies with provocative suggestion, while the dirty old pervert lay naked on the bed, masturbating under a running commentary of fantasy and filth.

A fat balding man in his mid-fifties - rumoured to be a teacher by day – with a fetish for dressing up in a baby's nappy, offered to pay them twice their normal fee if they acted out a mother and baby routine, treating him like a toddler and letting him suckle their breasts.

A sixty-year old man suffering with erectile dysfunction and an obsessive pain fetish wanted to be tied to a bed with handcuffs. The girls had to clip pegs to his nipples and attach several pegs to his scrotum and penis before covering him from head to toe in oil. Through a chorus of filthy name calling and shameless humiliation they had to spank him with a table tennis bat until his buttocks turned red.

There was an elderly client who they simply referred to as 'craggy face.'

Although the man had unattractive facial features he was extremely wealthy and with a passion for 'water-sport' he was prepared to pay a phenomenal fee if the girls would straddle his naked body and perform a 'golden fountain' over his rugged face.

A welcoming voice greeted them at the front door, the wheelchair, a chilling reminder of Gary's restrained and handicapped existence.

"Hi Gary. Happy birthday," Janice and Linda said in unison, stepping into the entrance hall and handing him a birthday card and a small gift.

"We've got another present for you. Its special. I think you'll like it," Janice smiled, flashing her eyes and pursing her lips with flirtatious intent.

"But not until we've had some of this," she added, shuffling inside a bag and removing a couple of bottles of wine.

"Here's to Gary," Linda toasted, raising her glass, the sound of clinking glasses and costume jewellery jangling on wrists and a rendition of 'Happy Birthday,' echoing off the kitchen walls.

"We're going to make this a special day for you, Gary," Janice smiled, brushing hair from her face and sipping her wine. "A happy ending to your birthday," she added, as the two happy-hookers eased into their professional roles, lifting the mood with laughter and flirtatious innuendo, the gaiety and intimate suggestion, bringing a smile to Gary's face.

"It's time for your special gift," Janice smiled, removing her blouse and bra and kicking her heels across the floor.

"You'll need an assistant," Linda volunteered, flashing her eyes and wriggling out of her skirt. "Oops. Silly me. I've got no knickers on," she smiled, turning around and bending over.

"Look Gary," she giggled, looking back over her shoulder and opening her legs. "I must have left them in the car."

It was time to go.

"Have a good holiday and don't worry about Gary," Janice smiled, lifting her glass to her mouth and catching a glimpse of the unsightly scratched tattoos on her right arm.

"Trust me, Gary will have a birthday that he won't forget," she said, with professional confidence, her throaty voice a reminder of too many hours of lost sleep, too much alcohol and too much sex.

"If we can't get his juices flowing, it won't be for the want of trying," she added, throwing back the last of her wine.

"And just to let you know were not on-the-clock for Gary," she confirmed, exaggerating a wink and running her tongue suggestively around the rim of the glass, a mischievous smile lifting the corners of her mouth.

"Our next appointment isn't until later tonight with craggy face," she mused, pausing momentarily and playing carelessly with a couple of gold bangles on her wrist.

"That reminds me.... We'll have to drink a lot more wine before we meet him."

Playground of Delights (circa-1986)

When he told his brother Frank he was going on holiday to Spain with his friend, Chris Hall he wasn't surprised to see him in the departure lounge at Newcastle Airport, but he didn't expect to see him still using his old army suitcase.
The Palm Beach Hotel was everything and more that the holiday company had described in their advertising literature. Air-conditioning and most of the bedrooms with panoramic views over the Mediterranean Sea. Two swimming pools, coloured fountains and water sculptures all set within private landscaped gardens.
With a compulsion for sleep walking and a fear of heights, Chris claimed the bed farthest away from the sliding doors to the balcony.
After unpacking his suitcase, he lit a cigarette and walked onto the balcony to take in the views over the Puerto Banus Marina.
An impressive arrangement of smaller crafts nestled in the blue water next to bigger and more prestigious boats and a luxury cruise ship sat motionless on the horizon. Sailboats charged in the breeze and a long-pointed speedboat with a tanned man at the wheel and a gaggle of teenage girls wearing micro-bikinis, flew by.
Life on the Mediterranean Sea seemed so exciting.
"That'll do for me," Frank uttered, from the adjoining balcony, wearing nothing but a pair of

white socks and pointing a finger at a magnificent luxury motor yacht, heading slowly into the harbour.
"Rich bastards," he added, pulling on a cigarette and flexing his muscular forearms, the tattoos on his arms mementoes of his many tours in Northern Ireland and the Middle East, the ugly scar on his left thigh a cruel reminder of a piece of shrapnel that ended his career in the British Armed Forces.
"The owners probably dealing in drugs," he grinned, watching a smart waiter skipping around the deck, serving food and drinks to eight people on a smoked glass table at the stern of the boat.
"Or porn," he laughed, pointing another finger at a speed boat with six young girls aboard, the white spray from the sea splashing over the boat as they circled the luxury yacht.
"If we stare long enough we might get an invite to lunch," Frank mocked, pulling on his cigarette and blowing smoke over the balcony.
"We'll gate crash later. After we've had a few drinks," he smiled, craning his neck and looking over the balcony.
"Where's Chris?" Frank asked.
"Vertigo," Mark replied, placing his hand on his forehead and feigning nausea.
"It's only seven fucking stories," Frank sniggered, pulling on his cigarette and scratching his balls, his suggestion to shower and change into fresh t-shirts and shorts and take a leisurely stroll along the sea front getting Chris on his feet.

"This is the life. Sun, drink and sex," Frank smiled, as they weaved their way through a knitted maze of never ending streets, the bars and restaurants buzzing with an electric mix of vibrant tourists all anxious to spend their hard-earned cash.

"I had a lot of this in the armed forces," Frank uttered. "But it's not the same when you're dodging bullets," he laughed, as they strolled along in the afternoon heat, rubbing shoulders with young people, old people, rich and poor, street sellers, artists, and beggars.

"I've had enough. My leg hurts. I need a drink. Let's go back to the hotel," Frank suggested.

A smart young man behind an impressive circular bar in the Palm Beach Hotel greeted them like long lost friends.

"Ramon Cortez," he said, with pride, pointing a finger at the nametag pinned to his black waistcoat, wiping a cloth across the counter and placing mats in front of them.

"This is better than walking the streets," Frank said, sitting on stools at the bar, nursing cold beers and smoking cigarettes, letting their bodies cool under the air-conditioning unit above the bar.

"You couldn't have picked a better hotel," Frank said, placing a friendly hand on his brother's shoulder. "After we've had a couple of drinks we'll have a stroll by the pool and see if we can pick up a couple of classy chicks," he added, the melodramatic voice of a middle-aged fat man approaching the bar, interrupting their brief moment of relaxation.

"Hello Ramon," he gasped, pausing to catch his breath and lighting a big fat cigar.

"Will you inform Salvador that my corporate clients have arrived," he added, forcing a smile at the three men sitting on stools at the bar and glancing at a Rolex Oyster Perpetual gold watch strapped to his wrist.

"It's urgent, Ramon," he barked, waving his hand with authority and puffing on his cigar, the glint of gold sovereign rings on all eight fingers and a tattoo of a dragon running the entire length of his left arm, getting Ramon's urgent attention.

"Yes, sir," Ramon responded, disappearing through a private door as an entourage of charismatic people of mixed ages and gender walked into the room.

Six blonde Barbie wannabe-famous-dolls, all in their late teens and all wearing the same white t-shirts displaying the corporate logo of *'Millio Sports & Leisure'* across their breasts laughed and giggled as they entered the room. Slim and curvaceous and sleek as cats, they strutted around the room in well-rehearsed-model walks, swaying their hips suggestively and flaunting their hour-glass figures to perfection, their nothing-to-hide sprayed-on lycra shorts attracting inquisitive eyes.

Two gay men with dazzling white teeth, walked into the room holding hands. One of them was dressed in a smart pink suit with a red flower attached to the lapel. His hair was pulled tight over his head and tied in a neat pony tail at the back.

The other gay man was dressed casually in a blue shirt and tight fitting blue jeans.

A chubby, loud mouthed brash woman - with a lot of mileage on the clock - wrapped in a colourful sarong and wearing a black beret tilted on one side of her head above a mass of bright red hair, skipped across the room in bare feet.

An older couple arrived but stood quietly by themselves.

The woman looked to be in her early-seventies. She was smartly dressed in a two-piece cream suit and her grey hair was held in a neat bun at the back of her head.

The man was tall and skinny and wore a white linen suit and a jaunty fedora on his head.

He looked a lot older than the woman. He also had an unhealthy look. One side of his mouth sagged a little, presumably the cruel aftermath of a stroke.

He looked as if he had lost touch with reality and was hovering in a modicum of confusion and uncertainty, somewhere between consciousness and unconsciousness.

Clearly too old to stand up without help, to him it was just another day nearer to death.

After Salvador, had finished hugging and kissing the fat man on both cheeks he was told to prepare drinks for everyone, including the three men sitting on bar stools.

"Yes, Mr Griffin," Salvador said. "Drinks for everyone," he repeated, disappearing behind the bar

and stacking a row of wine glasses on the counter in the shape of a pyramid.
"Champagne, Ramon," Salvador instructed, snapping his fingers. "Con rapidez. Quickly," he added, forcing a smile and making motioning gestures with his hands.
"Yes sir," Ramon acknowledged, taking two bottles of champagne from a cooler and standing on a footstool behind the bar, all eyes staring in his direction as he raised one of the bottles over the top glass.
"Bravo Ramon," someone cheered, as a waterfall of sparkling liquid spilled slowly from the top before reaching the lower glasses.
"Magnifico…Magnifico," the Barbie-girls echoed, chanting and clapping their hands as if they had just seen a miracle unfold.
'Get yourselves a drink, a friendly voice announced, the welcoming hospitality of a glass of champagne and the fat man's extended hand of introduction, inviting some trivial conversation, a little light-hearted humour and inevitable enquiry.
"I see we have something in common," the fat man added, pointing a finger at a tattoo of three red and white plumes on Frank's left arm. "Salute," he added, raising his glass and proudly confirming his former regiment in the British Armed Forces.
"To lost friends," Frank acknowledged, clinking his glass in a toast.
"If we were all fucking instead of fighting the world would be a much better place," Frank barked,

pulling on a cigarette and reaching for another glass of champagne.

"Talking about fucking," Frank whispered, as a beautiful woman with a deep olive complexion and long legs growing from a pair of towering heels, walked into the room.

Her figure was stunning. Her smile was captivating, and her eyes were so dark they were almost black.

After pausing to light a cigarette and take a drink from a passing waiter, she smiled at everyone before glancing around the room.

"She's absolutely gorgeous. I think she's looking for someone," Chris uttered.

"I'm over here. Come and get me," Frank said in mocking jest, almost spilling his drink when she waved her hand and headed towards the bar.

"There you are," she smiled, swaying her hips to perfection and skipping across the floor, a figure hugging white silk dress dipping into every curve, the diaphanous material providing fleeting hints of the exquisite treasures that lay beneath.

"I couldn't see you with all the commotion at the bar," she smiled, kissing the fat man on the cheek.

As the evening gathered speed, they discovered that the fat man was a successful business man called Jack Griffin.

Jack was the chairman and the main shareholder of Griffin Construction Ltd, a multi-national building construction and civil engineering organisation, with offices in London, Glasgow, Birmingham, Liverpool and Belfast.

He also owned the largest scrap metal businesses in North London and three car dealerships in East London. One showroom was exclusive to prestige cars featuring Porsche, Ferrari, Aston Martin, BMW, Jaguar and the occasional Rolls Royce or Bentley.

The other showrooms were devoted to the run-of-the-mill new and used family type cars.

The beautiful woman was an Italian called Martina Sasso. She came from a small village on the outskirts of Milan. One-day Jack called into the restaurant for a business lunch, where she worked as a waitress, and made her an offer she couldn't refuse.

They had been together for six years.

The gay man in the sharp pink suit was Joseph Millio the owner of the fashion and leisure empire Millio Sports and Leisure. His boyfriend was a young man called Julian Greco, son of the shipping magnet, Andrea Greco.

The chubby brash woman with a cavernous mouth and red hair was Sally Morgan, the agent and P.R. advertising executive for Joseph Millio.

The dead looking man was a retired entrepreneur called Max Holden, who had made his fortune in the textile industry. The grey-haired woman linking his bony arm was his wife and accomplished author of a dozen crime novels.

The Barbie girls were invited for their playground skills.

"Can I have your attention please," Jack announced, banging his glass on the counter and clearing his throat to speak.

"Joseph Mellio and his corporate team have spent most of the day on my yacht launching their new range of Millio Sports and Leisure" he confirmed, puffing on his fat cigar and glancing at his expensive watch, before continuing.
"Because the day had been such a success we have decided to continue the campaign into the late evening," he smiled, glancing at the young girls. "Or for those who have the *joie-de-vivre*...into the early morning."
For the next twenty-minutes he talked in length about his loyal clients and introduced some of his corporate team but after too many introductions, punctuated by too many toasts, he realised that his audience were getting bored, so he decided to bring his speech to a close.
After a round of applause, he smiled and pointed a finger at the ceiling. "You're all welcome to join me and my corporate team in the penthouse suite to celebrate the continued success of Joseph Millio Sports and Leisure."

The penthouse suite and conference centre took up most of the top floor. There were eight bedrooms, three bathrooms, a large kitchen and dining area and a cavernous living-room with a full-length sliding door providing access to a huge terracotta balcony offering breath-taking views over the marina and the Mediterranean Sea.

In the corner of the room a middle-aged man dressed in a black suit, white shirt and bow-tie played soft jazz music from a white Steinway piano.
Four waiters dressed in stiff white jackets looked after the guests. Two of the waiters served drinks behind a bar while the other two weaved their way through crowds of spirited people, offering hors d'oeuvres and flutes of champagne from silver trays.
In the dining-room, a chef dressed in a smart white tunic with the obligatory tall hat, stood behind an imposing buffet table, serving a delicious spread of hot and cold meats, fish, savouries and deserts.
Through a haze of cigarette smoke, Salvador and his trusty employee, Ramon Cortez, pushed their way through and a wall of bubbly people, pushing a trolley stacked with several cases of Dom Perignon and Bollinger champagne.
Jack Griffin was clearly not ashamed of having lots of money and he certainly didn't feel guilty about spending it.
Through the cacophonous noise of spirited people, Sally Morgan announced to the guests that a photo-shoot was underway.
The Barbie girls suddenly appeared from one of the bathrooms, scantily dressed in white lace panties and wet t-shirts, bearing the corporate logo of Millio Sports & Leisure, printed across their pert young breasts.
"Bravo. Delightful," someone hailed. "Yes. Very sexy," another voice echoed, their risqué outfits

prompting a few raised eyebrows and several furtive glances.

The interaction of playful expression, the gaiety and innocence of youth, six young girls moving with graceful ease around the room, t-shirts clinging enticingly to shapely breasts and nipples blossoming beneath the wet fabric, panties hugging hips and dipping between legs, offering a tantalising glimpse of the mysterious dark triangle hidden beneath the fabric.

"Tania," Sally smiled, pointing a finger at the piano. "Give me your hand," she offered, helping her up until she was kneeling on all-fours on the top of the piano.

"You know what to do," Sally added, as Tania shuffled on the slippery surface, arching her back and pouting her bottom, opening her legs and wriggling her hips until the lace fabric had disappeared between the cheeks of her bottom.

"Hold it there, Margarita," Sally smiled, giving artistic instructions to one of the other girls wearing red lace knickers and a red bandana around her forehead, posing provocatively on top of the bar.

"Excellent. Let's have more of that," Sally insisted, walking out onto the terrace and giving advice to two other girls orchestrating their bodies in glamorous positions. "That's good. Very good," she added, every movement carefully choreographed by Sally Morgan, ensuring maximum exposure to the seasoned professional, flashing the Nikon camera.

Frank had heard enough stories from Jack Griffin about his time in the armed forces and had gone in pursuit of Sally Morgan. His friend, Chris Hall was outside on the terrace kissing and groping one of the Barbie girls.

With his brother, pre-occupied with Sally Morgan and Chris heading out the door with the young girl and a noticeable lump in his shorts, he took a glass of champagne from the tray of a passing waiter, lit a cigarette and walked onto the terrace.

"Have you enjoyed the party?" a voice whispered from the darkness of the terrace.

"Yes," he replied, turning on his heels to see the Italian beauty lying on a reclining chair with her white dress pulled up high over her thighs and sipping a glass of champagne.

"Your husband certainly knows how to throw a party," he smiled, a flash of white panties at the top of her thighs keeping his interest, as he pulled up a chair next to hers.

"Are you and Jack staying at this hotel?" he enquired, sipping his wine and gazing into her sleepy dark eyes, wondering if she kept them open during a kiss.

"Jack's not my husband. We're not married," she sighed, pausing long enough to light a long black cigarette before answering his other question.

"Yes and No," she replied, blowing plumes of white smoke above her head.

"We usually sleep on the boat, although we do have a permanent room at the hotel," she confirmed,

leaning over and flicking her cigarette into an ash tray.
"Jack's retired to the yacht. He had to leave the party early. He's got a business meeting in London tomorrow with his accountants," she smiled, brushing hair from her face and sipping her wine.
"He's flying to the UK in the morning on the Millio corporate jet. He should be back in a couple of days. It'll give him a chance to see his dogs. Two Doberman Pincers - Laurel and Hardy. The dogs are the love of his life," she sighed, raising an eyebrow and stubbing her cigarette into an ash tray, an insincere smile lingering long after she had finished talking.
"Have you been to the marina yet?" she asked, lifting from the lounger, an infectious smile sweeping away the apprehensive silence, the invitation to take in the spectacular views of the Puerto Banus marina, getting him to his feet.
"Not yet," he replied, returning her smile and handing her a glass of champagne.
"It certainly looks impressive," he offered, sipping his wine and gazing into her dark eyes, wondering if she kept them open during sex.
"It's worth a visit," she smiled, moving closer until their hands were almost touching, the warmth of her body brushing against his legs, heightening expectation and fuelling a growing lump inside his shorts.
"Is there anything out there that catches your eye?" she asked, lifting her glass to her mouth, the

unexpected question interrupting his hand making subtle adjustments to the untimely growth below his waist.

"That's rather nice," he replied, pointing a finger at the luxury motor yacht that he had seen from his balcony, earlier in the day.

"Then I must show you around. It was a birthday gift from Jack," she said, rather matter-of-fact, a thin smile lifting the corners of her mouth with flirtatious suggestion.

'Tomorrow night would be good. About eight o'clock. My names on the side of the yacht…Sasso," she smiled, the determination in her voice and the flirtatious invitation leaving little or no room for negotiation. "I must warn you. I'm fond of a little bondage and domination," she added, with playful amusement, brushing hair from her face and flashing her dark eyes with flirtatious intent.

"Sasso. Eight o'clock. I won't be late," he confirmed, the promise of furtive entertainment getting his full attention.

"It's getting late. I'll have to get back to the yacht. Jack will be wondering where I am. Will you be a gentleman and walk me back to the marina," she smiled, glancing at her watch and lifting to her feet.

"So, she likes a bit of bondage and domination. That sounds promising" he thought, waiting until Martina had waved goodnight before heading along a dark footpath back to the Palm Beach Hotel, a shadowy silhouette appearing from the darkness of a narrow

side street, interrupting his thoughts and stopping him in his tracks.

"I'm sorry if I startled you," Frank uttered, blowing lazy smoke rings from his cigarette into the air above his head, the bright red ash lighting up a triumphant face.

"Have you had a good night, Frank? You look like the cat that got the cream."

"Not bad," Frank replied, pulling on his cigarette. "That Sally Morgan got well and truly fucked tonight," he added, notching up his conquest by punching the air above his head.

"She was gagging for it. I had her screaming for mercy," he said, with a hint of smugness. "The couple next door said they couldn't sleep because of the noise of the headboard banging against the wall for most of the night," he chuckled, dropping his cigarette on the ground and crushing it under his foot.

Although he had no reason to doubt his brother's description of the night's events he was aware that any emotion Frank had was delivered from below his waist.

Frank was never particular with his choice of women. In fact, with some of his conquests, a dimmer switch and a bottle of Jack Daniels were compulsory.

He never really got into a permanent relationship with any woman and if you asked him about marriage his reply was always the same.

'Marriage is like a pack of playing cards. In the beginning, all you need is two hearts and a diamond. By the end, you wished you had a club and a spade.'

"I think I should mention that I had a confrontation with that pretty boy Julian Greco," Frank said, twisting his face and holding his nose, the putrid smell of an overloaded sewer, forcing them to move away from the narrow street.

"As soon as I met that bloke I knew he was a dodgy geezer and someone who couldn't be trusted," he added, lighting another cigarette, as they headed back to the hotel.

"I know, I've got a suspicious mind, but I kept my eye on him when I noticed he was going to the toilets too many times during the evening. Nobody needs to piss that often," he said, pulling on his cigarette and rolling his eyes.

"And then I spotted a small speck of white powder in one of his nostrils. At first, I let it go, thinking it was none of my business. But when I saw him taking a couple of the young girls into the toilet, I couldn't ignore it so I followed them in," he sighed, lifting his shoulders and brushing his hand across the back of his neck.

"I caught him trying to get the girls to snort the white stuff," he said, pulling on his cigarette and shaking his head from side-to-side.

"That's when I got angry," he said, clenching his fists in a gesture of aggression. "Julian told me to fuck off and mind my own business, or he would have me thrown out of the party. Well at that particular time I

had a raging hard-on and I was about to take Sally back to my room, so I ignored his threats," he grinned, lowering his hand and scratching his balls.
"I told him I was about to leave, but before I did I was going to cleanse his body of that filth," he said, his brothers questioning voice interrupting his flow.
"What did you do?" he asked, waiting patiently while Frank lit another cigarette from the one he was already holding.
"I grabbed him by the hair and pushed his head down the toilet. I flushed it a couple of times until he was gasping for air and begging for forgiveness.
I would have left it at that, but he kept telling me how sorry he was and then he offered to give me money if I promised not to hurt him," he laughed, pulling on his cigarette and making begging gestures with his hands.
"Hola," greeted a tired looking security man, smoking a fat cigar and smelling of alcohol.
"Hola," Frank replied, the revolving door squeaking in quiet protest, as they entered the solitude of the hotel foyer.
"He's had a few too many," Frank barked, the volume in his voice breaking the early morning silence and attracting suspicious looks from a couple of concierge staff sitting behind a reception desk.
"Sorry," Frank whispered, raising his hand in the way of an apology and lowering his voice.
"There are some things in life that I can't tolerate. Drugs, Fools, Cowards or Pity and Julian Greco had

them all," he smiled, hunching his shoulders and pressing a button for the lift.
"So, I smacked him across the face a couple of times, flushed the white stuff down the toilet and left him in the bathroom crying like a little girl."

"Fucking sun," he cursed, rolling off the bed and closing the curtains, glancing at his watch
and cursing again when he realised he had only been in bed for two-hours.
"Fucking heat. I must have turned the air-conditioning off before going to meet Martina," he thought, the mere mention of her name and the unforgettable sex on the beach, filling his head with erotic images and stirring the fleshy limb between his legs.
Her elegance and beauty, her passion and sexuality, her dark bewitching eyes and captivating smile, her long smooth legs and shapely curves. The blow-job...The fuck over the upturned boat...Martina was a beautiful woman. She had style. She was rich. She had a figure to die for and a smile that made wedding rings vanish from fingers. Martina had everything…Except fidelity.
It was a strange name for a pub that didn't have a piano, but the sign in the window reading, 'WE ONLY CLOSE FOR ONE HOUR TO ALLOW THE STAFF TO EAT AND SLEEP' was all the information Frank needed, to convince his brother and his friend, Chris Hall that a few drinks in 'The Piano Bar,' mixing with gorgeous women, would help to take his mind off what Frank referred to as, 'that fucking Italian woman.'

A shower of rain had forced most people to seek shelter inside bars and restaurants, so 'The Piano Bar,' was unexpectedly busy for an afternoon. The music was loud and the fragrance of feminine scents mingling with male testosterone, filled the room with the unmistakable smell of sex and infidelity.

"Watch the master at work," Frank smirked, as he approached two attractive girls sitting on stools at the end of the bar.

He didn't have time to find out their names before he was spinning on his heels in retreat, a dismissive hand gesture and a string of verbal abusive following in his wake.

"Fucking lesbians," he barked, pulling up a stool at the bar and lighting a cigarette, reaching for his drink and burying the bitter rejection inside his glass.

"After you get through fucking that Italian woman, I'll see you in the Piano Bar, later tonight," he mocked, swirling his glass on the wet surface of the table and tapping his feet beneath the bar stool, as Thin Lizzy launched into *'The Boys Are Back in Town.'*

He didn't want to keep Martina waiting. He wanted to look his best. He chose a pair of white
chinos and a striking white designer shirt, which he thought would be appropriate for a surreptitious night of bondage and domination.

He left the hotel just after seven-thirty, taking the fifteen-minute walk to the marina, a yellow orange glow settling just above the distant hills signalling the final minutes of the day would soon be slipping away and a galaxy of stars would be lighting up the Mediterranean sky.

A cruise ship sounded a horn as it headed into port and several yachts and motor launches were mooring up for the evening.

"What a magnificent sight. There's lots of money in here. How the other half live," he thought, strolling aimlessly along the marina, following a myriad of brilliant white crafts and endless rows of gleaming white boats, some of them small, some medium in size and others bigger than houses.

"Wow," he gasped, blinking his eyes and pausing to read the name 'Sasso' written in bold script letters along the bow of one of the most prestigious boats in the harbour.

"Hello," she smiled, brushing hair from her face and sipping a glass of champagne, a black silk dress moulding like a second skin to impossible curves.

"Welcome aboard. You look very handsome," she said, raising an eyebrow of approval and kissing him on the lips, a trace of perfume just enough to heighten her femininity and just enough to catch his attention.

"I wasn't sure you'd turn up," she whispered, handing him a glass of champagne.

"Have something to eat," she added, pointing a finger at a bowl of strawberries and an assortment of hors d'oeuvres on a white table cloth.

"I thought my erotic fantasies might have scared you off," she smiled, flashing her dark eyes and slipping a strawberry between her lips, biting half and offering him the rest.

"Memories," she toasted, raising her glass in salute, a deep cleavage and mouth-watering breasts getting his undivided attention.

"Scared me off. I don't think so" he laughed. "That's one of the reasons why I'm here," he smiled, lifting his glass to his mouth and stealing another glance at her tits.

"And what's the other?" she asked.

"I think you know the answer to that," he replied.

"Me. I'm just an innocent woman. I hope you're not going to take advantage of me," she said, in playful jest, skipping playfully around the deck with the elegance of a dancer, a long split up both sides uncovering endless legs growing from a pair of five-inch black heels.

"I've come here to make love to a beautiful woman," he said, pulling her into his arms in a meaningful kiss, tongues meeting in a moment of intimate union, the promise of bondage and domination, awakening the sleeping limb inside his pants.

"Later," she smiled, flashing her eyes and breaking from the kiss, the movement inside his pants, teasing her senses and fuelling the fire of passion between her legs.

"Let me show you around the yacht, first," she volunteered, handing him the ice bucket and the bottle of champagne.

During the leisurely stroll around the boat she talked briefly about her estranged relationship with Jack.

After telling him a little bit about her upbringing in Milan and how she first met Jack in a restaurant where she worked as a waitress, she talked about their business activities, although from what she was saying it appeared that he kept her at arms-length with most of his business interests and certainly his finances.

However, it was clear to see that Jack had made them filthy rich, and all Martina had to do was to spend his money.

"That's enough boring information for one night," she sighed, brushing her hand through her hair and closing her eyes, the soft caress of the wind sweeping away the painful memories of Milan and Jack Griffin.

"It's a beautiful night," she smiled, a full moon reflecting a white beam of light stretching as far as the eye could see over the black still waters of the Mediterranean Sea.

"A romantic night," she whispered, her elegance and charm captured in the hide and seek of shadows, the silhouette of personified perfection dancing and twirling in perpetual motion around the deck.

"A night for sex," she smiled, sucking in air through her nose, feasting on the intoxicating smell of arousal and breathing in the unmistakable aroma of sex.

"A night of bondage and domination," she giggled, sipping her wine and flashing her eyes in a gesture of flirtatious intent.

"You're quiet. What are you thinking about?" she asked, wrapping her arms around his neck and

pulling him close, feeling the swollen muscle pressing against her thigh.
"Silly question," she laughed, lowering her hand and squeezing the lump inside his pants.
"We'll have to do something about that. We don't want another premature occurrence," she sighed, a teasing smile lifting the corners of her mouth.
"You're overheating. I need to cool you down," she giggled, removing an ice cube from the champagne bucket and placing it inside his mouth.
"Kiss me," she whispered, lips meeting in romantic unity and tongues duelling in an exchange of heated breath, sweeping and dancing over teeth on a mission of playful pursuit, probing the cold object with her warm wet tongue and holding the embrace long enough until the ice cube melted away in a cool stream of liquid passion.
"Unhook my dress," she whispered, brushing water from his chin and flashing her eyes with flirtatious intent.
"You're very demanding," he jested, loosening the tiny hook and eye and slipping the straps from her shoulders, watching the capture of silk, sliding over shapely curves, before dropping to the floor at her feet.
"I can be. You just have to ask," she smiled, hovering precariously on a pair of towering heels, wearing nothing but a smile and a pair of black lace knickers, her shapely breasts bouncing invitingly in the breeze and two nipples that couldn't be ignored, blossoming from dark areolas.

"I'm on a promise, remember," she grinned, holding his arm for support, lifting one foot and then the other, before stepping out of the dress with the grace of a ballerina.

"Or have you forgotten already," she smiled, flashing her dark eyes and kicking her shoes playfully across the deck.

"You're very beautiful," he said, cupping her breasts in his hands, feeling their weight and softness filling his hands, caressing one and squeezing the other, twisting and pulling both nipples in playful capture between his fingers and thumbs.

"Oh yes. I like that," she breathed, sweeping her hands across his chest and opening the buttons on his shirt. "And I like this," she smiled, lowering her hand and squeezing the growing limb inside his pants.

"I've thought about you all day," she whispered, sucking his bottom lip into her mouth and holding it in gentle capture between her teeth.

"All day," he smiled, pulling her close, hormonal chaos fuelling emotions, gestures responding to impulsive urges, bodies pushing together in a simulation of coital foreplay, impatient hands moving with sensitive meaning, sweeping over curves, over soft feminine flesh, over hard masculine flesh, two lovers swimming in a sea of frustrated emotions, two people engaging in a courtship of mutual enquiry, two strangers desperate for carnal connection.

"Now I'm overheating," she smiled, lowering slowly to her knees, sucking his hard nipples on the way down, wiggling her tongue and holding each one in erogenous capture between her teeth, before lowering his zip and slipping her hands inside the waistband of his pants.

"Let's see what's in here," she whispered, pulling his pants down his thighs, nine-and-a-half-inches of liberated flesh, springing free from the dark confines of his briefs, lifting the corners of her mouth and bringing a smile to her face.

"It's so big," she gasped, staring wide eyed at the gruesome muscle bobbing and swaying in front of her eyes.

"And so, thick," she added, wrapping her fingers around the meaty girth, working the fleshy limb up and down, pulling and tugging, watching the bulbous head playing hide and seek beneath a shroud of loose foreskin, before easing him into her hungry mouth.

"And so, delicious," she whispered, feasting on the meaty shaft, sucking and blowing and easing him out, dragging her teeth slowly along the swollen limb, before pulling him back and taking him deep, swallowing the length from the head to the root before blowing him out in choking gasps for air.

"It's getting cold," she sighed, running her hands up and down her arms and shuffling uncomfortably on her knees.

"Let's go inside. You can warm me up in the bedroom" she smiled, taking his hand and gathering her clothes from the floor.

The bedroom was spacious. An arrangement of scented candles lit up a mirrored ceiling above a king-sized bed and lavender scented rose petals and an oasis of pillows were spread over black satin sheets.

"I'm impressed," he smiled, a bottle of champagne cooling in an ice bucket and a bowl of strawberries and a bottle of lubricant on a small table by the bed, hinting at the promise of erotic theatre and a carnal arena for endless hours of illicit entertainment.

"Just relax. I'm going to cover your muscular body in oil and then I want you to fuck me until I tell you to stop," she smiled, brushing hair from her face, squatting over his back and taking the bottle of strawberry scented oil from the bedside table.

"This'll make you feel relaxed," she whispered, shuffling on the bed, shifting her weight and walking on her knees, letting him feel the moist lips of her vulva opening and closing over the cheeks of his bottom.

"I'm good at this. I've had a lot of practice" she added, spilling a generous amount of oil from the container before sweeping her slippery hands over his back, massaging his neck and arms and working his shoulders with her fingers and thumbs, pressing gently at first and then applying a little more pressure when she thought it appropriate.

"You've got a cute little bottom," she whispered, pouring oil over his lower back and buttocks, smoothing it into the valley between the cheeks and sliding a fingernail along the perineum.

"And a gorgeous body," she added, twisting and pulling the hairs around his anus before dipping into the crack of his arse and probing the dark orifice with her finger.

"You are good at this," he uttered, a familiar movement in his groin reacting to the persuasion of touch. "You hit all the right places," he added, knowing that if he didn't turn over quickly he might end up fucking the mattress.

She was on top of him before his back hit the mattress. "Keep still. Let me do the work," she smiled, smoothing oil over both their bodies, flashing her eyes with flirtatious intent, before giving a little extra lubrication to his swollen limb.

"You've got a beautiful sculptured body," she whispered, shifting her weight on the bed and straddling over him, letting him feel the warmth, the softness and the weight of her tits flattening against his chest.

"So, muscular," she smiled, slipping and sliding in a sexual orientation of sixty-nine, lifting and lowering, swaying and bouncing, grunting and panting, wriggling her bottom, lifting up and dipping down, smothering his face in a sea of warm secretions and filling his nostrils with the musky smell of mature sex.

"So, hard," she moaned, moving to the persuasion of touch, sweeping her hands in a creative dance over his thighs, fondling and groping in an urgent enquiry of intimate exploration and a carnal mission of sexual discovery.

"So, big," she gasped, cupping her breasts in both hands, pushing her tits together and wrapping them around the gruesome muscle.

"What a magnificent cock," she breathed, holding the meaty length in promising capture between her cleavage, sliding up and down in a seductive rhythm of pleasure, massaging the length and embracing the girth before sweeping her tongue over the swollen head and feasting on his pulse of life.

"Give me the oil and turn over," he said, laying her face down on the satin sheets and tucking a pillow under her tummy.

"Now who's demanding," she smiled, opening her legs wide when she felt his probing hands and slippery fingers, smoothing oil over her lower back.

"I'm also good at this," he uttered, sweeping his hands over her back, focussing his eyes and taking in the feminine curves of perfection and the delightful invitation of a pouting bottom.

"You've got a beautiful bottom," he whispered, kissing and biting both cheeks and pulling them gently apart in a calculated intrusion of playful intimacy, bathing the dark orifice with his tongue and breathing in the musty odours of sex before proceeding down her legs until he reached her feet.

His grip was firm, but his fingers were sensuous, teasing the tight gaps between each painted toe, applying increased pressure on the arches and working the soft textures of her instep before gliding back up her long legs, peppering warm kisses and soft bites on her thighs before coming to rest on her shapely bottom.

"You smell delicious," he said, pulling the cheeks apart and exposing the dark valley of hidden secrets, teasing and probing the anal opening before easing a slippery finger slowly and gently inside her anal passage.

"Oh. That feels good," she breathed, hormonal chaos fuelling a turbulence of impossible urges, kneeling on the bed on all fours with her arms outstretched on the bed and both hands flat on the mattress.

"No more games," she whispered, a heartbeat smothered under a chorus of breathless whispers, arching her back and opening her legs with her bottom perched on the edge of the bed in submissive invitation.

"I want you to fuck me," she said, brushing hair from her face and looking back over her shoulder, watching him shuffling his feet on the floor and manoeuvring into position, the threatening limb swaying about like a thoroughbred colt preparing to mount a mare in heat, bringing a smile to her face and an impulsive gesture of approval.

"Wow," she gasped, shifting her weight on the bed and opening her legs in a responsive gesture of commitment, clenching her teeth and bracing her body for entry.

"Let me help you with that," she whispered, reaching back with a guiding hand, curling her fingers around the throbbing muscle and easing the fearsome object inside her body.

It was slippery and wet, the entry hard and physical, the penetration deep, strokes long, powerful and urgent, buttocks tightening and hips thrusting, hard male flesh smacking urgently against soft feminine flesh, easing in and easing out, plunging in and pulling out, moving back and forth with increasing determination, the sticky flaps and folds clinging to the fleshy column and the vaginal vault stretching to accommodate the perilous length and formidable girth.

"Ah. Fuck. Oh. Fuck. Fuck yes," she cried, looking back over her shoulder and twisting her face, a chorus of filthy curses and uncompromising demands, spilling from a helpless mouth.

"Faster," she insisted, wriggling and swaying her hips and pushing back in a mutual exchange of give and take. "Harder," she urged, brushing hair from her face and breathing in short gasps of air through her nose. "Deeper," she croaked, nine-and-a-half-inches of hard flesh breaching the limits of her inner core, the demanding voice of a wanting woman, fading in a chorus of emotional pleas for calm and painful cries of pleasure.

"You're a fucking machine," she breathed, looking up at the mirrored ceiling, the reflection throwing back an image of a submissive woman, kneeling on the bed on all fours, with her back glistening in oil and rose petals sticking to her skin.

"You're on a promise," remember, he smiled, glancing up at the ceiling, the erotic view in the mirror forcing another visceral surge of blood and adrenaline, flooding into vital organs.

"I always keep my promises," he added, holding her waist and thrusting his hips, moving back and forth with renewed determination, breathing in short gasps of air and increasing the momentum, his libido relentless and his stamina in overdrive, entering and retreating, in and out, breaching and penetrating the vaginal vault in a marathon of turbulent engagement and a synchronised motion of give and take.

"You're hitting the spot," she whispered, breathing in pants and gasps and moving to the persuasion of touch, wriggling her bottom and pushing back in a coital exchange of genitalia embracing genitalia, easing him in and easing him out, in and out, back and forth, pushing in and pulling out, faster and faster and deeper and deeper, penetrating the depths of the vaginal vault and flooding her body in a delirium of orgasmic glory.

"Oh...Fuck. Ah....Yes. Fuck…Fuck…Fuck" she cursed, her declaration of filthy obscenities smothered in the wet bed sheet, her body shuddering and stiffening, a woman responding to the sensation of an approaching orgasmic, filthy curses and crude obscenities growing into guttural cries of euphoric elation.

"Oh. Ah. I'm coming. I'm...I'm....Comminnggg…Arrggghhhh....Fuck-Fuck-Fuucckkk, she screamed, curling her toes and blinking stinging sweat from her eyes, the irreversible surge of ultimate pleasure starting at her feet and rushing up her legs, the release powerful and sustained, an outpouring of emotional fluids flooding her vulva in a sea of liquid passion.

"I'm drained. I need a moment," she sighed, brushing wet hair from her face and removing oil and perspiration from her eyes.

"I can hardly breathe," she gasped, sucking in air through her nose and looking back over her shoulder, a worshipping veil of uncertainty clouding her vision as she watched him squeezing the last of the strawberry oil from the container.

"It's okay. I'll wait until you're ready," he said, unconvincingly, ignoring her plea for calm, smoothing the oil between the cheeks of her bottom and coating the dark brown pigmented skin around the anal opening.

"The oil will help," he said, feeling the sphincter muscles opening and closing around his finger, sliding in gently and pulling out slowly, preparing the dark orifice for entry.

"Lift up," he gestured, motioning with his hand until she had resumed her position on all fours, with her legs open and her bottom raised invitingly in the air.

"Be gentle with me," she pleaded, sucking in short gasps of air through her nose, her heart banging like a drum inside her chest and her breathing increasing by the second.

"I'm a back-door virgin," she whispered, forcing a smile and gritting her teeth in anticipation of the assault, a little fearful of an unfamiliar object penetrating her most sacred place.

"I'll be gentle," he lied, gripping the throbbing flesh in his hand and guiding the smooth head against the anal opening, the dark shrine resisting entry, before yielding to the force.

He enters. He penetrates. He violates the dark abyss. The dark ring tightening like a vice around the swollen length and thickening girth and the sphincter muscles pulsing in quiet protest against the unfamiliar visitor.

"Oh. Ah," she cried, her rectal passage burning with the brutal invasion, the swollen limb held in tender confinement, two lovers momentarily fused together in a bond of intimate connection.

"Not too fast," she begged, gestures of discomfort pleading in urgent cries for calm, gripping the bed sheet with one hand, reaching back and grabbing his thigh with the other.

"Gently," she whispered, as he eased the slippery length inside her bottom, the dark entrance giving way to the persuasion of momentum, the anal passage adjusting to the carnal invasion and the tight anal muscles contracting and relaxing around the thick girth.

"I'm okay now," she whispered, regaining her composure and looking back over her shoulder, her willingness to continue dancing in a promise behind flashing eyes.

"Slow down. Be gentle. You're too big," she sighed, hesitancy turning into commitment and cautious whispers chasing hesitant cries, moans and groans getting louder and longer and gasps and sighs stumbling over painful cries, a tortured voice rising to that abandoned pitch where discomfort gives way to pleasure.

"Fuck, that's good," she cursed, a mutual connection embroiled in a harness of unfamiliar pursuit, balls deep inside the dark shrine of intimacy, the tight ring of her sphincter embracing the length and gripping the girth, easing in gently and easing out slowly in a slow momentum of breach and abuse.

"I'm going to come again," she announced, arching her back and lowering her hand between her legs, sliding her long-painted fingers between the slippery folds of flesh and dancing in playful circles over the swollen clitoris with her finger and thumb, the solo stimulation and a running commentary of filth, lifting the corners of her mouth in a chorus of vocal persuasion.

"Fuck…Fuck. Yes…Yes," she cursed, wriggling and swaying her hips and thrashing her head from side to side. "Yes…Yes," she cried, the tight anal muscles gripping the gruesome muscle in an uncompromising vice. "Yes…Yes, she moaned, a long-painted finger working the clitoris before slipping inside the fleshy folds. "Ah yes. Oh...Ah," she blurted, her legs tightening and her toes curling, euphoric muttering dancing behind gritted teeth, glancing over her shoulder, her eyes vacant and her mouth opening and closing, words having no meaning and making no sense, her face twisting in a theatrical mask of pleasure and a euphoric smile betraying her fast-approaching orgasm.

"Oh Yes," she moaned. "Fuck…Ah Fuck," she cursed, puffing and panting and gasping and wheezing, waves of euphoric contractions flooding her vulva in a warm sea of liquid passion.

"Ah…Ah Yes, Oh…Oh Fuck….Ahhhhhh," she screamed, an earth-shattering orgasm flooding her thighs in a turbulent outpouring of burning heat, euphoric whimpers and painful cries of pleasure, echoing off the walls inside the room.

"Don't move," he insisted, sucking in air through his nose and gripping her waist, ignoring

her pleas for tenderness and dismissing her cries for calm, the carnal invasion quickly gathering speed, frictionless movements of hard flesh lubricated in oil plunging seamlessly into her dark interior, all the way in and all the way out, reaching places inside her body that had never been touched before.

"Ah…Ah. Oh…Fuck," he cursed. "I'm coming. I'm coming," he hissed, through gritted teeth, the hot ballast shooting up the shaft and exploding inside her bottom with surprising force, seminal eruptions, copious and endless, multiple loads of emotional fluids spilling into the dark abyss and washing the walls of her bruised and tortured bottom, bleeding out the last of his creamy mess until his balls were empty and his legs were giving way.

In a sliding stream of warm secretions and a voice pleading caution, he eased the blockage from her burning bottom and they both fell on the bed.

"I'm exhausted," he gasped, sucking in short gasps of air through his nose, his body soaked in water, strawberry oil and sweat, two lovers trembling in the aftershocks of euphoric release, laying in silence and waiting for calm, breathing in the aroma of lingering sex.

"That's a vision I'll never forget," he said, staring at the reflexion in the mirrored ceiling above the bed, the Italian beauty glistening in oil and perspiration, a curtain of wet hair masking her face and a fusion of rose petals sticking to her skin.

"Me too," she smiled, brushing hair from her face and staring at the sleeping effigy of beauty hanging over his thigh.

"Will you remember the memories we shared together?" she asked.

"I will always think of you," he replied, rolling off the bed and gathering his clothes from the floor, the candles burning themselves out and their lips meeting in a parting kiss.

He wasn't surprised to find the place was still open at four in the morning, but he didn't expect to see Frank and Chris sitting on the same bar stools.

A friendly smile from the resident DJ and The Eagles singing, *'Hotel California,'* welcomed him into the Piano Bar.

Some of the bar staff were busy clearing away the day's business, while a young girl with a mop and bucket was cleaning the contents of someone's stomach from the floor.

A couple of drunks trying to find the door stumbled unsteadily on their feet and two people waving their hands on the dance floor, looked as if they were swatting away flies.

'Some dance to remember, some dance to forget,' he sang, as he approached Frank and Chris at the bar.

"The bottle of pink champagne on ice looks impressive. Are you two expecting some female company?" he asked, sarcastically. "I hope you haven't been here all night?" he added.

"No. No, we haven't," Frank replied, pulling up a stool for his brother, draining his glass and signalling to the barman to bring more drinks.

"We had a casual stroll through the old town. The streets were littered with prostitutes and most of the pubs offered negotiable entertainment," Frank said, pausing to pay the barman for the drinks.

"After a couple of beers in some shady places we eventually found Hannah's bar, hidden away up a narrow side street. The sign in the window was too tempting, so we went in," he said, lifting his drink to his mouth and mumbling the name into the glass.

'LIQUOR IN THE FRONT-POKER IN THE REAR.

"It was another fucking brothel," Frank and Chris barked in unison.

"Anyway," Frank continued, swallowing his pride in his glass, his demeanour growing in confidence and a broad smile tugging at his lips.

"When we got back to the Piano Bar, we got chatting to a couple of gorgeous women."

He was aware of Frank's moral code and he also knew his brother would flirt with any woman as long a she had a pulse. He also knew what Frank's idea of gorgeous was, on a scale of one-to-ten, so he just smiled and let it go over his head.

"The night was showing promise, so I decided it was fitting to impress the girls with a bottle of champagne," Frank smiled, sipping his drink before continuing.

"After talking to one of them for the best part of an hour she invited me back to her room," he said, pulling on his cigarette and pausing long enough for Mark to interrupt his flow.

"So where are they now?"

"Well," Frank said, wearing an expression of anxiety and defeat.

"I needed to use the toilet, so I asked Chris to get the drinks in while I was away," he sighed, shaking his head in despair.

"Chris said, without lowering his voice, that it wasn't his turn, because he had bought the drinks in the second brothel."

'The fucking second brothel," Frank repeated.

"I' could hear the girls laughing as they made a hasty retreat to the ladies' toilet," he sighed, rolling his eyes and pointing an accusing finger at Chris.

"That was about an hour ago."

'The last thing I remember; they were running for the door.' Don Henley chirped in.

"They might still be in the toilet. Do you want me to have a look?" Chris slurred, a comical mask of innocence and naivety smiling back through glazed and empty eyes.

"I've had too much to drink. I think I'm going to be sick," he announced, his head bobbing around like a balloon on a string and drool spilling from his mouth, the young girl with the mop and bucket waiting patiently for the inevitable.

"Hey....Ugh," he managed to splutter into his glass. "I think I can smell strawberries," he giggled, before sliding off the bar stool and crashing to the floor in a heap.

A Moment of Madness (circa-1988)

The six-mile Metro journey to Newcastle was relaxing and uneventful. The train was packed with Monday morning commuters heading for their all too boring and familiar places of work.

As usual, everyone was wearing their trademark sour faces, and no one offered a kind look, or even a hint of a smile.

Men reading 'the tabloids' had their eyes fixed on either today's naked image on page three or the back page for the sport and a smartly dressed man reading a 'broadsheet' newspaper held a pen precariously between his thumb and index finger, studying the daily crossword puzzle.

A middle-aged woman with her head buried in a romantic novel shuffled uncomfortably in her seat and a younger woman sitting opposite casually thumbed through a glossy magazine, pausing occasionally when the article featured men, sex or the occasional celebrity gossip.

The rest of the commuters just sat in silence, wishing they were home in bed.

He was nervous. His head was in chaos. He hadn't slept. He couldn't eat. His heart was banging like a drum inside his chest, the true reality of the court hearing at Newcastle Crown Court at ten-o'clock today, was hanging like a lead weight in the pit of his stomach.

"Fuck me," a voice cursed from the chaos inside his head. 'I could find himself out of a job by the end of the day.

Fucking hell,' the voice echoed. 'I could be spending the night in Durham Prison, he sighed, shuffling uncomfortably in his seat and sucking in air through his nose, trying to calm the racing heartbeat inside his chest, the confident words of his solicitor the previous day, giving him some comfort.

"Bring your cheque book to court rather than a tooth-brush," he told him, with reassurance. "With an unblemished record and exemplary character, it's more likely that you'll receive a community service order and a substantial fine rather than a custodial sentence.

The wind and rain hammered mercilessly against the carriage windows sending waterfalls streaming in uneven patterns across the dirty glass, making visibility almost impossible.

The soft seductive voice of a woman - who could have earned a fortune on one of those telephone sex lines - breathed the name of the approaching station through the tannoy system, the noise of the brakes screeching on metal tracks and the sound of a door buzzer signalling the train had stopped at the station.

"I hope my solicitor knows what he's talking about," he sighed, running his hand over the murky glass and looking out onto the platform, a warning sign fixed to a steel post catching his eye and bringing a smile to his face.

'DONT STAND TOO CLOSE TO THE PLATFORM EDGE OR YOU MIGHT GET SUCKED OFF.'

A wall of impatient commuters all surged forward towards the automatic doors, shaking wet brollies and stamping their feet, pushing and squeezing their way through a gap in the doors and into the comfort of the warm carriage.

A fat man with a jolly face, waited patiently until everyone had boarded the train before helping a blind woman and her guide dog into the overcrowded carriage. After placing her hand firmly on a vertical support rail, the golden Labrador obeyed her command and sat down next to her.

As the train gathered speed, tightly pressed bodies with arms outstretched above their heads, held onto high level support rails, swaying precariously with the momentum and shuffling unsteadily on their feet, trying to find purchase on the wet floor.

The dog's ears suddenly pricked, and his black nose started to twitch. He lowered his head, following the scent of a familiar smell, searching between the legs of unsuspecting commuters, before pushing his wet nose between the pleats of a middle-aged woman's rain coat, the unexpected acquaintance of something sniffing her bottom, forcing her to let go of the high-level rail and turn quickly on her heels.

Her eyes were instinctively drawn to the fat jolly man standing directly behind her, the force of an umbrella across his arm and a string of verbal abuse, taking the smile off his face.

"Dirty old man," she barked, her hasty departure to another part of the carriage, leaving the blind woman and her faithful companion oblivious to the unfolding events and a cluster of nervous commuters shuffling uncomfortably on their feet, trying to gain as much distance between them and the lecherous man.

The fat man fiddled nervously with his shirt collar, before brushing a layer of perspiration from his forehead and forcing a cough into a clenched fist.

"It wasn't...It wasn't," he stammered, shaking his head and lifting his shoulders in his defence, pointing an accusing finger at the dog and offering an *'I'm-not-guilty'* smile at the other commuters.

But his crimson face and virtuous gestures of mitigation, did little to proclaim his innocence.

The train was warm and comfortable. The peaceful rhythm of the metal tracks clicking over joints and the gentle rocking of the carriage giving him time to gather his thoughts and reflect on his life and his appearance in court today.

"The calm before the storm," he sighed. *"I've got a good life. I've got a beautiful wife and daughter. I've got a good job. I've got a business. What was I thinking. Did I really believe I would get away with it? A moment of fucking madness. What an idiot"* he muttered to himself, thoughts and images of the last few years of his life, gathering inside his sleepy head.

It was a bitterly cold morning in January when he walked into the main reception area at Durham County Council Civic Centre to begin his first day in a new job. The multidisciplinary offices occupied the first three floors of the entire building, employing two hundred professional and administration staff. The technical and professional disciplines included architects, technicians, building surveyors, mechanical and electrical engineers, quantity surveyors, structural engineers, and landscape architects.

The architectural design office on the third floor alone, comprised of about sixty professional staff, a mixture of architects, technicians and building surveyors.

His first morning was moderately uneventful, most of his time was taken up settling into the working environment and meeting the rest of the architectural staff.

The afternoon followed much of the same routine, visiting member of staff on all three floors, greeting faceless people, endless introductions, too many handshakes and certainly too many names to remember.

Then he was faced with a vision of purity and wonder.

Jill Wallis worked in the medical room on the ground floor of the building. She had a Mona Lisa smile, sparkling blue eyes, long dark hair and a stunning hour-glass figure.

Jill Wallis was without doubt the Holy-Grail of feminine beauty.

For the rest of the day he couldn't get her out of his head.

His second day at work was just as bad. He feigned a headache just to visit the medical room, a little disappointed when he was greeted by an overweight nurse, who gave him a couple of tablets and sent him on his way.

The third day started out much the same, until he was invited to a lunchtime retirement party at a pub across the road from the office. *A glimmer of hope... She might be there.*

Jill was there, but unfortunately for him, so was her fiancée.

He gave her his best smile. It worked. Jill invited him over. She introduced him to her fiancée. He was immature and disrespectful. He was certainly punching above his weight. Jill Wallis deserved better.

On the fourth day, he was already forging a plan.

It wasn't going to be easy. It was certainly a challenge. But he knew that if he wanted to be part of this woman's life, he would have to be patient, using all his charm to gain her trust, melt her heart and win her affections. But he was old enough to know that patience was a virtue and experience had told him that if he employed all these factors into the chase, Jill Wallis would eventually belong to him.

Weeks turned slowly into months. He worked tirelessly. He made any excuse to visit the ground floor on the off-chance that he might see her in the foyer. He even volunteered for first-aid courses and feigned a range of different ailments just to visit the medical room.

He made a mental note of when she arrived and left the office. On a couple of occasions, he waited in his car until she left the office and headed for the bus stop, his chivalrous offer of a lift home, always greeted with a friendly smile and a kind word.

Was he making it a little too obvious? Was he turning into a 'voyeur' as well as a 'stalker'? But time was running out and he was becoming frustrated. Fuck it he thought. He decided to throw caution to the wind and make the call.

He wasn't sure if it was his heart-melting charm or his shameless pride that wouldn't take no for an answer, but it didn't matter in the end. Jill Wallis agreed to go out with him.

They might have ended up having sex in the multi-storey car park, if it wasn't for a prying CCTV camera pointing directly at his car.

He had just pulled the car into a parking bay when their eyes met, a quick check on the dashboard clock reminding him that they were already running late for their reservation at the restaurant.

The connection of hungry mouths, the endearment of two people alive with the sensation of touch, engaging in a flirtatious exchange of intimate enquiry, hormonal chaos exploding inside a young impulsive body, tremors of emotional bliss plunging into the well of her stomach, any thoughts of reservations or food, lost in the heat of passion.

A sour faced Italian waiter looked at his watch and rolled his eyes before showing them to a table next to the kitchen. After settling into seats and ignoring the pandemonium of the noisy kitchen, a bottle of wine and the romantic voice of Eric Clapton singing *"Wonderful Tonight,"* eased the anxiety and lifted the mood.

Jill did most of the talking. He just pretended to study the menu.

Behind the surreptitious mask of the menu, he watched her fingers playing carelessly with an engagement ring on her left hand, staring openly into her beauty and breathing in her essence of youth.

"Have you been here before?" he enquired, catching a glimpse of her shapely breasts, watching her lips forming words and listening to her soft innocent voice, offering a sincere reply to every question, always responsive and never critical, making sure he laughed and smiled at every appropriate junction.

"No, I haven't," she answered, her blue eyes sparkling with excitement and her sensuous lips almost begging to be kissed. "This is my first time in a restaurant," she whispered across the table, their faces almost touching, and their eyes locked together in a courtship of promising intimacy.

"You'll have to help me with the menu," she smiled, reaching over the table and touching his hand, the closeness and intimacy, fuelling the fire of passion between her legs.

After eating and drinking wine under a soft ambience of romantic music and a warm exchange of compliments and endearment, they thanked the sour faced waiter and left the restaurant.

"I've got something for you," he announced, reaching into the glove compartment and handing her a gift wrapped in silver paper and a red bow.

"I hope you like it," he added, hoping that his efforts of finding out her favourite perfume would gain him precious brownie points.
"It's my favourite," she smiled, spraying a light mist over her neck as he pulled the car out of the multi-storey car park and into the city traffic.
"I know it is," he replied, the headlights beaming on a green road sign with a white arrow pointing right to his flat in Gateshead and another arrow pointing left to Walker, where Jill lived with her parents.
"It's my favourite too," he said, through a genuine smile, dropping down a gear at the approaching roundabout.
"How did you know?"
"The first day I met you," he lied, discreetly adjusting the growing lump inside his pants and trying to calm the voices doing battle inside his head.
"Turn right at the roundabout. Take her back to your flat and give her a damn good fucking," the voice of dishonour insisted. *"You'll be sorry if you don't. She's engaged. She's going to marry that moron. She doesn't want commitment from a man old enough to be her father. If you don't fuck her she'll think you're homosexual."*
"Turn left at the roundabout. Remember your pledge. Be Patient. Gain her trust. Melt her heart. Win her affections," the voice of virtue pleaded. *"You can deal with that nuisance inside your pants as soon as you get back to your flat."*
He turned left at the roundabout.
The second date was much like the first. A candle lit dinner for two at Marco Polo's. Plenty of

compliments and lots of endearment. The same music. The same sour faced Italian waiter and the same seat next to the kitchen.

Only this time when they left the restaurant, he turned right at the roundabout.

The third time they met she wasn't wearing her engagement ring.

They skipped the restaurant and went straight to his flat.

They almost fell through the front door.

"This way. Follow me," he croaked, grabbing her hand and unbuttoning his shirt, the pursuit of coital expectation fuelling a visceral surge of sexual energy.

"I want to make love to you," they both said, almost in unison, pausing momentarily at the bottom of the stairs to kiss and remove each other's clothes.

"The bedroom," he urged, breaking from the kiss and dropping clothes on the floor, pulses throbbing and heart beats racing, two people overwhelmed in the heat of passion, any thoughts of engagement rings or wedding bells, smothered under the sound of urgent footfalls thudding up the stairs to the bedroom.

They were naked and almost sprinting by the time they hit the mattress, a tangle of hands sweeping over naked flesh in a courtship of playful foreplay, touching and feeling, squeezing and groping, exploring the boundaries and testing the limits, embracing the warm sensation of each other's nakedness, laughing one minute and moaning the next, rejoicing in their intimate moment of human sexual discovery.

"That's so good," she smiled, a young woman swimming in a sea of mixed emotions, a vibrant young body hovering on a plateau somewhere in heaven, a thousand butterflies fluttering inside her stomach and a burning compulsion manifesting between her legs.

"Oh…Ah. Oh…Ahhh. Yes," she moaned, shaking her head from side to side, gripping his arm with one hand and clutching the bedsheet with the other. "Oh. Yes…Oh. Fuck," she cursed, as an earth-shattering orgasm claimed her body, stinging her eyes, curling her toes and distorting her face.

They never slept that Friday night. Two devoted bodies celebrating a special union of sexual discovery until the early hours of the next morning. Saturday and Sunday smothered in the heat of passion. The entire weekend devoted to hours of mind-blowing sex.

They fucked on the bed. They fucked on the floor. They fucked in the kitchen. They fucked on the stairs. Him on top of her. Her on top of him. Catching brief moments of sleep. Showering together. Eating together. Returning to the bedroom to continue their marathon of impetuous copulation. Multiple orgasms until their bodies were drained of energy and their natural defences had surrendered to exhaustion.

They needed each other so much that she moved into his flat. They were deeply in love and their sex life was extremely active. Life couldn't be better. So why did he decide to invest in a newsagent's business with his brother Frank? And what was he thinking about when he put their life savings into a business partnership with a man whose sole outlook in life was viewed through the bottom of a whiskey glass?

After being discharged from the British Armed Forces on medical grounds, Frank had tried different jobs but none of them seemed to fit his undisciplined lifestyle. He started to get depressed and started drinking heavily and there were times when his drinking got so bad, he ended up in trouble with the police.

On the day, Frank arrived at his house his life was empty, and his self-respect was in the gutter, but he was wearing his entrepreneurial head when he offered his proposals for a business venture and partnership.

It wasn't as if he wanted to invest his time or his money in a newsagent's shop, and if the truth were known, Frank was probably the last person he could think of to form a business partnership.

Nevertheless, Frank was very persuasive.

He said that he intended putting up most of the initial capital from the money he had received
from his early retirement from the army. He also said that he didn't expect him to leave his job and become proactive in the business, because he was going to move into the vacant flat above the premises with his girlfriend, Maureen Turnbull and together they would manage the day-to-day running of the business.

Frank was so full of optimism and enthusiasm that day and it had been a long time since he had seen him feeling more alive and looking more like his old self.

So, when he declared on oath that he had changed for the better, he felt an overwhelming obligation to help him to get back on his feet.

The first year of settling into the new business arrangement was hard work, but things were going to plan. The profits were small, but trading was reasonable, and the bank manager was happy with the annual business accounts.

Frank continued to collect the day-to-day supplies from the local cash-and-carry warehouse and Maureen managed the shop with a couple of part time staff. Things were going quite well, and it appeared that their future in the retail business held great promise.

After eighteen months of trading and Frank's insatiable appetite for success, they approached the bank for a business loan and purchased another newsagents shop.

After trying for a baby for almost ten months, Jill happily announced that she was pregnant. They were both overjoyed with the news. Nothing was more important as they both prepared for the birth of their first child.

He continued to work hard at his job in the council offices and because Frank and Maureen appeared to have the business fully under control, he felt confident that he could leave it in his safe hands and concentrate on devoting all his free time to Jill.

In the next financial year, the business accounts continued to declare small profits.
Then Frank and Maureen met John and Monica Hastings.
The couple owned a transport business in a large industrial building, on the banks of the River Tyne.
John drove a Jaguar and Monica drove a Mercedes sports.
They lived in a six-bedroom house on four acres of land, with mature trees and a tennis court and they spent most of their time, either holidaying in the Caribbean, or frequenting the casinos in London.
Monica wore skirts that were too short and blouses that were too tight and John flashed his money like a millionaire.
That's when things started to go seriously wrong with the business.
Frank and Maureen wanted to live a lifestyle like John and Monica.
In a short period of time, they somehow managed to find the money to place a large deposit on a four-bedroom detached house and purchase a new 3.0 litre Ford Granada.
So, when the business overdraft crept up to a level that alerted the bank manager, they were asked to attend an urgent meeting at the bank with their accountants.
At the meeting, the bank manager confirmed that the recent year ending accounts for the business had accrued substantial losses, and furthermore neither Mark nor Frank could give a satisfactory explanation

for the deficit. To protect the banks interests, the manager said that he had no alternative but to remove the business overdraft facility, until the situation improves.

Without financial help from the bank it proved extremely difficult to continue trading and it soon became clear that if the economic situation couldn't be improved, the outcome of the business was inevitable.

Their accountants advised them that they had about six-months to correct their trading account otherwise they were looking at the probability of going into voluntary receivership.

The threats against the business didn't seem to register with Frank and Maureen.

They continued to socialise in the same upper-class circles as their friends John and Monica Hastings, spending money irresponsibly, living well beyond their means and going about their lives as if the problems didn't exist. They even arranged to go on a Caribbean holiday with their friends and like a fool he agreed to take time off work to look after the business while they were away.

Because Jill was close to giving birth to their first child he was up to his neck in matrimonial duties as well as trying to balance the finances and the accruing debts of the failing business.

Late one evening after closing one of the newsagent shops, he was just about to get into his car when he was approached by a couple of dodgy geezers.

They told him that they had a large quantity of cigarettes for sale and asked him if he was interested in doing a deal.
At first, he was a little apprehensive, but after a quick calculation he realised that the return from the sale of the cigarettes would substantially reduce the business deficit and remove the underlying pressure that was now beginning to affect his health.
Trapped in a financial dilemma and seeing no better alternative to get them out of a hole that was getting deeper by the day, he purchased the cigarettes.
Jill Brand gave birth to a baby girl.
Apart from the ongoing problems with his brother Frank and the business finances, life in the Brand household couldn't have been more fulfilling.
Motherhood seemed to come naturally to Jill. She spent most of her time looking after their daughter Catherine, adapting to the inevitable changes and performing her maternal duties with the utmost care and attention.
Three weeks later while Frank and Maureen were away on a week-end break in London with John and Monica Hastings, Gateshead CID swooped on both newsagent's shops.
He was arrested and charged with receiving stolen goods.

The Last Time (circa-1990)

Justice Adrian Bradshaw removed his wire-rimmed spectacles from his tweed jacket pocket and after slipping them over his nose he stared at the nine defendants in the dock.

All nine had pleaded guilty to theft or the receiving of stolen goods.

Of the nine defendants, three men in their mid-twenties had pleaded guilty to the theft of three-million cigarettes stolen from a cash-and-carry warehouse, in the west-end of the city.

The men had disabled the security alarm system and close circuit television cameras before crashing a heavy goods vehicle through a roller-shutter door.

The other three men in the dock consisted of two Asian men and one white male.

They were the owners of newsagent's shops and all three had pleaded guilty to receiving in the region of one-million cigarettes each.

The remaining members in the dock were three women in their mid-fifties who had pleaded guilty to the handling of stolen goods.

Justice Bradshaw had been listening for most of the morning, to the respective barristers representing the three young men who carried out the initial theft. They asked his lordship to consider a range of mitigating circumstances that had resulted in bringing their clients to this unfortunate situation. They said that if their clients hadn't come from broken families, living in depressed neighbourhoods with little or no prospects and had they been given a better start in life in a more secure environment, they felt sure that their paths would have taken a different route and they most certainly wouldn't be standing in front of his lordship today.

Leaning forward on his elbows with his fingers laced together in front of his face in that universal sign for prayer and his half-moon glasses balanced precariously on the end of his nose he casually flicked through a lengthy summary report of their previous convictions, ranging from GBH and ABH, assault with a deadly weapon, arson, burglary, resisting arrest, breaking and entry, theft, drinking and driving….the list went on.

Mr Bradshaw sighed and folded his arms across his chest, waiting patiently for the barrister to describe how these three men – when they weren't engaged in crime – felt it was their duty to help little old ladies to cross a busy road.

The barristers representing the proprietors of the newsagent's shops who had received the stolen cigarettes, generally summarised their clients as happily married men with children, who were respected and upstanding members of the communities they served.

The barristers reminded his lordship that if you discounted unpaid parking fines, all three men had outstanding and unblemished records. They respectfully suggested to his lordship that given their clients circumstances and background, on this occasion a suspended sentence rather than a custodial sentence would be more appropriate.

Justice Bradshaw had heard enough bullshit for one day. There were more important things on his mind. Like the vintage bottle of Claret, he had removed from his wine cellar earlier that morning and the sizzling roast beef dinner that his wife will have waiting for him when he gets home from his bureaucratic kingdom of justice.

He pushed his spectacles back onto the bridge of his nose and cleared his throat to announce his intention to deliver the verdicts. His voice was calm but delivered with an intellectual maturity that you would expect from a man who administers the law.

He first directed his attention at the two men who he described as the ring-leaders in a well organised, ruthless and well executed crime, with only one objective. He suggested that in

their desperate attempt to steal a quantity of goods they had left a trail of destruction with no thought or consideration of others.

Growling his dissatisfaction in a vocal outburst full of genuine hatred, he launched into a fiery attack on their characters, describing how men like these play an egotistical but unworthy part in today's society. His words were conveyed with a hint of patronising sarcasm, only just avoiding the word 'scumbags, when he talked about the substantial costs that had incurred and the tireless hours spent by the police in their efforts to have these two men extradited from the Mediterranean island of Cyprus.

The two men both received a five-year prison sentence.
The third man in the dock described as the get-away driver, who allegedly only received a payment of a few hundred pounds and a couple of cartons of cigarettes, received a two-year prison sentence.
A brief moment of the most uncomfortable silence filled the court room, eventually broken by a flatulent movement from someone in the dock. It was at this point when the haunting reality of a custodial sentence looked almost certain.
His freedom. His wife. His job. His life hanging by a thread. He took the matter a little more seriously, sat up straight, cleared his throat and adjusted the knot in his tie.
Justice Bradshaw gathered a few papers from his desk before turning his attention to the two Asian men and the white male who he referred to as, 'the shopkeepers.'
Looking out over the top of his half-moon spectacles, his eyes were unforgiving, and the tone of his voice was assertive.
"You have been described as three professional men who are supposed to be respected pillars of the community. But men of your status in society should know better than to break the law. If you weren't so eager to take stolen goods, then crimes of this nature wouldn't be so appealing to the criminals."
After sentencing the three men to eighteen-months in prison, he took a deep intake of breath before facing

the three middle-aged women who had pleaded guilty to handling stolen goods.
Innocent faces shrouded in paper tissues, forcing sniffles and false tears and shuffling nervously on their feet, stared back at the judge, waiting anxiously for the outcome.
After placing the palms of his hands flat together directly in front of his face in that collective sign common to prayer or begging, he looked at the three women and cleared his throat.
"I believe that you three women were unfortunately caught up in a ruthless criminal web of deceit. I also accept that your involvement in the handling of these stolen goods did in fact play a small part in the scale of the overall crime. Notwithstanding this, you are all old enough to understand that your conscience is that part of you which separates right from wrong and for that reason I can't let you go unpunished."
After pausing to regain his composure and adjusting his spectacles, he continued.
"I therefore sentence all three of you to…" There was a brief moment of crippling silence before one of the three women almost collapsed in the dock and another began sobbing uncontrollably. But after a court usher dutifully provided a glass of water and the judge informed them that they would each receive a twelve-month suspended prison sentence, they all made a remarkable recovery.
Overcome with relief, the three women hugged and kissed each other before extending their thanks to Justice Bradshaw. One of them composed a curtsy

and addressed him as, 'Your Highness' which brought a sanctimonious smile to the face of one of the barristers.

The holding cell in the bowels of the court was cold and depressing. Two rows of bench seating fixed along a white-washed painted wall covered in shameful graffiti provided the condemned men with a place to contemplate their adversity, as they sat without protest, awaiting their final destination.

He glanced at the artwork and graffiti decorating the walls. It was mostly filth and impulsive inscriptions of lovers proclaiming their everlasting love for each other. Some had written insults and others had made promises that would never be kept.

The inmate's reception at H.M.P. Durham held an unhealthy black gloom of helplessness and inevitable depression.

A sour faced, arrogant and overweight prison officer had the mundane task of registering each inmate as he entered his domain.

"Name," he barked, without emotion and avoiding eye contact, followed by the usual confirmation of address and date of birth.

"Empty the contents of your pockets on the desk. Remove any watches, rings and jewellery," he bellowed his authority. "Strip off and turn around in a full circle," was his next instruction.

"Enter the showers and then pick up a set of prison clothing," was his final command.

From that moment and throughout the remainder of his sentence, he would only be referred to by his Surname, and never by his Christian name.

For many years H.M.P. Durham had been a top-security jail, holding some of the country's most violent prisoners. But now it operated solely as an allocation prison and therefore most inmates would only spend a short time in custody, before being relocated to another prison.

His barrister had informed him that he would probably spend about four-weeks in Durham before being transferred to H.M.P. Tollgate open prison. He also said that with good behaviour and a recommendation by the Parole Board, he could be released on licence after serving a third of his original sentence.

His first night of incarceration was always going to be the most difficult to deal with.

He couldn't stop thinking about Jill and how she would cope on her own with their four-month old baby girl, Catherine. But although he agonised with her predicament he was fully aware that Jill was a strong and rational person, who would manage and deal with any problem or difficult situation.

Stepping into the haunting claustrophobia of a cold prison cell on E-Wing, to be greeted by a violent and foul-mouthed man in his mid-twenties who had been convicted of stealing and ringing cars, didn't help him in his moment of despair. Neither did the metal framed bed with a badly stained mattress and perpetual use from countless inmates who had shed more than tears during their long sleepless nights. Or the foul-smelling bucket of urine in the corner of the cell, a bowel moving reminder of the dignity lost in the disposal of bodily functions.

He climbed into bed. He couldn't sleep. He couldn't think straight. He tried hard to ignore the friendship of the foul-mouthed man sharing the cell.

He waited until he had fallen asleep before spilling a few silent tears on the pillow. He buried his face in the mattress and prayed, hoping that when he woke up, this would all turn out to be some regrettable nightmare.

After a sleepless night with a homicidal maniac, he was relieved when a prison officer told him he was being transferred to another cell on C-Wing, later that day.

His new cell mate was a tall stocky man in his early-fifties with long grey hair, a huge head and a cavernous mouth, displaying more gum than teeth.

He was serving three-years for arson.

"Tom Bradley," he announced, shaking his hand and almost crushing his fingers.

"Mark Brand," he replied, dropping his belongings on one of the bunk-beds.

"You're on the top bunk," Tom said, without compromise, waiting patiently until he had moved his stuff off his bed.

"Cigarette," Tom offered, his face shrouded in smoke from a burning cigarette dangling precariously from his mouth.

"Is this your first time inside?" Tom asked, handing him his lighter.

"Is it that obvious," he replied, lighting his cigarette.

"It is, so, I'd better give you a brief rundown of the rules and protocols inside the prison," he said with reassurance, slipping his lighter back into his pocket.

"This is a shit-hole, son. In nearly one-hundred years there has only been two changes to improve the welfare and conditions for inmates," he sighed, pausing to pull on his cigarette. "After a fucking hundred-years, you can now have corn flakes for breakfast and a radio in your cell," he said, twisting his face and staring at the radio, the resonating power-chord of AC/DC, launching into 'A *Whole Lotta Rosie,'* interrupting his flow.

"You can't hear yourself speak with that fucking racket," he barked, shaking his head from side-to-side and lowering the volume, pulling on his cigarette and gathering his thoughts, before continuing with his lecture.

"The screws get you up at six the morning and they put you to bed at 10 p.m. You collect your meals from the kitchen and you eat your food inside your cell. You shower on a Thursday and you get a change of clothing on Friday. They allow you a forty-five-minute break each day for 'Association, which consists of a casual stroll inside the prison yard," he said, coughing into a clenched fist and pausing to roll two more cigarettes.

"Jobs inside the prison are scarce son. Kitchen...Laundry...Library...Scrubbing or Mopping

floors can all get you away from the boredom of the prison cell," he smiled, handing him a cigarette between two nicotine stained fingers.
"If you don't have a job you are banged-up in your cell for most of the day," he concluded, flicking his lighter over the cigarettes.
"Oh. There's one more thing. Never ask anybody why they are in here and be careful how you go, this place is full of thieves and fucking villains."
A week later Tom informed him that he was expecting to be transferred to another prison.
"That squeaky clean image of yours is only going to get you into trouble," Tom said, raising a concerned eyebrow.
"It's a fucking time bomb in here," Tom snorted. "The place is full of fucking maniacs," he added, placing a friendly hand on his shoulder.
"It's a place where the strong fuck the weak son and you look vulnerable," he said, brushing his hand over the back of his neck and staring out through the steel bars on a small window, a faint glimmer of light the only reminder of the world outside.
"Over the years this prison has held some of the most violent criminals. Ronnie Kray. John McVicar. Frankie Fraser. They've all done time in here," he sighed, blowing smoke between the vertical steel bars and stubbing his cigarette out on a fossilised spider.
"If you want to stay clear of trouble son, you need to mix with the right people," he said, with reassurance, smiling through a toothless mouth.

"I'll introduce you to two friends of mine who will look after you when I'm gone. Nobody messes with Tony and Darren…Not even the screws," he grinned, as he proceeded to empty his bladder into a bucket of piss.

When Tom Bradley introduced him to Tony Elliott and Darren Adams, he knew immediately that these were two ruthless hard-men who should always be respected.

Tony Elliott had the physique of a gladiator and the look of a man who ate his meat raw.

Over six-feet tall and built like the proverbial brick-shit-house, he towered over most people and there were occasions when he had to lower his head when he entered a room.

A huge muscular man with a threatening look and a venomous voice, he had the biggest pair of hands he had ever seen.

Prior to his conviction, Tony worked on his parent's farm, but in his younger days he had been a semi-professional boxer, until he lost his licence. After one of his fights, Tony was enraged when the referee awarded the fight to the other man. After the fight he confronted the referee and after a heated exchange of words Tony hit him with a punch to the face that left him unconscious on the dressing room floor.

Tony was serving a two-year sentence for the theft of a tanker full of diesel fuel.

Darren Adams was similar in build, although only six feet tall with normal size hands that displayed the

prison trademark of 'LOVE' and 'HATE' tattooed across each hand.
When he wasn't doing time, he worked on-and-off as a night-club doorman.
Darren was serving a three-year sentence for grievous bodily harm.
It was a timely coincidence that Darren was a good friend of the two men who had been convicted of the stolen cigarettes, and furthermore he had flown to Cyprus to visit the men prior to their extradition back to the UK.
When he said the worst job in the prison was scrubbing floors, Tom Bradley was right.
With a scrubbing brush in one hand and a bucket of dirty water in the other, he worked his way down the stairs under the watchful eye of a prison officer.
His task for that day was to ensure the quality of workmanship was up to his demanding standards, and if it wasn't he would find himself out of a job.
"BRAND!" growled the prison officer, the sound of two fingers snapping together and that unmistakable voice of authority interrupting his thoughts and his enthusiastic momentum.
"Move to the side and let the probation officers pass," he insisted, waving his hand in a gesture of direction.
"Yes sir," he answered, dragging his bucket of dirty water to one side, as two women in uniforms headed down the stairs.
One of them was a fat abrasive woman in her mid-fifties with a round face and a few strands of hair

growing from a hideous mole on her chin. The other woman was in her mid-thirties. She was slim and attractive with incredibly long legs growing out of a pair of black heels.

Their eyes met and the sound of heels tapping on the concrete stairs, suddenly stopped.

He froze, and she gasped, almost losing her balance in embarrassing recoil. She looked at him and he looked at her. She lowered her eyes and then looked up again, the expression on her face a haunting mask of shock and disbelief.

With a deep shade of crimson colouring her face and her heels clicking in an urgent descent down the concrete stairs, Caroline Spencer walked out of his life for the second time.

The coach journey to H.M.P. Tollgate open prison took just over an hour. And even though the panoramic views of the autumnal countryside were a welcoming sight from his dismal cell in Durham, he was still a little apprehensive about his next destination, knowing he wouldn't have the friendship or the protection of Tony Elliott and Darren Adams.

Before his untimely departure from HMP-Durham, Tom Bradley had explained some of the advantages and disadvantages of being inside an open prison.

He told him that the main advantage was the flexibility to move freely around the camp and mix with the other inmates. And because you weren't locked in a cell for most of the day you could take a shower and get a change of clothing whenever you liked.

He said that although all inmates were allocated a job, when your working day had ended the rest of your time was devoted to the social and leisure facilities inside the prison.

The main disadvantage of the move to an open prison would be the monthly visit for Jill. Durham prison was only a short bus ride from Gateshead, but now she would be faced with a lengthy journey and it wouldn't be easy, considering Catherine was only four months old.

Another disadvantage of the open prison was that although you had the freedom to move around inside the camp, the night-shift prison staff were few in numbers, which added to the risk of attacks from other inmates.

Surrounded by a three-metre-high steel security fence the open prison covered a vast area of land. The buildings for both inmates and the prison service were a mixture of pre-fabricated timber and brickwork construction. They had that despondent look that you often associate with old institutional buildings and army barracks.

There was a range of social and activity rooms for inmates. Television Room. Gymnasium. Snooker and Pool Room. Arts and Crafts Room. Music Room, which consisted of a tired looking piano with several broken keys. He counted six. It was certainly not a Steinway.

His accommodation for the remainder of his sentence would be undertaken in one of the pre-fabricated buildings, where he would spend most of his time living with eleven other inmates. Apart from himself and a man in his late-forties, all the other inmates were in their early to late-twenties.

For the next few days he went about adjusting to his new environment, mixing socially with some of the younger inmates, finding his way around the prison and getting familiar with the recreational facilities, all the time making sure he followed Tom Bradley's advice, avoiding any confrontation with violent lunatics.

It was a cold wet morning, waiting for the daily roll-call-register to get underway.

"Adams!" shouted the duty officer. "Yes," a voice echoed, the mere mention of his name getting him on his toes and craning his neck, looking over a sea of heads and searching for the compulsory raised hand of the inmate.

'Darren Adams,' the fingers of 'LOVE' and 'HATE,' informed him, craning his neck again and looking over an ocean of blue denim uniforms, the towering silhouette of Tony Elliott, lifting the corners of his mouth and bringing a smile to his face.

'Never in his wildest dreams would he have thought that a couple of ruthless hard-men could be such a welcoming sight,' he thought, breathing a sigh of relief and waving a friendly hand.

It didn't take long before the prison officers recognised the authority and respect that Tony and

Darren were given, amongst the other inmates. It was also evident that the screws played a part in passing information to certain inmates, especially when it concerned a 'nonce' who was attempting to slip through the net.

Most inmates who were inside for normal criminal activities that weren't associated with interfering with children, or attacks on elderly people were reasonably accepted by other inmates and most of the prison officers. No one tolerated paedophiles and if they were discovered they were dealt with in a brutal and violent manner.

Tom Bradley had told him that convicted sex offenders were given the opportunity to be protected under prison 'Rule 43,' which meant they could spend their sentence in solitary confinement. However, there was the occasional 'nonce' that preferred to mix and socialise with the other inmates and thought the risk was worth taking.

It was meant to be a friendly gesture, but the gruesome hand of Tony Elliott gripping his shoulder and the threatening voice in his ear, always made him feel uneasy, especially when he was alone in the toilet block.

"There's a 'nonce' in your building," Tony barked, spitting skilfully into the sink next to the urinal, the urgency in his voice demanding that he should finish his piss and listen to what he had to say.

"The older man," Darren confirmed, stepping from the shadows. "He's been convicted of sex offences with children," he added, blowing smoke above his head, pulling his zip down and levelling up at one of the urinals.

"After midnight roll-call, we're going to pay him a visit," Tony grinned, his grip intensifying and his voice uncompromising.

"I want you to warn the other inmates not to get involved. And if the screws ask questions, tell them to keep their mouths shut."

Thirty-minutes after midnight roll-call, Tony and Darren walked casually into the pre-fabricated building and after pushing a sock into the older man's mouth they dragged him along the corridor and into a nearby toilet block.

The paedophile was beaten without remorse, his desperate cries for help fading into muffled echoes inside the toilet enclosure, until everything went deathly silent.

It didn't take long for the rumours to circulate around the prison the next day. All the inmates were being questioned by the prison officers, although everyone including the screws knew who had carried out the assault. Apparently, the man had been attacked by someone yielding two snooker balls wrapped inside a sock. The beating was so violent his face was unrecognisable, and his testicles had been crushed.

After being rushed to a local hospital the 'nonce' was on a life support machine in a critical condition. A prison officer confirmed that if he hadn't managed to crawl from the toilet block and into the corridor, he probably would have died from his injuries.

The weather was showing signs that they were heading for a cold winter, so when he was told he would be employed in the main administration block, he considered himself rather fortunate, especially when the other inmates told him that working in the Governor's office was considered to be the best job in the prison.

The administration block was predominantly a brick built flat roof building. The building footprint formed the shape of a letter T. On the immediate left of the T were the offices for about thirty civilian staff. To the right were the offices of the Governor and the Deputy Governor, Principal Prison Officers and the Probation Service.

The leg of the T contained the staff toilets, store rooms, a kitchen, and an inmate's toilet.

Jack Wilson was a desperately thin and frail old man who looked as if he needed a good meal and a doctor. With snowy white hair combed flat on his head and shining with cream, his face was tired and gaunt, and his expression always held a bitter sadness.

After spending four-weeks of his sentence at H.M.P. Armley, he was transferred to Tollgate open prison, where he had spent the last five-months working in the administration block.

He had been convicted of stealing goods from a supermarket, where he was employed as an assistant manager.

After giving the company forty-years of his life and never once having a day's sickness, Jack was overlooked for promotion. He was deeply hurt and for a long time he suffered from anxiety and depression.

Insulted by their oversight, he decided that an alternative way to top-up his pension and savings account was to remove goods from the supermarket store room.

At first, things were going reasonably well, and his thefts went undetected. He started by taking a few items home in the boot of his car and sold them to friends and neighbours.

But with all crime comes greed and it wasn't long before the quantities increased, and he ended up having to make use of a truck.

For his crime, Jack was sent to prison for two-years.

"Fucking rain," he cursed, lifting his collar and sprinting like an athlete through the storm, soaking wet and gasping for breath when he eventually reached the administration block.

"Fucking weather," he repeated, pausing in the dark lobby to catch his breath and clear water from his face and hair.

Apart from the sound of the rain drumming against the air-conditioning units on the roof, there was an uncanny silence.

Once he had regained his composure, he headed towards a bright light spilling into the corridor from an open door, pausing momentarily when he heard the feint sound of someone muttering inside the room.

He courteously signalled his approach with a couple of forced coughs, before stepping into the warmth of the kitchen.

"I'll be with you in a moment," said an old man holding a felt-tip pen, marking a calendar on the wall and circling today's date. "Nearly done," he added, his bony fingers counting out the next six days, leading up to the seventh day marked with the words, 'FREEDOM.'

"Only six-days to go," the old man smiled, pointing a finger at the calendar, before extending his hand.

"Jack Wilson," he invited, unable to disguise the cheer in his voice. "You must be the new boy," he said, forcing a smile that quickly faded.

"Mark Brand," he offered, letting go of his hand.

"The Parole Board recommended that I could be released on licence after serving a third of my sentence," Jack said, raising two fingers at the establishment. "I can't wait to get away from this fucking shit-hole," he added, frowning when he realised his words were a little insensitive.

Before his release, Jack explained some of the important protocols and procedures involved with his many duties. He told him he was the tea-boy. The subservient dogs-body. The whipping-boy and anything else they could think of. Jack also advised him who he should look out for, who he could trust, and most of all, who he should avoid.

Once he had accepted the indignity of delivering tea and coffee to the staff and cleaning the toilets, life was

reasonably comfortable, and the privacy of the kitchen gave him time to relax and write letters to Jill.
David Jefferies had been the Governor of H.M.P. Tollgate for the past twenty-five years. He was a tired looking man who looked his age and should have retired from the prison service at least two-years ago.
Boasting a large sweeping moustache that curled upwards at the ends, the yellow nicotine streak in the centre confirmed his weakness for his twenty-a-day foul smelling cigars. And with a soft baritone voice and easy-going manner he was polite and respectful to everyone.
He was calm. He was sophisticated. He was intelligent. He was known to complete the Times cross-word puzzle, in under fifteen minutes.
Douglas Wood had held the position of Deputy Governor for the last eight years. He was a fit looking man in his early-fifties and from his six-foot-four-inch height, he looked down on those around him with contempt. He was a foul mouthed arrogant man who demanded respect from everyone and there were occasions when his mood swings could often lead to a demonstration of his violent temper. He made it clear that he wasn't interested in exchanging pleasantries with anyone, apart from the Governor.
Douglas Wood was also aware that the announcement of David Jefferies declaring the date of his retirement, was long overdue.
It didn't take him long to find out that some of the prison officers and most of the civilian office staff

were decent and friendly people, even a fat middle-aged woman with an obvious moustache that would have made a lot of young men very proud.
But the one person working in the admin office that caught his attention, was an attractive woman in her early-thirties, called Christine Noble.

It was a bitterly cold night in November when he walked into the administration block.
The Governor and Deputy Governor and some of the select Principal Prison Officers were entertaining members from the Prison Officers Association and Parole Board.
His job for the evening was to serve the guests with tea, coffee or alcoholic drinks.
He was given a white jacket especially for the occasion.
He was a little apprehensive about his first function, but when he discovered that Christine Noble had volunteered to help with the buffet, he felt more relaxed and looked forward to the event and the opportunity of getting to know more about her.
After a brief introduction and a busy hour, serving the guests with food and drinks, they sat in the kitchen, smoking cigarettes and making small-talk.
But as the evening progressed, that despondent silence that always brings strangers together, miraculously produced a spark of chemistry.
After gaining her trust, they sampled the wine and continued to share intimate details about each other

with surprising ease, slowly guiding each other towards a sexual and more flirtatious conversation.
They laughed and took turns in telling each other about their backgrounds and their likes and dislikes. Christine managed to compress her entire life storey into about fifteen-minutes of rambling trivia, some of which was interesting, but other information about her family and pets were less important and ultimately boring.
As the night reached a close, it was evident that Christine had consumed too much wine.
In a slurred voice and a cute giggle, she said that she hoped she might see him again at the 'Big-Bash' in December.
He wasn't sure what she meant and the embarrassment of a baseball bat inside his pants, forced him to remain seated. But there was a soft tenderness in her voice that hinted maybe Christine Noble wanted something more.

With the offer of free cigarettes, coffee and chocolate biscuits, the monthly visit from members of Alcoholics Anonymous always attracted a large number of inmates.
With a mouth permanently fixed in a contented smile, a large framed woman in her early-fifties stood up at the visitors table and introduced herself and two other people with her.
Staring into the faces of about thirty restless and uninterested inmates, she looked a little

apprehensive as she announced the purpose of her visit to the prison.

After talking with assurance for about fifteen-minutes, about the serious consequences that alcohol can have and how it can seriously affect your social, domestic and physical way of life, she introduced the first speaker.

"My name is Stuart Bell and I'm an alcoholic," said a tall skinny man with a nasal voice and bulging eyes. "I'm thirty-four years old and after a divorce about three years ago, I now live on my own in a single bed flat."

After a chorus of sniggers and a string of crude remarks from a few inmates, Stuart took a deep intake of breath and continued.

"I used to work as a telecommunication engineer for a large telephone company. Each day I was given a job sheet with a list of installations or maintenance items which I had to complete. The company provided me with a van to get to the appropriate destinations," he said, scratching his testicles and lowering his head, trying to ignore the crude and impatient comments from the mutinous and unforgiving audience.

"I've been a member of Alcoholics Anonymous for the last two-years," he declared, pausing to smile at the large framed woman and waiting long enough until she returned his smile.

"Let me tell you about a typical day in my life," he offered, pausing to sip a glass of water and gather his thoughts. "Each day would start with a thumping hangover. Breakfast would usually consist of a piece of toast, followed by a couple of cans of beer or a glass of whisky. Once I had arrived at my first job for that particular day, I would make a mental note of the pubs in the area and before my lunch break, I would have probably had another can of beer," he sighed, pausing and hunching his shoulders to indicate his stupidity.

"When I was inside the pub at lunch-time, I would consume about three pints and sometimes a whisky to wash down a sandwich. In the late afternoon, I would drink another can or two before driving home. For the remainder of the evening I would just sit at home, drinking beer, whiskey or vodka…I never went to bed until I was pissed," he sighed, looking into the eyes of a group of inmates staring back at him with contempt, before gathering his thoughts to speak.

"I will never let alcohol ruin my life again," he declared, with the conviction of a minister and the look of a defeated man who had been used to too many disappointments in his life.

After twisting his face in miserable apology, Stuart Bell sat down in his chair and for a few seconds the room went deathly quiet.

Someone sitting at the back of the room, with a strong Liverpool accent and a foul mouth, broke the crippling silence. "IS THAT FUCKING ALL?" he chuckled. "I've spilt more down me fucking shirt."

Everyone in the room, except Stuart Bell and the large framed woman sitting next to him, exploded into fits of laughter.

It was a cold December night when he arrived in a hasty panic at the administration block. Because his guests would be arriving at 7.p.m. Douglas Wood had instructed him to be there no later than six-thirty, to offer reception drinks on their arrival.

After hanging his coat in the lobby and walking into the kitchen, Christine Noble greeted him with a welcoming smile and a reassuring voice.

"I told you we'd meet again at the Governors Christmas party."

Douglas Wood was a little nervous but also excited about the occasion. Tonight, was a high-profile event with delegates from the Chair of Prison Governors, The Chief Constable and members of the Association of Police Officers and representatives from the National Probation Service and the Parole Board.

Douglas Wood, knew that this social gathering, could determine his future of becoming the next prison governor, so there was no surprise when he delivered his instructions with determination and authority, that made him feel like he was something, he had just scraped off his shoe.

"Look smart. No alcohol and don't fuck up."

Although he found his remarks about alcohol almost laughable, he just nodded his head and left the tempting *'arrogant fucking arsehole'* waiting at the back of his throat.

Inside the confines of the pre-fabricated buildings, the inmates were also making preparation for their festive party. The regular 'fence-drops' had provided an abundance of canned beers and various bottles of wines and spirits, and the cartons of cigarettes and dope would ensure the inmates celebrated the Christmas and New Year, in the traditional way.

David Jefferies waited until all the guests had received a glass of champagne before announcing his retirement from the prison service.

Douglas Wood's eagerness broke the silence inside the room. "Three cheers for the Governor," Douglas hailed, raising his glass and inviting a toast. "The Governor. To a long and happy retirement," he added, unable to disguise the enthusiasm in his voice and the glowing look of self-congratulation on his face.

For the first couple of hours, Mark and Christine skipped between the kitchen and the governor's office, making sure everyone had been watered and fed. But as the night gathered speed and the guests became less demanding, they were able to spend more time in the kitchen, chatting over a cigarette and a glass of wine.

On one occasion when he returned to the kitchen, he discovered a cigar had been carefully placed on his chair. David Jefferies was a considerate man.

It was becoming evident in her voice and a piece of mistletoe stuck in her hair that Christine had been sampling the champagne a little too much and a little too often. And not only did the alcohol relax her mood, it also removed any defences that she might have had and prompted several flirtatious comments and sexual innuendoes.

"Haven't you noticed what I've got in my hair?" she smiled, flashing her eyes and pointing a finger at the mistletoe tangled in her hair, the unexpected acquaintance of his lips meeting hers in a meaningful kiss, bringing her quickly back to sobering reality.

"Oh, she gasped, stepping back and breaking away from the kiss, her face registering uncertainty, as if contemplating a situation that she really wanted, but never expected could actually happen.

"I'm not sure," she added, pulling the mistletoe from her hair and letting it drop on the floor, a commotion gathering between her legs, letting her know the moment was real.

"What are you not sure about?" he whispered, blowing in her ear and peppering her neck with soft, meaningful kisses, a playful interaction of touch and feel, and a brief exchange of persuasive gestures, melting her heart and gaining her approval.

Even though he was a little surprised at the speed of her submission, the touch of her lips and her warm tongue probing inside his mouth, quickly eroded any indecision from his mind.

But he was aware that the real challenge he faced with Christine wasn't because she was naive or inexperienced. It was more that her impetuous desire for stimulation, might be compromised because of the bizarre and precarious circumstances.

Faces touched, and lips met, tongues flirting and dancing over teeth, in a courtship of mutual engagement, hormonal chaos and the promise of expectation, stirring emotions and increasing arousal, caution and rational melting away in the heat of passion.

The risk. The danger. The excitement. The reality of sex fuelling the fire of passion. A wanting woman with emotional needs and a familiar wetness gathering between her legs, brushing away the need for caution.

Although fearful of the incriminations should she be caught fucking an inmate, the desire to have him between her legs, far outweighed any complications or uncertainties.

"Follow me," she smiled, curling a finger invitingly and heading into the corridor.

"I'm coming. Wait for me," he croaked, obeying her command and following quickly on her heels, the promise of surreptitious intimacy, stimulating and exciting and washing away the need for caution, although the consequences of being caught, never too far from his thoughts.

The inmate's toilet at the end of the corridor was desperately small and left little room for movement. And with only a toilet pan and a small wash hand basin and a single light bulb hanging from a bare wire, it certainly lacked romantic ambience.

It certainly wasn't designed for two people anticipating intercourse.

It was dangerous. It was outrageous. It was insane. It would have to be hurried.

His pants were at his feet before her bottom hit the toilet seat.

"Oh, Wow," she gasped, lifting the swollen muscle from his briefs and blinking her eyes, staring with alluring fascination at the gruesome limb, bobbing and swaying between the folds of his shirt.

"It's big," she smiled, shifting her weight on the toilet seat and curling her fingers around the thick veiny shaft, cradling the throbbing muscle in her hand, feeling the weight and the pulse between her fingers.

"And so heavy," she whispered, working the length with proficient ease, pulling and tugging, up and down, pulling and dragging, tugging and releasing, long strokes fast and meaningful, short strokes slow and deliberate, dragging the loose foreskin down the length and pulling it back until it shrouded the bulbous head.

"It looks good enough to eat," she smiled, flashing her eyes and brushing hair from her face, sweeping her tongue suggestively over her top lip, curiosity and responsive gestures, increasing arousal and fuelling impulsive urges.

"Do you want me to put it in my mouth. Would you like me to suck it? "she breathed, dragging her long fingernails across the scrotum and cradling his testicles in her hand, giving each one a gentle squeeze before curling her fingers around the long-veined column and easing him into her hungry mouth.

"I think you do," she smiled, easing him in and easing him out, working the length with sensuous ease, before sweeping her tongue over the sensitive head and holding his cock in tender capture between her teeth.

"You're a prisoner in my mouth," she gasped, through a stretched mouth and a swollen cock pulsing between her lips, sucking in air through her nose and dragging her teeth over the swollen head, easing him in and easing him out, feasting on the sticky fluids oozing from the small eye.

"Stand up," he croaked, the urgency in his voice getting her quickly to her feet. "I want you naked," he added, unbuttoning her blouse and fumbling nervously with the bra clasp until it yielded and both garments fell to the floor.

"What was that. I thought I heard a noise," she whispered, staring at the door and placing a finger against her mouth.

"We can't be away too long. Someone might get suspicious," she added, her heart banging like a drum inside her chest, her breathing ragged and heavy and her knickers getting wetter by the minute.

"Just long enough to…," she breathed, two mouths colliding in a crushing kiss, curious hands sweeping over curves, over bulges, over soft flesh, over hard flesh, moans chasing groans and hips moving back and forth in a simulation of coital foreplay.

"Fuck," she cursed, genitalia pushing together in a courtship of promising expectation, fondling and squeezing, biting and mauling, groping and scratching, touching and feeling, the receptive and reckless interaction accompanied by a running

commentary of compliments and filthy obscenities, echoing off the walls inside the small enclosure.
"You're right. We'd better make it quick. The last thing we need is Douglas Wood, sniffing around the kitchen," he replied, sliding his hand inside her knickers, feeling the thick bush of pubic hair slipping between his fingers, before parting the moist flaps and folds and sliding a finger inside her body.
"Oh, yes. That feels good," she breathed, heart beats racing and pulses buzzing and humming, chemicals charging adrenaline and hormonal chaos dancing in a tango of carnal uncertainty.
"Put another one in," she insisted, moaning and groaning as he slid two fingers inside her body, her confidence growing in urgent gestures of persuasive simulation, her libido increasing by the second and her body preparing for the invasion she knew was coming and desperately needed.
"Fuck Douglas wood," she said, turning around to face the wall and shamelessly pulling her knickers to the floor. "I want you inside me," she insisted, lifting her skirt over the contours of her hips until the fabric had gathered at her waist.
"This isn't going to be easy," she sighed, leaning forward with one knee on the toilet seat and one foot on the floor, one hand flat against the tiled wall and the other hand gripping the hand basin.
Christine was hot and impatient. She had given up worrying about making too much noise. It was far too late to agonise over such trivial matters now.
"Fuck me," was all she said.

No preliminary. No finesse. A single thrust of his hips and he was inside her body.

A carnal connection of urgent commitment, both hands holding her waist and his hard thighs smacking against her soft buttocks, the treacherous limb stretching the moist flaps and folds, opening the inner walls and filling her body with nine-and-a-half-inches of hard flesh.

"Oh yes," she moaned. "Faster. Faster" she urged, a visceral surge of adrenalin and oxygen rushing through her bloodstream, stealing the life source from other vital organs and fuelling genitalia.

"Fuck me. Fuck me Harder," she cried, brushing hair from her face and looking over her shoulder, the expression on her face a twisted mask of pleasure.

She was swimming in a sea of hormonal chaos. He was drowning in an ocean of testosterone. Two strangers caught in a raging sea of emotional tides and turbulent currents, riding the waves of an unpredictable storm, testing the troubled waters of risk, danger and uncertainty, a responsive expression of carnal lust and submissive persuasion, a physical demonstration of tireless stamina and endless libido, entering and retreating, pushing in and pulling out, hard and fast, penetrating deep, plunging into the depths of her burning interior, thrusting and pushing, hammering and grinding, in and out, back and forth, banging her like a screen door in a hurricane.

"Slow down. You're hurting me," she pleaded, through tight lips and gritted teeth, the brief pause giving her just enough time to adjust her knee on the toilet seat and tighten her grip on the wash-hand basin.

"Sorry," he offered, aware that her voice was a little too loud. "Keep quiet. You're making too much noise," he sighed, slowing the momentum, easing in slowly and easing out in a seamless exit, in and out, slow and methodical, allowing her to adjust to the brutal force, watching and waiting for the signal to unleash the energy of a well-oiled machine, letting her feel the tireless stamina of a man in need of euphoric release.

"I'm okay now," she whispered, her willingness to continue acknowledged in an invitation of motioning gestures and verbal suggestion. "But be gentle," she added, wriggling and swivelling her bottom, the curves of perfection and the cheeks of her bottom open and inviting and the sphincter muscles around her anal opening, pulsing with renewed arousal.

"Yes. That's better," she said, pushing back to meet the full impact of his swollen limb, giving and taking, taking and giving, entering and retreating, giving more, taking more, in a mutual engagement of intimate connection, moans and groans and whimpering cries, fading in a monologue of breathless curses and choking gasps for air.

"I want to come," she breathed, shuffling on her knee in a precarious but well-practiced vulva squeezing action and gripping his cock in a vice-like-grip, the obscene length and formidable girth stretching her body and almost tearing her apart.

"Christine wanted a good hard fucking. She was getting that...But how would she deal with an orgasm," he thought, glancing at his watch, the fast ticking timepiece reminding him that after being locked behind closed doors for twenty-minutes, it was time to find out.

With the musky odours of sex filling his nostrils and beads of sweat dripping off his chin and onto the floor, he moved inside her body with uncompromising determination, pushing in and pulling out in a seamless expression of domination over submissiveness, two people groaning out their pleasure under the rhythmic sounds of hard masculine flesh slapping against soft feminine flesh, the wet sloppy noises from their tireless copulation, echoing in a musical overture off the tiled walls inside the toilet.

"Oh. Yes. Oh. Fuck," she gasped, compliments and promises following a string of curses and filthy demands, moans and groans smothered under a chorus of euphoric mutterings, a woman reaching the heights of no return, a wanting woman freefalling towards orgasm.

"Oh God," she cried. "Oh God," she repeated. "Oh yes…Ah yes. I'm fucking coming," she cursed in an outburst of unholy pledges and filthy vocabulary, sucking in short gasps of air through her nose, her body shuddering and jerking, tensing and stiffening, her legs buckling under her weight and her vaginal muscles tightening around the custodial visitor.

"Yes. Yes. Yes," she blurted, gripping his cock in tender confinement, orgasmic mutterings growing in pace and volume, an active volcano of immense proportions erupting from her toes and up her legs, into her chest and face, tingling her fingertips and rattling her teeth, reaching the farthest recess of her brain, an earth-shattering orgasm stinging her eyes and flooding through her body in a plateau of euphoric waves and a turbulent sea of emotional ecstasy, the ultimate release of a knee-trembling orgasm celebrated in shimmering silence.

"You need to come," she said, with urgent persuasion, glancing back over her shoulder and shuffling her feet on the floor.

After a couple of determined thrusts accompanied by a vocal chorus of teeth grinding moans and groans, his balls exploded, firing a sea of seminal fluids gushing up his shaft and spilling from the single eye with the intensity of a flash flood, multiple loads of his life creation, splashing against the threshold of the cervix and flooding the vaginal vault with endless streams of liquid passion.

After a short interlude of rearranging clothes and making sure that all signs of mischief had been removed, they shared a smile and a kiss and with as much dignity as they could manage, they walked back into the kitchen and casually resumed their duties.

Neither of them said a word for a while, two strangers sitting in silence, staring at each other and forcing smiles, red faces betraying their moment of risky fornication, breathing in the fear and excitement, both aware that they had been outrageously daring and extremely lucky not to have been caught.

"I don't think we've been missed," Christine said, breaking the silence hanging between them, lighting a cigarette and pouring wine into a glass, trying to calm her nerves and regain her composure. "We needn't have hurried. Shall we do it again," she giggled, lifting the glass to her mouth and draining the contents in a couple of mouthfuls.

"That was amazing," she smiled, speaking in conspiratorial whispers and pulling on her cigarette, her post coital flush fading and her confidence growing. "I can't wait for your release date," she added, flashing her eyes with flirtatious intent and forcing a smile.

He was aware that Christine was responsible for sending out the inmates visiting orders and would therefore have a record of his personal details, including his home address, telephone number and marital status.

He returned her smile but said nothing in reply.

Christmas and New Year slipped quietly away.

A few inmates risked going over the fence to celebrate Christmas and New Year with friends or loved ones, although it didn't take long before the police picked them up, and once they were back in prison they faced the consequences of an extended sentence.

Christmas in prison was lonely and depressing, but like many complicated or challenging scenarios, light always follows darkness.

The Parole Board had recommended that he could be released early on licence and therefore he would only have to serve six-months of his initial eighteen-month sentence.

Nothing else mattered. He had a new vitality to his life. All he could think about was his new release date and the eventual home comforts with Jill and their daughter Catherine.

'Keep your nose clean...Stay out of trouble,' the words of Tom Bradley, repeated inside his head.

Time in prison seemed to stand still. Long tedious days, predictable weeks and monotonous months, all seemed to move desperately slow and for most inmate's, boredom was inevitable.

Sometimes a letter or a monthly visit with a friend or loved one was the only thing that kept them going.

He should have listened to Tom Bradley when he told him to 'stay out of trouble' and don't get involved with the personal grievances of other inmates.

But when the 'Dear John' letters started to arrive, and he discovered that many inmates lacked a basic academic education, and some couldn't even read or write, he volunteered his literary services.

However, his skills as an 'Agony Aunt' therapist, didn't last long. Most of his letters proved to have a negative response which led to some inmates becoming aggressive and threatening, so for the sake of his health, he decided to decline any further assistance to inmates concerning matrimonial issues or matters of infidelity.

After teaching a couple of inmates to play Chess, one of them wrote a letter to his sister, who lived in Canada, which triggered a lot of interest from her family and friends, who were keen to set up a game.

They accepted that the game would have to be communicated via the postal service and would inevitably be a time-consuming event. Nevertheless, everyone was enthusiastic and subsequently England-v-Canada began positively.

But after only four-weeks into the game, Douglas Wood got wind of what was taking place and decided it was inappropriate and subsequently prevented any further postal contact overseas. The game was terminated with all black and white pieces still in play.

Once again, the 'King' had looked down on his 'Pawns' with amusement and contempt.

Christine Noble always made sure his visiting order was delivered on time, so when the day arrived he was always well prepared for his monthly visit with Jill and Catherine.

It was only half-past one on a cold Saturday afternoon and he was already sitting in the visiting room anxiously waiting for his two-o'clock visit with Jill.

His mind was in chaos. He was eating cigarettes. He had just risked everything.

'Keep your nose clean...Stay out of trouble...Don't do anything that could affect your parole,' the mantra kept repeating inside his head.

He couldn't get the thought of the prison officer's irresponsible and careless action out of his head. It was a typical Saturday morning, working for a few hours in the administration block, cleaning the offices and toilets and making beverages for the three prison officers on duty.

He was almost at the end of his shift when one of the prison officer in his mid-fifties with a cigarette permanently dangling from his mouth and a face shrouded in a cloud of smoke, called him into his office.

"Brand," he barked, snapping two fingers together, as if he was calling his pet dog.

"Come into my office. I've got an errand for you," he gasped, crushing his cigarette into an overflowing ashtray, squeezing his fat arse into a chair and lighting another cigarette, his lack of enthusiasm a clear sign that he had been given a desk-job to ease him into early retirement.

"I want you to go to the central store and ask for Fred," he grunted, handing him two large empty coffee-jars, his breath smelling of alcohol and cigarettes and his emphysema making him breathe in quick short gasps.

"Give these two jars to Fred and he will fill them with gloss paint," he said, lifting from the chair and slapping him dismissively on the shoulder. "And be quick about it. My wife wants me to paint some fucking doors when I get home today," he cursed, pulling on his cigarette, coughing and wheezing and spitting phlegm into a handkerchief.

It wasn't until he was back inside the pre-fabricated building and getting ready for his monthly visit with Jill and Catherine, when he realised the Prison Officer was stealing paint from HMP stores, and furthermore he had implicated him in his crime.

'Keep your nose clean...Stay out of trouble...Don't do anything that could affect your parole. The voice of caution kept nagging away inside his head, as he waited for Jill to arrive.

"There's another 'nonce' in the prison and this time Tony and Darren want an audience," said a faceless man with a Northern Irish accent, the volume in his voice, interrupting his thoughts.

He turned quickly in his chair. The speaker was a fat unkempt man holding a cigarette between his fingers and swearing at a lighter that wouldn't work.

"What...When?" he prompted the fat man, reaching into his pocket and lighting his cigarette, just avoiding setting fire to his long hair hanging over his face.

"It's going to happen at six o'clock tonight," the fat man confirmed, pausing to look over his shoulder and pulling nervously on his cigarette.

"Tony and Darren said you have to be there," he whispered, before disappearing into the crowd of anxious visitors, filling the room.

The painful screams echoed off the walls inside the pre-fabricated building as Tony Elliott and Darren Adams, exploded into a frenzied and violent attack.

With one foot pushed inside a metal dustpan, Tony Elliott lost control, inflicting the paedophile with an onslaught of continuous kicks and punches to the lower body and head.

"Fucking nonce...Fucking cunt...Dirty fucking bastard," Tony barked, kicking the man repeatedly in the head, his growling aggression, synonymous with a chained scrap-yard dog.

The battered man struggled helplessly on the floor, pleading for his life and trying to manoeuvre his body into a tight ball, in a desperate attempt to protect his face from Darren's burning cigarette. But his efforts were futile and his cries for help were smothered under the cacophonous chants from an audience of bloodthirsty inmates, demanding nothing less than serious injury or death from their defiant gladiators.

The beating was swift and brutal and as the inmates slowly melted away, the 'nonce' was left lying unconscious on the floor, in a pool of blood with the wooden handle of the dustpan inserted into his anus and a letter 'N' burned into his forehead, a permanent reminder of his heinous and unforgiving crime.

It was a freezing cold morning in March, as he headed towards the main entrance gates, although the weather was the last thing on his mind.

He was going home.

After a cursory smile and a muttered *'don't come back,'* the security officer opened the prison gates and he walked back into the civilised world of sanity and normality.

Blinking tears of euphoric release from his eyes, the sound of a car horn and flashing lights informed him that his brother, Frank was waiting to take him home.

As he headed towards the car, he wondered whether the best part of his life was already behind him. How he had missed the simple but precious moments that life had to offer.

"I'm going home. Nothing else matters," he sighed, an unexpected smile that had been hibernating for the last six-months, lifting the corners of his mouth.

He looked back over the prison for the last time, catching sight of hundreds of inmates dressed in blue denim uniforms, flooding the forecourt like a swarm of locusts, waiting patiently for the early morning roll-call.

The haunting vision of incarceration brought him quickly back to reality.

"Fucking shit-hole," he cursed, turning on his heels, the biting wind in his face sweeping away the memories. The filth...The maniacs...The perverts...The screws...Douglas Wood...Tony Elliott...Darren Adams...Christine Noble.

Gone and forgotten…Forever.

Never again, he vowed...Never again.
Few things in life are more fulfilling than the euphoria of sex, although the feeling of walking through the main gates of a prison to freedom, must rank as a close contender.

Nothing Else Matters (Nov-2005)

The rain pounded the dirty streets and footpaths and the wind raged in a swirling tornado, propelling litter from the ground and sending it high into the dark sky.

In a narrow alleyway, a row of overflowing bins filled the night air with the smell of rotting refuse, alcohol and urine and a broken neon sign above a Chinese restaurant buzzed and crackled in the rain and a roller shutter door rattled loudly in the wind.

In the darkness of the alley, the white glow from a street light shone down on a mysterious figure, throwing ominous shadows against the walls, as he silently approached the main-entrance door to an old Victorian building.

After brushing water from his face and blinking his eyes into focus, a feint light inside a first-floor window and the distorted image of a shadowy figure moving around inside, signalled that someone was working late.

The old oak door groaned on its rusty hinges, as he entered the ground-floor lobby. After closing the door gently against the frame and engaging the dead lock, he paused momentarily to focus his eyes in the darkness and regain his composure.

He waited...He listened...Nothing.

In the crippling silence, he climbed the creaking stairs, each step slow and deliberate, his footfalls hitting the outer treads, making sure he avoided attracting attention. As he reached the first-floor landing a sudden flash of lightning lit up the entire corridor and stopped him in his tracks.

After wiping a layer of sweat from his brow and taking a deep intake of breath, he waited patiently for the thunder that always followed. The cacophonous noise echoed off the walls inside the building, shaking the old window frames and rattling the glass, the timely commotion helping to mask his silent approach.

The old floorboards groaned in quiet protest as he moved slowly and precariously in the darkness, running his hand along a dusty wall and feeling the occasional cobweb slipping between his fingers, breathing in the smell of old leather books and that familiar musty smell, that old building, always seem to have.

A tired floorboard suddenly creaked under his weight as he approached a dimly lit door, the impulsive recoil and cautious hesitation giving him a moment to regain his composure and read the engraving on the office door.

Kenneth Barnaby - Solicitor LLB, the brass plaque on the door, informed him.

"Well, Mr Kenneth Barnaby, let's see if you're still a big man with this stuck in your face," he thought, removing a Colt Magnum semi-automatic pistol from his coat pocket and opening the door just enough to see the back of a man's head sitting in a leather chair in front of a messy desk, littered with books, papers and client's files.

The old leather chair creaked as Kenneth Barnaby lifted to his feet, a single light above his desk silhouetting his movements and casting haunting shadows across the wall, as he paced back and forth across the room, staring at a piece of paper in his hand, as if deep in thought.

He was nervous. His hand was shaking. The gun was sweating in his hand. He hadn't killed a man before.

With his heart beating like a drum inside his chest and every part of his body shaking and trembling, he steadied his hand, gripped the gun and peered through a small gap in the door. *'There was never going to be a better time for murder,'* a voice inside his head told him, wiping a layer of sweat from his forehead and blinking his eyes, taking a deep intake of breath and bursting through the door, the adrenaline inspired energy, sending it crashing against the wall with a deafening bang.

A parrot in a cage that had been chirping noisily, suddenly stopped.

"Remember me, Kenneth Barnaby. You don't look so fucking big now," he barked, raising his hand and pointing the gun in his face. "I'm going to beat you until you beg for mercy and then I'm going to kill you," he sniggered, grabbing him by the throat and raising the gun above his head.

"Smug fucking bastard," he shouted, before hitting him a couple of times over the head with the gun handle, his cries and screams for help smothered under the continuous breaks of thunder, the cacophonous interlude ensuring that the unfolding murder was never going to attract attention from the street below.

"Arrogant bastard," he croaked, hitting him with the gun again and throwing him against the desk, sending a large glass ashtray, overflowing with cigar butts, crashing to the floor.

"Please don't hurt me," Kenneth cried. "I'm sorry. Please don't kill me," he added, wiping blood from his nose and mouth and begging and pleading for his worthless life.

"It's too late to be sorry, Kenneth," he grinned, pressing the barrel of the gun against his thigh and pulling the trigger.

"Christ, you've shot me," Kenneth howled, grabbing his right leg and watching blood seeping through his grey cotton trousers, his painful cries for mercy, echoing off the plastered walls.

"Please. You can stop this now," Kenneth pleaded, limping across the floor and searching his desk for his bible, begging for self-pity and confessing he was a shameful person.

"Will this help," he offered, holding the bible in one hand and raising the other, pledging on oath that if he spared his life, he would change his ways.

"Like I said, Kenneth. It's too late for forgiveness," he said, pointing the gun at his other leg.

He wanted to see Kenneth Barnaby begging on his knees for forgiveness. He wanted to see him squirm before pulling the trigger again.

The next bullet sent an excruciating pain into his left leg.

"Please. No more. It's not too late," Kenneth pleaded, gripping his bloody wounds with both hands, his painful cries for mercy spilling from a helpless mouth.

"If you let me go, I can help you. I can give you money," he offered, reaching into his jacket pocket and removing a key. "It's for the safe under the desk. Take as much money as you want," he said, forcing a smile and handing him the key.

"I don't want your fucking money. I want your fucking life," he barked, slapping his face and throwing him on the floor.

"Please don't kill me," he pleaded, dragging his limp body in the direction of the door and leaving a blood trail snaking over the vinyl floor. "I need to go to a hospital," he begged, sucking in short gasps of air through his nose and trying to calm the erratic beating of his heart.

"I won't tell the police," he offered, reaching up and grabbing the circular door handle. "I won't tell anyone," he added, pulling himself up from the floor. "I promise. You have my word," he sighed, covering his face with his bloody hands and peeking nervously through the gaps between his fingers, the wet patch on the front of his trousers, betraying his inability to control his bladder.

"I have your word," he laughed, pulling his hands from his face and looking him in the eyes.

"So, let me just remind you what you said at our meeting. She can have the house…The Bank account…The Car and our Daughter, and I can keep my fucking job!" he barked, through clenched teeth, raising the gun and placing the barrel between his bulging eyes.

"Fuck you, arsehole," he shouted, squeezing the trigger, the deafening noise and the force from the recoil, throwing him slightly backwards.

"Good riddance," he added, a smile of satisfaction tugging at the corners of his mouth, as Kenneth Barnaby's lifeless body fell to the floor in a pool of blood.

"What a fucking mess," he sighed, letting the gun drop to the floor and staring at the blood spatter and shattering bits of body tissue, decorating the inside of the door.

Other than a couple of muted squawks from the parrot the room fell silent.

A sudden flash of lightening illuminated the inside of the room, followed immediately by a thunderous explosion, making the entire building shake on its foundations and waking him from his chilling nightmare.

"What the fuck," he croaked, jerking upright on the bed in a state of panic, blinking his eyes and trying to focus through the nausea and fog, clouding his vision.

"What an awful fucking dream. I think I'm going to be sick," he thought, wiping beads of sweat from his forehead and sucking in air through his nose, trying to calm the racing heart banging like a drum inside his chest.

"Kenneth fucking Barnaby. The arrogant little weasel. He hated that man so much, it's no wonder he's finding his way into his subconscious and plaguing his mind with evil thoughts," he muttered silently to himself, the mere mention of his name sending a cold chill sweeping across the back of his neck and filling his head with images of his brutal death.

"I need a piss," he thought, the urgency of nature's calling getting him quickly on his feet.

"Be careful. Steady on," a voice inside his head cautioned, a sudden rush of dizziness clouding his vision, as he staggered unsteadily towards the bathroom.

"Wow, that smell, and that throbbing head feels all too familiar," he thought, leaning forward with both hands flat against the toilet wall and his flaccid penis hanging like a length of fire hose over the toilet bowl.

"Beer and Vodka, if I'm not mistaken," he muttered, breathing in the early morning urine, drifting up from the ceramic shrine.

"I knew there was something else," he smiled, the smell of vagina on his fingers a timely reminder of the previous night's drinking session, followed by a night of sex with a woman whose name he couldn't even remember.

He glanced into the bathroom mirror. The ghostly image of a dead man stared back.

The sound of the kettle whistling in the kitchen refocused his attention.

"I'm coming," he told the kettle, glancing at his watch. *'Christ, its nearly three in the afternoon,'* he thought, removing the kettle from the cooker and pouring the hot water into a cup.

'I'd better get a move on. I don't want to be late. Jill had invited him to her house for dinner to celebrate his birthday. She had asked him to be there before six o'clock because Catherine was going out early with some of her friends. The night certainly looked promising. 'Just the two of them alone in the house with no interference and no complications. A timely opportunity for a meaningful discussion and the possibility of a reconciliation looking more and more hopeful, especially when she suggested that he could sleep the night,' he smiled, taking four paracetamol tablets from a container and washing them down with a cup of black coffee, before heading to the shower.

His new landlord said he was calling tomorrow morning, to check the waste pipes in the bathroom. He knew it was only an excuse for his landlord to inspect his property, but because he was spending the night at Jill's and wouldn't be there to meet him, he had to make sure that everything was looking clean and tidy for his arrival.

Once he had the place looking reasonably respectable and he had just about recovered from his alcohol induced haze, he drained the last of his coffee and opened the door. As he turned the key in the lock, he could already feel the cold breeze from the North Sea, biting through his cotton shirt and into his skin.

Even after taking too many tablets and a surge of caffeine, his head was still clouded, and he hadn't gotten very far when his OCD questioned his security actions.

He couldn't remember if he had locked the door.

Because of his financial status, a friend of his had been kind enough to negotiate a reduction in the rent on his new home, so he didn't want to be neglectful with the owner's property, especially if he called tomorrow and discovered that he hadn't locked the door.

He walked back to check the door. It was locked.

"Fucking weather," he cursed, the cold wind biting his face, as he headed the short distance to the bus stop on the hill. "Fucking wind," he added, lifting the collar on his coat and trying to light a cigarette in the wind.

"Got it," he smiled, pausing momentarily to pull on his cigarette and watch the winter waves from the North Sea, rising high above the promenade walls, before crashing against the beach in a thunderous crescendo of swirling white foam.

'What was that woman's name?' he thought, through the fog and haze of a painful hangover and his brain struggling with a touch of memory deficiency.

He was sure it began with a J. *"Jean…. or was it Jackie. Or maybe Janice,"* he thought, pulling on his cigarette, hoping the intake of nicotine into his bloodstream might give him the answer.

"Fuck it," he conceded, flicking his cigarette into the wind. *"It wasn't the first woman he had slept with and*

forgotten her name and it certainly wasn't going to be the last," he thought, breathing in the cold sea air and trying to clear the cobwebs of nameless women from his mind.

"Judith, he suddenly remembered, a jubilant smile lifting the corners of his mouth, as he reached the bus stop on the hill. "Yes. Judith," he repeated, twisting his face in bitter recoil and cursing under his breath when he realised he had no recollection of their night together.

"I'm drinking too much. I'd better slow down." he sighed, looking down over a myriad of white metal structures, knowing that when his landlord arrived tomorrow morning, he would find his caravan in pristine condition.

There was no surprise to find that Jill had prepared a delicious three-course meal.

After they had eaten, and he had gone through the usual protocols of blowing out too many candles and Jill and Catherine had sung a couple of verses of 'Happy Birthday,' Catherine announced that her taxi would be here at any minute.

After a quick visit to her bedroom and a change of clothing, she was heading for the door.

"Where are you going," Catherine? he politely asked.

"I'm going to a party at a friend's house," she replied. "Her mum and dad have gone on holiday to Spain for two weeks. Don't wait up. I won't be back until midnight," she smiled.

"Have fun," he sighed, casting an eye of disapproval over the shortness of her skirt.

"Be careful. And keep out of trouble" he added, remembering when a friend of his returned from a holiday in Italy to discover that his daughter had also had a party while he was away and the damages to his property had left him with a substantial repair bill.

He said nothing to Catherine about the length of her skirt or having respect for someone else's property.

Tonight, they would have the house to themselves.

The conversation over dinner and the birthday celebrations had gone better than expected, so the rest of the evening was beginning to look promising, although she hadn't given him any indication that he would be sharing her bed tonight.

After touching their wine glasses together in a toast to long life and happiness they sat on the sofa for a while, talking about some of the better times they had shared together and some memories that were best forgotten.

They talked a little about his heart attack, his family's medical history, his unhealthy lifestyle and the sudden death of his brother Frank from a massive heart attack, the subject inevitably leading to another lecture from Jill.

"I see you're still smoking," she sighed, handing him an ashtray that she kept in a drawer.

"I don't know why you ignore the advice of your doctor, especially after having a heart attack," she sighed, choking back a lump in her throat. "What did the doctor tell you. High cholesterol. High blood pressure. Control your alcohol intake, consider a healthier diet and exercise regularly," she added, wagging a finger in his face.

"You were lucky. You could have ended up like your brother Frank," she said, brushing a tear from the corner of her eye.

Jill had her lecturers head on. He wasn't going to interrupt her flow. He knew better. He just nodded his head and listened to what she had to say.

"You're only fifty-six. You've still got a long life ahead of you. If you look after yourself," she sighed, pointing a finger of disapproval at the cigarette in his hand.

"I want you to promise me that you'll make some changes to your lifestyle. Do it for Catherine. She loves you and she needs a father," she said, wafting away cigarette smoke above her head.

"Let's start now," she insisted, taking his cigarette from his hand and crushing it into the ashtray. "We don't want cigarette smoke drifting up into our bedroom," she smiled, brushing hair from her face and flashing her eyes with flirtatious suggestion, the slightest hint of sharing her bed bringing a smile to his face and a stirring inside his pants.

"Enough lecturing for one night. It's time to give you your birthday present. I think you'll like it. It's in the bedroom," she smiled.

"Fifty-fucking-six. Christ I'm nearly sixty," he cursed, lying naked on the bed, his mind capturing nostalgic images when he was a fit and healthy teenager and every decision was centred on three subjects. Sex. Football and Cars and everything else in his life was nothing more than an obstacle in his way.

"I'm getting old, and it's beginning to affect my sex life," he thought, glancing at the sleeping limb hanging over his thigh, before slipping a Viagra tablet into his mouth, knowing his mind and his drive and his libido were still willing, but with the fire now dampened by age, it certainly took him longer to recover after a fuck.

An insistent voice interrupted his reverie.

"Sorry It took so long," said the attractive nurse, snapping him out of his dreamy thoughts.

"Well. What do you think?" she smiled, skipping around the room on four-inch heels, white stockings and suspenders and a white tunic clinging like a second skin to shapely curves.

"Do you like it?" she breathed, flashing her eyes suggestively and twirling on her toes, a white nurses cap tilted on her head, above a mass of blonde hair.

"Wow. Yes. I do. I like it a lot. You must be nurse naughty," he mocked, the vision of erotic suggestion and the stimulation of an increased blood flow from the blue tablet, bringing a smile to his face and a movement on his thigh.

"I've left a key in the front door. Just in case," she smiled, bending over to light two scented candles on the bedside tables. "We don't want to be disturbed," she added, her white tunic lifting just enough to reveal the string of a thong disappearing between the cheeks of her bottom and flossing the dark anal valley with alluring authority.

"A little music and I'm all yours, Mr Brand," she giggled, slipping a disc into the CD player.

"I Dreamed a Dream," she sang, skipping playfully around the room, bending over and parting her legs, sweeping her hands over her bottom and orchestrating her body with alluring effect.

"I dreamed that love would never die," she smiled, flashing her eyes and running her tongue suggestively over her top lip before removing her white tunic and letting it fall to the floor.

"Happy birthday, she whispered, wearing nothing but a thong and a pair of white stockings and suspenders, posing like an underwear model and smiling into his eyes before kicking her heels playfully across the floor.

"Nurse naughty's here to make you feel good on your birthday," she smiled, pursing her lips and slipping a finger into her mouth with provocative suggestion.

"You just have to ask, and she'll oblige," she breathed, rolling her stockings down each leg and slipping them off her feet, the sheer shrouds joining the white thong on the bedroom floor.

"Can the nurse help me with this?" he mockingly asked, pointing at the fleshy object hanging over his thigh. "With a little help, it can grow to nearly nine-inches," he smiled, gripping the gruesome muscle in his hand, the flickering light from the candles casting distorted shadows of a phallic object on the bedroom wall.

"I think I can help you with that," nurse naughty confirmed. "I specialise in big cocks," she smiled, her wide eyes taking in the full glory of the phallic images on the bedroom wall.

"I think you need some therapeutic stimulation," she smiled, flashing her eyes and climbing on the bed. "I'm going to give you a massage," she smiled, reaching for a bottle of baby oil on the bedside table.

"A happy birthday and a happy ending," she added, squeezing the oil into her hands and smoothing the glistening liquid generously over his shoulders and muscular arms.

"Just relax. Let Olga do her job," she said, getting into character with a spurious Russian accent. "If I don't please you they will send me back to the workhouse," she sighed, pursing her bottom lip and rolling her eyes.

"Let me please you, Mr Brand" she whispered, running her slippery hands over the fine hairs on his chest, before travelling south over his abdomen, pausing momentarily to give his manhood a generous smearing of oil.

"You Englishmen are so big," she smiled, giving his cock and balls a playful squeeze. "And so strong," she added, sweeping her hands over his muscular thighs, gazing into his eyes to see his reaction before smoothing the oil slowly and gently over one leg and then the other.

"Now your feet, Mr Brand" she volunteered, gripping his ankles with both hands and working the tight tissues around his toes with her fingers and thumbs.

"Your feet are too important to ignore," she smiled, kneading the arches and the soft insoles of his feet, like a skilled masseur.

"Now. Let's get down to business," she smiled, spilling the oil liberally over his swollen limb and testicles, dragging a fingernail playfully over the rough skin of the scrotum and cradling his hairy balls in her slippery hands.

"I think that'll do nicely," she smiled, squeezing each one gently and making sure she had covered all his bits.

"I'm going to fuck you now? She breathed, curling her fingers around the thick girth, working the length up and down, squeezing the girth on the down stroke and pulling the length on the way up, up and down, back and forth, tugging and pulling, slow and methodical and then fast and precise, a whispered voice in his ear fuelling the fire of passion and increasing the flow of blood into his genitals.

"Would you like Olga to suck your cock before she fucks you?" she asked, smiling into his eyes before easing the fleshy muscle into her mouth.

"Whatever you say nurse," he croaked, the warmth of her mouth and the stimulus of Viagra, sending his heart rate souring and a visceral surge of blood flowing into his penis and leaving him with a very impressive erection.

A shrieking voice in the street below the bedroom window that they both recognised, suddenly interrupted their romantic interlude.
"It's Catherine," Jill shouted, letting his cock slip from her mouth and rolling off the bed.
"I thought she said she wouldn't be back until midnight," she sighed, slipping into a dressing gown and leaning her head out the window, the familiar silhouette of her daughter staring up with a questioning eye.
"Can you let me in. I can't get my key in the door," Catherine barked, shivering in the biting cold wind and pulling her short skirt over her knees.
"You're back early. What happened to the party?" Jill enquired, choking back a lump in her throat, her question interrupted by two faceless shadows joining Catherine at the door.
"There was a disturbance from a couple of gate-crashers. It looked like there was going to be trouble, so we left. I've invited two of my friends back to the house for coffee."
A crippling silence hung in the air between them before Catherine eventually broke the silence with a question that caught Jill by surprise.
"What's that on your head, mother?" Catherine shouted, raising both eyebrows.
"What…Its nothing." Jill panicked, grabbing the white cap from her head with lightning speed.
"Omigod!" Catherine squirmed, stepping back in shameful recoil. "It's a nurse's cap and you're

wearing a…a…blonde wig," she snorted, in a choking stammer.
"That's Gross," she scowled, her two friends trying to hide their embarrassment behind closed eyes and making sure they avoided any direct eye contact with Catherine.
"Omigod! You're wearing a nurse's outfit and you and dad are having sex," she yelled. "How disgusting," she sighed, putting two fingers inside her mouth in that universal gesture for 'I-need-to-vomit.'
But it wasn't enough to deter Catherine who continued with a barrage of accusing insults at her mother while her two friends shivered helplessly in the cold.
"This is so humiliating," Catherine said, turning to face her two friends and raising her voice an octave higher than it ought to be.
"My father is fifty-six and recovering from a heart attack and my mother is…," she paused, counting numbers in her head. "Forty-something," she muttered silently, rolling her eyes with increasing frustration and tracing through the memory bank of embarrassing parent files stored inside her head.
"One night they were seen by one of the neighbours having sex over the picnic table in the back garden," she sighed, shaking her head in defeat.
"The police arrived at the door the next day. My father told them it was an outrageous and untruthful accusation, so they never pressed charges," she croaked, pointing a finger at the front door

"I know why you left the key in the door. I'm not stupid," Catherine growled, stepping into the entrance hall, her two friends following cautiously on her heels.

"Dressing up in a nurse's outfit, at your age," mother, she hissed her disapproval through tight lips and gritted teeth, her two friends shuffling nervously in the entrance hall with blushing faces and that universal look of disgust that all teenagers seem to have when they hear their parents talking about sex.

"Don't go upstairs, Catherine," Jill insisted. "I need to remove the handcuffs from your father's wrists. He's naked and he's tied to the bed," she smiled, with mocking tease.

"You did the right thing, leaving the party early when you thought there might be trouble," Jill said, approvingly, aware that her two friends were caught up in the crossfire of parental innuendo and looked anxious to be away.

"You know where the coffee is. If you have no objection, I've got some unfinished business in the bedroom. We'll try not to make too much noise," Jill smiled.

"I'm not in the mood for coffee. My friends are going home and I'm going to my room. I never want to see or speak to you ever again," Catherine bellowed, showing her friends to the door and disappearing up the stairs to her bedroom.

"Catherine's upset. Why do teenagers think sex is only for young people," Jill sighed, pouring wine into

two glasses and humming along to the throaty voice of Steven Tyler singing *'I Don't Want to Miss a Thing.'*
"She'll grow out of it. Trust me. It's just a hormonal thing," he smiled. "Dance with me," he whispered, stealing a kiss and slipping her robe from her shoulders.
"We'll have to be quiet. I don't want another confrontation with Catherine," she smiled, the gentle breeze from the window cooling their heated bodies and the candles on the bedside tables almost burning themselves out.
"She's probably fast asleep by now," he said, smiling into her eyes and pulling her into his arms. Two bodies joined together in harmonious union. Two people back for good. Two lovers about to make up for lost time....
"Mother....Mum...Will you come and get this spider on my bedroom wall?"

Printed in Great Britain
by Amazon

35290987R00288